The human is a highly complex organism, motivated by a variety of emotions—curiosity, courage, cussedness, love, hatred, boredom, and combinations of several more.

The puppeteers were gentle—in fact, one of their most laudable and dominant characteristics was cowardice. Which made for a very high survival factor. At least for puppeteers.

The most admirable thing, of course, was that they were willing (and very able) to pay other aliens to take the risks they were morally obliged not to take themselves.

Which appealed hugely to the greed in certain life-forms.

Notably *homo sapiens. . . .*

NEUTRON STAR

Larry Niven

Ballantine Books • New York
An Intext Publisher

BALLANTINE BOOKS, INC.
101 Fifth Avenue, New York, N.Y. 10003

TO DAD & HOPE

Who early suspected that I might
know what I was doing.

CONTENTS

NEUTRON STAR

THE *Skydiver* DROPPED out of hyperspace an even million miles above the neutron star. I needed a minute to place myself against the stellar background, and another to find the distortion Sonya Laskin had mentioned before she died. It was to my left, an area the apparent size of the Earth's moon. I swung the ship around to face it.

Curdled stars, muddled stars, stars that had been stirred with a spoon.

The neutron star was in the center, of course, though I couldn't see it and hadn't expected to. It was only eleven miles across, and cool. A billion years had passed since BVS-1 burned by fusion fire. Millions of years, at least, since the cataclysmic two weeks during which BVS-1 was an X-ray star, burning at a temperature of five billion degrees Kelvin. Now it showed only by its mass.

The ship began to turn by itself. I felt the pressure of the fusion drive. Without help from me my faithful metal watchdog was putting me in a hyperbolic orbit that would take me within one mile of the neutron star's surface. Twenty-four hours to fall, twenty-four hours to rise . . . and during that time something would try to kill me. As something had killed the Laskins.

The same type of autopilot, with the same program, had chosen the Laskins' orbit. It had not caused their ship to collide with the star. I could trust the autopilot. I could even change its program.

I really ought to.

How did I get myself into this hole?

The drive went off after ten minutes of maneuvering. My orbit was established, in more ways than one. I knew what would happen if I tried to back out now.

All I'd done was walk into a drugstore to get a new battery for my lighter!

Right in the middle of the store, surrounded by three floors of sales counters, was the new 2603 Sinclair intrasystem yacht. I'd come for a battery, but I stayed to admire. It was a beautiful job, small and sleek and streamlined and blatantly different from anything that'd ever been built. I wouldn't have flown it for anything but I had to admit it was pretty. I ducked my head through the door to look at the control panel. You never saw so many dials. When I pulled my head out, all the customers were looking in the same direction. The place had gone startlingly quiet.

I can't blame them for staring. A number of aliens were in the store, mainly shopping for souvenirs, but they were staring too. A puppeteer is unique. Imagine a headless, three-legged centaur wearing two Cecil the Seasick Sea Serpent puppets on its arms, and you'll have something like the right picture. But the arms are weaving necks, and the puppets are real heads, flat and brainless, with wide flexible lips. The brain is under a bony hump set between the bases of the necks. This puppeteer wore only its own coat of brown hair, with a mane that extended all the way up its spine to form a thick mat over the brain. I'm told that the way they wear the mane indicates their status in society, but to me it could have been anything from a dock worker to a jeweler to the president of General Products.

I watched with the rest as it came across the floor, not because I'd never seen a puppeteer but because there is something beautiful about the dainty way they move on those slender legs and tiny hooves. I watched it come straight toward me, closer and closer. It stopped a foot away, looked me over, and said, "You are Beowulf Shaeffer, former chief pilot for Nakamura Lines."

Its voice was a beautiful contralto with not a trace of accent. A puppeteer's mouths are not only the most flexible speech organs around, but also the most sensitive hands. The tongues are forked and pointed; the wide, thick lips have little fingerlike knobs along the rims. Imagine a watchmaker with a sense of taste in his fingertips . . .

I cleared my throat. "That's right."

It considered me from two directions. "You would be interested in a high-paying job?"

"I'd be fascinated by a high-paying job."

"I am our equivalent of the regional president of General Products. Please come with me, and we will discuss this elsewhere."

I followed it into a displacement booth. Eyes followed me all the way. It was embarrassing, being accosted in a public drugstore by a two-headed monster. Maybe the puppeteer knew it. Maybe it was testing me to see how badly I needed money.

My need was great. Eight months had passed since Nakamura Lines folded. For some time before that I had been living very high on the hog, knowing that my back pay would cover my debts. I never saw that back pay. It was quite a crash, Nakamura Lines. Respectable middle-aged businessmen took to leaving their hotel windows without their lift belts. Me, I kept spending. If I'd started living frugally, my creditors would have done some checking . . . and I'd have ended in debtor's prison.

The puppeteer dialed thirteen fast digits with its tongue. A moment later we were elsewhere. Air puffed out when I opened the booth door, and I swallowed to pop my ears.

"We are on the roof of the General Products building." The rich contralto voice thrilled along my nerves, and I had to remind myself that it was an alien speaking, not a lovely woman. "You must examine this spacecraft while we discuss your assignment."

I stepped outside a little cautiously, but it wasn't the windy season. The roof was at ground level. That's the way we build on We Made It. Maybe it has something to do with the fifteen-hundred-mile-an-hour winds we get in summer and winter, when the planet's axis of rotation runs through its primary, Procyon. The winds are our planet's only tourist attraction, and it would be a shame to slow them down by planting skyscrapers in their path. The bare, square concrete roof was surrounded by endless square miles of desert, not like the deserts of other inhabited worlds, but an utterly lifeless expanse of fine sand just crying to be planted with ornamental cactus. We've tried that. The wind blows the plants away.

The ship lay on the sand beyond the roof. It was a No. 2 General Products hull: a cylinder three hundred feet long and twenty feet through, pointed at both ends and with a slight wasp-waist constriction near the tail. For some reason it was lying on its side, with the landing shocks still folded in at the tail.

Ever notice how all ships have begun to look the same? A good ninety-five percent of today's spacecraft are built around one of the four General Products hulls. It's easier and safer to build that way, but somehow all ships end as they began: mass-produced look-alikes.

The hulls are delivered fully transparent, and you use paint where you feel like it. Most of this particular hull had been left transparent. Only the nose had been painted, around the lifesystem. There was no major reaction drive. A series of retractable attitude jets had been mounted in the sides, and the hull was pierced with smaller holes, square and round, for observational instruments. I could see them gleaming through the hull.

The puppeteer was moving toward the nose, but something made me turn toward the stern for a closer look at the landing shocks. They were bent. Behind the curved transparent hull panels some tremendous pressure had forced the metal to flow like warm wax, back and into the pointed stern.

"What did this?" I asked.

"We do not know. We wish strenuously to find out."

"What do you mean?"

"Have you heard of the neutron star BVS-1?"

I had to think a moment. "First neutron star ever found, and so far the only. Someone located it two years ago, by stellar displacement."

"BVS-1 was found by the Institute of Knowledge on Jinx. We learned through a go-between that the Institute wished to explore the star. They needed a ship to do it.

They had not yet sufficient money. We offered to supply them with a ship's hull, with the usual guarantees, if they would turn over to us all data they acquired through using our ship."

"Sounds fair enough." I didn't ask why they hadn't done their own exploring. Like most sentient vegetarians, puppeteers find discretion to be the *only* part of valor.

"Two humans named Peter Laskin and Sonya Laskin wished to use the ship. They intended to come within one mile of the surface in a hyperbolic orbit. At some point during their trip an unknown force apparently reached through the hull to do this to the landing shocks. The unknown force also seems to have killed the pilots."

"But that's impossible. Isn't it?"

"You see the point. Come with me." The puppeteer trotted toward the bow.

I saw the point, all right. Nothing, but nothing, can get through a General Products hull. No kind of electromagnetic energy except visible light. No kind of matter, from the smallest subatomic particle to the fastest meteor. That's what the company's advertisements claim, and the guarantee backs them up. I've never doubted it, and I've never heard of a General Products hull being damaged by a weapon or by anything else.

On the other hand, a General Products hull is as ugly as it is functional. The puppeteer-owned company could be badly hurt if it got around that something *could* get through a company hull. But I didn't see where I came in.

We rode an escalladder into the nose.

The lifesystem was in two compartments. Here the Laskins had used heat-reflective paint. In the conical control cabin the hull had been divided into windows. The relaxation room behind it was a windowless reflective silver. From the back wall of the relaxation room an access tube ran aft, opening on various instruments and the hyperdrive motors.

There were two acceleration couches in the control cabin. Both had been torn loose from their mountings and wadded into the nose like so much tissue paper, crushing the instrument panel. The backs of the crumpled couches were splashed with rust brown. Flecks of the same color were all over everything, the walls, the windows, the viewscreens. It was as if something had hit the couches from behind: something like a dozen paint-filled toy balloons striking with tremendous force.

"That's blood," I said.

"That is correct. Human circulatory fluid."

Twenty-four hours to fall.

I spent most of the first twelve hours in the relaxation room, trying to read. Nothing significant was happening, except that a few times I saw the phenomenon Sonya Laskin had mentioned in her last report. When a star went directly behind the invisible BVS-1, a halo formed. BVS-1 was heavy enough to bend light around it, displacing most stars to the sides; but when a star went directly behind the neutron star, its light was displaced to all sides at once. Result: a tiny circle which flashed once and was gone almost before the eye could catch it.

I'd known next to nothing about neutron stars the day the puppeteer picked me up. Now I was an expert. And I still had no idea what was waiting for me when I got down there.

All the matter you're ever likely to meet will be normal matter, composed of a nucleus of protons and neutrons surrounded by electrons in quantum energy states. In the heart of any star there is a second kind of matter: for there, the tremendous pressure is enough to smash the electron shells. The result is degenerate matter: nuclei forced together by pressure and gravity, but held apart by the mutual repulsion of the more or less continuous electron "gas" around them. The right circumstances may create a third type of matter.

Given: a burnt-out white dwarf with a mass greater than 1.44 times the mass of the sun—Chandrasekhar's Limit, named for an Indian-American astronomer of the nineteen hundreds. In such a mass the electron pressure alone would not be able to hold the electrons back from the nuclei. Electrons would be forced against protons—to make neutrons. In one blazing explosion most of the star would change from a compressed mass of degenerate matter to a closely packed lump of neutrons: neutronium, theoretically the densest matter possible in this universe. Most of the remaining normal and degenerate matter would be blown away by the liberated heat.

For two weeks the star would give off X-rays as its core temperature dropped from five billion degrees Kelvin to five hundred million. After that it would be a light-emitting body perhaps ten to twelve miles across: the next best thing to invisible. It was not strange that BVS-1 was the first neutron star ever found.

Neither is it strange that the Institute of Knowledge on Jinx would have spent a good deal of time and trouble looking. Until BVS-1 was found, neutronium and neutron stars were only theories. The examination of an actual neutron star could be of tremendous importance. Neutron stars might give us the key to true gravity control.

Mass of BVS-1: 1.3 times the mass of Sol, approx.

Diameter of BVS-1 (estimated): eleven miles of neutronium, covered by half a mile of degenerate matter, covered by maybe twelve feet of ordinary matter.

Nothing else was known of the tiny hidden star until the Laskins went in to look. Now the Institute knew one thing more: the star's spin.

"A mass that large can distort space by its rotation," said the puppeteer. "The Laskins' projected hyperbola was twisted across itself in such a way that we can deduce the star's period of rotation to be two minutes twenty-seven seconds."

The bar was somewhere in the General Products building. I don't know just where, and with the transfer booths it doesn't matter. I kept staring at the puppeteer bartender. Naturally only a puppeteer would be served by a puppeteer bartender, since any biped life form would resent knowing that his drink had been made with somebody's mouth. I had already decided to get dinner somewhere else.

"I see your problem," I said. "Your sales will suffer if it gets out that something can reach through one of your hulls and smash a crew to bloody smears. But where do I come in?"

"We want to repeat the experiment of Sonya Laskin and Peter Laskin. We must find—"

"With me?"

"Yes. We must find out what it is that our hulls cannot stop. Naturally you may—"

"But I won't."

"We are prepared to offer one million stars."

I was tempted, but only for a moment. "Forget it."

"Naturally you will be allowed to build your own ship, starting with a No. 2 General Products hull."

"Thanks, but I'd like to go on living."

"You would dislike being confined. I find that We Made It has re-established the debtor's prison. If General Products made public your accounts—"

"Now, *just* a—"

"You owe money on the close order of five hundred thousand stars. We will pay your creditors before you leave. If you return—" I had to admire the creature's honesty in not saying "When"—"we will pay you the residue. You may be asked to speak to news commentators concerning the voyage, in which case there will be more stars."

"You say I can build my own ship?"

"Naturally. This is not a voyage of exploration. We want you to return safely."

"It's a deal," I said.

After all, the puppeteer had tried to blackmail me. What happened next would be its own fault.

They built my ship in two weeks flat. They started with a No. 2 General Products hull, just like the one around the Institute of Knowledge ship, and the lifesystem was practically a duplicate of the Laskins', but there the resemblance ended. There were no instruments to observe neutron stars. Instead, there was a fusion motor big enough for a Jinx warliner. In my ship, which I now called *Skydiver*, the drive would produce thirty gees at the safety limit. There was a laser cannon big enough to punch a hole through We Made It's moon. The puppeteer wanted me to feel safe, and now I did, for I could fight and I could run. Especially I could run.

I heard the Laskins' last broadcast through half a dozen times. Their unnamed ship had dropped out of hyperspace a million miles above BVS-1. Gravity warp would have prevented their getting closer in hyperspace. While her husband was crawling through the access tube for an instrument check, Sonya Laskin had called the Institute of Knowledge. "... We can't see it yet, not by naked eye. But we can see where it is. Every time some star or other goes behind it, there's a little ring of light. Just a minute, Peter's ready to use the telescope. . . ."

Then the star's mass had cut the hyperspacial link. It was expected, and nobody had worried—then. Later, the same effect must have stopped them from escaping whatever attacked them into hyperspace.

When would-be rescuers found the ship, only the radar and the cameras were still running. They didn't tell us much. There had been no camera in the cabin. But the forward camera gave us, for one instant, a speed-blurred view of the neutron star. It was a featureless disk the orange color of perfect barbecue coals, if you know someone who can afford to burn wood. This object had been a neutron star a long time.

"There'll be no need to paint the ship," I told the president.

"You should not make such a trip with the walls transparent. You would go insane."

"I'm no flatlander. The mind-wrenching sight of naked space fills me with mild but waning interest. I want to know nothing's sneaking up behind me."

The day before I left, I sat alone in the General Products bar letting the puppeteer bartender make me drinks with his mouth. He did it well. Puppeteers were scattered around the bar in twos and threes, with a couple of men for variety, but the drinking hour had not yet arrived. The place felt empty.

I was pleased with myself. My debts were all paid, not

that that would matter where I was going. I would leave with not a minicredit to my name, with nothing but the ship . . .

All told, I was well out of a sticky situation. I hoped I'd like being a rich exile.

I jumped when the newcomer sat down across from me. He was a foreigner, a middle-aged man wearing an expensive night-black business suit and a snow-white asymmetric beard. I let my face freeze and started to get up.

"Sit down, Mr. Shaeffer."

"Why?"

He told me by showing me a blue disk. An Earth government ident. I looked it over to show I was alert, not because I'd know an ersatz from the real thing.

"My name is Sigmund Ausfaller," said the government man. "I wish to say a few words concerning your assignment on behalf of General Products."

I nodded, not saying anything.

"A record of your verbal contract was sent to us as a matter of course. I noticed some peculiar things about it. Mr. Shaeffer, will you really take such a risk for only five hundred thousand stars?"

"I'm getting twice that."

"But you only keep half of it. The rest goes to pay debts. Then there are taxes . . . But never mind. What occurred to me was that a spaceship is a spaceship, and yours is very well armed and has powerful legs. An admirable fighting ship, if you were moved to sell it."

"But it isn't mine."

"There are those who would not ask. On Canyon, for example, or the Isolationist party of Wunderland."

I said nothing.

"Or, you might be planning a career of piracy. A risky business, piracy, and I don't take the notion seriously."

I hadn't even thought about piracy. But I'd have to give up on Wunderland.

"What I would like to say is this, Mr. Shaeffer. A single entrepreneur, if he were sufficiently dishonest, could do terrible damage to the reputation of all human beings everywhere. Most species find it necessary to police the ethics of their own members, and we are no exception. It occurred to me that you might not take your ship to the neutron star at all; that you would take it elsewhere and sell it. The puppeteers do not make invulnerable war vessels. They are pacifists. Your *Skydiver* is unique.

"Hence I have asked General Products to allow me to install a remote-control bomb in the *Skydiver*. Since it is inside the hull, the hull cannot protect you. I had it installed this afternoon.

"Now, notice! If you have not reported within a week, I will set off the bomb. There are several worlds within a week's hyperspace flight of here, but all recognize the dominion of Earth. If you flee, you must leave your ship within a week, so I hardly think you will land on a nonhabitable world. Clear?"

"Clear."

"If I am wrong, you may take a lie-detector test and prove it. Then you may punch me in the nose, and I will apologize handsomely."

I shook my head. He stood up, bowed, and left me sitting there cold sober.

Four films had been taken from the Laskins' cameras. In the time left to me I ran through them several times, without seeing anything out of the way. If the ship had run through a gas cloud, the impact could have killed the Laskins. At perihelion they were moving at better than half the speed of light. But there would have been friction, and I saw no sign of heating in the films. If something alive had attacked them, the beast was invisible to radar and to an enormous range of light frequencies. If the attitude jets had fired accidentally—I was clutching at straws—the light showed on none of the films.

There would be savage magnetic forces near BVS-1, but that couldn't have done any damage. No such force could penetrate a General Products hull. Neither could heat, except in special bands of radiated light, bands visible to at least one of the puppeteers' alien customers. I hold adverse opinions on the General Products hull, but they all concern the dull anonymity of the design. Or maybe I resent the fact that General Products holds a near-monopoly on spacecraft hulls, and isn't owned by human beings. But if I'd had to trust my life to, say, the Sinclair yacht I'd seen in the drugstore, I'd have chosen jail.

Jail was one of my three choices. But I'd be there for life. Ausfaller would see to that.

Or I could run for it in the *Skydiver*. But no world within reach would have me. If I could find an undiscovered Earth-like world within a week of We Made It . . .

Fat chance. I preferred BVS-1.

I thought that flashing circle of light was getting bigger, but it flashed so seldom, I couldn't be sure. BVS-1 wouldn't show even in my telescope. I gave that up and settled for just waiting.

Waiting, I remembered a long-ago summer spent on Jinx. There were days when, unable to go outside because a dearth of clouds had spread the land with raw blue-white sunlight, we amused ourselves by filling party balloons with tap water and dropping them on the sidewalk from three stories up. They made lovely splash patterns, which dried out too fast. So we put a little ink in each balloon before filling it. Then the patterns stayed.

Sonya Laskin had been in her chair when the chairs collapsed. Blood samples showed that it was Peter who had struck them from behind, like a water balloon dropped from a great height.

What could get through a General Products hull?

Ten hours to fall.

I unfastened the safety net and went for an inspection tour. The access tunnel was three feet wide, just right to push through in free fall. Below me was the length of the fusion tube; to the left, the laser cannon; to the right, a set of curved side tubes leading to inspection points for the gyros, the batteries and generator, the air plant, the hyperspace shunt motors. All was in order—except me. I was clumsy. My jumps were always too short or too long.

There was no room to turn at the stern end, so I had to back fifty feet to a side tube.

Six hours to go, and still I couldn't find the neutron star. Probably I would see it only for an instant, passing at better than half the speed of light. Already my speed must be enormous.

Were the stars turning blue?

Two hours to go—and I was sure they were turning blue. Was my speed that high? Then the stars behind should be red. Machinery blocked the view behind me, so I used the gyros. The ship turned with peculiar sluggishness. And the stars behind were blue, not red. All around me were blue-white stars.

Imagine light falling into a savagely steep gravitational well. It won't accelerate. Light can't move faster than light. But it can gain in energy, in frequency. The light was falling on me, harder and harder as I dropped.

I told the dictaphone about it. That dictaphone was probably the best-protected item on the ship. I had already decided to earn my money by using it, just as if I expected to collect. Privately I wondered just how intense the light would get.

Skydiver had drifted back to vertical, with its axis through the neutron star, but now it faced outward. I'd thought I had the ship stopped horizontally. More clumsiness. I used the gyros. Again the ship moved mushily, until it was halfway through the swing. Then it seemed to fall automatically into place. It was as if the *Skydiver* preferred to have its axis through the neutron star.

I didn't like that.

I tried the maneuver again, and again the *Skydiver* fought back. But this time there was something else. Something was pulling at me.

So I unfastened my safety net—and fell headfirst into the nose.

The pull was light, about a tenth of a gee. It felt more like sinking through honey than falling. I climbed back into my chair, tied myself in with the net, now hanging face down, and turned on the dictaphone. I told my story in such nitpicking detail that my hypothetical listeners could not but doubt my hypothetical sanity. "I think this is what happened to the Laskins," I finished. "If the pull increases, I'll call back."

Think? I never doubted it. This strange, gentle pull was inexplicable. Something inexplicable had killed Peter and Sonya Laskin. Q.E.D.

Around the point where the neutron star must be, the stars were like smeared dots of oilpaint, smeared radially. They glared with an angry, painful light. I hung face down in the net and tried to think.

It was an hour before I was sure. The pull was increasing. And I still had an hour to fall.

Something was pulling on me, but not on the ship.

No, that was nonsense. What could reach out to me through a General Products hull? It must be the other way around. Something was pushing on the ship, pushing it off course.

If it got worse, I could use the drive to compensate. Meanwhile, the ship was being pushed *away* from BVS-1, which was fine by me.

But if I was wrong, if the ship was not somehow being pushed away from BVS-1, the rocket motor would send the *Skydiver* crashing into eleven miles of neutronium.

And why wasn't the rocket already firing? If the ship was being pushed off course, the autopilot should be fighting back. The accelerometer was in good order. It had looked fine when I made my inspection tour down the access tube.

Could something be pushing on the ship *and* on the accelerometer, but not on me? It came down to the same impossibility: something that could reach through a General Products hull.

To hell with theory, said I to myself, said I. I'm getting out of here. To the dictaphone I said, "The pull has increased dangerously. I'm going to try to alter my orbit."

Of course, once I turned the ship outward and used the rocket, I'd be adding my own acceleration to the X-force. It would be a strain, but I could stand it for a while. If I came within a mile of BVS-1, I'd end like Sonya Laskin.

She must have waited face down in a net like mine, waited without a drive unit, waited while the pressure rose and the net cut into her flesh, waited until the net snapped and dropped her into the nose, to lie crushed and broken until the X-force tore the very chairs loose and dropped them on her.

I hit the gyros.

The gyros weren't strong enough to turn me. I tried it three times. Each time the ship rotated about fifty degrees and hung there, motionless, while the whine of the gyros went up and up. Released, the ship immediately swung back to position. I was nose down to the neutron star, and I was going to stay that way.

Half an hour to fall, and the X-force was over a gee. My sinuses were in agony. My eyes were ripe and ready to fall out. I don't know if I could have stood a cigarette, but I didn't get the chance. My pack of Fortunados had fallen out of my pocket when I dropped into the nose. There it was, four feet beyond my fingers, proof that the X-force acted on other objects besides me. Fascinating.

I couldn't take any more. If it dropped me shrieking into the neutron star, I had to use the drive. And I did. I ran the thrust up until I was approximately in free fall. The blood which had pooled in my extremities went back where it belonged. The gee dial registered one point two gee. I cursed it for a lying robot.

The soft-pack was bobbing around in the nose, and it occurred to me that a little extra nudge on the throttle would bring it to me. I tried it. The pack drifted toward me, and I reached, and like a sentient thing it speeded up to avoid my clutching hand. I snatched at it again as it went past my ear, and again it was moving too fast. That pack was going at a hell of a clip, considering that here I was practically in free fall. It dropped through the door to the relaxation room, still picking up speed, blurred and vanished as it entered the access tube. Seconds later I heard a solid *thump*.

But that was *crazy*. Already the X-force was pulling blood into my face. I pulled my lighter out, held it at arm's length and let go. It fell gently into the nose. But the pack of Fortunados had hit like I'd dropped it from a *building*.

Well.

I nudged the throttle again. The mutter of fusing hydrogen reminded me that if I tried to keep this up all the way, I might well put the General Products hull to its toughest test yet: smashing it into a neutron star at half lightspeed. I could see it now: a transparent hull containing only a few cubic inches of dwarf-star matter wedged into the tip of the nose.

At one point four gee, according to that lying gee dial, the lighter came loose and drifted toward me. I let it go. It was clearly falling when it reached the doorway. I pulled the throttle back. The loss of power jerked me violently forward, but I kept my face turned. The lighter slowed and hesitated at the entrance to the access tube. Decided to go through. I cocked my ears for the sound, then jumped as the whole ship rang like a gong.

And the accelerometer was right at the ship's center of mass. Otherwise the ship's mass would have thrown the needle off. The puppeteers were fiends for ten-decimal-point accuracy.

I favored the dictaphone with a few fast comments, then got to work reprogramming the autopilot. Luckily what I wanted was simple. The X-force was but an X-force to me, but now I knew how it behaved. I might actually live through this.

The stars were fiercely blue, warped to streaked lines near that special point. I thought I could see it now, very small and dim and red, but it might have been imagination. In twenty minutes I'd be rounding the neutron star. The drive grumbled behind me. In effective free fall, I unfastened the safety net and pushed myself out of the chair.

A gentle push aft—and ghostly hands grasped my legs. Ten pounds of weight hung by my fingers from the back of the chair. The pressure should drop fast. I'd programmed the autopilot to reduce the thrust from two gees to zero during the next two minutes. All I had to do was be at the center of mass, in the access tube, when the thrust went to zero.

Something gripped the ship through a General Products hull. A psychokinetic life form stranded on a sun twelve miles in diameter? But how could anything alive stand such gravity?

Something might be stranded in orbit. There is life in space: outsiders and sailseeds, and maybe others we haven't found yet. For all I knew or cared, BVS-1 itself might be alive. It didn't matter. I knew what the X-force was trying to do. It was trying to pull the ship apart.

There was no pull on my fingers. I pushed aft and landed on the back wall, on bent legs. I knelt over the door, looking aft/down. When free fall came, I pulled myself through and was in the relaxation room looking down/forward into the nose.

Gravity was changing faster than I liked. The X-force was growing as zero hour approached, while the compensating rocket thrust dropped. The X-force tended to pull the ship apart; it was two gee forward at the nose, two gee backward at the tail, and diminished to zero at the center of mass. Or so I hoped. The pack and lighter had behaved as if the force pulling them had increased for every inch they moved sternward.

The back wall was fifteen feet away. I had to jump it with gravity changing in midair. I hit on my hands, bounced away. I'd jumped too late. The region of free fall was moving through the ship like a wave as the thrust dropped. It had left me behind. Now the back wall was "up" to me, and so was the access tube.

Under something less than half a gee, I jumped for the access tube. For one long moment I stared into the three-foot tunnel, stopped in midair and already beginning to fall back, as I realized that there was nothing to hang on to. Then I stuck my hands in the tube and spread them against the sides. It was all I needed. I levered myself up and started to crawl.

The dictaphone was fifty feet below, utterly unreachable. If I had anything more to say to General Products,

I'd have to say it in person. Maybe I'd get the chance. Because I knew what force was trying to tear the ship apart.

It was the tide.

The motor was off, and I was at the ship's midpoint. My spread-eagled position was getting uncomfortable. It was four minutes to perihelion.

Something creaked in the cabin below me. I couldn't see what it was, but I could clearly see a red point glaring among blue radial lines, like a lantern at the bottom of a well. To the sides, between the fusion tube and the tanks and other equipment, the blue stars glared at me with a light that was almost violet. I was afraid to look too long. I actually thought they might blind me.

There must have been hundreds of gravities in the cabin. I could even feel the pressure change. The air was thin at this height, one hundred and fifty feet above the control room.

And now, almost suddenly, the red dot was more than a dot. My time was up. A red disk leapt up at me; the ship swung around me; I gasped and shut my eyes tight. Giants' hands gripped my arms and legs and head, gently but with great firmness, and tried to pull me in two. In that moment it came to me that Peter Laskin had died like this. He'd made the same guesses I had, and he'd tried to hide in the access tube. But he'd slipped ... as I was slipping ... From the control room came a multiple shriek of tearing metal. I tried to dig my feet into the hard tube walls. Somehow they held.

When I got my eyes open the red dot was shrinking into nothing.

The puppeteer president insisted I be put in a hospital for observation. I didn't fight the idea. My face and hands were flaming red, with blisters rising, and I ached as though I'd been beaten. Rest and tender loving care, that's what I wanted.

I was floating between a pair of sleeping plates, hideously uncomfortable, when the nurse came to announce a visitor. I knew who it was from her peculiar expression.

"What can get through a General Products hull?" I asked it.

"I hoped you would tell me." The president rested on its single back leg, holding a stick that gave off green incense-smelling smoke.

"And so I will. Gravity."

"Do not play with me, Beowulf Shaeffer. This matter is vital."

"I'm not playing. Does your world have a moon?"

"That information is classified." The puppeteers are cowards. Nobody knows where they come from, and nobody is likely to find out.

"Do you know what happens when a moon gets too close to its primary?"

"It falls apart."

"Why?"

"I do not know."

"Tides."

"What is a tide?"

Oho, said I to myself, said I. "I'm going to try to tell you. The Earth's moon is almost two thousand miles in diameter and does not rotate with respect to Earth. I want you to pick two rocks on the moon, one at the point nearest the Earth, one at the point farthest away."

"Very well."

"Now, isn't it obvious that if those rocks were left to themselves, they'd fall away from each other? They're in two different orbits, mind you, concentric orbits, one almost two thousand miles outside the other. Yet those rocks are forced to move at the same orbital speed."

"The one outside is moving faster."

"Good point. So there *is* a force trying to pull the moon apart. Gravity holds it together. Bring the moon close enough to Earth, and those two rocks would simply float away."

"I see. Then this 'tide' tried to pull your ship apart. It was powerful enough in the lifesystem of the Institute ship to pull the acceleration chairs out of their mounts."

"And to crush a human being. Picture it. The ship's nose was just seven miles from the center of BVS-1. The tail was three hundred feet farther out. Left to themselves, they'd have gone in completely different orbits. My head and feet tried to do the same thing when I got close enough."

"I see. Are you molting?"

"What?"

"I notice you are losing your outer integument in spots."

"Oh, *that*. I got a bad sunburn from exposure to starlight. It's not important."

Two heads stared at each other for an eyeblink. A shrug? The puppeteer said, "We have deposited the residue of your pay with the Bank of We Made It. One Sigmund Ausfaller, human, has frozen the account until your taxes are computed."

"Figures."

"If you will talk to reporters now, explaining what happened to the Institute ship, we will pay you ten thousand stars. We will pay cash so that you may use it immediately. It is urgent. There have been rumors."

"Bring 'em in." As an afterthought I added, "I can also tell them that your world is moonless. That should be good for a footnote somewhere."

"I do not understand." But two long necks had drawn back, and the puppeteer was watching me like a pair of pythons.

"You'd know what a tide was if you had a moon. You couldn't avoid it."

"Would you be interested in—"

"A million stars? I'd be fascinated. I'll even sign a contract if it states what we're hiding. How do *you* like being blackmailed for a change?"

A RELIC OF THE EMPIRE

WHEN THE SHIP arrived, Dr. Richard Schultz-Mann was out among the plants, flying over and around them on a lift belt. He hovered over one, inspecting with proprietary interest an anomalous patch in its yellow foliage. This one would soon be ripe.

The nature-lover was a breadstick of a man, very tall and very thin, with an aristocratic head sporting a close-cropped growth of coppery hair and an asymmetric beard. A white streak ran above his right ear, and there was a patch of white on each side of the chin, one coinciding with the waxed spike. As his head moved in the double sunlight, the patches changed color instantly.

He took a tissue sample from the grayish patch, stored it, and started to move on. . . .

The ship came down like a daylight meteor, streaking blue-white across the vague red glare of Big Mira. It slowed and circled high overhead, weaving drunkenly across the sky, then settled toward the plain near Mann's *Explorer*. Mann watched it land, then gave up his bumble-bee activities and went to welcome the newcomers. He was amazed at the coincidence. As far as he knew, his had been the first ship ever to land here. The company would be good . . . but what could anyone possibly want here?

Little Mira set while he was skimming back. A flash of white at the far edge of the sea, and the tiny blue-white dwarf was gone. The shadows changed abruptly, turning the world red. Mann took off his pink-tinged goggles. Big Mira was still high, sixty degrees above the horizon and two hours from second sunset.

The newcomer was huge, a thick blunt-nosed cylinder twenty times the size of the *Explorer*. It looked old: not damaged, not even weathered, but indefinably old. Its nose

29

was still closed tight, the living bubble retracted, if indeed it had a living bubble. Nothing moved nearby. They must be waiting for his welcome before they debarked.

Mann dropped toward the newcomer.

The stunner took him a few hundred feet up. Without pain and without sound, suddenly all Mann's muscles turned to loose jelly. Fully conscious and completely helpless, he continued to dive toward the ground.

Three figures swarmed up at him from the newcomer's oversized airlock. They caught him before he hit. Tossing humorous remarks at each other in a language Mann did not know, they towed him down to the plain.

The man behind the desk wore a captain's hat and a cheerful smile. "Our supply of Verinol is limited," he said in the trade language. "If I have to use it, I will, but I'd rather save it. You may have heard that it has unpleasant side effects."

"I understand perfectly," said Mann. "You'll use it the moment you think you've caught me in a lie." Since he had not yet been injected with the stuff, he decided it was a bluff. The man had no Verinol, if indeed there was such an animal as Verinol.

But he was still in a bad hole. The ancient, renovated ship held more than a dozen men, whereas Mann seriously doubted if he could have stood up. The sonic had not entirely worn off.

His captor nodded approvingly. He was huge and square, almost a cartoon of a heavy-planet man, with muscularity as smooth and solid as an elephant's. A Jinxian, for anyone's money. His size made the tiny shipboard office seem little more than a coffin. Among the crew his captain's hat would not be needed to enforce orders. He looked like he could kick holes in hullmetal, or teach tact to an armed Kzin.

"You're quick," he said. "That's good. I'll be asking questions about you and about this planet. You'll give truthful, complete answers. If some of my questions get too personal, say so; but remember, I'll use the Verinol if I'm not satisfied. How old are you?"

"One hundred and fifty-four."

"You look much older."

"I was off boosterspice for a couple of decades."

"Tough luck. Planet of origin?"

"Wunderland."

"Thought so, with that stick-figure build. Name?"

"Doctor Richard Harvey Schultz-Mann."

"Rich Mann, hah? Are you?"

Trust a Jinxian to spot a pun. "No. After I make my reputation, I'll write a book on the Slaver Empire. Then I'll be rich."

"If you say so. Married?"

"Several times. Not at the moment."

"Rich Mann, I can't give you my real name, but you can call me Captain Kidd. What kind of beard is that?"

"You've never seen an asymmetric beard?"

"No, thank the Mist Demons. It looks like you've shaved off all your hair below the part, and everything on your face left of what looks like a one-tuft goatee. Is that the way it's supposed to go?"

"Exactly so."

"You did it on purpose then."

"Don't mock me, Captain Kidd."

"Point taken. Are they popular on Wunderland?"

Dr. Mann unconsciously sat a little straighter. "Only among those willing to take the time and trouble to keep it neat." He twisted the single waxed spike of beard at the right of his chin with unconscious complacence. This was the only straight hair on his face—the rest of the beard being close-cropped and curly—and it sprouted from one of the white patches. Mann was proud of his beard.

"Hardly seems worth it," said the Jinxian. "I assume it's to show you're one of the leisure classes. What are you doing on Mira Ceti-T?"

"I'm investigating one aspect of the Slaver Empire."

"You're a geologist, then?"

"No, a xenobiologist."

"I don't understand."

"What do you know about the Slavers?"

"A little. They used to live all through this part of the

galaxy. One day the slave races decided they'd had enough, and there was a war. When it was over, everyone was dead."

"You know quite a bit. Well, Captain, a billion and a half years is a long time. The Slavers left only two kinds of evidence of their existence. There are the stasis boxes and their contents, mostly weaponry, but records have been found too. And there are the plants and animals developed for the Slavers' convenience by their tnuctip slaves, who were biological engineers."

"I know about those. We have bandersnatchi on Jinx, on both sides of the ocean."

"The bandersnatchi food animals are a special case. They can't mutate; their chromosomes are as thick as your finger, too large to be influenced by radiation. All other relics of tnuctipun engineering have mutated almost beyond recognition. Almost. For the past twelve years I've been searching out and identifying the surviving species."

"It doesn't sound like a fun way to spend a life, Rich Mann. Are there Slaver animals on this planet?"

"Not animals, but plants. Have you been outside yet?"

"Not yet."

"Then come out. I'll show you."

The ship was very large. It did not seem to be furnished with a living bubble, hence the entire lifesystem must be enclosed within the metal walls. Mann walked ahead of the Jinxian down a long unpainted corridor to the airlock, waited inside while the pressure dropped slightly, then rode the escalator to the ground. He would not try to escape yet, though the sonic had worn off. The Jinxian was affable but alert, he carried a flashlight-laser dangling from his belt, his men were all around them, and Mann's lift belt had been removed. Richard Mann was not quixotic.

It was a red, red world. They stood on a dusty plain sparsely scattered with strange yellow-headed bushes. A breeze blew things like tumbleweeds across the plain, things which on second glance were the dried heads of former bushes. No other life-forms were visible. Big Mira sat on the horizon, a vague, fiery semicircular cloud, just dim enough to look at without squinting. Outlined in sharp black silhouette against the red giant's bloody disk were three slender, improbably tall spires, unnaturally straight and regular, each with a vivid patch of yellow vegetation surrounding its base. Members of the Jinxian's crew ran, walked, or floated outside, some playing an improvised variant of baseball, others at work, still others merely enjoying themselves. None were Jinxian, and none had Mann's light-planet build. Mann noticed that a few were using the thin wire blades of variable-knives to cut down some of the straight bushes.

"Those," he said.

"The bushes?"

"Yes. They used to be tnuctip stage trees. We don't know what they looked like originally, but the old records say the Slavers stopped using them some decades before the rebellion. May I ask what those men are doing in my ship?"

Expanded from its clamshell nose, the *Explorer*'s living bubble was bigger than the *Explorer*. Held taut by air pressure, isolated from the surrounding environment, proof against any atmospheric chemistry found in nature, the clear fabric hemisphere was a standard feature of all camper-model spacecraft. Mann could see biped shadows moving purposefully about inside and going between the clamshell doors into the ship proper.

"They're not stealing anything, Rich Mann. I sent them in to remove a few components from the drives and the comm systems."

"One hopes they won't damage what they remove."

"They won't. They have their orders."

"I assume you don't want me to call someone," said Mann. He noticed that the men were preparing a bonfire, using stage bushes. The bushes were like miniature trees, four to six feet tall, slender and straight, and the brilliant yellow foliage at the top was flattened like the head of a dandelion. From the low, rounded eastern mountains to the western sea, the red land was sprinkled with the yellow dots of their heads. Men were cutting off the heads and roots, then dragging the logs away to pile them in conical formation over a stack of death-dry tumbleweed heads.

"We don't want you to call the Wunderland police, who happen to be somewhere out there looking for us."

"I hate to pry—"

"No, no, you're entitled to your curiosity. We're pirates."

"Surely you jest. Captain Kidd, if you've figured out a way to make piracy pay off, you must be bright enough to make ten times the money on the stock market."

"Why?"

By the tone of his voice, by his gleeful smile, the Jinxian was baiting him. Fine; it would keep his mind off stage trees. Mann said, "Because you can't *catch* a ship in hyperspace. The only way you can match courses with a ship is to wait until it's in an inhabited system. Then the police come calling."

"I know an inhabited system where there aren't any police."

"The hell you do."

They had walked more or less aimlessly to the *Explorer*'s airlock. Now the Jinxian turned and gazed out over the red plain, toward the dwindling crescent of Big Mira, which now looked like a bad forest fire. "I'm curious about those spires."

"Fine, keep your little secret. I've wondered about them myself, but I haven't had a chance to look at them yet."

"I'd think they'd interest you. They look definitely artificial to me."

"But they're a billion years too young to be Slaver artifacts."

"Rich Mann, are those bushes the only life on this planet?"

"I haven't seen anything else," Mann lied.

"Then it couldn't have been a native race that put those spires up. I never heard of a space-traveling race that builds such big things for mere monuments."

"Neither did I. Shall we look at them tomorrow?"

"Yes." Captain Kidd stepped into the *Explorer*'s airlock, wrapped a vast hand gently around Mann's thin wrist and pulled his captive in beside him. The airlock cycled and Mann followed the Jinxian into the living bubble with an impression that the Jinxian did not quite trust him.

Fine.

It was dark inside the bubble. Mann hesitated before turning on the light. Outside he could see the last red sliver of Big Mira shrinking with visible haste. He saw more. A man was kneeling before the conical bonfire, and a flickering light was growing in the dried bush-head kindling.

Mann turned on the lights, obliterating the outside view. "Go on about piracy," he said.

"Oh, yes." The Jinxian dropped into a chair, frowning. "Piracy was only the end product. It started a year ago, when I found the puppeteer system."

"The—"

"Yes. The puppeteers' home system."

Richard Mann's ears went straight up. He was from Wunderland, remember?

Puppeteers are highly intelligent, herbivorous, and very old as a species. Their corner on interstellar business is as old as the human Bronze Age. And they are cowards.

A courageous puppeteer is not regarded as insane only by other puppeteers. It *is* insane, and usually shows disastrous secondary symptoms: depression, homicidal tendencies, and the like. These poor, warped minds are easy to spot. No sane puppeteer will cross a vehicular roadway or travel in any but the safest available fashion or resist a thief, even an unarmed thief. No sane puppeteer will leave his home system, wherever that may be, without his painless method of suicide, nor will it walk an alien world without guards—nonpuppeteer guards.

The location of the puppeteer system is one of the puppeteer's most closely guarded secrets. Another is the painless suicide gimmick. It may be a mere trick of preconditioning. Whatever it is, it works. Puppeteers cannot be tortured into revealing anything about their home world, though they hate pain. It must be a world with reasonably earthlike atmosphere and temperature, but beyond that nothing is known . . . or was known.

Suddenly Mann wished that they hadn't lit the bonfire so soon. He didn't know how long it would burn before the logs caught, and he wanted to hear more about this.

"I found it just a year ago," the Jinxian repeated. "It's best I don't tell you what I was doing up to then. The less you know about who I am, the better. But when I'd got safely out of the system, I came straight home. I wanted time to think."

"And you picked piracy? Why not blackmail?"

"I thought of that—"

"I should hope so! Can you imagine what the puppeteers would pay to keep that secret?"

"Yes. That's what stopped me. Rich Mann, how much would you have asked for in one lump sum?"

"A round billion stars and immunity from prosecution."

"Okay. Now look at it from the puppeteer point of view. That billion wouldn't buy them complete safety, because you might still talk. But if they spent a tenth of that on detectives, weapons, hit men, et cetera, they could shut your mouth for keeps and also find and hit anyone you might have talked to. I couldn't figure any way to make myself safe and still collect, not with that much potential power against me.

"So I thought of piracy.

"Eight of us had gone in, but I was the only one who'd guessed just what we'd stumbled into. I let the others in on it. Some had friends they could trust, and that raised our number to fourteen. We bought a ship, a very old one, and renovated it. She's an old slowboat's ground-to-orbit auxiliary fitted out with a new hyperdrive; maybe you noticed?"

"No. I saw how old she was."

"We figured even if the puppeteers recognized her, they'd never trace her. We took her back to the puppeteer system and waited."

A flickering light glimmered outside the bubble wall.

Any second now the logs would catch . . . Mann tried to relax.

"Pretty soon a ship came in. We waited till it was too deep in the system's gravity well to jump back into hyperspace. Then we matched courses. Naturally they surrendered right away. We went in in suits so they couldn't describe us even if they could tell humans apart. Would you believe they had six hundred million stars in currency?"

"That's pretty good pay. What went wrong?"

"My idiot crew wouldn't leave. We'd figured most of the ships coming into the puppeteer system would be carrying money. They're misers, you know. Part of being a coward is wanting security. And they do most of their mining and manufacturing on other worlds, where they can get labor. So we waited for two more ships, because we had room for lots more money. The puppeteers wouldn't dare attack us inside their own system." Captain Kidd made a sound of disgust. "I can't really blame the men. In a sense they were right. One ship with a fusion drive can do a hell of a lot of damage just by hovering over a city. So we stayed.

"Meanwhile the puppeteers registered a formal complaint with Earth.

"Earth hates people who foul up interstellar trade. We'd offered physical harm to a puppeteer. A thing like that could cause a stock-market crash. So Earth offered the services of every police force in human space. Hardly seems fair, does it?"

"They ganged up on you. But they still couldn't come after you, could they? The puppeteers would have to tell the police how to find their system. They'd hardly do that; not when some human descendant might attack them a thousand years from now."

The Jinxian dialed himself a frozen daiquiri. "They had to wait till we left. I still don't know how they tracked us. Maybe they've got something that can track a gravity warp moving faster than light. I wouldn't put it past them to build it just for us. Anyway, when we angled toward

Jinx, we heard them telling the police of We Made It just where we were."

"Ouch."

"We headed for the nearest double star. Not my idea; Hermie Preston's. He thought we could hide in the dust clouds in the trojan points. Whatever the puppeteers were using probably couldn't find us in normal space." Two thirsty gulps had finished his daiquiri. He crumpled the cup, watched it evaporate, dialed another. "The nearest double star was Mira Ceti. We hardly expected to find a planet in the trailing trojan point, but as long as it was there, we decided to use it."

"And here you are."

"Yeah."

"You'll be better off when you've found a way to hide that ship."

"We had to find out about you first, Rich Mann. Tomorrow we'll sink the *Puppet Master* in the ocean. Already we've shut off the fusion drive. The lifters work by battery, and the cops can't detect that."

"Fine. Now for the billion-dollar—"

"No, no, Rich Mann. I will not tell you where to find the puppeteer planet. Give up the whole idea. Shall we join the campfire group?"

Mann came joltingly alert. *How* had the stage trees lasted this long? Thinking fast, he said, "Is your autokitchen as good as mine?"

"Probably not. Why?"

"Let me treat your group to dinner, Captain Kidd."

Captain Kidd shook his head, smiling. "No offense, Rich Mann, but I can't read your kitchen controls, and there's no point in tempting you. You might rashly put someth—"

WHAM!

The living bubble bulged inward, snapped back. Captain Kidd swore and ran for the airlock. Mann stayed seated, motionless, hoping against hope that the Jinxian had forgotten him.

WHAM! WHAM! Flares of light from the region of the campfire. Captain Kidd frantically punched the cycle button, and the opaque inner door closed on him. Mann came to his feet, running.

WHAM! The concussion hurt his ears and set the bubble rippling. Burning logs must be flying in all directions. The airlock recycled, empty. No telling where the Jinxian was; the outer door was opaque too. Well, that worked both ways.

WHAM!

Mann searched through the airlock locker, pushing sections of spacesuit aside to find the lift belt. It wasn't there. He'd been wearing it; they'd taken it off him after they shot him down.

He moaned: a tormented, uncouth sound to come from a cultured Wunderlander. He *had* to have a lift belt.

WHAMWHAMWHAM. Someone was screaming far away.

Mann snatched up the suit's chest-and-shoulder section and locked it around him. It was rigid vacuum armor, with a lift motor built into the back. He took an extra moment to screw down the helmet, then hit the cycle button.

No use searching for weapons. They'd have taken even a variable-knife.

The Jinxian could be just outside waiting. He might have realized the truth by now.

The door opened.... Captain Kidd was easy to find, a running misshapen shadow and a frantic booming voice. "Flatten out, you yeastheads! It's an attack!" He hadn't guessed. But he must know that the We Made It police would use stunners.

Mann twisted his lift control to full power.

The surge of pressure took him under the armpits. Two standard gees sent blood rushing to his feet, pushed him upward with four times Wunderland's gravity. A last stage log exploded under him, rocked him back and forth, and then all was dark and quiet.

He adjusted the attitude setting to slant him almost straight forward. The dark ground sped beneath him. He moved northeast. Nobody was following him—yet.

Captain Kidd's men would have been killed, hurt, or at

least stunned when the campfire exploded in their faces. He'd expected Captain Kidd to chase him, but the Jinxian couldn't have caught him. Lift motors are all alike, and Mann wasn't as heavy as the Jinxian.

He flew northeast, flying very low, knowing that the only landmarks big enough to smash him were the spires to the west. When he could no longer see the ships' lights, he turned south, still very low. Still nobody followed him. He was glad he'd taken the helmet; it protected his eyes from the wind.

In the blue dawn he came awake. The sky was darker than navy blue, and the light around him was dim, like blue moonlight. Little Mira was a hurtingly bright pinpoint between two mountain peaks, bright enough to sear holes in a man's retinae. Mann unscrewed his helmet, adjusted the pink goggles over his eyes. Now it was even darker.

He poked his nose above the yellow moss. The plain and sky were empty of men. The pirates must be out looking for him, but they hadn't gotten here yet. So far so good.

Far out across the plain there was fire. A stage tree rose rapidly into the black sky, minus its roots and flowers, the wooden flanges at its base holding it in precarious aerodynamic stability. A white rope of smoke followed it up. When the smoke cut off, the tree became invisible ... until, much higher, there was a puff of white cloud like a flak burst. Now the seeds would be spreading across the sky.

Richard Mann smiled. Wonderful, how the stage trees had adapted to the loss of their masters. The Slavers had raised them on wide plantations, using the solid-fuel rocket cores inside the living bark to lift their ships from places where a fusion drive would have done damage. But the trees used the rockets for reproduction, to scatter their seeds farther than any plant before them.

Ah, well ... Richard Mann snuggled deeper into the yellow woolly stuff around him and began to consider his next move. He was a hero now in the eyes of humanity-

at-large. He had badly damaged the pirate crew. When
the police landed, he could count on a reward from the
puppeteers. Should he settle for that or go on to bigger
stakes?

The *Puppet Master*'s cargo was bigger stakes, certainly.
But even if he could take it, which seemed unlikely, how
could he fit it into his ship? How escape the police of We
Made It?

No. Mann had another stake in mind, one just as
valuable and infinitely easier to hide.

What Captain Kidd apparently hadn't realized was that
blackmail is not immoral to a puppeteer. There are well-
established rules of conduct that make blackmail perfectly
safe both for blackmailer and victim. Two are that the
blackmailer must submit to having certain portions of his
memory erased, and must turn over all evidence against
the victim. Mann was prepared to do this if he could force
Captain Kidd to tell him where to find the puppeteer
system.

But how?

Well, he knew one thing the Jinxian didn't. . . .

Little Mira rose fast, arc blue, a hole into hell. Mann
remained where he was, an insignificant mote in the yellow
vegetation below one of the spires Captain Kidd had
remarked on last night. The spire was a good half mile
high. An artifact that size would seem impossibly huge to
any but an Earthman. The way it loomed over him made
Mann uncomfortable. In shape it was a slender cone with
a base three hundred feet across. The surface near the
base was gray and smooth to touch, like polished granite.

The yellow vegetation was a thick, rolling carpet. It
spread out around the spire in an uneven circle half a mile
in diameter and dozens of feet deep. It rose about the
base in a thick turtleneck collar. Close up, the stuff wasn't
even discrete plants. It looked like a cross between moss
and wool, dyed flagrant yellow.

It made a good hiding place. Not perfect, of course; a
heat sensor would pick him out in a flash. He hadn't
thought of that last night, and now it worried him. Should
he get out, try to reach the sea?

The ship would certainly carry a heat sensor, but not a portable one. A portable heat sensor would be a weapon, a nighttime gunsight, and weapons of war had been illegal for some time in human space.

But the *Puppet Master* could have stopped elsewhere to get such implements. Kzinti, for example.

Nonsense. Why would Captain Kidd have needed portable weapons with night gunsights? He certainly hadn't expected puppeteers to fight hand-to-hand! The stunners were mercy weapons; even a pirate would not dare kill a puppeteer, and Captain Kidd was no ordinary pirate.

All right. Radar? He need only burrow into the moss/wool. Sight search? Same answer. Radio? Mental note: Do not transmit anything.

Mental note? There was a dictaphone in his helmet. He used it after pulling the helmet out of the moss/wool around him.

Flying figures. Mann watched them for a long moment, trying to spot the Jinxian. There were only four, and he wasn't among them. The four were flying northwest of him, moving south. Mann ducked into the moss.

"Hello, Rich Mann."

The voice was low, contorted with fury. Mann felt the shock race through him, contracting every muscle with the fear of death. It came from behind him!

From his helmet.

"Hello, Rich Mann. Guess where I am?"

He couldn't turn it off. Spacesuit helmet radios weren't built to be turned off: a standard safety factor. If one were fool enough to ignore safety, one could insert an "off" switch; but Mann had never felt the need.

"I'm in your ship, using your ship-to-suit radio circuit. That was a good trick you played last night. I didn't even know what a stage tree was till I looked it up in your library."

He'd just have to endure it. A pity he couldn't answer back.

"You killed four of my men and put five more in the autodoc tanks. Why'd you do it, Rich Mann? You must have known we weren't going to kill you. Why should we? There's no blood on *our* hands."

You lie, Mann thought at the radio. *People die in a market crash. And the ones who live are the ones who suffer. Do you know what it's like to be suddenly poor and not know how to live poor?*

"I'll assume you want something, Rich Mann. All right. What? The money in my hold? That's ridiculous. You'd never get in. You want to turn us in for a reward? Fat chance. You've got no weapons. If we find you now, we'll kill you."

The four searchers passed far to the west, their headlamps spreading yellow light across the blue dusk. They were no danger to him now. A pity they and their fellows should have been involved in what amounted to a vendetta.

"The puppeteer planet, of course. The modern El Dorado. But you don't know where it is, do you? I wonder if I ought to give you a hint. Of course you'd never know whether I was telling the truth. . . ."

Did the Jinxian know how to live poor? Mann shuddered. The old memories came back only rarely; but when they came, they hurt.

You have to learn not to buy luxuries before you've bought necessities. You can starve learning which is which. Necessities are food and a place to sleep, shoes and pants. Luxuries are tobacco, restaurants, fine shirts, throwing away a ruined meal while you're learning to cook, quitting a job you don't like. A union is a necessity. Boosterspice is a luxury.

The Jinxian wouldn't know about that. He'd had the money to buy his own ship.

"Ask me politely, Rich Mann. Would you like to know where I found the puppeteer system?"

Mann had leased the *Explorer* on a college grant. It had been the latest step in a long climb upward. Before that . . .

He was half his lifetime old when the crash came. Until then boosterspice had kept him as young as the ageless idle ones who were his friends and relatives. Overnight he

*was one of the hungry. A number of his partners in
disaster had ridden their lift belts straight up into eternity;
Richard Schultz-Mann had sold his for his final dose of
boosterspice. Before he could afford boosterspice again,
there were wrinkles in his forehead, the texture of his skin
had changed, his sex urge had decreased, strange white
patches had appeared in his hair, there were twinges in his
back. He still got them.*

*Yet always he had maintained his beard. With the white
spike and the white streak it looked better than ever.
After the boosterspice restored color to his hair, he dyed
the patches back in again.*

"Answer me, Rich Mann!"

Go ride a bandersnatch.

It was a draw. Captain Kidd couldn't entice him into
answering, and Mann would never know the pirate's
secret. If Kidd dropped his ship in the sea, Mann could
show it to the police. At least that would be something.

Luckily Kidd couldn't move the *Explorer*. Otherwise he
could take both ships half around the planet, leaving
Mann stranded.

The four pirates were far to the south. Captain Kidd
had apparently given up on the radio. There were water
and food syrup in his helmet; Mann would not starve.

Where in blazes were the police? On the other side of
the planet?

Stalemate.

Big Mira came as a timorous peeping Tom, poking its
rim over the mountains like red smoke. The land bright-
ened, taking on tinges of lavender against long, long navy
blue shadows. The shadows shortened and became vague.

The morality of his position was beginning to bother
Dr. Richard Mann.

In attacking the pirates, he had done his duty as a
citizen. The pirates had sullied humanity's hard-won reputation for honesty. Mann had struck back.

But his motive? Fear had been two parts of that motive. First, the fear that Captain Kidd might decide to
shut his mouth. Second, the fear of being poor.

That fear had been with him for some time.

Write a book and make a fortune! It looked good on paper. The thirty-light-year sphere of human space contained nearly fifty billion readers. Persuade one percent of them to shell out half a star each for a disposable tape, and your four-percent royalties became twenty million stars. But most books nowadays were flops. You had to scream very loud nowadays to get the attention of even ten billion readers. Others were trying to drown you out.

Before Captain Kidd, that had been Richard Schultz-Mann's sole hope of success.

He'd behaved within the law. Captain Kidd couldn't make that claim; but Captain Kidd hadn't killed anybody.

Mann sighed. He'd had no choice. His major motive was honor, and that motive still held.

He moved restlessly in his nest of damp moss/wool. The day was heating up, and his suit's temperature control would not work with half a suit.

What was that?

It was the *Puppet Master,* moving effortlessly toward him on its lifters. The Jinxian must have decided to get it under water before the human law arrived.

... Or had he?

Mann adjusted his lift motor until he was just short of weightless, then moved cautiously around the spire. He saw the four pirates moving to intersect the *Puppet Master.* They'd see him if he left the spire. But if he stayed, those infrared detectors ...

He'd have to chance it.

The suit's padded shoulders gouged his armpits as he streaked toward the second spire. He stopped in midair over the moss and dropped, burrowed in it. The pirates didn't swerve.

Now he'd see.

The ship slowed to a stop over the spire he'd just left.

"Can you hear me, Rich Mann?"

Mann nodded gloomily to himself. Definitely, that was it.

"I should have tried this before. Since you're nowhere

in sight, you've either left the vicinity altogether or you're hiding in the thick bushes around those towers."

Should he try to keep dodging from spire to spire? Or could he outfly them?

At least one was bound to be faster. The armor increased his weight.

"I hope you took the opportunity to examine this tower. It's fascinating. Very smooth, stony surface, except at the top. A perfect cone, also except at the top. You listening? The tip of this thing swells from an eight-foot neck into an egg-shaped knob fifteen feet across. The knob isn't polished as smooth as the rest of it. Vaguely reminiscent of an asparagus spear, wouldn't you say?"

Richard Schultz-Mann cocked his head, tasting an idea.

He unscrewed his helmet, ripped out and pocketed the radio. In frantic haste he began ripping out double handfuls of the yellow moss/wool, stuffed them into a wad in the helmet, and turned his lighter on it. At first the vegetation merely smoldered, while Mann muttered through clenched teeth. Then it caught with a weak blue smokeless flame. Mann placed his helmet in a mossy nest, setting it so it would not tip over and spill its burning contents.

"I'd have said a phallic symbol, myself. What do you think, Rich Mann? If these are phallic symbols, they're pretty well distorted. Humanoid but not human, you might say."

The pirates had joined their ship. They hovered around its floating silver bulk, ready to drop on him when the *Puppet Master*'s infrared detectors found him.

Mann streaked away to the west on full acceleration, staying as low as he dared. The spire would shield him for a minute or so, and then . . .

"This vegetation isn't stage trees, Rich Mann. It looks like some sort of grass from here. Must need something in the rock they made these erections out of. Mph. No hot spots. You're not down there after all. Well, we try the next one."

Behind him, in the moments when he dared look back, Mann saw the *Puppet Master* move to cover the second spire, the one he'd left a moment ago, the one with a gray streak in the moss at its base. Four humanoid dots clustered loosely above the ship.

"Peekaboo," came the Jinxian's voice. "And good-bye, killer."

The *Puppet Master*'s fusion drive went on. Fusion flame lashed out in a blue-white spear, played down the side of the pillar and into the moss/wool below. Mann faced forward and concentrated on flying. He felt neither elation nor pity, but only disgust. The Jinxian was a fool after all. He'd seen no life on Mira Ceti-T but for the stage trees. He had Mann's word that there was none. Couldn't he reach the obvious conclusion? Perhaps the moss/wool had fooled him. It certainly did look like yellow moss, clustering around the spires as if it needed some chemical element in the stone.

A glance back told him that the pirate ship was still spraying white flame over the spire and the foliage below. He'd have been a cinder by now. The Jinxian must want him extremely dead. Well—

The spire went all at once. It sat on the lavender plain in a hemisphere of multicolored fire, engulfing the other spires and the Jinxian ship; and then it began to expand and rise. Mann adjusted his attitude to vertical to get away from the ground. A moment later the shock wave slammed into him and blew him tumbling over the desert.

Two white ropes of smoke rose straight up through the dimming explosion cloud. The other spires were taking off while still green! Fire must have reached the foliage at their bases.

Mann watched them go with his head thrown back and his body curiously loose in the vacuum armor. His expression was strangely contented. At these times he could forget himself and his ambitions in the contemplation of immortality.

Two knots formed simultaneously in the rising smoke trails. Second stage on. They rose very fast now.

"Rich Mann."

Mann flicked his transmitter on. "You'd live through anything."

"Not I. I can't feel anything below my shoulders. Listen, Rich Mann, I'll trade secrets with you. What happened?"

"The big towers are stage trees."

"Uh?" Half question, half an expression of agony.

"A stage tree has two life cycles. One is the bush, the other is the big multistage form." Mann talked fast, fearful of losing his audience. "The forms alternate. A stage tree seed lands on a planet and grows into a bush. Later there are lots of bushes. When a seed hits a particularly fertile spot, it grows into a multistage form. You still there?"

"Yuh."

"In the big form the living part is the tap root and the photosynthetic organs around the base. That way the rocket section doesn't have to carry so much weight. It grows straight up out of the living part, but it's as dead as the center of an oak except for the seed at the top. When it's ripe, the rocket takes off. Usually it'll reach terminal velocity for the system it's in. Kidd, I can't see your ship; I'll have to wait till the smoke—"

"Just keep talking."

"I'd like to help."

"Too late. Keep talking."

"I've tracked the stage trees across twenty light-years of space. God knows where they started. They're all through the systems around here. The seed pods spend hundreds of thousands of years in space; and when they enter a system, they explode. If there's a habitable world, one seed is bound to hit it. If there isn't, there's lots more pods where that one came from. It's immortality, Captain Kidd. This one plant has traveled farther than mankind, and it's much older. A billion and a—"

"Mann."

"Yah."

"Twenty-three point six, seventy point one, six point nil. I don't know its name on the star charts. Shall I repeat that?"

Mann forgot the stage trees. "Better repeat it."

"Twenty-three point six, seventy point one, six point

nothing. Hunt in that area till you find it. It's a red giant, undersized. Planet is small, dense, no moon."

"Got it."

"You're stupid if you use it. You'll have the same luck I did. That's why I told you."

"I'll use blackmail."

"They'll kill you. Otherwise I wouldn't have said. Why'd you kill me, Rich Mann?"

"I didn't like your remarks about my beard. Never insult a Wunderlander's asymmetric beard, Captain Kidd."

"I won't do it again."

"I'd like to help." Mann peered into the billowing smoke. Now it was a black pillar tinged at the edges by the twin sunlight. "Still can't see your ship."

"You will in a moment."

The pirate moaned . . . and Mann saw the ship. He managed to turn his head in time to save his eyes.

AT THE CORE

I

I couldn't decide whether to call it a painting, a relief mural, a sculpture, or a hash; but it was the prize exhibit in the Art Section of the Institute of Knowledge on Jinx. The Kdatlyno must have strange eyes, I thought. My own were watering. The longer I looked at "FTL-SPACE," the more blurred it got.

I'd tentatively decided that it was *supposed* to look blurred when a set of toothy jaws clamped gently on my arm. I jumped a foot in the air. A soft, thrilling contralto voice said, "Beowulf Shaeffer, you are a spendthrift."

That voice would have made a singer's fortune. And I thought I recognized it—but it couldn't be; *that* one was on We Made It, light-years distant. I turned.

The puppeteer had released my arm. It went on: "And what do you think of Hrodenu?"

"He's ruining my eyes."

"Naturally. The Kdatlyno are blind to all but radar. 'FTLSPACE' is not meant to be seen but to be touched. Run your tongue over it."

"My tongue? No, thanks." I tried running my hand over it. If you want to know what it felt like, hop a ship for Jinx; the thing's still there. I flatly refuse to describe the sensation.

The puppeteer cocked its head dubiously. "I'm sure your tongue is more sensitive. No guards are nearby."

"Forget it. You know, you sound just like the regional president of General Products on We Made It."

"It was he who sent me your dossier, Beowulf Shaeffer. No doubt we had the same English teacher. I am the regional president on Jinx, as you no doubt recognized from my mane."

Well, not quite. The auburn mop over the brain case

between the two necks is supposed to show caste once you learn to discount variations of mere style. To do that, you have to be a puppeteer. Instead of admitting my ignorance, I asked, "Did that dossier say I was a spendthrift?"

"You have spent more than a million stars in the past four years."

"And loved it."

"Yes. You will shortly be in debt again. Have you thought of doing more writing? I admired your article on the neutron star BVS-1. 'The pointy bottom of a gravity well ...' 'Blue starlight fell on me like intangible sleet ...' Lovely."

"Thanks. It paid well, too. But I'm mainly a spaceship pilot."

"It is fortunate, our meeting here. I had thought of having you found. Do you wish a job?"

That was a loaded question. The last and only time I took a job from a puppeteer, the puppeteer blackmailed me into it, knowing it would probably kill me. It almost did. I didn't hold that against the regional president of We Made It, but to let them have another crack at me—? "I'll give you a conditional 'Maybe.' Do you have the idea I'm a professional suicide pilot?"

"Not at all. If I show details, do you agree that the information shall be confidential?"

"I do," I said formally, knowing it would commit me. A verbal contract is as binding as the tape it's recorded on.

"Good. Come." He pranced toward a transfer booth.

The transfer booth let us out somewhere in Jinx's vacuum regions. It was night. High in the sky, Sirius B was a painfully bright pinpoint casting vivid blue moonlight on a ragged lunar landscape. I looked up and didn't see Binary, Jinx's bloated orange companion planet, so we must have been in the Farside End.

But there was something hanging over us.

A No. 4 General Products hull is a transparent sphere a thousand-odd feet in diameter. No bigger ship has been built anywhere in the known galaxy. It takes a government to buy one, and they are used for colonization projects only. But this one could never have been so used; it was all machinery. Our transfer booth stood between two of the landing legs, so that the swelling flank of the ship looked down on us as an owl looks down at a mouse. An access tube ran through vacuum from the booth to the airlock.

I said, "Does General Products build complete spacecraft nowadays?"

"We are thinking of branching out. But there are problems."

From the viewpoint of the puppeteer-owned company, it must have seemed high time. General Products makes the hulls for ninety-five percent of all ships in space, mainly because nobody else knows how to build an indestructible hull. But they'd made a bad start with this ship. The only room I could see for crew, cargo, or passengers was a few cubic yards of empty space right at the bottom, just above the airlock, and just big enough for a pilot.

"You'd have a hard time selling that," I said.

"True. Do you notice anything else?"

"Well ..." The hardware that filled the transparent hull was very tightly packed. The effect was as if a race of ten-mile-tall giants had striven to achieve miniaturization. I saw no sign of access tubes; hence there could be no in-space repairs. Four reaction motors poked their appropriately huge nostrils through the hull, angled outward from the bottom. No small attitude jets; hence, oversized gyros inside. Otherwise ... "Most of it looks like hyperdrive motors. But that's silly. Unless you've thought of a good reason for moving moons around?"

"At one time you were a commercial pilot for Nakamura Lines. How long was the run from Jinx to We Made It?"

"Twelve days if nothing broke down." Just long enough to get to know the prettiest passenger aboard, while the autopilot did everything for me but wear my uniform.

"Sirius to Procyon is a distance of four light-years. Our ship would make the trip in five minutes."

"You've lost your mind."

"No."

But that was almost a light-year per minute! I couldn't visualize it. Then suddenly I did visualize it, and my mouth fell open, for what I saw was the galaxy opening before me. We know so little beyond our own small neighborhood of the galaxy. But with a ship like that—!

"That's goddam fast."

"As you say. But the equipment is bulky, as you note. It cost seven billion stars to build that ship, discounting centuries of research, but it will only move one man. As is, the ship is a failure. Shall we go inside?"

II

The lifesystem was two circular rooms, one above the other, with a small airlock to one side. The lower room was the control room, with banks of switches and dials and blinking lights dominated by a huge spherical mass pointer. The upper room was bare walls, transparent, through which I could see air- and food-producing equipment.

"This will be the relaxroom," said the puppeteer. "We decided to let the pilot decorate it himself."

"Why me?"

"Let me further explain the problem." The puppeteer began to pace the floor. I hunkered down against the wall and watched. Watching a puppeteer move is a pleasure. Even in Jinx's gravity the deerlike body seemed weightless, the tiny hooves tapping the floor at random. "The human sphere of colonization is some thirty light-years across, is it not?"

"Maximum. It's not exactly a sphere—"

"The puppeteer region is much smaller. The Kdatlyno sphere is half the size of yours, and the Kzinti is fractionally larger. These are the important space-traveling species. We must discount the Outsiders since they do not use ships. Some spheres coincide, naturally. Travel from one sphere to another is nearly nil except for ourselves, since our sphere of influence extends to all who buy our hulls. But add all these regions, and you have a region sixty light-years across. This ship could cross it in seventy-five minutes. Allow six hours for takeoff and six for landing, assuming no traffic snarls near the world of destination, and we have a ship which can go anywhere in thirteen hours but nowhere in less than twelve, carrying one pilot and no cargo, costing seven billion stars."

"How about exploration?"

"We puppeteers have no taste for abstract knowledge. And how should we explore?" Meaning that whatever race flew the ship would gain the advantages thereby. A puppeteer wouldn't risk his necks by flying it himself. "What we need is a great deal of money and a gathering of intelligences, to design something which *may* go slower but *must* be less bulky. General Products does not wish to spend so much on something that may fail. We will require the best minds of each sentient species and the richest investors. Beowulf Shaeffer, we need to attract attention."

"A publicity stunt?"

"Yes. We wish to send a pilot to the center of the galaxy and back."

"Ye . . . gods! Will it go *that* fast?"

"It would require some twenty-five days to reach the center and an equal time to return. You can see the reasoning behind—"

"It's perfect. You don't need to spell it out. Why me?"

"We wish you to make the trip and then write of it. I have a list of pilots who write. Those I have approached have been reluctant. They say that writing on the ground is safer than testing unknown ships. I follow their reasoning."

"Me too."

"Will you go?"

"What am I offered?"

"One hundred thousand stars for the trip. Fifty thousand to write the story, in addition to what you sell it for."

"Sold."

From then on, my only worry was that my new boss

would find out that someone had ghost-written that neutron star article.

Oh, I wondered at first why General Products was willing to trust me. The first time I worked for them I tried to steal their ship, for reasons which seemed good at the time. But the ship I now called *Long Shot* really wasn't worth stealing. Any potential buyer would know it was hot; and what good would it be to him? *Long Shot* could have explored a globular cluster; but her only other use was publicity.

Sending her to the Core was a masterpiece of promotion.

Look: It was twelve days from We Made It to Jinx by conventional craft, and twelve hours by *Long Shot*. What's the difference? You spent twelve years saving for the trip. But the Core! Ignoring refueling and reprovisioning problems, my old ship could have reached the galaxy's core in three hundred years. No known species had ever *seen* the Core! It hid behind layer on layer of tenuous gas and dust clouds. You can find libraries of literature on those central stars, but they all consist of generalities and educated guesses based on observation of other galaxies, like Andromeda.

Three centuries dropped to less than a month! There's something anyone can grasp. And with pictures!

The lifesystem was finished in a couple of weeks. I had them leave the control-room walls transparent and paint the relaxroom solid blue, no windows. When they finished, I had entertainment tapes and everything it takes to keep a man sane for seven weeks in a room the size of a large closet.

On the last day the puppeteer and I spoke the final version of my contract. I had four months to reach the galaxy's center and return. The outside cameras would run constantly; I was not to interfere with them. If the ship suffered a mechanical failure, I could return before reaching the center; otherwise, no. There were penalties. I took a copy of the tape to leave with a lawyer.

"There is a thing you should know," the puppeteer said

afterward. "The direction of thrust opposes the direction of hyperdrive."

"I don't get it."

The puppeteer groped for words. "If you turned on the reaction motors and the hyperdrive together, the flames would precede your ship through hyperspace."

I got the picture then. Ass backward into the unknown. With the control room at the ship's bottom, it made sense. To a puppeteer, it made sense.

III

And I was off.

I went up under two standard gees because I like my comfort. For twelve hours I used only the reaction motors. It wouldn't do to be too deep in a gravity well when I used a hyperdrive, especially an experimental one. Pilots who do that never leave hyperspace. The relaxroom kept me entertained until the bell rang. I slipped down to the control room, netted myself down against free fall, turned off the motors, rubbed my hands briskly together, and turned on the hyperdrive.

It wasn't quite as I'd expected.

I couldn't see out, of course. When the hyperdrive goes on, it's like your blind spot expanding to take in all the windows. It's not just that you don't see anything; you forget that there's anything to see. If there's a window between the kitchen control bank and your print of Dali's "Spain," your eye and mind will put the picture right next to the kitchen bank, obliterating the space between. It takes getting used to, in fact it has driven people insane, but that wasn't what bothered me. I've spent thousands of man-hours in hyperspace. I kept my eye on the mass pointer.

The mass pointer is a big transparent sphere with a number of blue lines radiating from the center. The direction of the line is the direction of a star; its length shows the star's mass. We wouldn't need pilots if the mass pointer could be hooked into an autopilot, but it can't. Dependable as it is, accurate as it is, the mass pointer is a psionic device. It needs a mind to work it. I'd been using mass pointers for so long that those lines were like real stars.

A star came toward me, and I dodged around it. I thought that another line that didn't point *quite* straight ahead was long enough to show dangerous mass, so I dodged. That put a blue dwarf right in front of me. I shifted fast and looked for a throttle. I wanted to slow down.

Repeat, *I wanted to slow down.*

Of course there was no throttle. Part of the puppeteer research project would be designing a throttle. A long fuzzy line reached for me: a protosun. . . .

Put it this way: Imagine one of Earth's freeways. You must have seen pictures of them from space, a tangle of twisting concrete ribbons, empty and abandoned but never torn down. Some lie broken; others are covered with houses. People use the later rubberized ones for horseback riding. Imagine the way one of these must have looked about six o'clock on a week night in, say, nineteen seventy. Groundcars from end to end.

Now, let's take all those cars and remove the brakes. Further, let's put governors on the accelerators, so that the maximum speeds are between sixty and seventy miles per hour, not all the same. Let something go wrong with all the governors at once, so that the maximum speed also becomes the minimum. You'll begin to see signs of panic.

Ready? Okay. Get a radar installed in your car, paint your windshield and windows jet black, and get out on that freeway.

It was like that.

It didn't seem so bad at first. The stars kept coming at me, and I kept dodging, and after a while it settled down to a kind of routine. From experience I could tell at a glance whether a star was heavy enough and close enough to wreck me. But in Nakamura Lines I'd only had to take that glance every six hours or so. Here I didn't dare look away. As I grew tired, the near-misses came closer and closer. After three hours of it I had to drop out.

The stars had a subtly unfamiliar look. With a sudden jar I realized that I was entirely out of known space. Sirius, Antares—I'd never recognize them from here; I wasn't even sure they were visible. I shook it off and called home.

"*Long Shot* calling General Products, *Long Shot* calling—"

"Beowulf Shaeffer?"

"Have I ever told you what a lovely, sexy voice you have?"

"No. Is everything going well?"

"I'm afraid not. In fact, I'm not going to make it."

A pause. "Why not?"

"I can't keep dodging these stars forever. One of them's going to get me if I keep on much longer. The ship's just too goddam fast."

"Yes. We must design a slower ship."

"I hate to give up that good pay, but my eyes feel like peeled onions. I ache all over. I'm turning back."

"Shall I play your contract for you?"

"No. Why?"

"Your only legal reason for returning is a mechanical failure. Otherwise you forfeit twice your pay."

I said, "Mechanical failure?" There was a tool box somewhere in the ship, with a hammer in it. . . .

"I did not mention it before, since it did not seem polite, but two of the cameras are in the lifesystem. We had thought to use films of you for purposes of publicity, but—"

"I see. Tell me one thing, just one thing. When the regional president of We Made It sent you my name, did he mention that I'd discovered your planet has no moon?"

"Yes, he did mention that matter. You accepted one million stars for your silence. He naturally has a recording of the bargain."

"I see." So that's why they'd picked Beowulf Shaeffer, well-known author. "The trip'll take longer than I thought."

"You must pay a penalty for every extra day over four months. Two thousand stars per day late."

"Your voice has acquired an unpleasant grating sound. Good-bye."

I went on in. Every hour I shifted to normal space for a ten-minute coffee break. I dropped out for meals, and I dropped out for sleep. Twelve hours per ship's day I spent traveling, and twelve trying to recover. It was a losing battle.

By the end of day two I knew I wasn't going to make the four-month limit. I might do it in six months, forfeiting one hundred and twenty thousand stars, leaving me almost where I started. Serve me right for trusting a puppeteer!

Stars were all around me, shining through the floor and between the banked instruments. I sucked coffee, trying not to think. The milky way shone ghostly pale between my feet. The stars were thick now; they'd get thicker as I approached the Core, until finally one got me.

An idea! And about time, too.

The golden voice answered immediately. "Beowulf Shaeffer?"

"There's nobody else here, honey. Look, I've thought of something. Would you send—"

"Is one of your instruments malfunctioning, Beowulf Shaeffer?"

"No, they all work fine, as far as they go. Look—"

"Then what could you possibly have to say that would require my attention?"

"Honey, now is the time to decide. Do you want revenge, or do you want your ship back?"

A small silence. Then, "You may speak."

"I can reach the Core much faster if I first get into one of the spaces between the arms. Do we know enough about the galaxy to know where our arm ends?"

"I will send to the Institute of Knowledge to find out."

"Good."

Four hours later I was dragged from a deathlike sleep by the ringing of the hyperphone. It was not the president, but some flunky. I remembered calling the puppeteer "honey" last night, tricked by my own exhaustion and that seductive voice, and wondered if I'd hurt his puppeteer feelings. "He" might be a male; a puppeteer's sex is one of his little secrets. The flunky gave me a bearing and distance for the nearest gap between stars.

It took me another day to get there. When the stars began to thin out, I could hardly believe it. I turned off the hyperdrive, and it was true. The stars were tens and hundreds of light-years apart. I could see part of the Core peeking in a bright rim above the dim flat cloud of mixed dust and stars.

IV

From then on, it was better. I was safe if I glanced at the mass pointer every ten minutes or so. I could forget the rest breaks, eat meals and do isometrics while watching the pointers. For eight hours a day I slept, but during the other sixteen I moved. The gap swept toward the Core in a narrowing curve, and I followed it.

As a voyage of exploration the trip would have been a fiasco. I saw nothing. I stayed well away from anything worth seeing. Stars and dust, anomalous wispy clusters shining in the dark of the gap, invisible indications that might have been stars—my cameras picked them up from a nice safe distance, showing tiny blobs of light. In three weeks I moved almost seventeen thousand light-years toward the Core.

The end of those three weeks was the end of the gap. Before me was an uninteresting wash of stars backed by a wall of opaque dust clouds. I still had thirteen thousand light-years to go before I reached the center of the galaxy.

I took some pictures and moved in.

Ten-minute breaks, mealtimes that grew longer and longer for the rest they gave, sleep periods that left my eyes red and burning. The stars were thick and the dust was thicker, so that the mass pointer showed a blur of blue broken by sharp blue lines. The lines began to get less sharp. I took breaks every half hour. . . .

Three days of that.

It was getting near lunchtime on the fourth day. I sat watching the mass pointer, noting the fluctuations in the blue blur which showed the changing density of the dust around me. Suddenly it faded out completely. Great! Wouldn't it be nice if the mass pointer went out on me? But the sharp starlines were still there, ten or twenty of them pointing in all directions. I went back to steering. The clock chimed to indicate a rest period. I sighed happily and dropped into normal space.

The clock showed I had half an hour to wait for lunch. I thought about eating anyway, decided against it. The routine was all that kept me going. I wondered what the sky looked like, reflexively looked up so I wouldn't have to look down at the transparent floor. That big an expanse of hyperspace is hard even on trained eyes. I remembered I wasn't in hyperspace and looked down.

For a time I just stared. Then, without taking my eyes off the floor, I reached for the hyperphone.

"Beowulf Shaeffer?"

"No, this is Albert Einstein. I stowed away when the *Long Shot* took off, and I've decided to turn myself in for the reward."

"Giving misinformation is an implicit violation of contract. Why have you called?"

"I can see the Core."

"That is not a reason to call. It was implicit in your contract that you would see the Core."

"Dammit, don't you care? Don't you want to know what it looks like?"

"If you wish to describe it now, as a precaution against accident, I will switch you to a dictaphone. However, if your mission is not totally successful, we cannot use your recording."

I was thinking up a really searing answer when I heard the click. Great, my boss had hooked me into a dictaphone. I said one short sentence and hung up.

The Core.

Gone were the obscuring masses of dust and gas. A billion years ago they must have been swept up for fuel by the hungry, crowded stars. The Core lay before me like a great jeweled sphere. I'd expected it to be a gradual thing, a thick mass of stars thinning out into the arms. There was nothing gradual about it. A clear ball of multicolored light five or six thousand light-years across nestled in the heart of the galaxy, sharply bounded by the last of the dust clouds. I was ten thousand four hundred light-years from the center.

The red stars were the biggest and brightest. I could actually pick some of them out as individuals. The rest was a finger painting in fluorescent green and blue. But those red stars ... they would have sent Aldebaran back to kindergarten.

It was all so *bright*. I needed the telescope to see black between the stars.

I'll *show* you how bright it was.

Is it night where you are? Step outside and look at the stars. What color are they? Antares may show red, if you're near enough; in the System, so will Mars. Sirius may show bluish. But all the rest are white pinpoints. Why? Because it's *dark*. Your day vision is in color, but at night you see black-and-white, like a dog.

The Core suns were bright enough for color vision.

I'd pick a planet here! Not in the Core itself, but right out here, with the Core on one side and on the other the dimly starred dust clouds forming their strange convoluted curtain. Man, what a view! Imagine that flaming jeweled sphere rising in the east, hundreds of times as big as Binary shows on Jinx; but without the constant feeling Binary gives you, the fear that the orange world will fall on you; for the vast, twinkling Core is only starlight, lovely and harmless. I'd pick my world *now* and stake a claim. When the puppeteers got their drive fixed up, I'd have the finest piece of real estate in the known universe! If I could only find a habitable planet.

If only I could find it twice.

Hell, I'd be lucky to find my way *home* from here. I shifted into hyperspace and went back to work.

V

An hour and fifty minutes, one lunch break and two rest breaks, and fifty light-years later, I noticed something peculiar in the Core.

It was even clearer then, if not much bigger; I'd passed through the almost transparent wisps of the last dust cloud. Not too near the center of the sphere was a patch of white, bright enough to make the green and blue and red look dull around it. I looked for it again at the next break, and it was a little brighter. It was brighter again at the next break. . . .

"Beowulf Shaeffer?"

"Yah. I—"

"Why did you use the dictaphone to call me a cowardly two-headed monster?"

"You were off the line. I *had* to use the dictaphone."

"That is sensible. Yes. We puppeteers have never understood your attitude toward a natural caution." My boss was peeved, though you couldn't tell from his voice.

"I'll go into that if you like, but it's not why I called."

"Explain, please."

"I'm all for caution. Discretion is the better part of valor, and like that. You can even be good businessmen, because it's easier to survive with lots of money. But you're so damn concerned with various kinds of survival that you aren't even interested in something that isn't a threat. Nobody but a puppeteer would have turned down my offer to describe the Core."

"You forget the Kzinti."

"Oh, the Kzinti." Who expects rational behavior from Kzinti? You whip them when they attack; you reluctantly decide not to exterminate them; you wait till they build up their strength; and when they attack, you whip 'em again. Meanwhile you sell them foodstuffs and buy their metals and employ them where you need good games theorists.

It's not as if they were a real threat. They'll *always* attack before they're ready.

"The Kzinti are carnivores. Where we are interested in survival, carnivores are interested in meat alone. They conquer because subject peoples can supply them with food. They cannot do menial work. Animal husbandry is alien to them. They must have slaves or be barbarians roaming the forests for meat. Why should they be interested in what you call abstract knowledge? Why should any thinking being, if the knowledge has no chance of showing a profit? In practice, your description of the Core would attract only an omnivore."

"You'd make a good case if it were not for the fact that most sentient races are omnivores."

"We have thought long and hard on that."

Ye cats. I was going to have to think long and hard on *that*.

"Why did you call, Beowulf Shaeffer?"

Oh, yeah. "Look, I know you don't want to know what the Core looks like, but I see something that might represent personal danger. You have access to information I don't. May I proceed?"

"You may."

Hah! I was learning to think like a puppeteer. Was that good? I told my boss about the blazing, strangely shaped white patch in the Core. "When I turned the telescope on it, it nearly blinded me. Grade two sunglasses don't give any details at all. It's just a shapeless white patch, but so bright that the stars in front look like black dots with colored rims. I'd like to know what's causing it."

"It sounds very unusual." Pause. "Is the white color uniform? Is the brightness uniform?"

"Just a sec." I used the scope again. "The color is, but the brightness isn't. I see dimmer areas inside the patch. I think the center is fading out."

"Use the telescope to find a nova star. There ought to be several in such a large mass of stars."

I tried it. Presently I found something: a blazing disk of

a peculiar blue-white color with a dimmer, somewhat smaller red disk half in front of it. That *had* to be a nova. In the core of Andromeda galaxy, and in what I'd seen of our own Core, the red stars were the biggest and brightest.

"I've found one."

"Comment."

A moment more and I saw what he meant. "It's the same color as the patch. Something like the same brightness, too. But what could make a patch of supernovas go off all at once?"

"You have studied the Core. The stars of the Core are an average of half a light-year apart. They are even closer near the center, and no dust clouds dim their brightness. When stars are that close, they shed enough light on each other to increase materially each other's temperature. Stars burn faster and age faster in the Core."

"I see that."

"Since the Core stars age faster, a much greater portion are near the supernova stage than in the arms. Also, all are hotter considering their respective ages. If a star were a few millennia from the supernova stage, and a supernova exploded half a light-year away, estimate the probabilities."

"They might both blow. Then the two could set off a third, and the three might take a couple more. . . ."

"Yes. Since a supernova lasts on the order of one human standard year, the chain reaction would soon die out. Your patch of light must have occurred in this way."

"That's a relief. Knowing what did it, I mean. I'll take pictures going in."

"As you say." Click.

The patch kept expanding as I went in, still with no more shape than a veil nebula, getting brighter and bigger. It hardly seemed fair, what I was doing. The light which the patch novas had taken fifty years to put out, I covered in an hour, moving down the beam at a speed which made the universe itself seem unreal. At the fourth rest period I dropped out of hyperspace, looked down through the floor while the cameras took their pictures, glanced away from the patch for a moment, and found myself blinded by tangerine afterimages. I had to put on a pair of grade one sunglasses, out of the packet of twenty which every pilot carries for working near suns during takeoff and landing.

It made me shiver to think that the patch was still nearly ten thousand light-years away. Already the radiation must have killed all life in the Core if there ever had been life there. My instruments on the hull showed radiation like a solar flare.

At the next stop I needed grade two sunglasses. Somewhat later, grade three. Then four. The patch became a great bright amoeba reaching twisting tentacles of fusion fire deep into the vitals of the Core. In hyperspace the sky was jammed bumper to bumper, so to speak, but I never thought of stopping. As the Core came closer, the patch grew like something alive, something needing ever more food. I think I knew, even then.

Night came. The control room was a blaze of light. I slept in the relaxroom, to the tune of the laboring temperature control. Morning, and I was off again. The radiation meter snarled its death-song, louder during each rest break. If I'd been planning to go outside, I would have dropped that plan. Radiation couldn't get through a General Products hull. Nothing else can, either, except visible light.

I spent a bad half hour trying to remember whether one of the puppeteers' customers saw X-rays. I was afraid to call up and ask.

The mass pointer began to show a faint blue blur. Gases thrown outward from the patch. I had to keep changing sunglasses. . . .

Sometime during the morning of the next day I stopped. There was no point in going farther.

"Beowulf Shaeffer, have you become attached to the sound of my voice? I have other work than supervising your progress."

"I would like to deliver a lecture on abstract knowledge."

"Surely it can wait until your return."

"The galaxy is exploding."

There was a strange noise. Then: "Repeat, please."

"Have I got your attention?"

"Yes."

"Good. I think I know the reason so many sentient races are omnivores. Interest in abstract knowledge is a symptom of pure curiosity. Curiosity must be a survival trait."

"Must we discuss this? Very well. You may well be right. Others have made the same suggestion, including puppeteers. But how has our species survived at all?"

"You must have some substitute for curiosity. Increased intelligence, maybe. You've been around long enough to develop it. Our hands can't compare with your mouths for tool-building. If a watchmaker had taste and smell in his hands, he still wouldn't have the strength of your jaws or the delicacy of those knobs around your lips. When I want to know how old a sentient race is, I watch what he uses for hands and feet."

"Yes. Human feet are still adapting to their task of keeping you erect. You propose, then, that our intelligence has grown sufficiently to ensure our survival without depending on your hit-or-miss method of learning everything you can for the sheer pleasure of learning."

"Not quite. Our method is better. If you hadn't sent me to the Core for publicity, you'd never have known about this."

"You say the galaxy is exploding?"

"Rather, it finished exploding some nine thousand years ago. I'm wearing grade twenty sunglasses, and it's still too bright. A third of the Core is gone already. The patch is spreading at nearly the speed of light. I don't see that anything can stop it until it hits the gas clouds beyond the Core."

There was no comment. I went on. "A lot of the inside of the patch has gone out, but all of the surface is new novas. And remember, the light I'm seeing is nine thousand years old. Now, I'm going to read you a few instruments. Radiation, two hundred and ten. Cabin temperature normal, but you can hear the whine of the temperature control. The mass indicator shows nothing but a blur ahead. I'm turning back."

"Radiation two hundred and ten? How far are you from the edge of the Core?"

"About four thousand light-years, I think. I can see plumes of incandescent gas starting to form in the near side of the patch, moving toward galactic north and south. It reminds me of something. Aren't there pictures of exploding galaxies in the Institute?"

"Many. Yes, it has happened before. Beowulf Shaeffer, this is bad news. When the radiation from the Core reaches our worlds, it will sterilize them. We puppeteers will soon need considerable amounts of money. Shall I release you from your contract, paying you nothing?"

I laughed. I was too surprised even to get mad. "No."

"Surely you do not intend to enter the Core?"

"No. Look, why do you—"

"Then by the conditions of our contract, you forfeit."

"Wrong again. I'll take pictures of these instruments. When a court sees the readings on the radiation meter and the blue blur in the mass indicator, they'll *know* something's wrong with them."

"Nonsense. Under evidence drugs you will explain the readings."

"Sure. And the court will know you tried to get me to go right to the center of that holocaust. You know what they'll say to that?"

"But how can a court of law find against a recorded contract?"

"The point is they'll want to. Maybe they'll decide that we're both lying and the instruments really did go haywire. Maybe they'll find a way to say the contract was illegal. But they'll find against you. Want to make a side bet?"

"No. You have won. Come back."

VI

The Core was a lovely multicolored jewel when it disappeared below the lens of the galaxy. I'd have liked to visit it someday, but there aren't any time machines.

I'd penetrated nearly to the Core in something like a month. I took my time coming home, going straight up along galactic north and flying above the lens where there were no stars to bother me, and still made it in two. All the way I wondered why the puppeteer had tried to cheat me at the last. *Long Shot*'s publicity would have been better than ever; yet the regional president had been willing to throw it away just to leave me broke. I couldn't ask why, because nobody was answering my hyperphone. Nothing I knew about puppeteers could tell me. I felt persecuted.

My come-hither brought me down at the base in the Farside End. Nobody was there. I took the transfer booth back to Sirius Mater, Jinx's biggest city, figuring to contact General Products, turn over the ship, and pick up my pay.

More surprises awaited me.

1) General Products had paid one hundred and fifty thousand stars into my account in the Bank of Jinx. A personal note stated that whether or not I wrote my article was solely up to me.

2) General Products has disappeared. They are selling no more spacecraft hulls. Companies with contracts have had their penalty clauses paid off. It all happened two months ago, simultaneously on all known worlds.

3) The bar I'm in is on the roof of the tallest building in Sirius Mater, more than a mile above the streets. Even from here I can hear the stock market crashing. It started with the collapse of spacecraft companies with no hulls to build ships. Hundreds of others have followed. It takes a long time for an interstellar market to come apart at the seams, but, as with the Core novas, I don't see anything that can stop the chain reaction.

4) The secret of the indestructible General Products

hull is being advertised for sale. General Products' human representatives will collect bids for one year, no bid to be less than one trillion stars. Get in on the ground floor, folks.

5) Nobody knows anything. That's what's causing most of the panic. It's been a month since a puppeteer was seen on any known world. Why did they drop so suddenly out of interstellar affairs?

I know.

In twenty thousand years a flood of radiation will wash over this region of space. Thirty thousand light-years may seem a long, safe distance, but it isn't, not with this big an explosion. I've asked. The Core explosion will make this galaxy uninhabitable to any known form of life.

Twenty thousand years *is* a long time. It's four times as long as human written history. We'll all be less than dust before things get dangerous, and I for one am not going to worry about it.

But the puppeteers are different. They're scared. They're getting out right now. Paying off their penalty clauses and buying motors and other equipment to put in their indestructible hulls will take so much money that even confiscating my puny salary would have been a step to the good. Interstellar business can go to hell; from now on, the puppeteers will have no time for anything but running.

Where will they go? Well, the galaxy is surrounded by a halo of small globular clusters. The ones near the rim might be safe. Or the puppeteers may even go as far as Andromeda. They have the *Long Shot* for exploring if they come back for it, and they can build more. Outside the galaxy is space empty enough even for a puppeteer pilot, if he thinks his species is threatened.

It's a pity. This galaxy will be dull without puppeteers. Those two-headed monsters were not only the most dependable faction in interstellar business; they were like water in a wasteland of more-or-less humanoids. It's too bad they aren't brave, like us.

But is it?

I never heard of a puppeteer refusing to face a problem. He may merely be deciding how fast to run, but he'll never pretend the problem isn't there. Sometime within the next twenty millennia we humans will have to move a population that already numbers forty-three billion. How? To where? When *should* we start thinking about this? When the glow of the Core begins to shine through the dust clouds?

Maybe men are the cowards—at the core.

THE SOFT WEAPON

LOGICALLY JASON PAPANDREOU should have taken the *Court Jester* straight home to Jinx. But . . .

He'd seen a queer star once.

He'd been single then, a gunner volunteer on one of Earth's warships during the last stages of the last Kzinti war. The war had been highly unequal in Earth's favor. Kzinti fight gallantly, ferociously, and with no concept of mercy; and they always take on several times as much as they can handle.

Earth's ships had pushed the Kzinti back out of human space, then pushed a little farther, annexing two Kzinti worlds for punitive damages. The fleets had turned for home. But Jason's captain had altered course to give his crew what might be their last chance to see Beta Lyrae.

Now, decades later, Jason, his wife, and their single alien passenger were rattling around in a ship built for ten times their number. Anne-Marie's curiosity was driving her up the walls with the frustration of not being able to open the stasis box in the forward locker. Nessus, the mad puppeteer, had taken to spending all his time in his room, hovering motionless and morose between the sleeping plates. Jinx was still weeks away.

Clearly a diversion was in order.

Beta Lyrae. A six-degree shift in course would do it.

Anne-Marie glared at the locker containing the stasis box. "Isn't there *any* way to open it?"

Jason didn't answer. His whole attention was on the mass indicator, the transparent ball in which a green radial line was growing toward the surface—growing and splitting in two.

"Jay?"

"We can't open it, Anne. We don't have the equipment to break a stasis field. It's illegal anyway."

Almost time. The radial double-line must not grow too long. When a working hyperdrive gets too deep into a gravity well, it disappears.

"Think they'll tell us what's inside?"

"Sure, unless it's a new weapon."

"With our luck it will be. Jay, nobody's ever found a stasis box that shape before. It's bound to be something new. The Institute is likely to sit on it for years and years.

"Whup! Jay, what are you *doing?*"

"Dropping out of hyperspace."

"You might warn a lady." She wrapped both arms around her midsection, apparently making sure everything was still there.

"Lady, why don't you have a look out that side window?"

"What for?"

Jason merely looked smug. His wife, knowing she would get no other answer, got up and undogged the cover. It was not unusual for a pilot to drop out in the depths of interstellar space. Weeks of looking at the blind-spot appearance of hyperspace could wear on the best of nerves.

She stood at the window, a tall, slender brunette in a glowing-green falling jumper. A Wunderlander she had been, of the willowy low-gravity type rather than the fat, balloonlike low-gravity type, until Jason Papandreou had dropped out of the sky to add her to his collection of girls in every port. It hadn't worked out that way. In the first year of marriage she had learned space and the *Court Jester* inside out, until she was doubly indispensable. Jay, Anne, *Jester,* all one independent organism.

And she thought she'd seen everything. But she hadn't seen this! Grinning, Jason waited for her reaction.

"Jay, it's *gorgeous!* What *is* it?"

Jason moved up to circle her waist with one arm. She'd put on weight in the last year, muscle weight, from moving in heavier gravities. He looked out around her shoulder ... and thought of smoke.

There was smoke across the sky, a trail of red smoke

wound in a tight spiral coil. At the center of the coil was the source of the fire: a double star. One member was violet-white, a flame to brand holes in a human retina, its force held in check by the polarized window. The companion was small and yellow. They seemed to burn inches apart, so close that their masses had pulled them both into flattened eggs, so close that a red belt of lesser flame looped around them to link their bulging equators together. The belt was hydrogen, still mating in fusion fire, pulled loose from the stellar surfaces by two gravitational wells in conflict.

The gravity war did more than that. It sent a loose end of the red belt flailing away, away and out in a burning Maypole spiral that expanded and dimmed as it rose toward interstellar space, until it turned from flame-red to smoke-red, bracketing the sky and painting a spiral path of stars deep red across half the universe.

"They call it Beta Lyrae," said Jason. "I was here once before, back when I was free and happy. Mph. Hasn't changed much."

"Well, *no*."

"Now don't you take all this for granted. How long do you think those twins can keep throwing hydrogen away? I give it a million years, and then, pft! No more Beta Lyrae."

"Pity. We'd better hurry and wake Nessus before it disappears."

The being they called Nessus would not have opened his door for them.

Puppeteers were gregarious even among alien species. They'd had to be. For at least tens of thousands of years the puppeteers had ruled a trade empire that included all the races within the sixty-light-year sphere men called "known space" and additional unknown regions whose extent could not be guessed. As innate cowards the puppeteers had to get along with everyone. And Nessus, too, was usually gregarious. But Nessus was mad.

Nessus was cursed with courage.

In a puppeteer, courage is a symptom of insanity. As usual there were other symptoms, other peripheral indications of the central disorder. Nessus was now in the depressive stage of a manic-depressive cycle.

Luckily the depression had not hit him until his business with the Outsiders was over. In the manic stage he had been fun. He had spent every night in a different stateroom. He had charcoal-drawn cartoons which now hung in the astrogation room, cartoons that Jason could hardly believe were drawn by a puppeteer. Humor is generally linked to an interrupted defense mechanism. Puppeteers weren't supposed to have a sense of humor. But now Nessus spent all his time in one room. He wanted to see nobody.

There was one thing he might open his door for.

Jason moved to the control board and pushed the panic button. The alarm was a repeated recording of a woman's scream. It should have brought the puppeteer galloping in as if the angel of death were at his heel. But he trotted through the door seconds later than he should have. His flat, brainless heads surveyed the control room for signs of damage.

The first man to see a puppeteer had done so during a Campish revival of *Time for Beany* reruns. He had come running back to the scout ship, breathless and terrified, screaming, "Take off! The planet's full of monsters!"

"Whatta they look like?"

"Like a three-legged centaur with two Cecil the Seasick Sea Serpent puppets on its hands, and no head."

"Take a pill, Pierson. You're drunk."

Nessus was an atypical puppeteer. His mane was straggly and unkempt. It should have been twisted, brushed, and tied in a manner to show his status in puppeteer society. But it showed no status at all. Perhaps this was appropriate. There was no puppeteer society. The puppeteers had apparently left the galaxy en masse some twelve years earlier, leaving behind only their insane and their genetically deficient.

"What is wrong?" asked Nessus.

"There's nothing wrong," said Jason.

Anne-Marie said, "Have a look out the window. This window."

Their employer obediently moved to the window. He happened to stop just next to one of the cartoons he'd drawn while in the manic phase, and Jason, looking from the puppeteer to the cartoon, found it more difficult than ever to associate the two.

The cartoon showed two human gods. Only the lighting and the proportions showed that they were gods. Otherwise they were as individually human as a very good human artist could have drawn them. One, a child just about to become a teen-ager, was holding the galaxy in his hands. He wore a very strange grin as he looked down at the glowing multicolored spiral. The other figure, a disgruntled patriarch with flowing white hair and beard, was saying, "All right, now that you've had your little joke . . ."

Nessus claimed it was an attempt to imitate human humor. Maybe. Would an insane puppeteer develop a sense of humor?

Nessus (his real name sounded like a car crash set to music) was insane. There were circumstances under which he would actually risk his life. But the sudden puppeteer exodus had left a myriad broken promises made to a dozen sentient races. The puppeteers had left Nessus and his fellow exiles with money to straighten things out. So Nessus had rented the *Court Jester,* rented all twelve staterooms, and gone out to the farthest edge of known space to deal with a ship of the Outsiders.

"I recognize this star," he said now. "Amazing. I really should have suggested this stop myself. Had I not been so depressed, I certainly would have. Thank you, Jason."

"My pleasure, sir." Jason Papandrcou really sounded as though he'd invented the gaudy display just to cheer up a down-in-the-mouths puppeteer. Nessus cocked a sardonic head at him, and he hastily added, "We'll be on our way again whenever you're ready."

"I'll scan with deep-radar," Anne-Marie said helpfully.

Jason laughed. "Can you imagine how many ships must have scanned this system already?"

"Just for luck."

A moment later there was a beep.

Anne-Marie yelped.

Jason said, "I don't believe it."

"Two in one trip!" his wife caroled. "Jay, that's some sort of record!"

It was. Using deep-radar had been more of a habit than anything else. A deep-radar on high setting was an easy way to find Slaver stasis boxes, since only stasis fields and neutron stars would reflect a hyperwave pulse. But Beta Lyrae *must* have been searched many times before. Searching was traditional.

Nessus turned from the window. "I suggest that we locate the box, then leave it. You may send a friend for it."

Jason stared. "Leave it? Are you kidding?"

"It is an anomaly. Such a box should have been found long since. It has no reason to be here in the first place. Beta Lyrae probably did not exist a billion and a half years ago. Why then would the Slavers have come here?"

"War. They might have been running from a tnuctip fleet."

Anne-Marie was sweeping the deep-radar in a narrow beam, following the smoky spiral, searching for the tiny node of stasis her first pulse had found.

"You hired my ship," Jason said abruptly. "If you order me to go on, I'll do it."

"I will not. Your species has come a long way in a short time. If you do not have prudence, you have some workable substitute."

"There it is," said Anne-Marie. "Look, Jay. A little icy blob of a world a couple of billion miles out."

Jason looked. "Shouldn't be any problem. All right, I'll take us down."

Nessus said nothing. He seemed alert enough, but without the nervousness and general excitability that would have meant the onset of his manic stage. At least Beta Lyrae had cured his depression.

The *Traitor's Claw* was under the ice. Ice showed dark and deep outside her hexagonal ports. In lieu of sight her crew used a mechanical sense like a cross between radar and X-ray vision. The universe showed on her screens as a series of transparent images superimposed: a shadow show.

Four Kzinti watched a blob-shaped image sink slowly through other images, coming to a stop at a point no different from any other.

"Chuft-Captain, they're down," said Flyer.

"Of course they're down." Chuft-Captain spoke without heat. "Telepath, how many are there?"

"Two human." There was a quiet, self-hating resignation in Telepath's speech. His tone became disgust as he added, "And a puppeteer."

"Odd. That's a passenger ship. A puppeteer couldn't need all that room."

"I sense only their presence, Chuft-Captain." Telepath was pointedly reminding him that he had not yet taken the drug. He would do so only if ordered. Without an injection of treated extract of sthondat lymph, his powers were low. Little more than the knack for making an accurate guess.

"One human has left the ship," said Flyer. "No, two humans."

"Slaverstudent, initiate hostilities. Assume the puppeteer will stay safely inside."

The planet was no bigger than Earth's moon. Her faint hydrogen atmosphere must have been regularly renewed as the spiral streamer whipped across her orbit. She was in the plane of the hydrogen spiral, which now showed as a glowing red smoke trail cutting the night sky into two unequal parts.

Anne-Marie finished tucking her hair into her helmet, clamped the helmet to her neck ring, and stepped out to look around.

"I dub thee Cue Ball," she said.

"Cute," said Jason. "Too bad if she's named already."

They moved through the ship's pressure curtain, Jason toting a bulky portable deep-radar. The escalladder carried them down onto the ice.

They moved away, following the dark image in the

deep-radar screen. Jason was a head shorter than his wife and twice as wide; his typical Earther's build looked almost Jinxian next to hers. He moved easily in the low gravity. Anne-Marie, bouncing like a rubber clown, kept pace with him only by dint of longer legs and greater effort.

Jason was standing right over the image of the stasis box, getting ready to mark the ice so they could dig for it, when the image quietly vanished.

A sharp crack jerked his head around. He saw a cloud of steam explode into the near-vacuum, a cloud lit from below by a rosy light. Anne-Marie was already sprinting for the ship in low flying leaps. He turned to follow.

A form like a big roly-poly man shot through the light into what must by then have been a cloud of tiny ice crystals. It was a Kzin in a vac suit, and the thing in its hands was a police stunner. It landed running. Under the conditions its aim was inhumanly accurate.

Jason collapsed like a deflating balloon. Anne-Marie was pinwheeling across the ice, slowly as dreams in the low gravity. The Kzin ignored them both. It was using a jet backpac to speed it along.

The ship's heavy, flush-fitting door started to close over the pressure curtain. Too slowly. Jason clung to consciousness long enough to see the Kzin's backpac carry it up the escalladder and through the pressure curtain. His mind hummed and faded.

Present in the crew's relaxroom were two humans, one puppeteer, and a Kzin. The Kzin was Chuft-Captain. It had to be that way, since the prisoners had not yet had the chance to refuse to talk. Chuft-Captain was a noble, entitled to a partial name. Had he not been alone with the prisoners, he would have been showing fear. His crew watched the proceedings from the control room.

The puppeteer lifted a head at the end of a drunkenly weaving neck. The head steadied, stared hard. In Kzin he said, "What is the purpose of this action?"

Chuft-Captain ignored him. One did not speak as an

equal to a puppeteer. Puppeteers did not fight, ever. Hence they were mere herbivorous animals. Prey.

The male human was next to recover from the stunners. He stared in consternation at Chuft-Captain, then looked around him. "So none of us made it," he said.

"No," said the puppeteer. "You may remember I advised—"

"How could I forget? Sorry about that, Nessus. What's happening?"

"Very little at the moment."

The male looked back at Chuft-Captain. "Who're you?"

"You may call me Captain. Depending on future events, you are either my kidnap victims or my prisoners of war. Who are you?"

"Jason Papandreou, of Earth origin." The human tried to gesture, perhaps to point at himself, and found the electronic police-web binding him in an invisible grip. He finished the introductions without gestures.

"Very well," said Chuft-Captain. "Jason, are you in possession of a stasis box, a relic of the Slaver Empire?"

"No."

Chuft-Captain gestured to the screen behind the prisoners. Telepath nodded and switched off. The prisoner had lied; it was now permissible to bring in help to question him.

It had been a strange, waiting kind of war.

Legally it was no war at all. The *Traitor's Claw* showed in the Kzinti records as a stolen ship. If she had been captured at any time, all the Kzinti worlds would have screamed loudly for Chuft-Captain's head as a pirate. Even the ship's name had been chosen for that eventuality.

There had never been a casualty; never, until now, a victory. A strange war, in which the rules were flexible and the dictates of personal honor were often hard to define and to satisfy. Even now ... What does one do with a captured puppeteer? You couldn't eat him; puppeteers were officially a friendly power. A strange war. But better than no war at all. Perhaps it would now get better still.

The Kzin had asked one question and turned away. A bad sign. Apparently the question had been a formality.

Jason wriggled once more against the force field. He was embedded like a fly in flypaper. It must be a police web. Since the last war the Kzinti worlds had been living in probationary status. Though they might possess and use police restraint-devices, they were allowed no weapons of war.

Against two unarmed humans and a puppeteer, they hardly needed them.

Anne-Marie stirred. Jason said, "Easy, honey."

"Easy? Oh, my neck. What happened?" She tried to move her arm. Her head, above the soft grip of the police web, jerked up in surprise; her eyes widened. And she saw the Kzin.

She screamed.

The Kzin watched in obvious irritation. Nessus merely watched.

"All *right*," said Jason. "*That* won't do us any good."

"Jay, they're *Kzinti!*"

"Right. And they've got us. Oh, hell, go ahead and scream."

That shocked her. She looked at him long enough to read his helplessness, then turned back to the Kzin. Already she was calmer. Jason didn't have to worry about his wife's courage. He'd seen it tested before.

She had never seen a Kzin; all she knew about them she had heard from Jason, and little of that had been good. But she was no xenophobe. There was more sympathy of feeling between Anne-Marie and Nessus than there was between Nessus and Jason. She could face the Kzin.

But Jason couldn't read the puppeteer's expression. It was Nessus he was worried about. Puppeteers hated pain worse than they feared death. Let the Kzin threaten Nessus with pain and there was no telling what he'd do. Without the puppeteer they might have a chance to conceal the stasis box.

It might be very bad if the Kzinti got into a stasis box.

A billion and a half years ago there had been a war. The Slavers, who controlled most of the galaxy at the time, had also controlled most of the galaxy's sentient species. One such slave species, the tnuctipun, had at last revolted. The Slavers had had a power like telepathic hypnosis, a power that could control the mind of any sentient being. The tnuctipun slaves had possessed high intelligence, higher technology, and a slyness more terrifying than any merely mental power. Slavers and tnuctipun slaves alike, and every sentient being then in the galaxy, had died in that war.

Scattered through known and unknown space were the relics of that war, waiting to be found by species which had become sentient since the war's end. The Slavers had left stasis boxes, containers in stasis fields, which had survived unchanged through a billion and a half years of time. The tnuctipun had left mutated remnants of their biological engineering: the Frumious bandersnatch of Jinx's shorelines; the stage tree, which was to be found on worlds scattered all across known space; the tiny cold-world sunflower with its rippling, reflective blossoms.

Stasis boxes were rare and dangerous. Often they held abandoned Slaver weapons. One such weapon, the variable-sword, had recently revolutionized human society, bringing back swordplay and dueling on many worlds. Another was being used for peaceful ends; the disintegrator was too slow to make a good weapon. If the Kzinti found a new weapon, and if it were good enough . . .

Their Kzinti captor was a big one, thought Jason, though even a small one was a big one. He stood eight feet tall, as erect as a human on his short hind legs. The orange shade of his fur might have been inconspicuous to a Kzin's natural prey, but to human eyes it blazed like neon. He was thick all over, arms, legs, torso; he might have been a very fat cat dipped in orange dye, with certain alterations. You would have had to discount the naked-pink ratlike tail; the strangely colored irises, which were round instead of slitted; and especially the head, rendered nearly triangular by the large cranial bulge, more than large enough to hold a human brain.

"The trap you stumbled into is an old one," said the Kzin. "One ship or another has been waiting on this world since the last war. We have been searching out Slaver stasis boxes for much longer than that, hoping to find new weapons . . ."

A door opened and a second Kzin entered. He stayed there in the dilated doorway, waiting for the leader's attention. There was something about his appearance . . .

"But only recently did we hit upon this idea. You may know," said their orange captor, "that ships often stop off to see this unusual star. Ships of most species also have the habit of sending a deep-radar pulse around every star they happen across. No student of Slavers has ever found method behind the random dispersion of stasis boxes throughout this region of space.

"Several decades ago we did find a stasis box. Unfortunately it contained nothing useful, but we eventually found out how to turn the stasis field on and off. It made good bait for a trap. For forty Kzin years we have waited for ships to happen by with stasis boxes in their holds. You are our second catch."

"You'd have done better finding your own boxes," said Jason. He had been examining the silent Kzin. This one was smaller than their interrogator. His fur was matted. His tail drooped, as did his pointed ears. For a Kzin the beast was skinny, and misery showed in his eyes. As certainly as they were aboard a fighting ship, this was not a fighting Kzin.

"We would have been seen. Earth would have acted to stop our search." Apparently dismissing the subject, their interrogator turned to the smaller Kzin and spat out an imitation of cats fighting. The smaller Kzin turned to face them.

A pressure took hold of Jason's mind and developed into a sudden splitting headache.

He had expected it. It was a strange thing: put a sane alien next to an insane one, and usually you could tell them apart. And Kzinti were much closer to human than were any other species; so close that they must at one time have had common microbe ancestors. This smaller Kzin was obviously half crazy. And he wasn't a fighter. To be in this place at this time, he had to be a trained telepath, a forced addict of the Kzinti drug that sent nine hundred and ninety-nine out of a thousand Kzinti insane and left the survivor a shivering neurotic.

He concentrated on remembering the taste of a raw carrot—just to be difficult.

Telepath sagged against a wall, utterly spent. He could still taste yellow root munched between flat-topped teeth. Chuft-Captain watched without sympathy, waiting.

He forced himself to speak. "Chuft-Captain, they have not hidden the stasis box. It may be found in a locker to the left of the control room."

Chuft-Captain turned to the wall screen. "See to it. And get the puppeteer's pressure suit. Then seal the ship."

Flyer and Slaverstudent acknowledged and signed off.

"The relic. Where did they find it?"

"Chuft-Captain, they did not. The stasis box was found in deep interstellar space, considerably closer to the Core, by a ship of the Outsiders. The Outsiders kept it to trade in known space."

"What business did the prisoners have with the Outsiders?"

"The puppeteer had business with them. It merely used the humans for transportation. The humans do not know what business it was."

Chuft-Captain spit in reflex fury, but of course he could not ask a Kzin to read the mind of a herbivore. Telepath wouldn't, and would have to be disciplined; or he would, and would go insane. Nor could Chuft-Captain use pain on the puppeteer. He would get the information if it was worthless; but if the puppeteer decided it was valuable, the creature would commit suicide.

"Am I to assume that the Outsiders did in fact sell the relic to the prisoners?"

"Chuft-Captain, they did. The sum was a puppeteer's recorded word of honor for fourteen million stars in human money."

"A lordly sum."

"Perhaps more than lordly. Chuft-Captain, you may know that the Outsiders are long-lived. The male human has speculated that they intend to return in one or more thousands of years, when the recording of a puppeteer's voice is an antique worth eights of times its face value."

"Urrr. I shouldn't stray into such byways, but ... are they really that long-lived?"

"Chuft-Captain, the Outsider ship was following a star-seed in order to trace its migratory pattern."

"Urrr-rrrr!" Starseeds lived long enough to make mating migrations from the galactic core to the rim and back, moving at average speeds estimated at point eight lights.

A patterned knock. The others entered, wearing pressure suits with the helmets thrown back. Flyer carried the puppeteer's pressure suit, a three-legged balloon with padded mittens for the mouths, small clawed boots, an extra bulge for a food pouch, and a hard, padded shield to cover the cranial hump. Slaverstudent carried a cylinder with a grip-notched handle. Its entire surface was a perfectly reflecting mirror: the sign of the Slaver stasis field.

The prisoners, the human ones, were silently glaring. Their post-telepathy headaches had not helped their dispositions. Telepath was resting from the aftereffects of the drug.

"Open it," said Chuft-Captain.

Slaverstudent removed an empty cubical box from the table, set the stasis box in its place, and touched a pressure-sensitive surface at the table's edge. The cylinder ceased to be a distorting mirror. It was a bronzy metal box, which popped open of its own accord.

The Kzin called Slaverstudent reached in and brought out:

A silvered bubble six inches in diameter, with a sculptured handle attached. The handle would not have fit any gripping appendage Chuft-Captain knew of.

A cube of raw meat in something like a plastic sandwich wrap.

A hand. An alien hand furnished with three massive, clumsy-looking fingers set like a mechanical grab. It had been dipped in something that formed a clear, hard coating. One thick finger wore a chronometer.

"A bad thing has happened," said Nessus.

The Kzin who had opened the box seemed terribly excited. He turned the preserved hand over and over, yowrling in Kzinti. Then he put it down and picked up the sphere-with-a-handle.

"Let me guess," said Jason. "That's not a Slaver box. It's a tnuctipun box."

"Yes. The first to be found. The handle on the bubble tool is admirably designed to fit a tnuctipun hand. The preserved Slaver hand must be a trophy—I am quoting the student of Slavers. Jason, this may be a disaster. The tnuctipun were master technologists."

The "student of Slavers" was running his padded, retractile-clawed hands over the sphere-with-a-handle. No detail at all showed on the sphere; it was the same mirror color as the stasis field that had disgorged it. The handle was bronzy metal. There were grooves for six fingers and two long, opposed thumbs; there was a button set in an awkward position. A deep, straight groove ran down the side, with a guide and nine notched settings.

Anne-Marie spoke in a low voice. "It looks like the handle of a gun."

"We need information," said Jason. "Nessus, is that bigger Kzin the boss? The one who speaks Interworld?"

"Yes. The one with the bubble tool is a student of the Slaver Empire. The one with the white stripe is the pilot. The mind reader is resting. We need not fear him for several hours."

"But the boss Kzin understands Interworld. Do the others?"

"I think not. Your inaptly named Interworld is difficult for nonhumans to learn and to pronounce."

"Good. Anne, how are you doing?"

"I'm scared. We're in big trouble, aren't we, Jay?"

"We are. No sense fooling ourselves. Any ideas?"

"You know me, Jay. In a pinch I usually know who to call for help. The integrator if the house stops, the taxi company when a transfer booth doesn't work. Step into an autodoc when you feel sick. If your lift belt fails, you dial E for Emergency on your pocket phone. If someone answers before you hit the ground, scream." She tried a smile. "Jay? Who do we call about Kzinti kidnapings?"

He smiled back. "You write a forceful note to the Patriarch of Kzin. Right, Nessus?"

"Also you threaten to cut off trade. Do not worry too much, Anne-Marie. My species is expert at staying alive."

"Undoubtedly a weapon," said Slaverstudent. "We had best try it outside."

"Later," said Chuft-Captain.

Again Slaverstudent dipped into the cylindrical box. He removed small containers half filled with two kinds of small-arms projectiles, a colored cap that might easily have fitted a standard bowling ball, a transparent bulb of clear fluid, and a small metal widget that might have been anything. "I see no openings for bullets."

"Nor do I. Flyer, take a sample of this meat and find out what it is made of. Do the same with this trophy and this bulb. Telepath, are you awake?"

"Chuft-Captain, I am."

"When can you again read the—"

"Chuft-Captain, please don't make—"

"At ease, Telepath. Take time to recover. But I intend to keep the prisoners present while we investigate this find. They may notice some detail we miss. Eventually I will need you."

"Yes, Chuft-Captain."

"Test that small implement for radio or hyperwave emissions. Do nothing else to it. It has the look of a subminiature communicator, but it might be anything: a camera, even an explosive.

"Slaverstudent, you will come with me. We are going outside."

It took several minutes for the Kzinti to get the prisoners into their suits, adjust their radios so that everybody could hear everybody else, and move them through the double-door airlock.

To Jason, the airlock was further proof that this was a warship. A pressure curtain was generally more convenient than an airlock; but if power failed during a battle, all the air could leave the ship in one whoof. Warships carried double doors.

Two stunners followed them up the sloping ice tunnel. Jason had thought there would be four. He'd need to fight only the boss Kzin and one other. But both carried stunners and both seemed alert.

He took too much time deciding. The boss made Nessus stand on a flexible wire grid, then did the same with Anne-Marie and Jason. The grid was a portable police web, and it was as inflexibly restraining as the built-in web in the ship.

The Kzinti returned down the sloping tunnel, leaving Jason, Anne-Marie, and Nessus to enjoy the view. It was a lonely view. The blue and yellow stars were rising, invisibly. They showed only as a brighter spot at one foot of the red-smoke arch of hydrogen. Stars showed space-bright in curdled patterns across the sky; they all glowed red near the arch. The land was cold rock-hard ice, rippling in long, low undulations that might have been seasonal snowdrifts millions of years ago, when the Lyrae twins were bigger and brighter. Black-faceted rock poked through some of the high spots.

Several yards away was the *Court Jester*. A thick, round-edged, flat-bottomed disk, she sat on the ice like a painted concrete building. Apparently she intended to stay.

Jason stood at parade rest on the police web. Anne-Marie was six inches to his right, facing him. For all of his urge to touch her, she might have been miles away.

Two days ago she had carefully painted her eyelids with semipermanent tattoo. They showed as two tiny black-and-white-checked racing victory flags, rippling when she blinked. Their gaiety mocked her drawn face.

"I wonder why we're still alive," she said.

Nessus' accentless voice was tinny in the earphones. "The captain wants our opinions on the putative weapon. He will not ask for them, but will take them through the telepath."

"That doesn't apply to you, does it?"

"No. No Kzin would read my mind. Perhaps no Kzin would kill me; my race holds strong policies on the safety of individual members. In any case we have some time."

"Time for what?"

"Anne-Marie, we must wait. If the artifact is a weapon, we must recover it. If not, we must survive to warn your people that the Kzinti are searching out Slaver stasis boxes. We must wait until we know which."

"*Then* what?"

"We will find a way."

"We?" said Jason.

"Yes. Our motives coincide here. I cannot explain why at this time."

But why should a puppeteer risk his life, his *life*, for Earth? Jason wondered.

The boss Kzin emerged from the airlock carrying the sphere-with-a-handle. He stood before Jason and held it before his eyes. "Examine this," he commanded, and turned it slowly and invitingly in his four-fingered hands.

There was the reflecting sphere, and there was the bronzy-metal gun handle with its deeply scored groove and its alien sculpturing. The groove had nine notched settings running from top to bottom, with a guide in the top notch. Squiggles that must have been tnuctip numbers corresponded to the notches.

Jason prayed for the police web to fail. If he could snatch the artifact—

The Kzin moved away, walking uphill to a rise of icy ground. A second Kzin emerged from the pressure curtain carrying an unfamiliar gadget of Kzinti make. The two Kzinti spat phrases at each other. Kzinti language always sounds like insults.

Nessus spoke quietly. "The meat was protoplasmic, protein, and highly poisonous. The small, complex tnuctip implement does operate in hyperspace but uses no known method of communication. The fluid in the clear bulb is forty percent hydrogen peroxide, sixty percent hydrogen oxide, purpose unknown."

"What's the Slaver expert carrying?"

"That is an energy-output sensor."

The puppeteer seemed calm enough. Did he know of some way to interrupt a police web?

Jason couldn't ask, not when the boss Kzin could hear every word. But he had little hope. A police web belonged to the same family as a pilot's crash field, triggered to enfold the pilot when signaled by excessive pressure on his crash webbing. A crash web was as deliberately foolproof as any last-ditch failsafe device. So was a police web.

Probably the puppeteer was slipping back into the manic state and was now convinced that nothing in the universe could harm him. Somehow that made Jason's failure worse. "One thing you should know, Jason, is that my species judges me insane." It was one of the first things the puppeteer had told him. Unable to trust his own judgment, Nessus had warned him by implication that he would have to trust Jason's.

They'd both trusted him.

"I had to show you Beta Lyrae," he said bitterly.

"It was a nice idea, Jay, really it was."

If he'd been free, he'd have found a wall and tried to punch it down.

Chuft-Captain stood on a rise of permafrost and let his eyes scan the horizon. Those points of dark rock would make good targets.

The weapon was uncomfortable in his hand, but he managed to get one finger on the presumed trigger button. He aimed at the horizon and fired.

Nothing happened.

He aimed at a closer point, first pressing and releasing the trigger button repeatedly, then holding it down. Still nothing.

"Chuft-Captain, there is no energy release."

"The power may be gone."

"Chuft-Captain, it may. But the notches in the handle may control intensity. The guide is now set on 'nil.'"

Chuft-Captain moved the guide one notch down. A moment later he had to resist the panicky urge to throw the thing as far as possible. The mirror-faced sphere was twisting and turning like something alive, changing shape like a drug nightmare. It changed and flowed and became ... a long slender cylinder with a red knob at the end and a toggle near the handle. The handle had not changed at all.

"Chuft-Captain, there was an energy discharge. Eek! What happened?"

"It turned into this. What do I do next?"

Slaverstudent took the artifact and examined it. He would have liked to fire it himself, but that was the leader's privilege and right. And risk. He said, "Try the toggle."

At a forward motion of the toggle the red knob lit up and leapt away across the ice. Chuft-Captain wiggled the handle experimentally. The red knob, still receding, bobbed and weaved in response to stay in line with the cylindrical barrel. When the knob was a red point sixty yards distant, Chuft-Captain stopped it with the toggle.

"Variable-sword," he muttered. He looked for a target. His eyes lit on a nearby tilted spire of dark rock or dirty ice.

Chuft-Captain gripped the artifact in both furry hands, like a big-game fishing pole, and swung the red light behind the spire. The artifact fought his pressure, then gave way. The top half of the spire toppled, kicking up a spray of chipped ice.

"A variable-sword," he repeated. "But not of Slaver design. Slaverstudent, have you ever heard of a weapon that changes shape?"

"No, Chuft-Captain, neither of the past nor of the present."

"Then we've found something new."

"Yes!" The word was a snarl of satisfaction.

"That tears it," said Anne-Marie. "It's a weapon."

Jason tried to nod. The police web held him fast.

The other Kzinti came outside and moved up the rise. Four Kzinti stood spitting at each other, looking like four fat men, sounding like a catfight. Nessus said, "The first notch must have been neutral. They intend to find out what the other notches do."

"It changes shape," said Anne-Marie. "That's bad enough."

"Quite right," said the puppeteer. "The artifact is now our prime target."

Jason grinned suddenly. The puppeteer reminded him of a cartoon: Two bearded, dirty convicts hanging three feet off the ground by iron chains. One convict saying, "Now here's my plan...."

First we wish away the police web. Then ...

Again the Kzinti captain moved the guide. The gun reverted to sphere-and-handle, then flowed into something hard to see at a distance. The boss Kzin must have realized it. He came down the hill, followed by the others. One at a time the Kzinti moved them to the top of the rise, so that they stood several yards behind the firing line, but still in the police web.

The boss Kzin resumed his firing stance.

Position number two was a parabolic mirror with a silvery knob at the center. It did nothing at all to the rock Chuft-Captain was using for a target, though Slaverstudent reported an energy discharge. Chuft-Captain considered, then turned the weapon on the puppeteer.

The puppeteer spoke in the human tongue. "I can hear a faint high-pitched whine."

"Another control dial has formed," Slaverstudent pointed out. "Four settings."

Chuft-Captain nodded and tried the second setting. It did not affect the puppeteer. Neither did the third and fourth.

"Chuft-Captain, will you hold down the trigger?" Slaverstudent cautiously peeped over the lip of the parabolic mirror. "Urrr. I was right. The knob is vibrating rapidly. Setting number two is a sonic projector—and a powerful one—if the puppeteer can hear it through near-vacuum and the thickness of its suit."

"But it didn't knock him out or anything."

"Chuft-Captain, we must assume that it was designed to affect the Slaver nervous system."

"Yes." Chuft-Captain moved the guide to setting number three. As the gun changed and flowed, he said, "We have found. nothing new. Sonics and variable-swords are common."

"Mutable weapons are not."

"Mutable weapons could not win a war, though they might help. Urrrr. This seems to be a projectile weapon. Have you the small-arms projectiles from the stasis box?"

"Chuft-Captain, I do."

The magazine under the barrel swung out for loading. It took both kinds of projectiles. Chuft-Captain again sighted on the rock, using the newly formed telescopic sight.

His first shot put a nick exactly where he aimed it.

His second, with the second-variety projectile, blew the rock to flying shards. Everybody ducked but Chuft-Captain.

"Should I empty the magazine before moving the guide?"

"Chuft-Captain, I do not think it matters. The bullets should certainly be removed, but the tnuctipun must have known that occasionally they would not be. Will you indulge my curiosity?"

"Since your curiosity is a trained one, I will." Chuft-Captain moved the guide. The projectiles still in the gun popped out through the shifting surface. The artifact became a sphere-with-handle, and then ... a sphere-with-handle. The new sphere was smaller than the neutral setting. It had a rosy hue and a smooth, oily texture unmarred by gunsights or secondary controls.

The trigger button did nothing at all.

"I tire rapidly of these duds."

"Chuft-Captain, there is energy release."

"Very well." Chuft-Captain fired at the puppeteer, using his marksman's instinct in the absence of a gunsight. The puppeteer showed no ill effects.

Neither did the female human.

In momentary irritation Chuft-Captain thought of firing the dud at Telepath, who was standing nearby looking harmless and useless. But nothing would happen; he would only upset Telepath. He moved the guide to the fifth setting.

The artifact writhed, became a short cylinder with an aperture in the nose and two wide, flat metallic projections at the sides. Chuft-Captain's lips drew back from neatly filed feline teeth. *This* looked promising.

He drew aim on what was left of the target rock—a dark blot on the ice.

The gun slammed back against his hand. Chuft-Captain was whirled half around, trying to keep his feet and fighting the sudden pressure as a fireman fights a fire hose. Releasing the trigger didn't shut off the incandescent stream of plasma gas. Pressing the trigger again did. Chuft-Captain blinked his relief and looked around to assess damages.

He saw a twisting trail of melted ice like the path of an earthworm hooked on LSD. Telepath was screaming into his helmet mike. An ominously diminishing scream. The other Kzinti were carrying him toward the airlock at a dead run. From the trail of thin, icy fog his suit left on the air, the weapon's firestream must have washed across his body, burning holes in nearly heatproof fabric.

The human female was running toward her ship.

A glance told him that the other prisoners were still in the police web. Telepath must have knocked the female spinning out of the force field while trying to escape the firestream. She was plainly visible, running across flat ice.

Chuft-Captain shot her with the stunner, then trudged away to pick her up. He had her back in the web when Flyer and Slaverstudent returned.

Telepath was still alive but in critical shape. They had dumped him in the freeze box for treatment on Kzin.

As for position five on the tnuctip relic:

"It's a rocket motor," said Slaverstudent. "As a short-range weapon it could be useful, but primarily it is a one-Kzin reaction pistol. One-tnuctip, that is. I doubt it would lift one of us against respectable gravity. The flat projections at the sides may be holds for feet. The tnuctipun were small."

"Pity you didn't think of this earlier."

"Chuft-Captain, I acknowledge my failure."

Chuft-Captain dropped it. Privately he too acknowledged a failure: he had not considered the female dangerous. Humans were sentient, male and female both. He would not forget it again.

Position six was a laser. It too was more than a weapon. A telescopic sight ran along the side, and there was a microphone grid at the back. Focus it on the proper target, and you could talk voice-to-voice.

"This will be useful," said Slaverstudent. "We can find the voice and hearing ranges for tnuctipun from this microphone."

"Will that make it a better weapon?"

"Chuft-Captain, it will not."

"Then keep your passion for useless knowledge to yourself." Chuft-Captain moved the guide to the seventh setting.

"Darling?"

Anne-Marie didn't move. The police web held her in a slumped sitting position. Her chest rose and fell with shallow breathing. Her eyes were closed, her face relaxed.

"Nice try," Jason told her.

"She cannot hear you," said Nessus.

"I *know* she can't hear me."

"Then why——? Never mind. What did that rocket setting look like to you?"

"A rocket."

"Using what fuel source?"

"Is it important?"

"Jason, I know nothing of warfare or of weapons, but my species has been making and using machines for some considerable time. Why did the projectile weapon not include its own projectiles? Why did it throw them away when it changed shape?"

"Oh. Okay, it can't throw away its own mass." Jason thought about that. "You're right. It can't be using its own fuel. Nessus, it's a jet. There was an intake somewhere that nobody noticed. Waitaminute. You couldn't use it in space."

"One would affix a gas cartridge at the intake."

"Oh. Right."

"One could not be sure a given atmosphere would burn. How is the gas heated?"

"A battery in the handle? No, it couldn't put out enough power, not without— But there has to be one. Nessus? The Kzinti could be listening."

"I think it does not matter. The Kzinti will know all about the weapon soon enough. Only the captain can profit from learning more before he turns the weapon over to his superiors."

"Okay. That battery must use total conversion of matter."

"Could you not build a fusion motor small enough to fit into the handle?"

"You're the expert. Could you? Would it give enough power?"

"I do not think so. The handle must contain a wide variety of mechanisms to control the changing of shapes."

They watched the Kzin test out the laser form.

"You could do it direct," said Jason. "Change some of the matter in the reaction gas to energy. It'd give you a terrifically hot exhaust. Nessus, is there any species in known space that has total conversion?"

"None that I have heard of."

"Did the tnuctipun?"

"I would not know."

"Things weren't bad enough. Can you see Kzinti warships armed and powered with total conversion?"

A gloomy silence followed. The Kzinti were watching the weapon change shape. The boss Kzin had not spoken; he may or may not have been listening to their discussions.

Anne-Marie made small protesting sounds. She opened her eyes and tried to sit up. She swore feelingly when she found that the web was holding her in her cramped position.

"Nice try," said Jason.

"Thanks. What happened?" She answered herself, her voice brittle and bitter. "They shot me, of course. What have I missed?"

The seventh setting was a blank, flat-ended cylinder with a small wire grid near the back. No gunsight. It did nothing when Chuft-Captain clicked the trigger button; it did nothing when he held it down, and nothing when he clicked it repeatedly. It had no effect on the target rock, the puppeteer, the humans. Its only effect on Slaverstudent was to make him back warily away, saying, "Chuft-Captain, please, there is an energy discharge."

"A singularly ineffective energy discharge. Take this, Slaverstudent. Make it work. I will wait."

And wait he did, stretched comfortably on the permafrost, his suit holding the cold a safe tenth of an inch away. He watched Slaverstudent's nerves fray under the fixity of his stare.

"What have I missed?"

"Not much. We've decided the jet that knocked you down converts matter to energy."

"Is that bad?"

"Very." Jason didn't try to explain. "The sixth setting was a more-or-less conventional message laser."

"The seventh does not work," said Nessus. "This angers the captain. Jason, for the first time I regret never having studied weapons."

"You're a puppeteer. Why should you . . ." Jason let the sentence trail off. There was a thought he wanted to trace down. About the weapon. Not any particular form, but all forms together.

"No sentient mind should turn away from knowledge. Especially no puppeteer. We are not known for our refusal to look at unpleasant truths."

Jason was silent. He was looking at an unpleasant truth.

Nessus had said that it didn't matter what the boss Kzin overheard. He was wrong. This was a thing Jason dared not say aloud.

Nessus said, "The Slaver expert wants to go inside with the weapon. He has permission. He is going."

"Why?" asked Anne-Marie.

"There is a microphone grid on the seventh setting. Jason, could a soldier use a hand computer?"

"He—" *wasn't a soldier!* Jason clamped his teeth on the words. "Probably could," he said.

Presently the Slaver expert returned holding the tnuctipun weapon.

To Jason, the artifact had taken on a final, fatal fascination. If he was right about its former owner, then he could stop worrying about its reaching the Patriarch of Kzin. All he had to do was keep his mouth shut. In minutes he and Anne-Marie and Nessus and the four Kzinti would be dead.

Slaverstudent said, "I was right. The artifact answered me in an unknown speech."

"Then it is another—" signaling device, he had been about to say. But it would have been built to signal tnuctipun, and the tnuctipun had been extinct for ages ... yet the thing had answered back! Chuft-Captain felt his back arch with the fighting reflex. There were ghost legends among the Kzinti.

"Chuft-Captain, I believe it to be a computer. A hand computer could be very useful to a warrior. It could compute angles for him as he fired explosive projectiles. It—"

"Yes. Can we use it?"

"Not unless we can teach it the Hero's Tongue. It may be too simple to learn."

"Then we pass to setting number eight." Chuft-Captain moved the guide down to the bottom setting.

Again there was no gunsight. Most of the genuine weapons had had gunsights or telescopic sights. Chuft-Captain scowled, but raised the weapon and aimed once again at the distant, shattered rock.

Jason cringed inside his imprisoned skin. Again the weapon was writhing, this time to the final setting.

There were so many things he wanted to say. But he didn't dare. The boss Kzin must not know what was about to happen.

The gun had twisted itself into something very strange.

"That looks familiar," said Nessus. "I have seen something like that at some time."

"Then you're unique," said Anne-Marie.

"I remember. It was one of a series of diagrams on how to turn a sphere inside out in differential topology. Certainly there could be no connection . . ."

The boss Kzin assumed marksman stance. Jason braced for the end.

What happened next was not at all what he expected.

Unconsciously he'd been leaning on the police net's force field. Suddenly he was falling, overbalanced. He straightened, not quite sure what had happened. Then he got it. The police net was gone. He slapped Anne-Marie hard on the butt, pointed at the *Court Jester,* saw her nod. Without waiting to see her start running, he turned and charged at the boss Kzin.

Something brushed by him at high speed. Nessus. Not running away but also charging into battle. *I was right,* thought Jason. *He's gone manic.*

Chuft-Captain pushed the trigger button. Nothing happened.

It was really too much. He stood a moment, marshaling words for Slaverstudent. A brand-new kind of weapon, and it wouldn't *do* anything! Half the settings were duds!

He knew it as he turned: something was wrong. The danger instinct sang in his nerves. He got no other warning. He had not seen the ship lights go out. He heard no sign of pounding clawed feet. The sounds of breathing *had* become a trifle heavy . . .

He started to turn, and something hit him in the side.

It felt as though an armored knight had run him through with a blunt lance. It *hurt.* Chuft-Captain lost all his aplomb and all his air, bent sideways as far as he could manage, and toppled.

He saw the world turned sideways, glowing through a blue fog. He saw the human female struggling futilely in Slaverstudent's hands; he saw Flyer aiming a stunner across the ice. He saw two running figures, human and puppeteer, trying to reach the other ship. Flyer's stunner didn't seem to affect them. The human had the tnuctip artifact.

He could breathe again, in sharp, shallow gasps. That blow in the side must have broken ribs; it could hardly have failed to, since Kzinti ribs run all the way down. That blow had felt like a puppeteer's kick! But that was ridiculous. Impossible. A puppeteer kick a Kzin?

The puppeteer reached the ship far in advance of the slower human. He paused a moment, then turned and ran on across the white undulating plain. The human also paused at the ship's entrance, then followed the puppeteer. Flyer was running after them.

Behind Chuft-Captain the ship lights were dim, but brightening. Hadn't they been dark when he fell? And the stunners hadn't worked. And the police webs . . .

So. The eighth setting was an energy absorber. Not a new thing, but much smaller than anything he'd heard of.

But what had hit him?

There was a hissing in his ears, a sound he hadn't noticed. Not breathing. Had somebody's suit been punctured? But nobody had been attacked. Except—

Chuft-Captain slapped a hand over his side. He yelled with the pain of motion but kept his hand pressed tight while he reached for a meteor patch. He risked one look under his hand before applying the patch. There were four tiny holes in the fabric. They might easily have marked the claws of a puppeteer's space boot.

The boss Kzin held his marksman's stance. Jason was moving toward him at a dead run. He had to get the weapon before the Kzinti realized what had happened.

Nessus passed him like a live missile. The puppeteer reached the Kzin, turned skidding on two front legs, and lashed out. Jason winced in sympathy. That kick had been sincere! It would have torn a man in half, crushed his lungs and rib cage and spine and life.

The mad puppeteer had barely paused. He ran straight toward the *Court Jester*. Jason scooped up the fallen weapon, skidded to a halt, and turned.

A Kzin had Anne-Marie.

We'll see about that! His fingers moved to the weapon's adjustment guide.

A second Kzin held a stunner on him.

The stunner would start working the moment the tnuctip weapon shifted shape. He'd lose everything.

He could hear Anne-Marie swearing tearfully as she fought. Then her voice came loud and clear. "Run, dammit! Jay, run!"

He could throw the weapon to Nessus, then charge to the rescue! They'd get *him,* but ... but the puppeteer was well out of range ... and couldn't be trusted anyway. A puppeteer who kicked something that could kick back was beyond psychiatric help.

Anne-Marie was still kicking and using her elbows. Her Kzinti captor didn't seem to notice. The boss Kzin lay curled like a shrimp around the spot of agony in his side. But the third Kzin held his pose, still bathing Jason in an imaginary stunner beam.

Jason turned and ran.

He saw Nessus leave the *Jester*'s entrance and go on. He guessed what he would find, but he had to look. Sure enough, the door was soldered shut.

The laser setting would have melted the steel solder away from the hullmetal door. But the third Kzin was finally in motion, coming after him, still trying to use the stunner.

Jason ran on. The puppeteer was a diminishing point. Jason followed that point, moving into a cold waste lit by a fiery arch with one bright glare spot.

"Flyer, return to the ship at once."

"Chuft-Captain, he's around here somewhere. I can find him."

"Or he could find you. Return to the ship. The rules of this game have changed."

The Kzin was gone. Jason had stalked him for a time, with his weapon set to the energy-absorbing phase and with his thumb on the guide. If he had seen the Kzin, and if the Kzin hadn't seen him ... a variable-sword, a hair-thin wire sheathed in a stasis field, would have cut one enemy into two strangers. But it hadn't happened, and he wasn't about to follow the Kzin back to home base.

Now he lay huddled in the hole he'd dug with the rocket phase.

"Jay!" It was Anne-Marie. "Have to talk quick; they're taking off my helmet. I'm not hurt, but I can't get away. The ship's taking off. Bury the weapon somewh—"

Her voice faded and was gone. The public band was silent.

Nessus' voice broke that silence. "Jason, turn to the private band."

He had to guess which band Nessus meant. He was third-time lucky.

"Can you hear me?"

"Yah. Where are you?"

"I do not know how to describe my position, Jason. I ran six or seven miles east."

"Okay. Let's think of a way to find each other."

"Why, Jason?"

He puzzled over that. "You think you're safer alone? I don't. How long will your suit keep you alive?"

"Several standard years. But help will arrive before then."

"What makes you think so?"

"When the Kzinti pilot entered the pressure curtain, I was calling my people for help."

"What? How?"

"Despite recent changes in the fortunes of my people, that is still most secret."

Telepathy? Something in his baggage or surgically implanted under his skin? The puppeteers kept their secrets well. Nobody had ever found out how they could commit painless suicide at will. And how Nessus had done it didn't matter. "Are they coming for you all the way from Andromeda?"

"Hardly, Jason."

"Go on."

"I suppose I must. My people are still in this region of the galaxy, in the sixty-light-year volume you call known space. Their journey began only twelve years ago. You see, Jason, my people do not intend to return to this galaxy. Hence it does not matter how much objective time passes during their journey. They can reach Andromeda in a much shorter subjective time using normal space drives. Our ships approach very close to lightspeed. Further, they need brave only the dangers of normal space, which they can handle easily. Hyperspace is an unpredictable and uncomfortable thing, especially for those who would spend decades traveling in any case."

"Nessus, your whole species is crazy. How did they keep a secret like that? Everyone thinks they're halfway to Andromeda."

"Naturally. Who would stumble across the fleet in inter-stellar space? Between systems every known species travels in hyperspace—except the Outsiders, with whom we have agreements. In any case, my people are within reach. A scout will arrive within sixty days. The scouts are fitted with hyperdrive."

"Then you're safe if you stay hidden." Damn! thought Jason. He was all alone. It was a proud and lonely thing to be a costume hero. "Well, good luck Nessus. I've got to—"

"Do not sign off. What is your plan?"

"I don't have one. I've got to see the Kzinti don't get this back, but I've also got to get Anne-Marie away from them."

"The weapon should come first."

"My wife comes first. What's your stake in this, any-way?"

"With the principles behind the tnuctip weapon the Kzinti could command known space. My people will be in known space for another twenty-eight human years. Should the Kzinti learn of our fleet, it would be an obvious and vulnerable target."

"Oh."

"We must help each other. How long can you live in your suit?"

"Till I starve to death. I'll have air and water indefinite-ly. Say thirty days, upper limit."

"Your people should not cut costs on vital equipment, Jason. My people cannot arrive in time to save you."

"If I gave you the weapon, could you stay hidden?"

"Yes. If the ship came in sight, I could shoot it down with the laser setting. I think I could. I could force myself—Jason, will the Kzinti call other ships?"

"Damn! Of course they will. They'd find you easily. What'll we do?"

"Can we force entrance to the *Court Jester*?"

"Yah, but they took my keys. We couldn't use the drives or the radio or get into the lockers."

"The laser would let us into the lockers."

"Right."

"Have you weapons aboard?"

"No. Nothing."

"Then the *Court Jester* would be no more than a place from which to surrender. I have no suggestions."

"Chuft-Captain, the eighth setting must be the way the artifact is recharged. It does not itself seem to be a weapon."

"It can be used as one. As we have seen. Don't bother me now, Slaverstudent." Chuft-Captain strove to keep his tone mild. He knew that his rage was the companion of his pain, and Slaverstudent knew it too.

Neither had referred to the fact that Chuft-Captain now walked crouched to the side. Neither would. The Kzinti captain could not even bandage himself; though when they reached space, he could use the ship's medical equipment to set the bones.

The worst damage had been done to Chuft-Captain's ego.

Had the puppeteer known what he was doing? His small clawed foot had shattered more than a couple of ribs. One day Chuft-Captain might have been Chuft, the hero, who found the weapon that beat the human empire to its belly. Now he would be Chuft who was kicked by a puppeteer.

"Chuft-Captain, here comes Flyer."

"Good. Flyer! Get your tail in here and lift us fast."

Flyer went past at a quick shuffling run. Slaverstudent shut the airlock after him, helped Chuft-Captain strap down, and was strapping himself in when Flyer did his trick. The ship rose out of the ice, dripping opalescent chunks and shining blue-white at the stern.

On the smoky arch of Beta Lyrae the bright point had reached its zenith. Behind their permanent veil the two stars had pulled apart in their orbits, so that the vague brightness shaded into an orange tinge on one side and a green on the other.

"One thing we do have," said Jason, "and that's the weapon itself."

"True. We have a laser, a flame-throwing rocket, and a shield against police stunners. But not simultaneously."

"I think we may have overlooked a setting."

"Wishful thinking, Jason, is not a puppeteer trait."

"Neither is knowledge of weapons. Nessus, what kind of weapon is this? I'm talking about the whole bundle, not any single setting."

"As you say, I am not an expert on warfare."

"I don't think it's a soldier's weapon. I think it's for espionage."

"Would that be different? I gather the question is important."

Jason stopped to gather his thoughts. He held the gun cradled in his hands. It was still at the eighth setting, the peculiar, twisted shape that Nessus had compared to a diagram from differential topology.

He held history in his hands, history a billion and a half years dead. Once upon a time a small, compactly built biped had aimed this weapon at beings with ball-shaped heads, big single eyes, massive Mickey Mouse hands, great splayed feet, and lightly armored skin and clusters of naked-pink tendrils at the corners of wide mouths. What could he have been thinking the last time he stored away this weapon? Did he guess that fifteen million centuries later a mind would be trying to guess his nature from his abandoned possessions?

"Nessus, would you say this gadget is more expensive to produce than eight different gadgets to do similar jobs?"

"Assuredly, and more difficult. But it would be easier to carry than eight discrete gadgets."

"And easier to hide. Have you ever heard of Slaver records describing a shape-changing weapon?"

"No. The tnuctipun would understandably have kept it a secret."

"That's my point. How long could they keep it secret if millions of soldiers had models?"

"Not long. The same objections hold for its use in espionage. Jason, what kind of espionage could a tnuctip do? Certainly it could not imitate a Slaver."

"No, but it could hide out on a sparsely settled world, or it could pretend to be a tnuctip slave. It'd have to have some defense against the Slaver power . . ."

"The cap in the stasis box?"

"Or something else, something it was wearing when the Slavers caught it."

"These are unpleasant ideas. Jason, I have remembered something. The Outsiders found the stasis box in a cold, airless world with ancient pressurized buildings still standing. If a battle had been fought there, would the buildings have been standing?"

"Slaver buildings?"

"Yes."

"They'd have been standing if the Slavers won. But then the Slavers would have captured at least one of the weapons."

"Only if there were many such weapons. I concede your point. The owner of the weapon was a lone spy."

"Good. Now—"

"Why were you so sure?"

"Mainly the variety of settings. The average soldier would get stomped on while he was trying to decide which weapon to use. Then there's a sonic for taking live prisoners. Maybe other settings make them feel fear or pain. The rocket would be silly for a soldier; he'd get killed flying around a battlefield. But a spy could use it for the last stage of his landing."

"All right. Why is it important?"

"Because there ought to be a self-destruct setting somewhere."

"What did—? Ah. To keep the secret of the mutable weapon. But we have used all the settings."

"I thought it would be number eight. It wasn't. That's why we're still alive. An espionage agent's self-destruct button would be made to do as much damage as possible."

Nessus gasped. Jason hardly noticed. "They've hidden it somehow," he said.

The *Traitor's Claw* was big. She had to be. Redundantly, she carried both a gravity polarizer and a fusion-reaction motor. Probably she could have caught anything in real space, barring ships of her own class, many of which were serving as police and courier ships in Kzinti space. Kzinti records listed her as a stolen courier ship. She was a squat cone, designed as a compromise between landing ability and speed in an atmosphere. In contrast, the flat *Court Jester* had been designed for landing ability alone; she would not have tipped over on a seventy-degree slope.

There was more than speed to the courier ship's two drives. Before it had ever seen a gravity polarizer, the human empire had taught the Kzinti a lesson they would never forget. The more efficient a reaction drive, the more effective a weapon it makes. A gravity polarizer was not a reaction drive.

Flyer used both drives at once. The ship went up fast. Six thousand miles up, the *Traitor's Claw* went into orbit.

"We can find the prisoners with infrared," said Chuft-Captain. "But it will do us little good if they shoot us down. Can the laser setting prevent us from going after them?"

"We can call for more ships," Flyer suggested. "Surely the weapon is important enough."

"It is. But we will not call."

Flyer nodded submission.

Knowing what Flyer knew, Chuft-Captain snarled inside

himself with humiliation and the digging agony in his side.
He had been kicked by a puppeteer in full view of two
subordinates. Never again could he face a Kzin of equal
rank, never until he had killed the puppeteer with his own
teeth and claws.

Could that kick have been cold-bloodedly tactical?
Chuft-Captain refused to believe it. But, intended or not,
that kick had stymied Chuft-Captain. He could not call
for reinforcements until the puppeteer was dead.

He forced his mind back to the weapon. The only
setting that could harm the Kzinti was the laser ... unless
the rosy sphere unexpectedly began working. But that was
unlikely. He asked, "Is there a completely safe way to
capture them? If not—"

"There is the drive," said Slaverstudent.

"They have the laser," Flyer reminded him. "A laser
that size is subject to a certain amount of spreading. We
should be safe two hundred miles up. Closer than that and
a good marksman could burn through the hull."

"Flyer, is two hundred miles too high?"

"Chuft-Captain, they are wearing heatproof suits, and
we can hover only at one-seventh Kzin-gravity. Our flame
would barely warm the ice."

"But there is the gravity polarizer to pull us down while
the fusion flame pushes us up. The ship was designed for
just that tactic. Now, the fugitives' suits are heatproof, but
the ice is not. Suppose we hovered over them with a five-
Kzin-gravity flame ..."

Jason held a five-inch rosy sphere with a pistol-grip
handle. "It has to be here somewhere," he said.

"Try doing things you ordinarily wouldn't: moving the
gauge while holding the trigger down ... moving the
guide sideways ... twisting the sphere."

Silence on the private circuit. Then, "No luck yet."

"The fourth setting was the only one that showed no
purpose at all."

"Yah. What in—"

High overhead a star had come into being. It was

blue-white, almost violet-white, and for Jason it stood precisely at the zenith.

"The Kzinti," said Nessus. "Do not shoot back. They must be out of range of your laser setting. You would only help them find you."

"They've probably found me already with infrared scopes. What the Finagle do they think they're doing?"

The star remained steady. In its sudden light Jason went to work on the weapon. He ran quickly through the remaining settings, memorizing the forms that used the trigger as an on-off switch, probing and prodding almost at random, until he reached neutral and the relic was a silver sphere with a handle.

The guide would not go sideways. It would not remain between any two of the notches. It would not twist.

"Are you making progress?"

"Nothing, dammit."

"The destruct setting would not be too carefully hidden. If a weapon were captured, an agent could always hope the Slavers would destroy it by accident."

"Yah." Jason was tired of looking at the neutral setting. He changed to laser and fired up at the new star, using the telescopic sight. He expected and got no result, but he held his aim until distracted by a sudden change in pressure around his suit.

He was up to his shoulders in water.

In one surge he was out of his hole. But the land around him was gone. A few swells of wet ice rose glistening from a shallow sea that reached to all the horizon. The Kzinti ship's downblast had melted everything for miles around.

"Nessus, is there water around you?"

"Only in the solid form. From my viewpoint the Kzinti ship is not overhead."

"They've got me. As soon as they turn off the drive, I'll be frozen in my tracks."

"I have been thinking. Do you need the destruct setting? Suppose you change to the rocket setting, turn the weapon nose down, and fire. The flame will remain on, and the weapon will eat its way through the ice."

"Sure, if we could think of a way to keep it pointed down. Odds are it'd turn over in the first few feet. Then the Kzinti find it with deep-radar or seismics and dig it out."

"True."

The water was getting deeper. Jason thought about using the rocket to burn his way loose once the water froze about his ankles. It would be too hot. He would probably burn his feet off. But he might have to try it.

The blue Kzinti star hung bright and clear against the arch of dust and hydrogen. A bright pink glow showed the Lyrae stars forty-five degrees from sunset.

"Jason. Why is there a neutral setting?"

"Why not?"

"It is not for collecting energy. The eighth setting does that very nicely. It is not for doing nothing. The projectile setting does that, unless you put projectiles in it. Thus the neutral setting has no purpose. Perhaps it does something we do not know about."

"I'll try it."

The bright star above him winked out.

"Chuft-Captain, I cannot locate the puppeteer."

"Its pressure suit may be too efficient to lose heat. We will institute a sight search later. Inform me when the human stops moving."

Nessus' idea would be a good one, Jason thought, if only he could make it workable. Much better than the destruct setting. Because if the destruct setting existed, it would almost certainly kill him.

Probably it would kill Nessus too. The destruct setting on an espionage agent's weapon would be made to do as much damage as possible. And there had been total conversion involved in the rocket setting. Total conversion would make quite a bomb, even if it weighed only four pounds, and the converted mass a fraction of a milligram.

The Kzinti-produced swamp was congealing from the bottom up. His boots were getting heavy. Each had collected a growing mass of ice. He kept walking so that they wouldn't freeze to the bottom.

He'd searched the neutral setting, handle and sphere, for hidden controls. Nothing showed—nothing obvious. He tried twisting various parts of the handle. Nothing broke, which was good, but nothing would twist either.

Maybe something *should* break. Suppose he broke off the gauge?

He wasn't strong enough.

He tried twisting the ball itself. Nothing.

He tried it again, holding the trigger down.

The silvery sphere twisted one hundred and eighty degrees, then clicked. Jason released the trigger, and it started to change.

"I've found it, Nessus. I've found *something*."

"A new setting? What does it look like?"

Like a white flash, thought Jason, waiting for the single instant in which it *would* look like a white flash. It didn't come. The protean material solidified.

"Like a cone with a rounded base, pointing away from the handle."

"Try it. And if you are successful, good-bye, Jason. Knowing you was pleasant."

"The blast could include you, too."

"Is it thus you assuage my loss of you?"

"You sure you don't have a sense of humor? Good-bye, Nessus. Here goes."

The cone did not explode. A time bomb? Jason was about to start looking for a chronometer on the thing when he noticed something that froze him instantly.

A hazy blue line led away in the direction he happened to be pointing the cone. Led away and upward at forty degrees, wavering, as tremor in his fingers waved the cone's vertex.

Another weapon.

He released the trigger. The line disappeared.

The Kzinti ship wasn't in sight. Not that he would have used it as a target, not with Anne-Marie aboard.

A hidden weapon. More powerful than the others? He

had to find out. Like Chuft-Captain, he tried to assume marksman's stance.

His feet were frozen solidly into the ice. He'd been careless. He shrugged angrily, aimed the weapon a little above the horizon, and fired.

A hazy blue line formed. He slowly lowered the vertex until the line touched the horizon.

The light warned him. He threw himself flat on his back and waited for the blast. The light died almost instantly, and suddenly the shiny horizon-to-horizon ice rippled and shot from under him. It took his feet along. His body snapped like a whip, and then the ice tore away from his feet.

He was on his face, with agony in his ankles.

The backlash came. The ice jerked under him, harmlessly.

"Jason, what happened? There was an explosion."

"Hang ... on." Jason rolled over and pulled his legs up to examine them. The pain was bad. His ankles didn't feel broken, but he certainly couldn't walk on them. The boots were covered with cracked wet ice.

"Jason. Puppeteer. Can you hear me?" It was the slurred, blurry voice of the boss Kzin.

"Don't say anything, Nessus. I'm going to answer him." Jason switched his transmitter to the common channel. "I'm here."

"You have discovered a new setting to the weapon."

"Have I?"

"I do not intend to play pup games with you. As a fighter, you are entitled to respect, which your herbivorous friend is not—"

"How are your ribs feeling?"

"Do not speak of that again, please. We have something to trade, you and I. You have a unique weapon. I have a female human who may be your mate."

"Well put. So?"

"Give us the weapon. Show us where to find the new setting. You and your mate may leave this world in your own ship, unharmed and unrestricted."

"Your name as your word?"

No answer.

"You lying get of a . . ." Jason searched for the word. He could say two words of Kzin; one meant hello, and one meant—

"Do not say it. Jason, the agreement stands, except that I will smash your hyperdrive. You must return to civilization through normal space. With that proviso, you have my name as my word."

"Nessus?"

"The herbivore must protect itself."

"I think not."

"Consider the alternative. Your mate is not entitled to the respect accorded a fighter. Kzinti are carnivorous, and we have been without fresh meat for some years."

"Bluff me not. You'd lose your only hostage."

"We'd lose one arm of her. Then another. Then a lower leg."

Jason felt sick. They could do it. Painlessly, too, if they wished; and they probably would, to avoid losing Anne-Marie to shock.

He gulped. "Is she all right now?"

"Naturally."

"Prove it." He was stalling. Nessus could hear everything; he might come up with something . . . and was ever there a fainter hope?

"You may hear her," said the boss Kzin. There were clunking sounds; they must be dropping her helmet over her head. Then Anne-Marie's voice spoke swiftly and urgently.

"Jay, darling, listen. Use the seventh setting. The *seventh*. Can you hear me?"

"Anne, are you all right?"

"I'm fine," she shouted. "Use the seventh . . ." Her voice died abruptly.

"Anne!"

Nothing.

There was fast, muffled Kzinti speech in his earphones. Jason looked at the weapon a moment, then dropped the guide to setting number seven. Maybe she had something. The cone writhed, became a mirror-surfaced sphere . . .

"Jason, you now know your mate is unharmed. We must ask for your decision immediately."

He ignored the burry voice, watched the weapon become a flat-ended cylinder with a grid near the handle. He'd seen the Kzinti using that.

"Oh," he said.

It was the computer, of course. The tnuctip computer. He smiled, and it hurt inside him. His wife had given him the only help she had to give. She'd told him where to find the only tnuctipun expert in known space.

The hell of it was, she was perfectly right. But the computer couldn't hear him, and he couldn't hear the computer, and they didn't speak a common language anyway.

Wait a minute. This was setting number seven; but if you counted neutral as the first setting, then—no. Setting six was only the laser.

Finagle! The Belter oath fitted. Finagle's First Law was holding beautifully.

His ankles stopped hurting.

Decoyed! He twisted his head around to find his enemy. The bargain had been a decoy! Already his head buzzed with the stunner beam. He saw the Kzin, hiding behind a half-melted bulge of ice with only one eye and the stunner showing. He fired at once.

The weapon was on computer setting. His hand went slack, then his mind.

"I do not understand why she wanted him to use the seventh setting."

"The computer, was it not?"

"Chuft-Captain, it was."

"He could not have used the computer."

"No. Why then did the prisoner—"

"She may have meant the sixth setting. The laser was the only weapon a human could have used against us."

"Urrr. Yes. She counted wrong, then."

The ship-to-suit circuit spoke. "Chuft-Captain, I have him."

"Flyer, well done. Bring him in."

"Chuft-Captain, do we still need him?"

The Kzin was not in a mood to argue. "I hate to throw anything away. Bring him in."

His head floated, his body spun, his ankles hurt like fury. He shuddered and tried to open his eyes. The lids came up slowly, reluctantly.

He was standing in a police web, slack neck muscles holding his head upright in one-eighth gee. No wonder he hadn't known which way was up. Anne-Marie was twelve inches to his side. Her eyes held no hope, only exhaustion.

"Damn," he said. One word to cover it all.

The Kzinti yowrling had been so much a part of the background that he didn't notice it until it stopped. After a moment the boss Kzin stepped in front of him, moving slowly and carefully, and curled protectively around his left side.

"You are awake."

"Obviously."

One massive four-clawed hand held the tnuctip weapon, still at the computer setting. The Kzin held it up. "You found a new setting on this. Tell me how to reach it."

"I can't," said Jason. "I found it by accident and lost it the same way."

"That is a shame. Do you realize we have nothing to lose?"

Jason studied the violet eyes, fruitlessly. "What do you mean?"

"Either you will tell me of your own free will, or you can be persuaded to tell, or you cannot. In any case, we have no reason not to remove your mate's arm."

He turned and spoke in the Kzinti tongue. The other aliens left the room.

"We will be leaving this world in an hour." The boss Kzin turned and settled his orange bulk carefully in a Kzinti contour couch, grunting softly with the pain of movement.

He meant it. His position was too simple for doubt. The boss Kzin had a tnuctip weapon to take back to Kzin, and he had two human captives. The humans were of no use to him. But he had great use for Jason's knowledge. What he offered was a simple trade: knowledge for the meat on their bones.

"I can't talk," said Jason.

"All right," Anne-Marie said dully.

"I *can't*." The cone form was too powerful. Its beam must set up spontaneous mass conversion in anything it touched. And he couldn't explain. The boss Kzin might hear him, and the Kzinti didn't know just what they were after.

"All right, you can't. We've had it. How did they get you?"

"I got stupid. While the boss Kzin was talking to me, one of the others snuck up and used a sonic."

"The seventh setting—"

"I didn't have time to figure anything out. There isn't enough air to carry sound out there."

"I didn't think of that. How's Nessus?"

"Still free."

The boss Kzin broke in. "We will have it soon. The puppeteer has no place to hide and nothing with which to fight, not even the inclination. Do you expect it to rescue you?"

Anne-Marie smiled sourly. "Not really."

The other Kzinti returned, carrying things. There were pieces of indecipherable Kzinti equipment, and there was a medkit from the emergency doc in the *Court Jester*. They set it all down next to the police web and went to work.

One piece of Kzinti equipment was a small tank with a pump and a piece of soft plastic tubing attached. Jason watched them wrap the tubing three or four times around Anne-Marie's upper arm. They joined the other end to the pump and started it going.

"It's cold," she said. "Freezing."

"I can't stop them," said Jason.

She shivered. "You're sure?"

He gave up. He opened his mouth to shout out his surrender. The boss Kzin raised his furry head questioningly—and Jason's voice stopped in his throat.

He'd used the hidden setting just once. For only an instant had the blue beam touched the horizon, but the explosion had damn near killed him. Obviously the hidden setting was not meant to be used on the surface of a planet.

It could be used only from space. Was it meant to destroy whole worlds?

But Anne-Marie hurt!

She said, "All right, you're sure. Jay, don't *look* like that. Jay? I can grow a new arm. Relax! Stop *worrying* about it!" The anguish in Jason's face was like nothing she'd ever seen.

The burry voice said, "She will never reach an autodoc."

"Shut *up!*" Jason screamed.

Soft Kzinti noises entered the silence. One of the Kzinti left: the pilot, the one with a white streak. The others talked. They talked of cooking, Kzinti sex, human sex, Beta Lyrae, how to hunt puppeteers, or how to turn a sphere inside out without forming a cusp. Jason couldn't tell. They used no gestures.

Anne-Marie said, "They could have planted a mike on us."

"Yah."

"So you can't tell me what you're hiding."

"No. I wish I spoke Wunderlander."

"*I* don't speak Wunderlander. Dead language. Jay, I can't feel my arm any more. There must be liquid nitrogen in this tube."

"I'm sorry. I *can't help*."

"It is not working," said Chuft-Captain.

"It should work," said Slaverstudent. "We may not get results with the first limb. We probably will with the second. The second time, they will know that we mean what we threaten." He looked thoughtfully at the prisoners. "Also, I think we should eat our meals in here."

"They know that limbs can be regrown."

"Only by human-built machines. There are none here."

"You have a point."

"It will be good to taste fresh meat again."

Flyer returned. "Chuft-Captain, the kitchen is programmed."

"Good." Chuft-Captain incautiously shifted his bulk and tensed all over at the pain. It would have been nice if he could have put pressure bandages around his ribs. The ribs had been set and joined with pins, but he could not use pressure bandages; they would remind his crew of what had happened. He would be shamed.

Kicked by a puppeteer.

"I have been thinking," he said. "Regardless of what the human tells us, we must take the tnuctip relic to Kzin as quickly as possible. There I will drop you, Slaverstudent, along with the weapon and the freeze box containing Telepath. Flyer, you and I will return here for the herbivore. He cannot be rescued in that time. He will be easy to find. A sight search will find him unless he digs a hole, in which case we may use seismographs."

"He will have a month to anticipate."

"Yes. He will."

"Can you understand me?"

Three pairs of Kzinti eyes jerked around. The voice had belonged to none of them. It sounded foreign, artificial.

"Repeating. Can you understand me?"

It was the gun speaking. The tnuctip weapon.

"It's learned their language," said Jason. And all the hope drained out of him.

"It'll tell them where to find that setting you were trying to hide."

"Yah."

"Then tell me this, Jay." She was on the edge of hysteria. "What good will it do me to lose my arm?"

Jason filled his lungs and shouted. "Hey!"

Not one Kzin moved. They hovered around the weapon, all talking at once.

"Hey, Captain! What *sthondat* was your sister?"

They all jerked around. He must have pronounced the word right.

"You must not use that word again," said the boss Kzin.

"Get this thing off my wife's arm!"

The boss Kzin thought it over, spoke to the pilot. The pilot manipulated the police web to free Anne-Marie's arm, using a cloth to protect his hand while he removed the cold, deadly tube. He turned off the pump, readjusted the police web, and went back to the discussion, which by then had become a dialogue. The boss Kzin had shut the others up.

"How's your arm?"

"Feels dead. Maybe it is. What were we hiding, Jay?"

He told her.

"Ye gods! And now they've got it."

"Could you use an anesthetic?"

"It doesn't hurt yet."

"Let me know. They're all through torturing us. They may eat us, but it'll be all at once."

The computer was doing most of the talking.

A Kzin was holding up the tnuctip cap, the one they'd found in the stasis box. The computer spoke.

He held up the small metal object that might have been a communicator. The computer spoke again.

The boss Kzin spoke.

The computer spoke at length.

The boss Kzin picked up the weapon and did things to it. Jason couldn't see what. The Kzin was facing away from him. But the weapon writhed. Jason snarled in his throat. He commonly used curses for emphasis. He knew no words to cover this situation.

The boss Kzin spoke briefly and left, cradling the weapon. One of the others followed: the expert on Slavers. Jason caught one glimpse of the weapon as the boss Kzin went through the door.

The Kzin with the white stripe, the pilot, remained.

Jason felt himself starting to shake. The weapon, the soft, mutable weapon. When the boss Kzin had left the room, he'd carried a gun handle attached to a double cone with rounded bases and points that barely touched.

He didn't understand.

Then his eyes, restlessly searching the room as if for an answer, fell on the empty stasis box. There was a tnuctip cap and a small metal object that registered in hyperspace and a preserved Slaver hand.

It began to make sense.

Did the computer have eyesight? Obviously. The Kzinti had been showing it objects from the stasis box.

Take a computer smart enough to learn a language by hearing it spoken for an hour. Never mind its size; any sentient being will build a computer as small as possible, if only to reduce the time lag in thinking with impulses moving at lightspeed or less. Let the computer know only what its tnuctipun builders had taught it, plus what it had seen and heard in this room.

It had seen a tnuctip survival kit. It had seen members of a species it did not recognize. The unfamiliar beings had asked questions which made it obvious that they knew little about tnuctipun, and that they could not ask questions of a tnuctip. They didn't speak the tnuctip language. They were desperately anxious for details about a tnuctip top-secret weapon.

Obviously they were not allies of the tnuctipun.

They must be enemies. In the Slaver War there had been, could be, no neutrals.

He said, "Anne."

"Still here."

"Don't ask questions, just follow orders. Our lives depend on it. See that Kzin?"

"Right. You sneak up on him from behind; I'll hit him with my purse."

"This is not funny. When I give the word, we're both going to spit at his ear."

"You're right. That's not funny."

"I'm in dead earnest. And don't forget to compensate for low gravity."

"How are you going to give the word with a mouthful of saliva?"

"Just spit when I do. Okay?"

Jason's shot brushed the Kzin's furry scalp. Anne-

Marie's caught him square in the ear. The Kzin came to his feet with a howl. Then, as both humans cleared their throats again, the Kzin moved like lightning. The air stiffened about their heads.

The Kzin contemptuously returned to his crouch against a wall.

It became hard to breathe.

Blinking was a slow, excruciating process. Talking was out of the question. Warm air, laden with CO_2, did not want to dissipate. It stayed before their faces, waiting to be inhaled again and again. The Kzin watched them struggle.

Jason forced his eyes closed. Blinking had become too painful. He tried to remember that he'd planned this, that it had worked perfectly. Their heads and bodies were now entirely enclosed by the police web.

Now here's my plan.

"The puppeteer ran east," said Chuft-Captain. And he turned west. He didn't want to kill the puppeteer without knowing it.

The weapon was hard and awkward in his hand. He was a little afraid of it, and a little ashamed of being afraid: a hangover from that awful moment when the weapon spoke. There were ghost legends among the Kzinti. Some of the most fearsome spoke of captured weapons haunted by their dead owners.

Nobles weren't supposed to be superstitious, not out loud.

A computer that could learn new languages was logical. The only way to reach the setting for the matter-conversion beam had been to ask the computer setting, and that was logical too. A matter-conversion beam was a dangerous secret.

Briefly, Chuft-Captain wondered about that. It seemed that for an honorable Kzin every recent change was a change for the worse. The conquest of space had ended when Kzinti met humans. Then had come the puppeteers with their trade outposts; any Kzin who attacked a puppeteer invariably found himself not harmed physically, but ruined financially. No Kzin could fight power like that. Would the tnuctip weapon reverse these changes?

There had been a time, between the discoveries of atomic power and the gravity polarizer, when it seemed the Kzinti species would destroy itself in wars. Now the Kzinti held many worlds, and the danger was past. But was it? A matter-conversion beam ...

There is no turning away from knowledge.

Haunted weapons ...

He stopped on a rise of permafrost some distance from the ship. By now half the sky was blood red. An arm of the hydrogen spiral was sweeping across the world, preparing to engulf it. Hours or days from now the arm would pass, moving outward on the wings of photon pressure, leaving the world with a faintly thicker atmosphere.

But we'll be long gone by then, Chuft-Captain thought. Already he was looking ahead to the problem of reaching Kzin. If human ships caught the *Traitor's Claw* entering Kzin's atmosphere, the Kzinti would clearly be violating treaty rules. But they weren't likely to be caught, not if Flyer did everything right.

"Chuft-Captain, this setting has no gunsight."

"No? You're right, it doesn't." He considered. "Perhaps it was meant only for large targets. A world seen from close up. The explosion was fierce."

"Or its accuracy may be low. Or its range. I wonder. Logically the tnuctipun should have included at least a pair of notches for sighting."

Something's wrong. The danger instinct whispered in his ear. "Superstition," he snarled, and raised the weapon stiffly, aiming well above the horizon. "Let us find the answer," he said.

In this area of Cue Ball the ice had melted and refrozen. It was as flat as a calm lake.

Nessus had stopped at the edge. He'd faced around, stopped again, held the pose for several minutes, then faced back and started across the flat, red-tinged ice. Muscles rippled beneath his pressure suit.

It wasn't as if he expected to help his human employees. They had gotten themselves into this. And he had neither weapons nor allies nor even stealth to aid him. A human infantryman could have crawled on his belly, but Nessus' legs weren't built that way. On a white plain with no cover he had to trot upright, bouncing gaily in the low gravity.

His only weapon was his hind leg.

Thinking that, he remembered the jarring impact as he had planted his foot in the Kzin's side. Two hundred and forty pounds of charging puppeteer applied over five square inches of clawed space boot. The shock wave had jarred up through thigh and hip and spine, jerked at his skull and continued along the necks to snap his teeth shut with a sharp double *click*. Like kicking a mountain, a soft but solid mountain.

The next instant he was running, really terrified for the first time in his life. But behind him the Kzin had vented a long whistling scream and folded tightly around himself. . . .

Nessus went on. He'd trotted across the frozen lake without seeing Kzinti or Kzinti ship. Now the ice was beginning to swell and dip. He'd reached the periphery of the blast area. Now there was a touch of yellow light ahead. Small and faint, but unmistakably yellow against the pink ice.

Ship lights.

He went on. He'd never know why. He'd never admit it to himself.

Thock! Hind boot slamming solidly into hard meat. Whistling shriek of agony between sharp-filed carnivore teeth.

He wanted to do it again. Nessus had the blood lust.

He went up a rise, moving slowly, though his feet wanted to dance. He was weaponless, but his suit was a kind of defense. No projectile short of a fast meteorite could harm him. Like a silicone plastic, the pressure suit was soft and malleable under gentle pressures, such as walking, but it instantly became rigid all over when something struck it.

He topped the rise.

The ship lights might have come from the *Court Jester*. They didn't. Nessus saw the airlock opening, and he charged down the slope so the next rise hid him from view.

The Kzinti ship was down. They must have landed with the gravity polarizer; otherwise he would have seen them. If they had then captured Jason on foot, he might still be alive. He might not. The same went for Anne-Marie.

Now what? The Kzinti ship was beyond this next rise of ice. At least one Kzin was outside. Were they looking for *him?* No, they'd hardly expect him here!

He had reached the trough between the two swells. They were long and shallow and smooth, like waves near an ocean shoreline.

The top of the swell behind Nessus suddenly sparkled with harsh blue-white sunlight.

Nessus knew just what to do, and he did it instantly. No point in covering his cranial bulge with his necks; he'd only get his larynxes crushed. The padding would protect his brain, or it wouldn't. He folded his legs under him and tucked his heads tight between his forelegs. He didn't have to think about it. The puppeteer's explosion reflex was no less a reflex for being learned in childhood.

He saw the light, he curled into a ball, and the ground swell came. It batted him like a beach ball. His rigid, form-fitting shell retained his shape. It could not prevent the ground swell from slamming him away, nor his brain from jarring under its thick skull and its extra padding.

He woke on his back with his legs in the air. There was a tingly ache along his right side and on the right sides of his necks and legs. Half his body surface would be one bruise tomorrow. The ground still heaved; he must have been unconscious for only a moment.

He clambered shakily to his feet. The claws were an enormous help on the smooth ice. He shook himself once, then started up the rise.

Suddenly and silently the Kzinti ship topped the rise. A quarter of a mile down the swell it slid gracefully into space in a spray of ice. It was rotating on its axis, and

Nessus could see that one side was red hot. It skimmed through the near-vacuum above the trough, seeming to drift rather than fall. It hit solidly on the shallow far rise and plowed to a stop.

Still upright. Steam began to surround it as it sank into melting ice.

Nessus approached without fear. Surely any Kzin inside was dead, and any human too. But could he get in?

The outer airlock door was missing, ripped from its hinges. The inner door must have been bent, for it leaked a thin fog from the edges. Nessus pushed the cycle button and waited.

The door didn't move.

The puppeteer cast an eye around the airlock. There must be telltales to sense whether the outer door was closed and whether there was pressure in the lock. There was one, a sensitized surface in the maimed outer doorway. Nessus pushed it down with his mouth.

Air sprayed into the enclosure, turned to fog, and blew away. Nessus' other head was casting about for a pressure sensor. He found it next to the air outlet. He swung alongside it and leaned against it so that his suit trapped the air. He leaned into the pressure.

The inner door swung open. Nessus fought to maintain his position against the roaring wind. When the door was fully open, he dodged inside. The door slammed just behind him.

Now. What had happened here?

The Kzinti lifesystem was a howling hurricane of air replacing what he'd let out. Nessus poked into the kitchen, the control section, and two privacy booths without seeing anything. He moved down the hall and looked into what he remembered would be the interrogation room. Perhaps here . . .

He froze.

Anne-Marie and Jason were in the police web. Obviously; because both were standing, and both were unconscious. They appeared undamaged. But the Kzin!

Nessus felt the world swim. His heads felt lighter than air. He'd been through a lot . . . He turned his eyes away.

It occurred to him that the humans must be unconscious from lack of oxygen. The police web must surround them completely, even to their heads. Otherwise the shock would have torn their heads off. Nessus forced himself to move to the police web. He kept his eyes resolutely away from the Kzin.

There were the controls. Was that the power switch? He tried it. The humans drifted gracefully to the floor. Done.

And Nessus found his eyes creeping back to the Kzin.

He couldn't look away.

The carnivore had struck like a wet snowball thrown with awful force. He was a foot up the wall, all spread out on a border of splashed circulatory fluid, and he *stuck*.

Nessus fainted. He woke up, still standing because of the normal tone of his relaxed muscles, to find Anne-Marie shaking him gently and trying to talk to him.

"I'm worried about him," said Anne-Marie.

Jason turned away from the *Jester*'s control panel. "He can get treatment on Jinx. There are puppeteers in Sirius Mater."

"That's still a week away. Isn't there anything *we* can do for him? He spends all his time in his room. It must be *awful* to be manic-depressive." She was rubbing the stump where the emergency doc had amputated her arm—a gesture Jason hated. It roused guilt feelings. But she'd get a new arm on Jinx.

"I hate to tell you," he said, "but Nessus isn't in a depressive stage. He stays in his room because he's avoiding us."

"Us?"

"Yah. I think so."

"But Jay! *Us?*"

"Don't take it personally, Anne. We're a symbol." He lowered his head to formulate words. "Look at it this way. You remember when Nessus kicked the Kzin?"

"Sure. It was beautiful."

"And you probably know he was nerving himself to fire

on the Kzinti ship if I gave him the tnuctipun weapon.
Finally, you know that he came voluntarily to the Kzinti
ship. I think he was going to fight them if he got the
chance. He knew they'd captured me, and he knew they
had the weapon. He was ready to fight."

"Good for him. But Jay—"

"Dammit, honey, it *wasn't* good for him. For him, it
was purest evil. Cowardice is *moral* for puppeteers. He
was violating everything he'd ever learned!"

"You mean he's ashamed of himself?"

"That's part of it. But there's more. It was the way we
acted when we woke up.

"You remember how it was? Nessus was standing and
looking at what was left of the Kzinti pilot. You had to
shake him a few times before he noticed. Then what did
he find out? I, Jason Papandreou, who had been his
friend, had planned the whole thing. I had known that the
boss Kzin and the Slaver expert were walking to their
deaths because the computer form of the weapon had
given them the self-destruct setting and told them it was
the matter-conversion beam. I knew that, and I let them
walk out and blow themselves to smithereens. I tricked the
pilot into putting our heads in the police web, but I left
him outside to die. And I was proud of it! And you were
proud of me!

"Now do you get it?"

"No. And I'm still proud of you."

"Nessus isn't. Nessus knows that we, whom he probably
thought of as funny-looking puppeteers—you may remember we were thinking of him as almost human—he knows
we committed a horrible crime. Worse, it was a crime he
was thinking of committing himself. So he's transferred his
shame to us. He's ashamed of us, and he doesn't want to
see us."

"How far to Jinx?"

"A week."

"No way to hurry?"

"I never heard of one."

"Poor Nessus."

FLATLANDER

THE MOST BEAUTIFUL girl aboard turned out to have a husband with habits so solitary that I didn't know about him until the second week. He was about five feet four and middle-aged, but he wore a hellflare tattoo on his shoulder, which meant he'd been in Kzin during the war thirty years back, which meant he'd been trained to kill adult Kzinti with his bare hands, feet, elbows, knees, and whatnot. When we found out about each other, he very decently gave me a first warning, and broke my arm to prove he meant it.

The arm still ached a day later, and every other woman on the *Lensman* was over two hundred years old. I drank alone. I stared glumly into the mirror behind the curving bar. The mirror stared glumly back.

"Hey. You from We Made It. What am I?"

He was two chairs down, and he was glaring. Without the beard he would have had a round, almost petulant face ... I think. The beard, short and black and carefully shaped, made him look like a cross between Zeus and an angry bulldog. The glare went with the beard. His square fingers wrapped a large drinking bulb in a death grip. A broad belly matched broad shoulders to make him look massive rather than fat.

Obviously he was talking to me. I asked, "What do you mean, what are you?"

"Where am I from?"

"Earth." It was obvious. The accent said Earth. So did the conservatively symmetrical beard. His breathing was unconsciously natural in the ship's standard atmosphere, and his build had been forged at one point zero gee.

"Then what am I?"

"A flatlander."

The glare heat increased. He'd obviously reached the bar way ahead of me. "A flatlander! Dammit, everywhere I go I'm a flatlander. Do you know how many hours I've spent in space?"

"No. Long enough to know how to use a drinking bulb."

"Funny. Very funny. Everywhere in human space a flatlander is a schnook who never gets above the atmosphere. Everywhere but Earth. If you're from Earth, you're a flatlander all your life. For the last fifty years I've been running about in human space, and what am I? A flatlander. Why?"

"Earthian is a clumsy term."

"What is WeMadeItian?" he demanded.

"I'm a crashlander. I wasn't born within fifty miles of Crashlanding City, but I'm a crashlander anyway."

That got a grin. I think. It was hard to tell with the beard. "Lucky you're not a pilot."

"I am. Was."

"You're kidding. They let a crashlander pilot a ship?"

"If he's good at it."

"I didn't mean to pique your ire, sir. May I introduce myself? My name's Elephant."

"Beowulf Shaeffer."

He bought me a drink. I bought him a drink. It turned out we both played gin, so we took fresh drinks to a card table ...

When I was a kid, I used to stand out at the edge of Crashlanding Port watching the ships come in. I'd watch the mob of passengers leave the lock and move in a great clump toward customs, and I'd wonder why they seemed to have trouble navigating. A majority of the starborn would always walk in weaving lines, swaying and blinking teary eyes against the sun. I used to think it was because they came from different worlds with different gravities and different atmospheres beneath differently colored suns.

Later I learned different.

There are no windows in a passenger spacecraft. If

there were, half the passengers would go insane; it takes an unusual mentality to watch the blind-spot appearance of hyperspace and still keep one's marbles. For passengers there is nothing to watch and nothing to do, and if you don't like reading sixteen hours a day, then you drink. It's best to drink in company. You get less lushed, knowing you have to keep up your side of a conversation. The ship's doc has cured more hangovers than every other operation combined, right down to manicures and haircuts.

The ship grounded at Los Angeles two days after I met Elephant. He'd made a good drinking partner. We'd been fairly matched at cards, he with his sharp card sense, I with my usual luck. From the talking we'd done, we knew almost as much about each other as anyone knows about anyone. In a way I was sorry to see him leave.

"You've got my number?"

"Yah. But, like I said, I don't know just what I'll be doing." I was telling the truth. When I explore a civilized world, I like to make my own discoveries.

"Well, call me if you get a chance. I wish you'd change your mind. I'd like to show you Earth."

"I decline with thanks. Good-bye, Elephant. It's been fun."

Elephant waved and turned through the natives' door. I went on to face the smuggler baiters. The last drink was still with me, but I could cure that at the hotel. I never expected to see Elephant again.

Nine days ago I'd been on Jinx. I'd been rich. And I'd been depressed.

The money and the depression had stemmed from the same source. The puppeteers, those three-legged, two-headed professional cowards and businessmen, had lured me into taking a new type of ship all the way to the galactic core, thirty thousand light-years away. The trip was for publicity purposes, to get research money to iron out the imperfections in the very ship I was riding.

I suppose I should have had more sense, but I never do, and the money was good. The trouble was that the Core had exploded by the time I got there. The Core stars had gone off in a chain reaction of novas ten thousand years ago, and a wave of radiation was even then (and even now) sweeping toward known space.

In just over twenty thousand years we'll all be in deadly danger.

You're not worried? It didn't bother me much either. But every puppeteer in known space vanished overnight, heading for Finagle knows what other galaxy.

I was depressed. I missed the puppeteers and hated knowing I was responsible for their going. I had time and money and a black melancholia to work off. And I'd always wanted to see Earth.

Earth smelled good. There was a used flavor to it, a breathed flavor, unlike anything I've ever known. It was the difference between spring water and distilled water. Somewhere in each breath I took were molecules breathed by Dante, Aristotle, Shakespeare, Heinlein, Carter, and my own ancestors. Traces of past industries lingered in the air, sensed if not smelled: gasoline, coal fumes, tobacco and burnt cigarette filters, diesel fumes, ale breweries. I left the customs house with inflated lungs and a questing look.

I could have taken a transfer booth straight to the hotel. I decided to walk a little first.

Everyone on Earth had made the same decision.

The pedwalk held a crowd such as I had never imagined. They were all shapes and all colors, and they dressed in strange and eldritch ways. Shifting colors assaulted the eye and sent one reeling. On any world in human space, any world but one, you know immediately who the natives are. Wunderland? Asymmetric beards mark the nobility, and the common people are the ones who quickly step out of their way. We Made It? The pallor of our skins in summer and winter; in spring and fall, the fact that we all race upstairs, above the buried cities and onto the blooming desert, eager to taste sunlight while the murderous winds are at rest. Jinx? The natives are short, wide, and strong; a sweet little old lady's handshake can crush steel.

Even in the Belt, within the solar system, a Belter strip haircut adorns both men and women. But Earth—!

No two looked alike. There were reds and blues and greens, yellows and oranges, plaids and stripes. I'm talking about hair, you understand, and skin. All my life I've used tannin-secretion pills for protection against ultraviolet, so that my skin color has varied from its normal pinkish-white (I'm an albino) to (under blue-white stars) tuxedo black. But I'd never known that other skin-dye pills existed. I stood rooted to the pedwalk, letting it carry me where it would, watching the incredible crowd swarm around me. They were all knees and elbows. Tomorrow I'd have bruises.

"Hey!"

The girl was four or five heads away, and short. I'd never have seen her if everyone else hadn't been short too. Flatlanders rarely top six feet. And there was this girl, her hair a topological explosion in swirling orange and silver, her face a faint, subtle green with space-black eyebrows and lipstick, waving something and shouting at me.

Waving my wallet.

I forced my way to her, until we were close enough to touch, until I could hear what she was saying above the crowd noise.

"Stupid! Where's your address? You don't even have a place for a stamp!"

"What?"

She looked startled. "Oh! You're an offworlder."

"Yah!" My voice would give out fast at this noise level.

"Well, look ..." She shoved her way closer to me. "Look, you can't go around town with an offworlder's wallet. Next time someone picks your pocket he may not notice till you're gone."

"You picked my pocket?"

"Sure! Think I found it? Would I risk my precious hand under all those spike heels?"

"How if I call a cop?"

"Cop? Oh, a stoneface." She laughed merrily. "Learn or

go under, man. There's no law against picking pockets. Look around you."

I looked around me, then looked back fast, afraid she'd disappear. Not only my cash but my Bank of Jinx draft for forty thousand stars was in that wallet. Everything I owned.

"See them all? Sixty-four million people in Los Angeles alone. Eighteen billion in the whole world. Suppose there was a law against picking pockets? How would you enforce it?" She deftly extracted the cash from my wallet and handed the wallet back. "Get yourself a new wallet, and fast. It'll have a place for your address and a window for a tenth-star stamp. Put your address in right away, and a stamp too. Then the next guy who takes it can pull out the money and drop your wallet in the nearest mailbox—no sweat. Otherwise you lose your credit cards, your ident, everything." She stuffed two hundred-odd stars in cash between her breasts, flashing me a parting smile as she turned.

"Thanks," I called. Yes I did. I was still bewildered, but she'd obviously stayed to help me. She could just as easily have kept wallet and all.

"No charge," she called back, and was gone.

I stopped off at the first transfer booth I saw, dropped a half-star in the coin slot and dialed Elephant.

The vestibule was intimidating.

I'd expected a vestibule. Why put a transfer booth inside your own home, where any burglar can get in just by dialing your number? Anyone who can afford the lease on a private transfer booth can also afford a vestibule with a locked door and an intercom switch.

There was a vestibule, but it was the size of a living room, furnished with massage chairs and an autovendor. There was an intercom, but it was a flat vidphone, three hundred years old, restored at perhaps a hundred times its original cost. There was a locked door; it was a double door of what looked like polished brass, with two enormous carved handles, and it stood fifteen feet high.

I'd suspected Elephant was well off, but this was too

much. It occurred to me that I'd never seen him completely sober, that I had in fact turned down his offer of
guide, that a simple morning-after treatment might have
wiped me from his memory. Shouldn't I just go away? I
had wanted to explore Earth on my own.

But I didn't know the rules!

I stepped out of the booth and glimpsed the back wall.
It was all picture window, with nothing outside—just
fleecy blue sky. How peculiar, I thought, and stepped
closer. And closer.

Elephant lived halfway up a cliff. A sheer mile-high
cliff.

The phone rang.

On the third ear-jarring ring I answered, mainly to stop
the noise. A supercilious voice asked, "Is somebody out
there?"

"I'm afraid not," I said. "Does someone named Elephant live here?"

"I'll see, sir," said the voice. The screen had not lit, but
I had the feeling someone had seen me quite clearly.

Seconds crawled by. I was half minded to jump back in
the transfer booth and dial at random. But only half; that
was the trouble. Then the screen lit, and it was Elephant.
"Bey! You changed your mind!"

"Yah. You didn't tell me you were rich."

"You didn't ask."

"Well, no, of course not."

"How do you expect to learn things if you don't ask?
Don't answer that. Hang on, I'll be right down. You did
change your mind? You'll let me show you Earth?"

"Yes I will. I'm scared to go out there alone."

"Why? Don't answer. Tell me in person." He hung up.

Seconds later the big bronze doors swung back with a
bone-shaking boom. They just barely got out of Elephant's
way. He pulled me inside, giving me no time to gape,
shoved a drink in my hand, and asked why I was afraid
to go outside.

I told him about the pickpocket, and he laughed. He
told me about the time he tried to go outside during a We
Made It summer, and I laughed, though I've heard of

outworlders being blown away and to Hades doing the same thing. Amazingly, we were off again. It was just like it had been on the ship, even to the end of Elephant's anecdote. "They called me a silly flatlander, of course."

"I've been thinking about that," I said.

"About what?"

"You said you'd give a lot to do something completely original, so the next time someone called you a flatlander, you could back him into a corner and force him to listen to your story. You said it several times."

"I didn't say just that. But I would like to have some story to tell, something like your neutron star episode. If only to tell myself. The silly offworlder wouldn't know, but *I'd* know."

I nodded. I'd talked about the neutron star episode over gin cards—a habit I've developed for distracting my opponent—and Elephant had been suitably impressed.

"I've thought of a couple of things you could do," I said.

"Spill."

"One. Visit the puppeteer home world. Nobody's been there, but everyone knows there is one, and everyone knows how difficult it is to find. You could be the first."

"Great." He mused a moment. "Great! And the puppeteers wouldn't stop me because they're gone. Where *is* the puppeteer home world?"

"*I* don't know."

"What's your second idea?"

"Ask the Outsiders."

"Huh?"

"There's not a system in the galaxy that the Outsiders don't know all about. We don't know how far the puppeteer empire extended, though it was way beyond known space, but we do know about the Outsiders. They know the galaxy like the palm of their—uh . . . And they trade for information; it's just about the only business they do. Ask them what's the most unusual world they know of within reach."

Elephant was nodding gently. There was a glazed look

in his eyes. I had not been sure he was serious about seeking some unique achievement. He was.

"The problem is," I said, "that an Outsider's idea of what is unique may not—" I stopped, because Elephant was up and half running to a tridphone.

I wasn't sorry. It gave me an opportunity to gape in private.

I've been in bigger homes than Elephant's. Much bigger. I grew up in one. But I've never seen a room that soothed the eye as Elephant's living room did. It was more than a living room; it was an optical illusion, the opposite of those jittering black-and-white images they show in lectures on how we see. These clinical children of Op Art give the illusion of motion, but Elephant's living room gave the illusion of stillness. A physicist would have loved the soundproofing. Some interior decorator had become famous for his work here, if he hadn't been famous already, in which case he had become rich. How could tall, thin Beowulf Shaeffer fit a chair designed to the measure of short, wide Elephant? Yet I was bonelessly limp, blissfully relaxed, using only the muscles that held a double-walled glass of an odd-tasting, strangely refreshing soft drink called Tzlotz Beer.

A glass which would not empty. Somewhere in the crystal was a tiny transfer motor connected to the bar, but the bent light in the crystal hid it. Another optical illusion, and one that must have tricked good men into acute alcoholism. I'd have to watch that.

Elephant returned. He walked as if he massed tons, as if any Kzin foolish enough to stand in his path would have a short, wide hole in him. "All done," he said. "Don Cramer'll find the nearest Outsider ship and make my pitch for me. We should hear in a couple of days."

"Okay," said I, and asked him about the cliff. It turned out that we were in the Rocky Mountains, and that he owned every square inch of the nearly vertical cliff face. Why? I remembered Earth's eighteen billion and wondered if they'd otherwise have surrounded him up, down, and sideways.

Suddenly Elephant remembered that someone named

Dianna must be home by now. I followed him into the transfer booth, watched him dial eleven digits, and waited in a much smaller vestibule while Elephant used the more conventional intercom. Dianna seemed dubious about letting him in until he roared that he had a guest and she should stop fooling around.

Dianna was a small, pretty woman with skin the deep, uniform red of a Martian sky and hair like flowing quicksilver. Her irises had the same polished-silver luster. She hadn't wanted to let us in because we were both wearing our own skins, but she never mentioned it again once we were inside.

Elephant introduced me to Dianna and instantly told her he'd acted to contact the Outsiders.

"What's an Outsider?" she asked.

Elephant gestured with both hands, looked confused, turned helplessly toward me.

"They're hard to describe," I said. "Think of a cat-o'-nine-tails with a big thick handle."

"They live on cold worlds," said Elephant.

"Small, cold, airless worlds like Nereid. They pay rent to use Nereid as a base, don't they Elephant? And they travel over most of the galaxy in big unpressurized ships with fusion drives and no hyperdrives."

"They sell information. They can tell me about the world I want to find, the most unusual planet in known space."

"They spend most of their time tracking starseeds."

Dianna broke in. "Why?"

Elephant looked at me. I looked at Elephant.

"Say!" Elephant exclaimed. "Why don't we get a fourth for bridge?"

Dianna looked thoughtful. Then she focused her silver eyes on me, examined me from head to foot, and nodded gently to herself. "Sharrol Janss. I'll call her."

While she was phoning, Elephant told me, "That's a good thought. Sharrol's got a tendency toward hero worship. She's a computer analyst at Donovan's Brains Inc. You'll like her."

"Good," I said, wondering if we were still talking about

a bridge game. It struck me that I was building up a debt to Elephant. "Elephant, when you contact the Outsiders, I'd like to come along."

"Oh? Why?"

"You'll need a pilot. And I've dealt with Outsiders before."

"Okay, it's a deal."

The intercom rang from the vestibule. Dianna went to the door and came back with our fourth for bridge. "Sharrol, you know Elephant. This is Beowulf Shaeffer, from We Made It. Bey, this is—"

"You!" I said.

"You!" she said.

It was the pickpocket.

My vacation lasted just four days.

I hadn't known how long it would last, though I did know how it would end. Consequently I threw myself into it body and soul. If there was a dull moment anywhere in those four days, I slept through it, and at that I didn't get enough sleep. Elephant seemed to feel the same way. He was living life to the hilt; he must have suspected, as I did, that the Outsiders would not consider danger a factor in choosing his planet. By their own ethics they were bound not to. The days of Elephant's life might be running short.

Buried in those four days were incidents that made me wonder why Elephant was looking for a weird world. Surely Earth was the weirdest of all.

I remember when we threw in the bridge hands and decided to go out for dinner. This was more complicated than it sounds. Elephant hadn't had a chance to change to flatlander styles, and neither of us was fit to be seen in public. Dianna had cosmetics for us.

I succumbed to an odd impulse. I dressed as an albino.

They were body paints, not pills. When I finished applying them, there in the full-length mirror was my younger self. Blood-red irises, snow-white hair, white skin with a tinge of pink: the teen-ager who had disappeared ages ago, when I was old enough to use tannin pills. I found my mind wandering far back across the decades, to the days when I was a flatlander myself, my feet firmly beneath the ground, my head never higher than seven feet above the desert sands.... They found me there before the mirror and pronounced me fit to be seen in public.

I remember that evening when Dianna told me she had known Elephant forever. "I was the one who named him Elephant," she bragged.

"It's a nickname?"

"Sure," said Sharrol. "His real name is Gregory Pelton."

"O-o-oh." Suddenly all came clear. Gregory Pelton is known among the stars. It is rumored that he owns the thirty-light-year-wide rough sphere called *human space,* that he earns his income by renting it out. It is rumored that General Products—the all-embracing puppeteer company, now defunct for lack of puppeteers—is a front for Gregory Pelton. It's a fact that his great-to-the-eighth grandmother invented the transfer booth and that he is rich, rich, rich.

I asked, "Why Elephant? Why that particular nickname?"

Dianna and Sharrol looked demurely at the tablecloth. Elephant said, "Use your imagination, Bey."

"On what? What's an elephant, some kind of animal?"

Three faces registered annoyance. I'd missed a joke.

"Tomorrow," said Elephant, "we'll show you the Zoo."

There are seven transfer booths in the Zoo of Earth. That'll tell you how big it is. But you're wrong; you've forgotten the two hundred taxis on permanent duty. They're there because the booths are too far apart for walking.

We stared down at dusty, compact animals smaller than starseeds or bandersnatchi but bigger than anything else I'd ever seen. Elephant said, "See?"

"Yah," I said, because the animals showed a compactness and a plodding invulnerability very like Elephant's. And then I found myself watching one of the animals in a muddy pool. It was using a hollow tentacle over its mouth to spray water on its back. I stared at that tentacle ... and stared ...

"Hey, look!" Sharrol called, pointing. "Bey's ears are turning red!"

I didn't forgive her till two that morning.

And I remember reaching over Sharrol to get a tabac stick and seeing her purse lying on her other things. I said, "How if I picked your pocket now?"

Orange and silver lips parted in a lazy smile. "I'm not wearing a pocket."

"Would it be in good taste to sneak the money out of your purse?"

"Only if you could hide it on you."

I found a small flat purse with four hundred stars in it and stuck it in my mouth.

She made me go through with it. Ever make love to a woman with a purse in your mouth? Unforgettable. Don't try it if you've got asthma.

I remember Sharrol. I remember smooth, warm blue skin, silver eyes with a wealth of expression, orange-and-silver hair in a swirling abstract pattern that nothing could mess up. It always sprang back. Her laugh was silver, too, when I gently extracted two handfuls of hair and tied them in a hard double knot, and when I gibbered and jumped up and down at the sight of her hair slowly untying itself like Medusa's locks. And her voice was a silver croon.

I remember the freeways.

They were the first thing that showed coming in on Earth. If we'd landed at night, it would have been the lighted cities; but of course we came in on the day side. Why else would a world have three spaceports? There were the freeways and autostradas and autobahns, strung in an all-enclosing net across the faces of the continents.

From a few miles up, you still can't see the breaks. But they're there, where girders and pavement have collapsed. Only two superhighways are still kept in good repair. They are both on the same continent: the Pennsylvania Turnpike and the Santa Monica Freeway. The rest of the network is broken chaos.

It seems there are people who collect old groundcars and race them. Some are actually renovated machines, fifty to ninety percent replaced; others are handmade reproductions. On a perfectly flat surface they'll do fifty to ninety miles per hour.

I laughed when Elephant told me about them, but actually seeing them was different.

The rodders began to appear about dawn. They gathered around one end of the Santa Monica Freeway, the end that used to join the San Diego Freeway. This end is a maze of fallen spaghetti, great curving loops of prestressed concrete that have lost their strength over the years and sagged to the ground. But you can still use the top loop to reach the starting line. We watched from above, hovering in a cab as the groundcars moved into line.

"Their dues cost more than the cars," said Elephant. "I used to drive one myself. You'd turn white as snow if I told you how much it costs to keep this stretch of freeway in repair."

"How much?"

He told me. I turned white as snow.

They were off. I was still wondering what kick they got driving an obsolete machine on flat concrete when they could be up here with us. They were off, weaving slightly, weaving more than slightly, foolishly moving at different speeds, coming perilously close to each other before sheering off—and I began to realize things.

Those automobiles had no radar.

They were being steered with a cabin wheel geared directly to four ground wheels. A mistake in steering and they'd crash into each other or into the concrete curbs. They were steered and stopped by muscle power, but whether they could turn or stop depended on how hard four rubber balloons could grip smooth concrete. If the tires loosed their grip, Newton's First Law would take over; the fragile metal mass would continue moving in a straight line until stopped by a concrete curb or another groundcar.

"A man could get killed in one of those."

"Not to worry," said Elephant. "Nobody does, usually."

"Usually?"

The race ended twenty minutes later at another tangle of fallen concrete. I was wet through. We landed and met some of the racers. One of them, a thin guy with tangled, glossy green hair and a bony white face with a widely grinning scarlet mouth, offered me a ride. I declined with thanks, backing slowly away and wishing for a weapon. This joker was obviously dangerously insane.

I remember flatlander food, the best in known space, and an odd, mildly alcoholic drink called Taittinger Comtes de Champagne '59. I remember invading an outworlder bar, where the four of us talked shop with a girl rock-miner whose inch-wide auburn crest of hair fell clear to the small of her back. I remember flying cross-country with a lift belt and seeing nothing but city enclosing widely separated patches of food-growing land. I remember a submerged hotel off the Grand Banks of Newfoundland and a dolphin embassy off Italy, where a mixed group of dolphins and flatlanders seemed to be solving the general problem of sentient beings without hands (there are many, and we'll probably find more). It seemed more a coffee-break discussion than true business.

We were about to break up for bed on the evening of the fourth day when the tridphone rang. Don Cramer had found an Outsider.

I said, disbelieving, "You're leaving *right now?*"

"Sure!" said Elephant. "Here, take one of these pills. You won't feel sleepy till we're on our way."

A deal is a deal, and I owed Elephant plenty. I took the pill. We kissed Sharrol and Dianna good-bye, Dianna standing on a chair to reach me, Sharrol climbing me like a beanpole and wrapping her legs around my waist. I was a foot and a half taller than either of them.

Calcutta Base was in daylight. Elephant and I took the

transfer booth there, to find that the *ST∞* had been shipped ahead of us.

Her full name was *Slower Than Infinity*. She had been built into a General Products No. 2 hull, a three-hundred-foot spindle with a wasp-waist constriction near the tail. I was relieved. I had been afraid Elephant might own a flashy, vulnerable dude's yacht. The two-man control room looked pretty small for a lifesystem until I noticed the bubble extension folded into the nose. The rest of the hull held a one-gee fusion drive and fuel tank, a hyperspace motor, a gravity drag and belly-landing gear, all clearly visible through the hull, which had been left transparent.

She held fuel, food, and air. She must have been ready for days. We took off twenty minutes after arriving.

Using the fusion drive in Earth's atmosphere would have gotten us into the organ banks, in pieces. Flatlander laws are strict about air pollution. A robot rocket with huge wings lifted us to orbit, using air compressed nearly to degenerate matter as a propellant. We took off from there.

Now there was plenty of time for sleep. It took us a week at one gee just to get far enough out of the solar system's gravity well to use the hyperdrive. Somewhere in that time I removed my false coloring (it *had* been false; I'd continued to take tannin-secretion pills against Earth's sunlight), and Elephant turned his skin back to light tan and his beard and hair back to black. For four days he'd been Zeus, with marble skin, a metal-gold beard, and glowing molten-gold eyes. It had fitted him so perfectly that I hardly noticed the change.

Hyperdrive—and a long, slow three weeks. We took turns hovering over the mass indicator, though at first-quantum hyperdrive speeds we'd have seen a mass at least twelve hours before it became dangerous. I think I was the only man who knew there *was* a second quantum, a puppeteer secret. The Outsider ship was near the edge of known space, well beyond Tau Ceti.

"It was the only one around," Elephant had said. "Number fourteen."

"Fourteen? That's the same ship I dealt with before."

"Oh? Good. That should help."

Days later he asked, "How'd it happen?"

"The usual way Number fourteen was on the other side of known space then, and she sent out an offer of information exchange I was almost to Wunderland, and I caught the offer. When I dropped my passengers, I went back."

"Did they have anything worth while?"

"Yah. They'd found the *Lazy Eight II*."

The *Lazy Eight II* had been one of the old slowboats, a circular-flying wing taking colonists to Jinx. Something had gone wrong before turnover, and the ship had continued on, carrying fifty passengers in suspended animation and a crew of four, presumed dead With a ramscoop to feed hydrogen to her fusion drive, she could accelerate forever. She was five hundred years on her way.

"I remember," said Elephant. "They couldn't reach her "

"No. But we'll know where to find her when the state of the art gets that good." Which wouldn't be soon, I thought. A hyperdrive ship would not only have to reach her but would have to carry fuel to match her speed. Her speed was barely less than a photon's, and she was more than five hundred light-years away, seventeen times the diameter of known space.

"Did you have any problems?"

"Their translator is pretty good. But we'll have to be careful, Elephant. The thing about buying information is that you don't know what you're getting until you've got it. They couldn't just offer to sell me the present position of the *Lazy Eight II*. We'd have tracked their course by telescope until we saw the light of a fusion drive and gotten the information free."

The time came when only a small green dot glowed in the center of the mass indicator. A star would have shown as a line; no star would have shown no dot. I dropped out of hyperspace and set the deep-radar to hunt out the Outsider.

The Outsider found us first.

Somewhere in the cylindrical metal-pod near her center of mass, perhaps occupying it completely, was the reactionless drive. It was common knowledge that that drive was for sale and that the cost was a full trillion stars. Though nobody, and no nation now extant, could afford to pay it, the price was not exorbitant. In two or three minutes, while we were still searching, that drive had dropped the Outsider ship from above point nine lights to zero relative and pulled it alongside the *ST∞*.

One moment, nothing but stars. The next, the Outsider ship was alongside.

She was mostly empty space. I knew her population was the size of a small city, but she was much bigger because more strung out. There was the miniscule-seeming drive capsule, and there, on a pole two and a half miles long, was a light source. The rest of the ship was metal ribbons, winding in and out, swooping giddily around themselves and each other, until the ends of each tangled ribbon stopped meandering and joined the drive capsule. There were around a thousand such ribbons, and each was the width of a wide city pedwalk.

"Like a Christmas tree decoration," said Elephant. "What now, Bey?"

"They'll use the ship radio."

A few minutes of waiting, and here came a bunch of Outsiders. They looked like black cat-o'-nine-tails with grossly swollen handles. In the handles were their brains and invisible sense organs; in the whip ends, the clusters of motile root-tentacles, were gas pistols. Six of them braked to a stop outside the airlock.

The radio spoke. "Welcome to Ship Fourteen. Please step outside for conveyance to our office. Take nothing on the outsides of your pressure suits."

Elephant asked, "Do we?"

I said, "Sure. The Outsiders are nothing if not honorable."

We went out. The six Outsiders offered us a tentacle each, and away we went across open space. Not fast. The thrust from the gas pistols was very low, irritatingly weak.

But the Outsiders themselves were weak; an hour in the gravity of Earth's moon would have killed them.

They maneuvered us through the tangled clutter of silver ribbons, landing us on a ramp next to the looming convex wall of the drive capsule.

It wasn't quite like being lost in a giant bowl of noodles. The rigid ribbons were too far apart for that. Far above us was the light source, about as small and intense and yellowish-white as Earth's sun seen from a moon of Neptune. Shining down through the interstellar vacuum, it cast a network of sharp black shadows across all the thousand looping strands that made up the city.

Along every light-shadow borderline were the Outsiders. Just as their plantlike ancestors had done billions of years ago on some unknown world near the galactic core, the Outsiders were absorbing life-energy. Their branched tails lay in shadow, their heads in sunlight, while thermo-electricity charged their biochemical batteries. Some had root-tentacles dipped in shallow food-dishes; the trace elements which kept them alive and growing were in suspension in liquid helium.

We stepped carefully around them, using our headlamps at lowest intensity, following one of the Outsiders toward a door in the wall ahead.

The enclosure was dark until the door closed behind us. Then the light came on. It was sourceless, the color of normal sunlight, and it illuminated a cubicle that was bare and square. The only furnishing was a transparent hemisphere with an Outsider resting inside. Presumably the hemisphere filtered out excess light going in.

"Welcome," said the room. Whatever the Outsider had said was not sonic in nature. "The air is breathable. Take off your helmets, suits, shoes, girdles and whatnot." It was an excellent translator, with a good grasp of idiom and a pleasant baritone voice.

"Thanks," said Elephant, and we did.

"Which of you is Gregory Pelton?"

"Gronk."

The wall was not confused. "According to your agent, you want to know how to reach that planet which is most unusual inside or within five miles of the sixty-light-year-wide region you call known space. Is this correct?"

"Yes."

"We must know if you plan to go there or to send agents there. Also, do you plan a landing, a near orbit, or a distant orbit?"

"Landing."

"Are we to guard against danger to your life?"

"No." Elephant's voice was a little dry. The Outsider ship was an intimidating place.

"What kind of ship would you use?"

"The one outside."

"Do you plan colonization? Mining? Growth of food plants?"

"I plan only one visit."

"We have selected a world for you. The price will be one million stars."

"That's high," said Elephant. I whistled under my breath. It was; and it wouldn't get lower. The Outsiders never dickered.

"Sold," said Elephant.

The translator gave us a triplet set of coordinates some twenty-four light-years from Earth along galactic north. "The star you are looking for is a protosun with one planet a billion and a half miles distant. The system is moving at a point eight lights toward——" He gave a vector direction. It seemed the protosun was drawing a shallow chord through known space; it would never approach human space.

"No good," said Elephant. "No hyperdrive ship can go that fast in real space."

"You could hitch a ride," said the translator, "with us. Moor your ship to our drive capsule."

"That'll work," said Elephant. He was getting more and more uneasy; his eyes seemed to be searching the walls for the source of the voice. He would not look at the Outsider business agent in the vacuum chamber.

"Our ferry fee will be one million stars."

Elephant sputtered.

"Just a sec," I said. "I may have information to sell you."

There was a long pause. Elephant looked at me in surprise.

"You are Beowulf Shaeffer?"

"Yah. You remember me?"

"We find you in our records. Beowulf Shaeffer, we have information for you, already paid. The former regional president of General Products on Jinx wishes you to contact him. I have a transfer-booth number."

"That's late news," I said. "The puppeteers are gone. Anyway, why would that two-headed sharpie want to see me?"

"I do not have that information. I do know that not all puppeteers have left this region. Will you accept the transfer-booth number?"

"Sure."

I wrote down the eight digits as they came. A moment later Elephant was yelling just as if he were a tridee set turned on in the middle of a program. "—hell is going on here?"

"Sorry about that," said the translator.

"What happened?" I asked.

"I couldn't hear anything! Did that mon— Did the Outsider have private business with you?"

"Sort of. I'll tell you later."

The translator said, "Beowulf Shaeffer, we do not buy information. We sell information and use the proceeds to buy territory and food soil."

"You may need this information," I argued. "I'm the only man within reach who knows it."

"What of other races?"

The puppeteers might have told them, but it was worth taking a chance. "You're about to leave known space. If you don't deal with me, you may not get this information in time."

"What price do you set on this item?"

"You set the price. You've got more experience at putting values on information, and you're honorable."

"We may not be able to afford an honest price."

"The price may not exceed our ferry fee."

"Done. Speak."

I told him of the Core explosion and how I'd come to find out about it. He made me go into detail on what I'd seen: the bright patch of supernovae spreading out as my ship caught up with ancient light-waves, until all the bright multicolored ball of the Core was ablaze with supernovae. "You wouldn't have known this until you got there, and then it would have been too late. You don't use faster-than-light drives."

"We knew from the puppeteers that the Core had exploded. They were not able to go into detail because they had not seen it for themselves."

"Oh. Ah, well. I think the explosion must have started at the back side of the Core from here. Otherwise it would have seemed to go much more slowly."

"Many thanks. We will waive your ferry fee. Now, there is one more item. Gregory Pelton, for an additional two hundred thousand stars we will tell you exactly what is peculiar about the planet you intend to visit."

"Can I find out for myself?"

"It is likely."

"Then I will."

Silence followed. The Outsider hadn't expected that. I said, "I'm curious. Your galaxy is rapidly becoming a death trap. What will you do now?"

"That information will cost you—"

"Forget it."

Outside, Elephant said, "Thanks."

"Forget it. I wonder what they will do."

"Maybe they can shield themselves against the radiation."

"Maybe. But they won't have any starseeds to follow."

"Do they need them?"

Finagle only knew. The starseeds followed a highly rigid migratory mating-pattern out from the Core of the galaxy and into the arms, almost to the rim, before turning back down to the Core. They were doomed. As they returned to the Core, the expanding wave of radiation from the multiple novae would snuff out the species one by one. What would the Outsiders do without them? What the hell did they do *with* them? Why did they follow them? Did they need starseeds? Did starseeds need Outsiders? The Outsiders would answer these and related questions for one trillion stars apiece. Personal questions cost high with the Outsiders.

A crew was already bringing the $ST\infty$ into dock. We watched from the ramp, with crewmen sunbathing about our feet. We weren't worried. The way the Outsiders handled it, our invulnerable hull might have been made of spun sugar and sunbeams. When a spiderweb of thin strands fastened the $ST\infty$ to the wall of the drive capsule, the voice of the translator spoke in our ears and invited us to step aboard. We jumped a few hundred feet upward through the trace of artificial gravity, climbed into the airlock, and got out of our suits.

"Thanks again," said Elephant.

"Forget it again," I said magnanimously. "I owe you plenty. You've been putting me up as a house guest on the most expensive world in known space, acting as my guide where the cost of labor is—"

"Okay okay okay. But you saved me a million stars, and don't you forget it." He whopped me on the shoulder and hurried into the control room to set up a million-star credit base for the next Outsider ship that came by.

"I won't," I called at his retreating back, and wondered what the hell I meant by that.

Much later I wondered about something else. Had Elephant planned to take me to "his" world? Or did he think to go it alone, to be the first to see it and not one of the first two? After the Outsider episode it was already too late. He couldn't throw me off the ship then.

I wished I'd thought of it in time. I never wanted to be a batman. My stake in this was to gently, tactfully keep Elephant from killing himself if it became necessary. For all his vast self-confidence, vast riches, vast generosity, and vast bulk, he was still only a flatlander, and thus a little bit helpless.

We were in the expansion bubble when it happened. The bubble had inflatable seats and an inflatable table, and was there for exercising and killing time, but it also supplied a fine view; the surface was perfectly transparent. Otherwise we would have missed it.

There was no pressure against the seat of the pants, no crawling sensation in the pit of the stomach, no feel of motion. But Elephant, who was talking about a Jinxian frail he'd picked up in a Chicago bar, stopped just as she was getting ready to tear the place apart because some suicidal idiot had insulted her.

Somebody heavy was sitting down on the universe.

He came down slowly, like a fat man cautiously letting his weight down on a beach ball. From inside the bubble it looked like all the stars and nebulae around us were squeezing themselves together. The Outsiders on the ribbons outside never moved; but Elephant said something profane, and I steeled myself to look up.

The stars overhead were blue-white and blazing. Around us they were squashed together; below, they were turning red and winking out, one by one. It had taken us a week to get out of the solar system, but the Outsider ship could have done it in five hours.

The radio spoke. "Sirs, our crewmen will remove your ship from ours, after which you will be on your own. It has been a pleasure to do business with you."

A swarm of Outsider crewmen hauled us through the maze of basking ramps and left us. Presently the Outsider ship vanished like a pricked soap-bubble, gone off on its own business.

In the strange starlight Elephant let out a long, shaky sigh. Some people can't take aliens. They don't find puppeteers graceful and beautiful; they find them horrifying, *wrong*. They see Kzinti as slavering carnivores whose only love is fighting, which is the truth; but they don't see the rigid code of honor, or the self-control which allows a Kzinti ambassador to ride a human-city pedwalk without slashing out with his claws at the impertinent stabbing knees and elbows. Elephant was one of these people.

He said, "Okay," in amazed relief. They were actually gone. "I'll take the first watch, Bey."

He did not say, "Those bastards would take your heart

as collateral on a tenth-star loan." He didn't see them as that close to human.

"Fine," I said, and went into the control bubble. The Fast Protosun was a week away. I'd been in a suit for hours, and there was a shower in the extension bubble.

If Elephant's weakness was aliens, mine was relativity.

The trip through hyperspace was routine. I could take the sight of the two small windows turning into blind spots, becoming areas of nothing, which seemed to draw together the objects around them. So could Elephant; he'd done some flying, though he preferred the comfort of a luxury liner. But even the best pilot occasionally has to drop back into the normal universe to get his bearings and to assure his subconscious that the stars are still there.

And each time it was changed, squashed flat. The crowded blue stars were all ahead; the sparse, dim red stars were all behind. Four hundred years ago men and women had lived for years with such a view of the universe, but it hadn't happened since the invention of hyperdrive. I'd never seen the universe look like this. It bothered me.

"No, it doesn't bug me," said Elephant when I mentioned it. We were a day out from our destination. "To me, stars are stars. But I have been worried about something. Bey, you said the Outsiders are honorable."

"They are. They've got to be. They have to be so far above suspicion that any species they deal with will remember their unimpeachable ethics a century later. You can see that, can't you? Outsiders don't show up more often than that."

"Um. Okay. Why did they try to screw that extra two hundred kilostars out of me?"

"Uh—"

"See, the goddam problem is, what if it was a fair price? What if we *need* to know what's funny about the Fast Protosun?"

"You're right. Knowing the Outsiders, it's probably information we can use. All right, we'll nose around a little before we land. We'd have done that anyway, but now we'll do it better."

What was peculiar about the Fast Protosun?

Around lunchtime on the seventh ship's day, a short green line in the sphere of the mass indicator began to extend itself. It was wide and fuzzy, just what you'd expect of a protosun. I let it reach almost to the surface of the sphere before I dropped us into normal space.

The squashed universe looked in the windows, but ahead of us was a circular darkening and blurring of the vivid blue-white stars. In the center of the circle was a dull red glow.

"Let's go into the extension bubble," said Elephant.

"Let's not."

"We'll get a better view in there." He turned the dial that would make the bubble transparent. Naturally we kept it opaque in hyperspace.

"Repeat, let's not. Think about it, Elephant. What sense does it make to use an impermeable hull, then spend most of our time outside it? Until we know what's here, we ought to retract the bubble."

He nodded his shaggy head and touched the board again. Chugging noises announced that air and water were being pulled out of the bubble. Elephant moved to a window.

"Ever see a protosun?"

"No," I said. "I don't think there are any in human space."

"That could be the peculiarity."

"It could. One thing it isn't is the speed of the thing. Outsiders spend all their time moving faster than this."

"But planets don't. Neither do stars. Bey, maybe this thing came from outside the galaxy. That would make it unusual."

It was time we made a list. I found a pad and solemnly noted speed of star, nature of star, and possible extragalactic origin of star.

"I've found our planet," said Elephant.

"Whereabouts?"

"Almost on the other side of the protosun. We can get there faster in hyperspace."

The planet was still invisibly small where Elephant brought us out. The protosun looked about the same.

A protosun is the foetus of a star: a thin mass of gas and dust, brought together by slow eddies in interstellar magnetic fields or by the presence of a trojan point in some loose cluster of stars, which is collapsing and contracting due to gravity. I'd found material on protosuns in the ship's library, but it was all astronomical data; nobody had ever been near one for a close look. In theory the Fast Protosun must be fairly well along in its evolution, since it was glowing at the center.

"There it is," said Elephant. "Two days away at one gee."

"Good. We can do our instrument checks on the way. Strap down."

With the fusion motor pushing us smoothly along, Elephant went back to the scope, and I started checking the other instruments. One thing stood out like a beacon.

"Elephant. Have you noticed in me a tendency to use profanity for emphasis?"

"Not really. Why?"

"It's goddam radioactive out there."

"Could you be a little more specific, sir?"

"Our suit shields would break down in three days. The extension bubble would go in twenty hours."

"Okay, add it to your list. Any idea what's causing it?"

"Not one." I made a note on my list, then went back to work. We were in no danger; the GP hull would protect us from anything but impact with something big.

"No asteroid belts," said Elephant. "Meteor density zero, as far as I can tell. No other planets."

"The interstellar gas may clean away anything small, at these speeds."

"One thing's for sure, Bey. I've got my money's worth. This is a damn funny system."

"Yah. Well, we missed lunch. Shall we get dinner?"

"Philistine."

Elephant ate fast. He was back at the telescope before I was ready for coffee. Watching him move, I was again reminded of a juggernaut; but he'd never shown as much determination when I knew him on Earth. If a hungry Kzin had been standing between him and the telescope, he'd have left footprints in fur.

But the only thing that could get in his way out here was me.

"Can't get a close look at the planet," said Elephant, "but it looks polished."

"Like a billiard ball?"

"Just that. I don't see any sign of an atmosphere."

"How about blast craters?"

"Nothing."

"They should be there."

"This system's pretty clean of meteors."

"But the space around us shouldn't be. And at these speeds—"

"Uh huh. That better go on your list."

I wrote it down.

We slept on the disaster couches. In front of me were the yellow lights of the control panel; the stars glowed red through one side window, blue through the other. I stayed awake for a long time, staring through the forward window into the red darkness of the protosun. The window was opaque, but I saw the dark red blur clearly in my imagination.

The radiation held steady all through the next day. I did some more thorough checking, using temperature readings and deep-radar on both sun and planet. Everywhere I looked was a new anomaly.

"This star definitely shouldn't be glowing yet. It's too spread out; the gas should be too thin for fusion."

"Is it hot enough to glow?"

"Sure. But it shouldn't be."

"Maybe the theories on protosuns are wrong."

"Then they're way wrong."

"Put it on your list."

And, an hour later:

"Elephant."

"*Another* peculiarity?"

"Yah."

From under shaggy brows, Elephant's eyes plainly told me he was getting sick of peculiarities.

"According to the deep-radar shadow, this planet doesn't have any lithosphere. It's worn right down to what ought to be the magma but isn't because it's so cold out here."

"Write it down. How many entries have you got?"

"Nine."

"Is any one of them worth paying two hundred kilostars to know about beforehand?"

"The radiation, maybe, if we didn't have a GP hull."

"But," said Elephant, glaring out at the huge, dark disk, "they knew we had a GP hull. Bey, can anything get through a General Products hull?"

"Light, like a laser beam. Gravity, like tides crushing you into the nose of a ship when you get too close to a neutron star. Impact won't harm the hull, but it'll kill what's inside."

"Maybe the planet's inhabited. The more I think about it, the more sure I am it came from outside. Nothing in the galaxy could have given it this velocity. It's diving through the plane of the galaxy; it wouldn't have to push in from the rim."

"Okay. What do we do if someone shoots a laser at us?"

"We perish, I think. I had reflective paint spread around the cabin, except for the windows, but the rest of the hull is transparent."

"We can still get into hyperspace from here. And for the next twenty hours. Afterwards we'll be too close to the planet."

I went right to sleep that night, being pretty tired despite the lack of exercise. Hours later I slowly realized that I was being examined. I could see it through my closed eyelids; I could feel the heat of the vast red glare, the size of the angry eye, the awful power of the mind behind it. I tried to struggle away, smacked my hand on something, and woke with a shock.

I lay there in the red darkness. The edge of the protosun peeked through a window. I could feel its hostile glare.

I said, "Elephant."

"Mngl?"

"Nothing." Morning would be soon enough.

Morning.

"Elephant, would you do me a favor?"

"Sure. You want Dianna? My right arm? Shave off my beard?"

"I'll keep Sharrol, thanks. Put on your suit, will you?"

"Sure, that makes sense. We aren't nearly uncomfortable enough, just because we closed off the bubble."

"Right. And because I'm a dedicated masochist, I'm going to put my suit on this instant. Now, I hate to enjoy myself alone . . ."

"You got the wind up?"

"A little. Just enough."

"Anything for a friend. You go first."

There was just room to get our suits on one at a time. If the inner airlock door hadn't been open, there wouldn't have been that. We tried leaving our helmets thrown back, but they got in our way against the crash couches. So we taped them to the window in front of us.

I felt better that way, but Elephant clearly thought I'd flipped. "You sure you wouldn't rather eat with your helmet on?"

"I hate suit food syrup. We can reach our helmets if we get a puncture."

"*What puncture?* We're in a *General Products hull!*"

"I keep remembering that the Outsiders knew that."

"We've been through that."

"Let's go through it again. Assume they thought we might be killed anyway if we weren't prepared. Then what?"

"Gronk."

"Either they expected us to go out in suits and get killed, or they know of something that can reach through a General Products hull."

"Or both. In which case the suits do us no good at all.

Bey, do you know how long it's been since a General Products hull failed?"

"I've never heard of it happening at all."

"It never has. The puppeteers offer an enormous guarantee in case one does. Something in the tens of millions if someone dies as a result."

"You're dead right. I've been stupid. Go ahead and take off your suit."

Elephant turned to look at me. "And you?"

"I'll keep mine on. Do you believe in hunches?"

"No."

"Neither do I. Except just this once."

Elephant shrugged his shaggy eyebrows and went back to his telescope. By then we were six hours out from the nameless planet, and decelerating.

"I think I've found an asteroid crater," he said presently.

"Let's see." I had a look. "Yah, I think you're right. But it's damn near disappeared."

He took the telescope back. "It's round enough. Almost has to be a crater. Bey, why should it be so eroded?"

"It must be the interstellar dust. If it is, then that's why there's no atmosphere or lithosphere. But I can't see the dust being that thick, even at these speeds."

"Put it—"

"Yah." I reached for my list.

"If we find one more anomaly, I'll scream."

Half an hour later we found life.

By then we were close enough to use the gravity drag to slow us. The beautiful thing about a gravity drag is that it uses very little power. It converts a ship's momentum relative to the nearest powerful mass into heat, and all you have to do is get rid of the heat. Since the $ST\infty$'s hull would pass only various ranges of radiation corresponding to what the puppeteers' varied customers considered visible light, the shipbuilders had run a great big radiator fin out from the gravity drag. It glowed dull red behind us. And the fusion drive was off. There was no white fusion flame to hurt visibility.

Elephant had the scope at highest magnification. At

first, as I peered into the eyepiece, I couldn't see what he was talking about. There was a dull white plain, all the same color except for a few blobs of blue. The blobs wouldn't have stood out except for the uniformity of the surface around them.

Then one of them moved. Very slowly, but it was moving.

"Right," I said. "Let me run a temperature check."

The surface temperature in that region was about right for helium II. And on the rest of the planet as well; the protosun wasn't putting out much energy, though it was very gung ho on radiation.

"I don't think they match any species I know."

"I can't tell," said Elephant. He had the telescope and the library screen going at the same time, with a Sirius VIII blob on the library screen. "There are twenty different species of helium life in this book, and they all look exactly alike."

"Not quite. They must have a vacuum-proof integument. And you'll notice those granules in the—"

"I treasure my ignorance on this subject, Bey. Anyway, we aren't going to find any species we know on this world. Even a stage-tree seed would explode the moment it hit."

I let the subject die.

Once again Elephant ran the scope over "his" planet, this time looking for the blobby life-forms. They were fairly big for helium II life but not abnormally so. Lots of cold worlds develop life using the peculiar properties of helium II; but because it hasn't much use for complexity, it usually stays in the amoeba stage.

There was one peculiarity, which I duly noted. Every animal was on the back side of the planet with relation to the planet's course through the galaxy. They weren't afraid of protosun sunlight, but they seemed to fear interstellar dust.

"You promised to scream."

"It's not odd enough. I'll wait."

Two hours passed.

The red glow of the radiator fin became more pronounced. So did the dull uniformity of the planetary surface. The planet was a disk now beyond the front window; if you watched it for a while you could see it grow. Turning ship to face the planet had made no difference to the gravity drag.

"Cue Ball," said Elephant.

"No good. It's been used. Beta Lyrae I."

"Cannonball Express then."

"Elephant, what are you doing here?"

He turned, startled. "What do you mean?"

"Look, you know by now I'm with you all the way. But I do wonder. You spent a million stars getting here, and you'd have spent two if you had to. You could be home in the Rockies with Dianna or hovering near Beta Lyrae, which is unusual enough and better scenery than this snowball. You could be sampling oddball drugs in Crashlanding or looking for Mist Demons on Plateau. Why here?"

"Because it is there."

"What the blazes is that supposed to mean?"

"Bey, once upon a time there was a guy named Miller. Six years ago he took a ramscoop-fusion drive ship and put a hyperdrive in it and set out for the edge of the universe, figuring he could get his hydrogen from space and use the fusion plant to power his hyperdrive. He's probably still going. He'll be going forever unless he hits something. Why?"

"A psychiatrist I'm not."

"He wants to be remembered. When you're dead a hundred years, what will you be remembered for?"

"I'll be the idiot who rode with Gregory Pelton, who spent two months and more than a million stars to set his ship down on a totally worthless planet."

"Gronk. All right, what about abstract knowledge? This star will be out of known space in ten years. Our only chance to explore it is right now. What—"

There was an almost silent breeze of air, and a strangling pressure in my larynx, and a stabbing pain in my ears, simultaneously. I heard the bare beginning of an alarm, but I was already reaching for my helmet. I clamped it down hard, spun the collar, and gave vent to an enormous belch at the same time as the wind went shrieking from my lungs.

There was no way to realize what was happening—and no time. But vacuum was around us, and air was spraying into my suit, frigid air. Iron spikes were being driven through my ears, but I was going to live. My lungs held a ghastly emptiness, but I would live. I turned to Elephant.

The fear of death was naked in his face. He had his helmet down, but he was having trouble with the collar. I had to force his hands away to get it fastened right. His helmet misted over, then cleared; he was getting air. Had it come in time to save his life?

I was alive. The pain was leaving my ears, and I was breathing: inhale, pause, inhale, as the pressure rose to normal.

I'd seen what had happened. Now I had time to think it through, to remember it, to play it back.

What had happened was insane.

The hull had turned to dust. Just that. All at once and nothing first, the ship's outside had disintegrated and blown away on a whispering breath of breathing-air. I'd *seen* it.

And sure enough, the hull was gone. Only the innards of the ship remained. Before me, the lighted control board. A little below that, the manhole to the packed bubble, and the bubble package itself. Above the board, the half-disk of the mystery planet, and stars. To the left, stars. To the right, Elephant, looking dazed and scared, and beyond him, stars. Behind me, the airlock, the kitchen storage-block and dial board, a glimpse of the landing legs and glowing radiator fin, and stars. The *ST∞* was a skeleton.

Elephant shook his head, then turned on his suit radio. I heard the magnified click in my helmet.

We looked at each other, waiting. But there was nothing to say. Except, *Elephant, look! We don't have a hull no more! Isn't that remarkable?*

I sighed, turned to the control board and began nursing the fusion drive to life. From what I could see of the ship, nothing seemed to be floating away. Whatever had been fixed to the hull must also have been fixed to other things.

"What are you doing, Bey?"

"Getting us out of here. Uh, you can scream now."

"Why? I mean, why leave?"

He'd flipped. Flatlanders are basically unstable. I got the drive pushing us at low power, turned off the gravity drag, and turned to face him. "Look, Elephant. No hull." I swept an arm around me. "None."

"But what's left of the ship is still mine?"

"Uh, yah. Sure."

"I want to land. Can you talk me out of it?"

He was serious. Completely so. "The landing legs are intact," he went on. "Our suits can keep out the radiation for three days. We could land and take off in twelve hours."

"We probably could."

"And we spent going on two months getting here."

"Right."

"I'd feel like an idiot getting this close and then turning for home. Wouldn't you?"

"I would, except for one thing. And that one thing says you're landing this ship over my unconscious body."

"All right, the hull turned to dust and blew away. What does that mean? It means we've got a faulty hull, and I'm going to sue the hind legs off General Products when we get back. But do _you_ know what caused it?"

"No."

"So why do you assume it's some kind of threat?"

"Tell you what I'll do," I said. I turned the ship until it was tail down to Cannonball Express. "Now. We'll be there in three hours if you insist on landing. It's your ship, just as you say. But I'm going to try to talk you out of it."

"That's fair."

"Have you had space-pilot training?"

"Naturally."

"Did it include a history of errors course?"

"I don't think so. We got a little history of the state of the art."

"That's something. You remember that they started out

with chemical fuels and that the first ship to the asteroids was built in orbit around Earth's moon?"

"Uh huh."

"This you may not have heard. There were three men in that ship, and when they were launched, it was in an orbit that took them just slightly inside the moon's orbit, then out again and away. About thirty hours after launching, the men noticed that all their ports were turning opaque. A concentration of dust in their path was putting little meteor pits all through the quartz. Two of the men wanted to continue on, using instruments to finish their mission. But the third man was in command. They used their rockets and stopped themselves dead.

"Remember, materials weren't as durable in those days, and nothing they were using had been well tested. The men stopped their ship in the orbit of the moon, which by then was 230,000 miles behind them, and called base to say they'd aborted the mission."

"You remember this pretty well. How come?"

"They drilled these stories into us again and again. Everything they tried to teach us was illustrated with something from history. It stuck."

"Go on."

"They called base and told them about their windows fogging up. Somebody decided it was dust, and someone else suddenly realized they'd launched the ship through one of the moon's trojan points."

Elephant laughed, then coughed. "Wish I hadn't breathed so much vacuum. I gather you're leading up to something?"

"If the ship hadn't stopped, it would have been wrecked. The dust would have torn it apart. The moral of this story is, anything you don't understand is dangerous until you do understand it."

"Sounds paranoid."

"Maybe it does, to a flatlander. You come from a planet so kind to you, so seemingly adapted to you, that you think the whole universe is your oyster. You might remember my neutron star story. I'd have been killed if I hadn't understood that tidal effect in time."

"So you would. So you think flatlanders are all fools?"

"No, Elephant. Just not paranoid enough. And I refuse to apologize."

"Who asked you?"

"I'll land with you if you can tell me what made our hull turn to dust."

Elephant crossed his arms and glared forward. I shut up and waited.

By and by he said, "Can we get home?"

"I don't know. The hyperdrive motor will work, and we can use the gravity drag to slow us down to something like normal. Physically we should be able to do it."

"Okay. Let's go. But I'll tell you this, Bey. If I were alone, I'd go down, and damn the hull."

So we turned tail and ran, under protest from Elephant. In four hours we were far enough from Cannonball Express's gravity well to enter hyperspace.

I turned on the hyperdrive, gasped, and turned it off just as fast as I could. We sat there shaking, and Elephant said, "We can inflate the bubble."

"But can we get in?"

"It doesn't have an airlock."

We worked it, though. There was a pressure-control dial in the cabin, and we set it for zero; the electromagnetic field that folded the bubble would now inflate it without pressure. We went inside, pressurized it, and took off our helmets.

"We're out of the radiation field," said Elephant. "I looked."

"Good." You can go pretty far in even a couple of seconds of hyperdrive. "Now, there's one thing I've got to know. Can you take that again?"

Elephant shuddered. "Can you?"

"I think so. I can do all the navigating if I have to."

"Anything you can take, I can take."

"Can you take it and stay sane?"

"Yes."

"Then we can trade off. But if you change your mind, let me know that instant. A lot of good men have left their marbles in the Blind Spot, and all they had were a couple of windows."

"I believe you. Indeed I do, sir. How do we work it?"

"We'll have to chart a course through the least dense part of space. The nearest inhabited world is Kzin. I hate to risk asking help from the Kzinti, but we may have to."

"Tell you what, Bey. Let's at least try to reach Jinx. I want to use that number of yours to give the puppeteers hell."

"Sure. We can always turn off to something closer."

I spent an hour or so working out a course. When I'd finished, I was pretty sure we could navigate it without either of us having to leave the bubble more than once every twenty-four hours to look at the mass indicator. We threw fingers for who got the first watch, and I lost.

We put on our suits and depressurized the bubble. As I crawled through the manhole, I saw Elephant opaqueing the bubble wall.

I squeezed into the crash couch, all alone among the stars. They were blue ahead and red behind when I finished turning the ship. I couldn't find the protosun.

More than half the view was empty space. I found myself looking thoughtfully at the airlock. It was behind and to the left, a metal oblong standing alone at the edge of the deck, with both doors tightly closed. The inner door had slammed when the pressure dropped, and now the airlock mechanisms guarded the pressure inside against the vacuum outside in both directions. Nobody inside to use the air, but how do you explain that to a pressure sensor?

I was procrastinating. The ship was aimed; I clenched my teeth and sent the ship into hyperspace.

The Blind Spot, they call it. It fits.

There are ways to find the blind spot in your eye. Close one eye, put two dots on a piece of paper, and bring the paper toward you, focusing on one of the dots. If you hold the paper just right, the other dot will suddenly vanish.

Let a ship enter hyperspace with the windows transparent, and the windows will seem to vanish. So will the space enclosing them. Objects on either side stretch and draw closer together to fill the missing space. If you look long enough, the Blind Spot starts to spread; the walls and the things against the walls draw even closer to the missing space, until they are engulfed.

It's all in your mind, they tell me. So?

I turned the key, and half my view was Blind Spot. The control board stretched and flowed. The mass-indicator sphere tried to wrap itself around me. I reached for it, and my hands were distorted too. With considerable effort I put them back at my sides and got a grip on myself.

There was one fuzzy green line in the plastic distortion that had been a mass indicator. It was behind and to the side. The ship could fly itself until Elephant's turn came. I fumbled my way to the manhole and crawled through.

Hyperspace was only half the problem.

It was a big problem. Every twenty-four hours one of us had to go out there, see if there were any dangerous masses around, drop back to normal space to take a fix and adjust course. I found myself getting unbearably tense during the few hours before each turn. So did Elephant. At these times we didn't dare talk to each other.

On my third trip I had the bad sense to look up—and went more than blind. Looking up, there was nothing at all in my field of vision, nothing but the Blind Spot.

It was more than blindness. A blind man, a man whose eyes have lost their function, at least remembers what things looked like. A man whose optic brain-center has been damaged doesn't. I could remember what I'd come out here for—to find out if there were masses near enough to harm us—but I couldn't remember how to do it. I touched a curved glass surface and knew that this was the machine that would tell me, if only I knew its secret.

Eventually my neck got sore, so I moved my head. That brought my eyes back into existence.

When we got the bubble pressurized, Elephant said, "Where were you? You've been gone half an hour."

"And lucky at that. When you go out there, don't look up."

"Oh."

That was the other half of the problem. Elephant and I had stopped communicating. He was not interested in saying anything, and he was not interested in anything I had to say.

It took me a good week to figure out why. Then I braced him with it.

"Elephant, there's a word missing from our language."

He looked up from the reading screen. If there hadn't been a reading screen in the bubble, I don't think we'd have made it. "More than one word," he said. "Things have been pretty silent."

"One word. You're so afraid of using that word, you're afraid to talk at all."

"So tell me."

"Coward."

Elephant wrinkled his brows, then snapped off the screen. "All right, Bey, we'll talk about it. First of all, you said it, I didn't. Right?"

"Right. Have you been thinking it?"

"No. I've been thinking euphemisms, like 'overcautious' and 'reluctance to risk bodily harm.' But since we're on the subject, why were you so eager to turn back?"

"I was scared." I let that word soak into him, then went on. "The people who trained me made certain that I'd be scared in certain situations. With all due respect, Elephant, I've had more training for space than you have. I think your wanting to land was the result of ignorance."

Elephant sighed. "I think it would have been safe to land. You don't. We're not going to get anywhere arguing about it, are we?"

We weren't. One of us was right, one wrong. And if I was wrong, then a pretty good friendship had gone out the airlock.

It was a silent trip.

We came out of hyperspace near the two Sirius suns. But that wasn't the end of it, because we still faced a universe squashed by relativity. It took us almost two weeks to brake ourselves. The gravity drag's radiator fin glowed orange-white for most of that time. I have no idea how many times we circled round through hyperspace for another run through the system.

Finally we were moving in on Jinx with the fusion drive.

I broke a silence of hours. "Now what, Elephant?"

"As soon as we get in range, I'm going to call that number of yours."

"Then?"

"Drop you off at Sirius Mater with enough money to get you home. I'd take it kindly if you'd use my house as your own until I come back from Cannonball Express. I'll buy a ship here and go back."

"You don't want me along."

"With all due respect, Bey, I don't. I'm going to land. Wouldn't you feel like a damn fool if you died then?"

"I've spent about three months in a small extension-bubble because of that silly planet. If you conquered it alone, I would feel like a damn fool."

Elephant looked excruciatingly unhappy. He started to speak, caught his breath—

If ever I picked the right time to shut a man up, that was it.

"Hold it. Let's call the puppeteers first. Plenty of time to decide."

Elephant nodded. In a moment he'd have told me he didn't want me along because I was overcautious. Instead, he picked up the ship phone.

Jinx was a banded Easter egg ahead of us. To the side was Binary, the primary to which Jinx is a moon. We should be close enough to talk ... and the puppeteers' transfer-booth number would also be their phone number.

Elephant dialed.

A sweet contralto voice answered. There was no picture, but I could tell: no woman's voice is quite that good. The puppeteer said, "Eight eight three two six seven seven oh."

"My General Products hull just failed." Elephant was wasting no time at all.

"I beg your pardon?"

"My name is Gregory Pelton. Twelve years ago I bought a No. 2 hull from General Products. A month and a half ago it failed. We've spent the intervening time limping home. May I speak to a puppeteer?"

The screen came on. Two flat, brainless heads looked out at us. "This is quite serious," said the puppeteer. "Naturally we will pay the indemnity in full. Would you mind detailing the circumstances?"

Elephant didn't mind at all. He was quite vehement. It was a pleasure to listen to him. The puppeteer's silly expressions never wavered, but he was blinking rapidly when Elephant finished.

"I see," he said. "Our apologies are insufficient, of course, but you will understand that it was a natural mistake. We did not think that antimatter was available anywhere in the galaxy, especially in such quantity."

It was as if he'd screamed. I could hear that word echoing from side to side in my skull.

Elephant's booming voice was curiously soft. "Antimatter?"

"Of course. We have no excuse, of course, but you should have realized it at once. Interstellar gas of normal matter had polished the planet's surface with miniscule explosions, had raised the temperature of the protosun beyond any rational estimate, and was causing a truly incredible radiation hazard. Did you not even wonder about these things? You knew that the system was from beyond the galaxy. Humans are supposed to be highly curious, are they not?"

"The hull," said Elephant.

"A General Products hull is an artificially generated molecule with interatomic bonds artificially strengthened by a small power plant. The strengthened molecular bonds are proof against any kind of impact, and heat into the hundreds of thousands of degrees. But when enough of the atoms had been obliterated by antimatter explosions, the molecule naturally fell apart."

Elephant nodded. I wondered if his voice was gone for good.

"When may we expect you to collect your indemnity? I

gather no human was killed; this is fortunate, since our funds are low—"

Elephant turned off the phone. He gulped once or twice, then turned to look me in the eye. I think it took all his strength; and if I'd waited for him to speak, I don't know what he would have said.

"I gloat," I said. "I gloat. I was right, you were wrong. If we'd landed on your forsaken planet, we'd have gone up in pure light. At this time it gives me great pleasure to say, I Told You So."

He smiled weakly. "You told me so."

"Oh, I did, I did. Time after time I said, Don't Go Near That Haunted Planet! It's Worth Yore Life And Yore Soul, I said. There Have Been Signs In The Heavens, I said, To Warn Us From This Place—"

"All right, don't overdo it, you bastard. You were dead right all the way. Let's leave it at that."

"Okay. But there's one thing I want you to remember."

"If you don't understand it, it's dangerous."

"That's the one thing I want you to remember besides I Told You So."

And that should have ended it.

But it doesn't. Elephant's going back. He's got a little flag with a UN insignia, about two feet by two feet, with spring wires to make it look like it's flapping in the breeze, and a solid rocket in the handle so it'll go straight when the flag is furled. He's going to drop it in the antimatter planet from a great height, as great as I can talk him into.

It should make quite a bang.

And I'm going along. I've got a solidly mounted tridee camera and a contract with the biggest broadcasting company in known space. *This* time I've got a reason for going!

THE ETHICS OF MADNESS

TAU CETI IS a small cool-yellow GO dwarf with four planets. Strictly speaking, none of the planets is habitable. Two are gas giants. The third inward has no air; the innermost has too much.

That innermost world is about the size of Venus. With no oversized moon to strip away most of its air, it has an atmosphere like Venus': thick and hot and corrosive. No human explorer would have marked it for colonization.

But the ramrobots were not human.

During the twenty-first and twenty-second centuries, the ramrobots explored most of what later came to be called "known space." They were complexly programmed, but their mission was simple. Each was to find a habitable planet.

Unfortunately they were programmed wrong.

The designers didn't know it, and the UN didn't know it; but the ramrobots were programmed only to find a habitable point. Having located a world the right distance from the star to which it was sent, the ramrobot probe would drop and circle until it found a place at ground level which matched its criteria for atmospheric composition, average temperature, water vapor, and other conditions. Then the ramrobot would beam its laser pulse back at the solar system, and the UN would respond by sending a colony slowboat.

Unlike the ramrobots, the man-carrying slowboats could not use interstellar ramscoops. They had to carry their own fuel. It meant that the slowboats took a long time to get where they were going, and there were no round-trip tickets. The slowboats could not turn back.

So We Made It was colonized because a ramrobot elected to settle in spring. Had it landed in summer or winter, when the planet's axis of rotation points through its primary, Procyon, it would have sensed the fifteen-hundred-mile-per-hour winds.

So Jinx was colonized. Jinx, with a surface gravity of 1.78 and two habitable bands between the ocean, where there is too much air, and the Ends, where there is none at all. Jinx, the Easter Egg Planet, home of men and women who are five feet tall and five feet wide, the strongest bipeds in known space. But they die young, of heart trouble.

So Plateau was colonized. For the innermost world of Tau Ceti is like Venus in size and atmosphere, save for one mountain. That straight-sided mountain is forty miles tall, and its nearly flat top is half the size of California. It rises out of the searing black calm at the planet's surface to the transparent atmosphere above; and that air can be breathed. Snow covers the peaks near the center of the Plateau, and rivers run lower down—rivers that tumble off the void edges of the Plateau into the shining mist below. The ramrobot landed there. And founded a world.

Several centuries passed.

Up from the Plateau on Mount Lookitthat came Douglas Hooker, rising like a star. He was the only occupant of a four-man exploration craft. Fifteen years ago he had stolen that ship from the UN, the government of Earth, and taken it to Plateau. He didn't dare return it. The laws of Earth were far stricter than those of Plateau.

And he couldn't stay on Plateau.

Plateau would not have complained. Hooker was a cured maniac, a guaranteed model citizen. An autodoc had adjusted the chemistry of his body, canceling the biochemical cause of his insanity. Two years of psychoanalysis, hypnoanalysis, and conditioning had attacked his memories, altering them in some cases, reducing or enhancing their importance in others. Conditioning had seen to it that he would never remain far from an autodoc; his chemistry would never again have the chance to go haywire in that particular fashion.

But he'd done a terrible thing on Plateau. He couldn't stay. He couldn't bear the thought of someday facing Greg Loeffler.

The world below changed from a vast white plain to a

round white ball. Hooker's fusion drive glowed hotter and bluer than any sun. He was using the hydrogen in his tank. Though his ship carried a model of mankind's first "safe" ramscoop, he was not yet moving fast enough to use interstellar hydrogen for fuel.

When Plateau was in danger of being lost against the stellar background, he turned the ship toward Wunderland. He'd decided on Wunderland months ago, when he really began to believe that he would be well someday. Wunderland was small, of light gravity; a nice world, but distant from Earth. Wunderland's technology was always several decades behind the times. The Wunderlanders would appreciate an extra spaceship, especially one as modern as Hooker's.

They might jail him—though he had served a term on Plateau, concurrently with his cure. But they wouldn't kill him. And Hooker could wait out a jail sentence. His health was perfect. Though he was eighty-seven years old, he might have been twenty. Earth's medical sciences had become very good indeed. Men and women walked the Earth in places they had trod three centuries earlier, and the medicine of their time was long obsolete.

(Yet ... look again. Twenty? Never. He acts *scarred*. Neither years nor scars show in the flesh, nor around the eyes, nor in them. But behind the eyes there are scars. It takes decades to form scars so deeply in the crevices of the brain that they show through to the surface.)

Hooker turned toward Wunderland and set the autopilot. His motions were quicker and surer than they had been for a long time. He was leaving Plateau, and he left a weight behind. Now he could begin to forget.

Hours later a second star rose from the Plateau on Mount Lookitthat. It turned slowly, questing, like a hound sniffing out a trail. Then it fixed on Wunderland and began to accelerate.

OCTOBER, A.D. 2514   SAN FRANCISCO

He took the news as if he'd expected it. He looked at

the human doctor for a long moment after she had stopped talking; then he slumped, back and shoulders dropping, chin nearly touching his chest. He mumbled, "I always knew I was different."

"Is that a crime, Doug?" Dr. Doris Hahn might have been any age beyond thirty. She was small and oriental, and she had had that look of great wisdom long before she acquired the wisdom itself.

"Seems it is," said Doug Hooker. He was eighteen years old, thin, with blue eyes and straw-colored hair. "I can't do anything about it, can I?"

"Sure you can! Why, you need never know you've got it, any time during the rest of your life. There are millions of potential paranoids walking this world and others. And diabetics, and epileptics, and schizophrenics. Nobody knows the difference."

"*They* know."

"Well, yes."

Doug looked the doctor in the eye. "Why? If they need never know, why tell them? How will this affect me, Doctor? What am I supposed to do about it?"

She nodded. "You're right, of course. It will affect you in two ways.

"First, the Fertility Board will probably not pass a potential paranoid. If you want to have a child, you'll have to do something so spectacular that the Board itself must recognize you as a genius. Something like inventing hyperdrive."

Doug smiled at that. Hyperdrive was "the moon on a platter."

"Second," she said, "you must never be out of reach of an autodoc for more than a month, for the rest of your life. Do you understand? Up to now your parents have had this responsibility. Now you're an adult. You must get to a doc every month so that it can stabilize your metabolism. Your body is chemically unstable. Without anti-paranoia substances you can go insane."

"That's all?"

"That's all. Best go every two weeks to give yourself some leeway."

"I will," said Doug. He wanted to leave. The news had been as bad as he had expected, and he'd expected it for years. He had been born into a paranoid body. It was a thing he couldn't tell even to Greg. He wanted to leave, to hide somewhere, to lick his wounds. But . . .

"How bad is it, Doctor? I mean, what would happen to me if I missed six weeks instead of a month?"

"The first time, very little. Your thinking processes would change a little, not enough to notice. When the doc readjusted you, you wouldn't notice that change either. But the second and third times would be worse. You see, Doug, a large part of being insane is having been insane. If you were paranoid for a year, a doc couldn't cure you. Your year of insanity would have formed habits. The doc would change your metabolism without changing your paranoid habits of thinking. You'd need a human psychotherapist."

Doug wet his lips. He thought the question: What is it like to be paranoid? How does a paranoid think?

He didn't want to know. He said, " 'Bye, Doctor," and he got up and left. He thought he heard Dr. Hahn call something after him, but he wasn't sure.

JUNE, A.D. 2526   KANSAS CITY

At the age of thirty Douglas Hooker thought he knew himself pretty well. He had long known that he was a man of habits, so he had trained his habits. Each weekday he entered his office at just ten o'clock, and the first thing he did was to use the desk doc.

He came in that Thursday morning at just ten o'clock, still wearing the smile with which he had hailed his good mornings at the other employees of Skyhook Enterprises. He hadn't seen Greg, but Greg was always early or late—usually early. Probably at work already. Doug sat, opened the panel in his desk, and inserted his hands.

There were twin pricks in the balls of his middle fingers. The doc was taking a blood sample. Doug waited until the green light came on, then removed his hands. His nails gleamed.

The desk doc was small; it's repertoire was limited. It could not repair injuries or exercise small unused muscles, as could a full-sized drugstore doc. It could detect infections and fight them with wide-spectrum antibiotics; it could supply needed vitamins; it was a fine manicurist. It could stabilize Doug Hooker's unusual metabolism, using two phials of biochemicals stored in its innards. If it ran out of something or if it sensed the presence of some medical anomaly that should be treated, it would flash a red light.

Doug frowned at the papers in his In basket, then sighed and went to work. There was no sound from beyond his office; there was nothing to distract him. Yet he worked slowly. He couldn't concentrate. It was not spring fever; city men didn't get spring fever, living in a world which was mostly city. It was the feel of something impending.

It came at noon, with Greg Loeffler's voice in the intercom.

"Doug? It's here. Drop whatever you're doing and come over."

Doug put down half a sandwich and went out, walking fast. The bright morning sunlight made him blink. He took one of the carts in front of Admin and drove it across to Design. He was about to park in front when his eye caught a shadowy bulk standing four stories tall around to the side. He drove over.

Greg stood waiting for him, leaning one-armed against the huge truncated cone, grinning like a proud papa. "Isn't she gorgeous?"

"No," said Hooker, for it was not. "Will it work?"

"We'll sue if it doesn't. But we can't test it here. We'll have to ship it to the Moon."

"And then?" Doug felt adrenalin flooding his veins. All the decisions had been made two years ago; yet here was the tangible result, four stories tall, a decision on the verge of proving itself. And an ancient dream.

The safe ramscoop.

For centuries the ramrobots had been exploring space at just less than the speed of light, fueled by hydrogen scooped from between stars in conical electromagnetic fields two hundred miles across. For centuries men had followed at a quarter of the speed of light, carrying their own fuel. A ramscoop's magnetic field would kill any chordate organism within three hundred miles. No shield had ever been developed which would protect a chordate and still let the ramscoop work.

Until two years ago, when Moscow Motors had built—this.

There was a "dead pocket," a bubble in this generator's ramscoop field. A ship could be built into that bubble, and that ship would go anywhere, with a limitless fuel supply.

Two years ago Skyhook Enterprises had bought the contract to build that ship. It was a UN project, with all the wealth of Earth behind it. Doug Hooker's father was still president when that decision was made; only a year ago he had turned the company over to Doug and gone off to become a Belter. For a year the ramship had been Doug's responsibility. He had given Greg Loeffler a free rein, not for the sake of a friendship fifteen years old, but because Greg was a genius at design.

"And then we fit the ramscoop to the ship and take her for a trip. The ship's been ready for months. That's what I was doing in April and May, Doug. On the Moon, examining the ship. It's ready. All you have to do is get the ramscoop there."

Doug nodded. For a moment he almost envied Greg. The ship was Skyhook's project, Doug Hooker's project, but it was Greg's ship. Top to bottom. If it was successful, it would conquer all of nearby space.

He said, "How's Joanna?"

Loeffler grinned proudly. "Out to here, and beautiful. Another month and she can go back to playing tennis. How's Clarisse?"

"Fine, fine."

"We haven't gotten together in a while. How about dinner tonight? To celebrate the ramscoop."

"Good. Where?"

"Our place. You haven't seen our new house."

"That's true," Hooker said vaguely. He was not at his

best in a social situation. He was uncomfortable in crowds and with people he didn't know. With Greg and Joanna he could relax; but not during work hours, not even with them.

"Doug?"

"Yah?"

"You and Clarisse were married long before I was. Why haven't you had children yet? Waiting for Joanna and me to pioneer the field?"

Hooker was tempted to say, *Yah, why not let you take the risks first?* But then he'd be asked again. So he told the truth. "The Fertility Board turned me down."

"Oh?" Loeffler wasn't about to ask why, but he'd left the door open if Hooker wanted a sympathetic ear.

"Guess I'd better get back to work," said Doug. "Will you be going to the Moon to supervise the tests?"

"If Skyhook pays the fare."

"Slip me a requisition. And we'll see you tonight."

AUGUST, A.D. 2557   THE ROCKIES

They lay in full sunlight beside the pool, under Greg's weather dome. All three were wet, with water running off their bodies to form pools around them on the red tiles. The woman, Joanna, was a tall, solidly built brunette with lovely legs. Of the men, Doug Hooker was still too thin for his height and not well muscled; whereas Greg Loeffler had gymnasium muscles and a loafer's tan. They lay exhausted after the race across the pool.

Outside it would be cold, though not yet freezing. In winter snow would surround the house and run melting from the weather dome. Greg's house was high in the Rockies, halfway up a cliff. By its design it seemed to have grown as an organic part of the cliff. A good part of it was inside the rock.

Idly, with wistfulness but no pain, Doug thought Clarisse into existence alongside him. Golden hair in a stiff complex hairdo, deep all-over tan, she would have fallen asleep by now in the sunlight burning through the transparent weather dome. He hadn't seen her in ten years. She had remarried right after the divorce. Two years later she had been twice a mother.

Wistfulness, but no pain. She'd got no alimony, but she'd tried, and that had canceled the pain of losing her. Her ghost-image died, and Doug turned over on his back.

"We'll be leaving in a month," said Joanna. There was a touch of regret in her voice.

"You're out of your minds," said Doug.

Greg got up on an elbow. "Not at all. The future isn't on Earth any more, Doug—"

"Where is it, on Plateau? Any other world, I'd still say you were crazy. But teeny little Plateau? In five generations it'll be as crowded as Earth!"

"Then you admit Earth's crowded."

"Well, yah, but that's the price you pay for civilization."

"I won't pay. I'm leaving." Greg was enjoying himself. He had rehearsed the argument over and over in past months. "By the time Plateau gets really crowded, there'll be so many colony planets that anyone can take his pick. Meanwhile, Plateau is a nice place to be. You've seen the pictures."

"Suppose they're hoked?"

"They aren't."

"And why risk it anyway? A dozen light-years in a four-man ship! Suppose a meteor—"

"Suppose a goblin? For Pete's sake, Doug! I designed these ships myself. They're foolproof."

Doug turned on his belly, scowling. Even he didn't know why he kept fighting a lost cause. Greg was going, and Joanna was going; their oldest daughter, Marcia, was going, with her husband. The only reason Greg kept up his side of the argument was the hope that Doug would change his mind and come along, which Doug would not.

But the thought of Greg and Joanna leaving filled him with nameless dread.

"Is the ship ready yet?"

"Yes. Since yesterday. We could leave any time."

"Not until I inspect it," said Doug. "You promised."

"So I did. How about tomorrow? I'll give you the key."

"Good."

Skyhook Enterprises had built that ship. By now hundreds like it were scattered across the sky, anywhere within fifteen light-years of the solar system. Which meant that Earth's information was up to fifteen years out of date; but as far as anyone knew, no Skyhook ramship had ever failed. Skyhook was now designing a bigger ramship, big enough to carry a thousand colonists in stasis. But the four-man Skyhook exploring-model was the only ramship now flying.

It came in three parts, easy to connect or to disconnect for inspection. Ramscoop, lifesystem, drive. And boosters, but boosters didn't count. They didn't count because they had been used for centuries. Rockets they were, containing helium compressed to within an inch of its life. Autopilots would guide them down after they had lifted Greg's ship to where he could safely use the fusion motor. Hooker ignored them, as he would have ignored a bicycle in the cargo hold. Too simple, too foolproof.

He ignored the ramscoop because he wouldn't have understood it. He ignored the fusion drive for both reasons. If there was a flaw in either of them, he would not find it.

His only chance was in the lifesystem.

It was big and roomy, that lifesystem, even for four people. Most flatlanders did not have that much room in their homes. But a claustrophobic ramship passenger could not step outside for a breath of air. The lifesystem was a cylinder with the central core running through it, the central core that joined the ramscoop to the fusion drive. Somewhere in the control panel were emergency switches which would blow the core apart to release the lifesystem as a separate unit, to fall through space awaiting an unlikely rescue.

There were two master bedrooms, soundproofed, with locks—very private. There was a gymnasium with muscle-stretchers for use in ship's gravity or in free fall, with sunlight tubes and masseur couches and a steam bath.

There was a small dining room with the kitchen controls set in one wall.

Hooker walked the ship as if he were afraid of it. He was. He still wasn't sure why.

There was the autodoc, the most complex ever built. It would replace its own biochemicals, its own plastiskin, its own artificially grown organ-replacements; all this automatically, using materials culled from the ship's waste collectors. It could cure anything. In theory it could keep a man young and healthy indefinitely. Skyhook Enterprises had not built this beauty. Moscow Motors, that industrial giant subsidized by the substate USSR, had taken that contract as part of the deal that won Skyhook the ship contract.

Hooker knew autodocs. He inspected the coffin and the machinery that fed it, and found no flaw.

He went through the kitchen, as much of it as he understood. This too turned waste into food. The processes were infernally complicated; but any chemical process can be reversed, given sufficient sophistication and sufficient power. The ship's power came straight from a fusion drive with unlimited fuel.

The air plant was the simplest part of the ship. Hooker didn't even look at it. By the time he got around to it, he was bone tired. He flopped on one of the beds and stared at the softly glowing ceiling.

As far as he could tell, there was nothing wrong with the ship. Nothing. What was the point in looking? Any flaw Douglas Hooker, the executive, could recognize could probably be fixed in five minutes.

They were going; they were practically on their way now. Greg and Joanna and Marcia and—he'd forgotten the name of Marcia's husband. But why should he try to stop them? He had plenty of other friends. Didn't he?

He had conjured up eleven names and was trying hard for a twelfth when it occurred to him that all eleven were people he had met through Greg and Joanna. All but two, and he hadn't seen them since Clarissa flew to Vegas, leaving him a wedding cake on which the wax bride and bridegroom stood facing outward on opposite sides of the bottom layer. Nine people, then, whom he saw only at Joanna's parties and "talk nights."

He had never made friends easily. Strangers made him uncomfortable. He kept wondering what they thought of him.

Even friends. There was a barrier between him and everyone else, and the barrier was a secret. As far as he knew, only two other people on Earth knew that Hooker was a potential paranoid. There had been three; but his father had gone to the Belt to start life over, probably thinking that the more lenient Belt fertility laws would permit him to have a second child after seven years had made him a citizen. He had lasted two years. He had smoked, and his dashboard included an ash tray. One day, during the last seconds of a landing approach to some unnamed rock, he had somehow used the attitude jets in such a way as to spill ashes out of the tray and into his eyes. The rock had smashed his sight bubble and his faceplate. And now there were two people who knew Doug's secret, but both were doctors. Clarissa had not known. She would have talked,

His secret stopped his mouth and slowed his conversation and made it innocuous. It kept him from getting drunk, for he feared his tongue would loosen. No man knows his fellow until he has seen him drunk; and no man had seen Doug Hooker drunk.

He tried to face it squarely. Doug and Joanna were taking his social life with them to Plateau.

Why not regard it as a challenge?

Hooker rolled off the bed and left the ship. He would tell the Loefflers that it was perfect, foolproof. When they were gone, he would make new friends, create his own social world. He had wrapped himself around his work for far too long.

But he was sixty-one years old, and his habits were developed.

AUGUST, A.D. 2570   KANSAS CITY

It happened thus:

Every six months a man came to service Douglas Hooker's desk doc. Paul Jurgenson was his name. He had been servicing docs for most of his life; docs of all kinds, from the huge multiple-patient emergency docs at aero-spaceports to the desk-sized docs installed in planes and short-hop spacecraft and used by executives the world over. The work never bored him, for Jurgenson was not overly bright; but he was good at his job.

He came on a Thursday, the last day of the working week, and the last Thursday of August. As usual, Doug Hooker went home at noon to give him room to work. Jurgenson took the doc apart and began to examine the parts. He shook his head sadly when he found both of the two special-mix phials *that* close to empty. Hooker didn't know it, but Jurgenson was the third man on Earth who knew his secret. He had guessed it, of course, but the guess was a certainty. You can't hide baldness from your barber.

Jurgenson filled the phials, still saddened. Mr. Hooker always sent him a twenty-five-mark bill for a Christmas present. (A firm handled Christmas presents of that nature for Hooker, remembering for him, but Jurgenson didn't know that.) Now it seemed that Mr. Hooker was using more antiparanoia than ever. That meant trouble in his life. Jurgenson knew that from long experience. He wished he could do something.

He replaced the hypo ncedles, as usual, the phials of pure alcohol, the vitamin ampoules, and the testosterone. He checked various circuits and replaced two wires; not that they were really ready to fail, but you never know. The manicure implements were self-replacing. Jurgenson frowned at the doc for a moment, listening to an instinct he trusted. It must have been right, for he closed the doc and unscrewed the red and green bulbs to look at the dates on their bases.

They were ten years old. In those days men built to last. There were laws. But ten years was old enough, even for bulbs which might last thirty. Jurgenson dropped them in the waste chute and replaced them from his kit. He tripped appropriate relays and saw that both bulbs lit.

He left, waving to Mr. Hooker's personal secretary. They had known each other for close to half a century and never done more than say hello and good-bye to each other. Miss Peterson was a beauty. But Jurgenson thought his wife was too good for him, and had long feared she would find out. He never philandered.

DECEMBER, A.D. 2570

Hooker entered the outer office. "Hi, fans," he said, as he had said each working day for ... he didn't know how long. The answer, from several people at once, was a jumbled chorus. Hooker entered his own office at just ten o'clock.

The In basket was full. Hooker frowned at it as he shoved his hands into the doc. Was he making a mistake, cutting down on Skyhook's commitments? It made paperwork simpler and thus saved money. But ... sometimes Hooker felt that Skyhook was stagnating.

Other than the colony-model ramships, a few of which were now in use for the UN, Skyhook had not pioneered anything in nearly twenty years.

The Loefflers must be on Plateau by now. Had they sent him a laser message? If so, it would not get here for twelve years.

What was wrong with the 'doc? It should have released him by now.

Doug withdrew his hands. There was no resistance; no fluids dripped from his fingers; his nails shone. Oh, nuts, he said subvocally. The green light's burned out. He made a mental note to call Jurgenson.

But he never did. It had never happened before; there were no habits to help him. And Jurgenson would be here in February. Hooker simply got used to the absence of a green light. He knew to within seconds when the doc was through with him.

It was the red light that had failed. The red bulb's filament had been dead for months. It had snapped and died when Jurgenson clicked it off.

FEBRUARY, A.D. 2571

The change came slowly. At first Doug noticed nothing. Then, as weeks passed, it seemed to him that his thinking was becoming clearer. He didn't know why, but he was becoming more intelligent. These things that troubled him ... they had one linking cause. Of course they must. All he had to do was find it.

His employees came at ten and went home at four, usually with Doug Hooker striding with them toward the parking lot, trying to look anonymous, returning good-byes if they were given. On Thursday, the first of February, Hooker did not leave. He nodded when his personal secretary told him it was after hours; he smiled emptily at her when she said good night. And then he sat.

The world did not intrude. The office was soundproof; its light did not depend on the sun; its false windows looked upon alien worlds, and on each a Skyhook ramship was landing. Impressive, for visitors. So Hooker could ignore the passage of time.

He thought of things that had gone wrong with his life.

He had no friends.

He had no hobbies. He'd thought of taking one up, but it turned out that he hated games. Losing irritated him. He always lost interest before he could become good enough to win.

His life was his work and the Palace. The Palace was a house of ill repute with a reputation for being very good and very expensive. If only Hooker had had the ability to play ... but that he had never had. He went to the Palace when his gonads told him to, and he left when they quieted. Most of the girls could not have told you his name.

His work was all habit. He slid through life as in a dream, and the dream was a dull one of easy defeat. For a long time it had been that way. It had started ...

When Clarisse left him? His teeth bared in savagery. If she were the cause, he would track her down wherever she hid! And the children for whom she had deserted him. . . . No. He could remember periods of enjoyment, brief flashes of sunlight in his life, and some of them had happened since Clarisse.

That Christmas party at the office, decades ago. Someone's idea had sparked them all, and they had stayed until three in the morning, using plant facilities to build a robot. The body had been built of emergency foam-plastic from the failsafe systems in a ramship. It couldn't have weighed more than twenty pounds, excluding another twenty pounds of motors, but it had stood twenty feet tall, blank-visaged and horrifying, with huge flat feet. Yes, it had been Greg: his idea, and mostly his suggestions. They had turned it loose on 217th pedwalk downtown, walking east in the westbound lane, so that it stood in one place, marking time. Skyhook employees had waited four hours for the seven o'clock rush hour, in an automated restaurant above the walk. The panic had been a beautiful thing.

Loeffler?

Sure, Loeffler! He'd waited until Doug's dependence on him was complete. Then he had left. So diabolically simple. Doug had not had a moment of real enjoyment since.

Hooker's lips pulled back and away from his teeth. His nostrils flared and turned white. So simple! Why hadn't he seen it before? Since high school it had always been Loeffler, blocking every chance he'd ever had to make his own friends and his own way of life. A decades-old plot that had not come to fruition until Doug was sixty-one years old. Now, now that he was finally alert, Doug could see the bones of the plan. The ramship had been part of it; it made the business so rich and so complex that it took all of Doug's time to handle it. A very neat trap. Had Clarisse been involved? Perhaps. There was no way to tell. But . . . Greg had introduced him to Clarisse, hadn't he?

Doug settled back in his chair. His face became almost calm. Clarisse, wherever she was, did not count. She had been a pawn, but Greg Loeffler was the king. Greg Loeffler must die.

It was midnight before Doug decided what to do. His secretary was long gone, which puzzled him until he realized what time it was. But he could do the work himself. He knew how to handle a tape. He dictated an application to buy one ramship at standard prices. Purpose: to leave Earth. (No point in saying where he intended to go. Loeffler might have left spies anywhere.) He put the tape in an envelope and dropped it in a mailbox on his way home.

Greg had had his answer in three days. By Monday, Doug would own a Skyhook ship. And then . . .

"Hi, fans," Doug Hooker called as he entered the outer office. Ranks of secretaries returned the greeting. They noticed nothing odd about him. He always walked that way, eyes straight ahead, walk fast and slightly hurried, rebuffing friendship before it was offered.

He entered his office, put his hands in the doc, waited for an estimated two minutes, withdrew them. Have to call Jurgenson, he thought, and then sneered at the triviality of the thought. He had better things to do. Where was that UN envelope?

There. He opened it, took out the credit-card-sized tape and inserted it in his desk player.

The refusal jarred him to his bones. He played it again, refusing to accept it—and again. It was true. He'd been turned down.

The implications were terrifying. Doug had had three days to think things over. With every hour the nature of Loeffler's plot had become clearer . . . and had involved more people. Loeffler must have had an enormous amount of help.

But Doug had never dreamed that the UN was part of the plot!

He'd have to be very careful. He might have given himself away already.

FEBRUARY, A.D. 2571   EAST NEW YORK

Somebody had stolen a Skyhook ramship.

The call came shortly after noon from a lovely, frightened woman who said she was the president's personal secretary. "It was Mr. Hooker's ship," she explained. "He was thinking of designing an improved model. He ordered a complete working-model of the ship they're using now. This morning it was gone!"

Loughery asked, "Did the model have gas boosters?" He was thinking, *Of course it had boosters. It couldn't take off without them, not without fusing Kansas City. But maybe a truck hauled it away?*

"Yes, it had boosters."

"Why?"

"Mr. Hooker wanted it complete in every detail."

"Oh, Lord." Loughery rubbed the back of his head. *The idiot! Wanted a complete model, did he?* Now there was a fusion ship loose somewhere in the solar system. Cut a few safety relays, turn off the fusion shield, and any fusion ship becomes an exploding fusion-bomb. "We'll send someone over right away. Is Mr. Hooker there?"

"He didn't arrive this morning."

"Well, give me his home address. And if he shows up, have him call here immediately."

The pieces began to fall together.

First, Skyhook. The area was well guarded; it would have been difficult for anyone to get in without being spotted. There was no human guard, but any unauthorized entry would have been photographed a dozen times. There would have been alarms.

Second, the Belt called. Several million people owned most of the solar system and a political power equal to that of the UN. They were furious. A fusion ship had left Earth without proper notification and was now boring through space toward the system's edge, paying no attention to laser calls. Loughery promised payment of damages. It was all he could do.

Nobody found Hooker. If he was at home, he wasn't answering phone calls.

The gas boosters found their way home. Loughery's men took charge of them immediately, inspecting them for clues. Reentry had not burned the fingerprints off their shiny surfaces. The fingerprints were Hooker's—some of them.

Loughery filed a request for a warrant to search

Hooker's house. It began to look as if Hooker had stolen his own ship.

On the afternoon of the twenty-seventh, somebody found Hooker's request to buy a ramship. It had been turned down for several good reasons. For one, Hooker had named neither destination nor purpose. For another, the UN was careful about passing fusion drives out to anyone who might ask; whereas Hooker—

Loughery felt the hair stir on the back of his neck. Hooker was a potential paranoid.

Jurgenson called that evening. By then Loughery was in Kansas City. He went right over to interview Jurgenson personally.

"He was using too much of this guck," said Jurgenson. He indicated two phials, both bone dry. "That's bad. I got other people who use stuff like this, people who need special guck or something goes wrong in their heads. When they got troubles, they use more guck than usual."

"But there's a warning light."

Jurgenson wrung his hands. "It's my fault. I put in a bad light. It worked when I tried it. I can't understand why it went bad."

"Who was Hooker's doctor?"

"Human? I don't know. Miss Peterson might."

Loughery asked Miss Peterson.

By then the search warrant had come through. What privacy there was on a crowded Earth was highly regarded; search warrants were not passed around like advertising posters. Hooker's home turned out to be the top of a skyscraper in downtown Kansas City.

Hooker had left a note, a long one. It said that since Hooker had no friends and no particular purpose in life, he had decided to spend the rest of his life on a project all his own. He was going to try to reach the edge of the universe. He did not expect to succeed. The ramship would keep him alive indefinitely, but indefinitely was not forever. Yet he intended to try.

It was a sanely spoken tape. Syntax was in order; Hooker's voice seemed calm. Hooker's expressed purpose was the only crazy thing about it. But Hooker was guaranteed crazy, wasn't he?

Loughery called the Belt again. Hooker's ship was well out of the inner system, far enough so that the Belt could stop monitoring him; there was little chance of his deadly drive-flame crossing anyone's path before it dissipated. Yes, he was headed roughly toward the galactic rim.

It checked, thought Loughery. Hooker would have been better advised to head straight out along the galactic axis; there was less junk to get in his way. But perhaps he hadn't thought of that.

The excitement began to settle. Loughery had other problems. But there was one last thing he could do about the Hooker problem, and eventually he thought of it.

"Keep a monitor on Hooker," he told the Belt Political Section. "We'll pay the standard fee. We want to know if he turns back or if he changes course toward some inhabited world."

And that would do it, he thought. Eventually Hooker would use the ship's doc. That simple. It would cure him. Then he would either turn back to Earth, to face a charge of stealing a fusion motor, or he would move on to one of the colonies. Probably the latter. Stealing a fusion motor was a capital crime on Earth. But they could deal with him, offer him amnesty for the return of the ship.

Three weeks later the word came. The actinic spark that was Hooker's drive had definitely shifted toward Tau Ceti. Loughery had to admit that Plateau was a good choice.

Plateau had suffered badly from the organ-bank problem in the two centuries before alloplasty, the science of putting foreign materials in the human body, had overtaken the techniques of organic transplant. All the inhabited worlds had gone through that stage. Its worst feature was that there was only one way to get the most important organic transplants.

On Plateau a small ruling class had held the power of life and death over its citizens. Life, because with unlimited access to the organ banks one could live centuries.

Death, because any crime could be made a capital crime whenever the organ banks ran short. The citizens would not complain. They wanted to live centuries.

Then alloplasty had caught up. Now there were no organ banks at all on Plateau and no capital punishment.

Loughery sent a laser to Plateau, warning them that a stolen ship was due to land there. He wasn't sure which would get there first, the laser or the ship. Ramships were fast.

MARCH, A.D. 2571, SHIP'S TIME

The ship flew itself, of course. All Doug had to do was take it below the plane of the Belt, leave it alone for a couple of weeks, then aim for Tau Ceti. The two weeks were misdirection. With the note he had left, they might convince the police that he was going off to nowhere and would never bother them again.

He kept busy watching for goldskin ships, Belt police; reading instruction booklets over and over; getting familiar with his machines. It wasn't until he had passed Pluto's orbit that he began to relax.

Nobody was after him as far as he could tell. Not that they could have done anything; you can't stop a ship in space. You can only destroy it. But he was reassured. He had broken free of his long bondage. And now . . . the long wait. Tau Ceti was eleven point nine light-years away. It would take less subjective time than that with the velocities he would eventually reach, but still . . .

He frowned. He hadn't been in a doc in some time. It would be stupid to get sick and die just when vengeance was within his grasp.

He climbed into the doc tank and went to sleep.

The doc found it necessary to make drastic changes in his metabolism. Hooker felt very strange when he woke. The strangeness seemed to be in his thinking, and that made it horrible. He felt slow, stupid. He could no longer remember why he wanted to kill Greg. He remembered only that his lifelong friend had done him a great wrong.

He thought of turning back. But he couldn't do that; he'd end in the organ banks for stealing this ship.

Should he try another colony world? It was a confusing question. His mind was full of confusing questions. But it was obvious that Mount Lookitthat was his best bet, regardless of what happened when he got there. Plateau was the only world of Man that did not impose the death penalty. If they decided he'd committed a crime, he'd get medical treatment.

His head buzzed. Perhaps he needed medical treatment. But the ship's doc could do anything.

He went on.

And as the weeks passed, a strange thing happened. He remembered his grudge against Greg Loeffler, and he realized something that sent cold chills of rage through him. They'd booby-trapped the doc!

No, it was worse than that. Somehow, long ago, Greg Loeffler and his minions had managed to booby-trap every doc on Earth. For all of his life Hooker had been using the docs. And each time he did, the docs had made alterations in his mind and body to keep him docile.

What could he do? His very life depended on the doc!

It took him a few days to get over his sense of panic, or perhaps he merely got used to it. Then he went to work. There was a thick instruction booklet for repairing the doc. Hooker memorized it. When he felt he was ready, he began to disconnect things. It was difficult to decide what to cut out. Finally he tackled it from the other direction: what to leave running. Anesthetics, of course, and the luxuries: manicures, haircuts, massage. Vitamins, antibiotics, all diagnostic machinery, surgical repair—except in the region of the head. He didn't dare leave that! Anticholesterol, synthetic blood components, alloplasty components and insertion tools . . .

He finished in two months. The doc should be incapable of anything that could damage his mind. But still he was afraid of it.

He tried it anyway. He was insane, definitely, but not stupid.

When he woke up, he knew that the doc was safe.

Plateau was a silver ball hanging serene in the heavens. Hooker stopped nearby, not too near, and not in any particular orbit. He began to scan the surface.

Where was Mount Lookitthat?

He couldn't find it. He turned ship to circle the planet, an irritating delay for an impatient man. Then he thought of turning on his radio. He'd turned it off because Plateau's voices of authority kept trying to tell him what to do. Now he could use their directional signal.

"—calling Douglas Hooker. Douglas Hooker, will you please answer? Do you need help? The United Nations claims you are flying a stolen ship. Is this true? You will need reentry craft to land. Are you able to establish an orbit so that they can find you? Douglas Hook—"

Hooker frowned down at the silver field in his scope screen. That was where Mount Lookitthat ought to be, according to his directional finder. So where was it?

Overcast, of course. By water vapor. There must be fog there or rain.

Hooker smiled and moved in.

He dropped fast into the mist beyond the void edge. If there were finders on him, he was caught; but what could they do about him? They couldn't approach him with anything manned. His ramscoop field was as deadly as earlier models, save for that "dead pocket." All he had to do was turn it on.

He heard nothing on the radio. They weren't sending in his direction. Good. And he was somewhere off the void edge of Mount Lookitthat.

He'd passed through Loeffler's laser message just about a year ago, ship's time. It was mealymouthed friendliness, all of it, obviously designed to lull Hooker's suspicions. All the same, it was a bad mistake on Loeffler's part. It included pictures of his house and environs.

Loeffler's house resembled his old home on Earth. It was large, almost ostentatiously large; and it seemed designed to fit its surroundings, as if it had grown from the land. Loeffler no longer lived on a cliff. He had chosen a spot in hilly country, set a few hundred feet back from the void edge in one direction and from a river in another. The river had etched itself a canyon over the millennia, and that canyon led to the void edge.

Hooker kept his ship submerged in the mist. His drive must be giving off a hellish glow, but he hoped he was far enough down for the mist to hide it. He angled his ship toward the invisible Mount Lookitthat and moved slowly in that direction.

Look for a waterfall.

It might not show at this level. It might turn to spray and evaporate high above.

Something black and formless loomed in the lesser blackness. Simultaneously, Hooker's radar beeped. Something black and huge, indefinitely huge ... Hooker backed ship and raised the thrust. The ship shot up. Up and up. The mist began to thin ... and Hooker had his first look at the side of Mount Lookitthat. It seemed infinite. It went on and on, up and down and sideways, like the surface of a world tilted from horizontal to vertical.

(After four hours of hopeless searching, the pilot of Plateau's first colony slowboat had seen Mount Lookitthat rising suddenly out of an endless white furry plain. "Lookitthat!" he'd said, four hundred years ago, in the voice of one punched in the stomach.

Hooker took his ship straight up the fluted side. Mist boiled and churned below him. Now he got his first look at Plateau's big soft sun. Tau Ceti was smaller and cooler than Sol, so that Plateau had to huddle closer for warmth, making the star look bigger from Plateau's surface. But Hooker had been traveling for more than four years of ship's time. He'd all but forgotten what a sun looked like.

Above and to the left, a waterfall. He angled that way.

The ship shot past the void edge. Suddenly most of Plateau was below him. Doug cut his thrust and looked around.

He snarled. He'd picked the wrong waterfall.

There were no spacecraft; but he could see cars all across the land, all colors, most of them staying near the ground. There were houses, and all were large. Loeffler's house must be about average in size. *Sure,* Hooker rebuked himself. *They've got more room. Did he plan that too? Hiding from me!*

Could that be it?

Hooker dropped. It was a great rounded house, like an enormous boulder with picture windows built into it. There was a river ... and it was close to the void edge ...

That was it. But was Loeffler there?

It didn't matter. Hooker back-angled his ship and came to a stop over the house. His drive licked down. The house erupted in flame.

Hooker laughed. He shouted, "You won't use *that* as a hiding place! Are you dead, Greg? If you're not, I'll find you wherever you hide!" Still laughing, he increased thrust and rose into the sky. Below him was a boiling lava pit.

He needed a city. A city would have records. He could search them to find where Loeffler was now.

But he'd have to be careful. Loeffler had taken over Earth. Hooker didn't know how long it had taken him, but he'd been on Plateau more than twelve years; he must have made some progress here.

Hooker's radio sounded.

It was a sound Hooker had never heard before. It was very loud and very terrible. Hooker reached to turn off the radio. His arms stopped halfway. He couldn't move them. He settled back in his seat. A strange, peaceful expression spread across his face. Presently a voice began to give orders, and Hooker obeyed.

"Lucky he had his radio on."

The second man nodded. "He could have wiped out this whole world. I *hate* these fusion drives. Land him, will you? I'll call the Hospital."

"Whose house was that?"

"I don't know. Let's hope nobody was in it. Will you *please* get him down? If it wears off, he'll turn off the radio; and then where will we be?"

They quit work at five o'clock. Hooker was exhausted. The chain gang had been planting trees where a generation of special mold had made sufficient soil to support them. Machines did some of the work, but mainly the chain gang used their hands.

Planting trees gave Hooker a feeling of accomplishment. Even as president of Skyhook he had never felt so useful.

He was bone tired until dinner arrived, and then he was ravenous. By the time he finished dinner, he was no longer tired. He went to his room and read until eight o'clock.

Psychotherapy was at eight.

"What I've been thinking about . . ." he told the doctor. "I want to know if I killed anyone."

"Why?"

Words formed a bottleneck in Hooker's throat. It had stopped him before during other psychotherapy sessions. He never knew how to answer that particular question. This time he forced out some kind of an answer.

"I want to know how guilty I am!"

"You know what you were trying to do. Whatever you did is done. How will feeling guilty help anything?"

"I don't *know*. But if I'm not supposed to feel guilty, why am I in prison? And don't tell me it's a hospital. I know it's a hospital. It's also a prison."

"Of course it is."

He'd killed four people. He'd killed Joanna Loeffler and her daughter and son-in-law and grandson. Greg Loeffler had been elsewhere. They waited a year to tell Hooker.

"Doug!"

Hooker jumped.

The radio yelled, "Doug, this is Greg. Answer me!"

Hooker hesitated only a moment. This was what he had dreaded. Loeffler must have a com laser on him with a directional signal in it. Hooker told the autopilot to follow it back.

The radio didn't wait. "Answer me, damn you! You know what I want!"

What was with Greg? How could he possibly expect Hooker to answer immediately? It would take hours for Hooker's com laser to cross the gap to Plateau. Hooker shifted nervously. The autopilot beeped, and he said, "I'm here, Greg. I didn't want to talk to you. I left Plateau because I couldn't face you. You must know how sorry I am for what happened."

Greg's voice didn't wait. "Doug! Why don't you answer? Is it because you think I'm going to kill you?"

Hooker came bolt upright in his chair. *Oh!*

Suddenly it was appallingly clear. Loeffler, shouting into a com laser, forgetting the lightspeed gap, was not a sane Loeffler.

Tau Ceti was a white flare in the stern scope. Wunderland's sun was too dim to see from here. Hooker turned on his ramscoop field: a complex process, most of which would be handled by the autopilot. Then he got up and began to pace.

"You cowardly, murdering . . ." Loeffler's speech turned profane. His accusations, justified at first, became wildly imaginative. Hooker listened, trying to gauge the depth of Greg's insanity. It was one more item on his burden of guilt.

Why didn't somebody stop him? A com laser was too powerful not to leak. Plateau radios must be picking this up.

And where had he gotten a com laser? The Plateau station was closed to all but qualified personnel. But Greg owned a ship with a com laser . . .

A ship just like this one.

Almost calmly, Hooker sat down at the control board. He connected the autopilot screen to the stern scope. Tau Ceti glowed brightly off center. Hooker centered it, then began to enlarge it. The screen turned yellowish-white, with a blue point moving off screen near the top. Hooker centered that, enlarged it.

A deep-blue flare with a black dot in the center.

Loeffler was coming after him.

Loeffler's hoarse voice stopped suddenly. Then it giggled. "Tricked you," it said, suddenly calm.

The stern scope turned deep red.

Damn, thought Hooker. *He did trick me.* The scope screen would not transmit more light than human eyes could bear, but there was a dial to register the light falling on the scope. That dial registered maximum. Loeffler was using his com laser as a weapon. At maximum power it could easily have blanketed Earth's solar system with a clearly read signal, but Loeffler was firing it at an object only light-hours distant.

He could kill me, Hooker thought. *He could do it.*

It wouldn't be fast. Loeffler was firing from behind at that part of Hooker's ship which was built to stand fusion flame applied for years. But eventually things would melt.

Greg was jubilant. "I'm going to burn you, Doug! Just like you burned Joanna and Marcia and Tom and little Greg! But slower! Slower, you . . ." And there was more profanity.

Needles were rising. Hull-temperature indicators, power-consumption meters, climbed toward pink zones nobody had ever expected them to touch.

Doug Hooker rubbed his eyes. He waited for an inspiration, and none came. Needles touched their pink zones. Bells rang, and Doug turned them off. After a bit he left the control room and went downstairs and lay down on the masseur couch.

He's going to kill me. The thought seemed far away, drowned in the groaning comfort of the massage.

All I wanted was a new life. I wanted to go away and start over. The couch was a hard, enveloping caress.

He won't let me. He wants to kill me. And who has a better right?

Let him kill me.

No.

It was difficult to struggle out of the couch, for the couch was not finished with him. During a massage one must be in a defeatist frame of mind. Otherwise one tenses; one's automatic defenses take over. But somehow Doug pulled himself free of the gentle, grasping embrace, and somehow he got upstairs to the control room. He was still covered with massage oil.

A man attacked has the right to defend himself. I paid for my crime.

Doug sat down in the control chair, used a key to unlock a panel. There were override switches underneath. One turned off the ship's alarm bells; one allowed excess power in the ship's circuitry; three others set up the sequence that would blow the ship apart if the drive or the ramscoop failed. Everything under the panel was an override switch for the ship's automatic safety precautions. Doug flipped one switch and closed the panel. Then he twisted a dial hard over, as far as it would go.

His com laser was already fixed on Loeffler's ship. Now it would burn.

Hooker turned off his fusion drive to reduce the heat pouring in at the ship's stern. Now he had a good chance. He was firing his laser at Loeffler's nose, where there was less protection. The massive, almost invulnerable bulk of the ramscoop would absorb most of the beam; but the lifesystem was wider than the ramscoop, and it would catch a lot of light. Eventually its walls would melt.

Hooker would kill Loeffler before Loeffler could kill Hooker.

Doug went back to the masseur couch. He felt very tired.

The lifesystem became hot—unbearably hot. When Doug felt he could stand it no longer, he went upstairs to throw another override switch. When he had done that, the cooling equipment would get more power, and his lifesystem would be cool until relays or busbars burned out.

At the control panel he found that it wasn't necessary. The ruby glow was gone from the rear scope screen. Loeffler's laser had burned out or lost its target.

Loeffler's ship was still there, still following. Hooker started his drive and turned off his laser. He was on his way to Wunderland, with Loeffler following.

Turnover. Loeffler was still behind him. Hooker had
long been convinced that Loeffler's com laser was burned
out. He had used his own com laser, but Loeffler never
answered.

And now he used it again.

"Greg," he said, "you've been following me for three
and a half years. I assume that you want justice on Wunderland. You're entitled to state your case there. But now
it's turnover time, in case you hadn't noticed, and I'm
turning around. Please do the same."

He used the gyros to swing the ship.

He was as nearly sane as a doc could make him. In
three and a half years he had almost forgotten about
Loeffler or at least had learned to accept him as an
endurable evil. And there was this: Loeffler had a doc.
He must have used it. A doc would not keep a man sane
under undue stress, but Hooker could at least hope that
Loeffler would use the law instead of weapons. The law
might punish Hooker, despite double jeopardy laws, but it
would also protect him.

He fell tail first toward Wunderland.

Now a point of light showed in the front scope. Hooker
watched for it to turn. It was small, that dot of light; for
Loeffler had fallen far behind in the race toward Wunderland. Hooker's ramscoop was taking part of Loeffler's
fuel, since Loeffler was in his shadow.

Hours after turnover the point of light moved. Loeffler
had gotten his message . . . or seen him turn. The point of
light became a line of light, then swung back to a point.

It still had a dot in the center.

"No," said Hooker.

A black dot in the center of a blob which showed
mostly blue.

"No. You're going the wrong way. Turn around, you
idiot!"

The ships were diving nose-on at each other.

Hurriedly Hooker swung his ship around. *I should have
known,* he told himself. *Loeffler wants to ram. When I*

accelerate to the side, so does he, because otherwise I might get around him. But he won't let me slow down.

If I get within three hundred miles of his ramscoop . . .

It was a stalemate. Loeffler couldn't catch Hooker, and Hooker couldn't escape Loeffler. But only Loeffler had the power to give up the game.

2590.0

Loughery came to Plateau in a colonist ramship. It was a common practice in those days for Earth to finance one-way trips to the colony worlds simply to get people off the planet. On his sixtieth birthday Loughery, having had enough of being a UN official, took the UN up on its offer.

He could have chosen any of the colony worlds. He chose Plateau because the social structure fascinated him. When he had learned enough, he intended to become a lawyer.

"That won't be easy," the mountaineer cop told him. Loughery had stopped the guy as he was coming off duty and offered to buy him drinks and dinner in return for information. "The mountaineer laws aren't as difficult as Earth's, at least from what I hear, but you may have trouble understanding the ethics behind them."

"I gather a mountaineer is a Plateau dweller."

"Right. Like a crashlander comes from We Made It and a flatlander comes from Earth."

"About the ethics."

"Hmmm." The cop scratched the back of his head. "Tell you what. The records building is still open. Let's walk over and I'll find you a few examples."

He had to use three electronic keys to get to the files. Once inside, he looked around him, lips puckered judiciously. "I'll start you with an easy one," he said. And he pulled a tape out of a drawer filled with similar tapes. "Let's run this."

They played it.

"Hooker," said Loughery. "I remember him. Dammit,

I'm the one who sent out the warning. I thought the 'doc had cured him. I'm as guilty as he is."

The cop looked very coldly at Loughery. "Could you have stopped him?"

"No. But I could have stressed the warning."

"As long as there was a warning. Now, do you understand the logic behind Hooker's sentence?"

"I'm afraid not. He got two years imprisonment for negligent homicide, with simultaneous psychotherapy and conditioning. Psychotherapy is a lost art on Earth, by the way. I don't question why he only got two years, but why negligent homicide?"

"There's the crux. He wasn't guilty of murder, was he?"

"I'd say Yes."

"But we say he was insane. That's a legitimate plea."

"Then why was he punished?"

"For letting himself become insane. He knew he was a potential paranoid; all he had to do was stay in reach of a working autodoc. And he didn't. Four people died. Negligent homicide."

Loughery nodded. His head was spinning.

"What isn't here on the tape is the follow-up. Loeffler tried to kill Hooker."

"Oh?"

"Hooker left in a ramship. Loeffler went after him. They had a big duel with com lasers. Now, let's suppose Hooker had won that battle and killed Loeffler. What then?"

"Self-defense."

"Not at all. Murder."

"But why?"

"Loeffler was insane. And he was insane as a direct result of Hooker's crime, not through Loeffler's own negligence. Hooker could run or hide or yell for help or talk Loeffler into accepting treatment. He could not strike back. If he'd killed Loeffler, he'd have gotten fifty years for murder."

"Maybe I should be a farmer. What did happen?"

"I wouldn't know. Neither of them ever came back to Plateau."

120,000 APPROX.

Fifty years?

The flap of a gnat's wing.

The long chase was nearing its end. At first Hooker had gained on his pursuer, for Loeffler's ramscoop was not getting as much hydrogen as Hooker's. Loeffler's ship was in the shadow of Hooker's. At one time they had been light-years apart. But now Loeffler's ship was gaining, for Hooker's ship had reached terminal velocity.

There had to be a limit on the velocity of a fusion-powered ramship. It was this: when the exhaust velocity of the fusion drive was no greater than the velocity of the interstellar hydrogen hitting the ramscoop, the ship could go no faster. Hooker had reached that limit tens of thousands of years ago. And so had his pursuer.

But Loeffler's ship was using hydrogen that had slipped through Hooker's ramscoop. The hydrogen wasn't hitting Loeffler's ramscoop field as hard. It had absorbed velocity from Hooker's.

Loeffler was close behind.

The chase could end within decades.

Once upon a time Hooker had hoped Loeffler would give up and turn around. Surely he would realize that Hooker could not be caught! But the years had stretched to decades, and every year Loeffler waited meant four years trying to get back to Wunderland. He'd have had to decelerate before he could begin the long flight home, and deceleration would take as many decades as he had spent fleeing. So Hooker had spent two hours a day before the scope screen, watching the stars crawl past year by year, waiting for Loeffler to turn around.

The years had stretched into centuries, and still Hooker spent two hours a day watching the rear scope screen. Now there were no more stars ahead, but only the distant muddled dots of galaxies, and the stars behind were taking on a vagueness like curdled milk. And when the centuries had become millennia, Hooker no longer believed his enemy would let him go. But still he spent two hours per ship's day before the scope screen, watching the galaxy drop away.

He was totally a man of habits now. He had not had an original thought in centuries. The ship's clock governed his life in every detail, taking him to the autodoc or the kitchen or the gym or the steam room or the bedroom or the bathroom. You'd have thought he was an ancient robot following a circular tape, no longer able to respond to outside stimuli.

He looked more like an aged robot than an aged man. From a distance he would have looked twenty. The doc had taken good care of him, but there were things the doc could not do. The oldest living man had been short of four hundred years old when that machine was made. Moscow Motors had had no way of knowing what a man would need when his life could be measured in tens of thousands of years. So the face was young; but the veneer was cracked, and the muscles no longer showed any kind of expression, and the habit patterns of the man were deeply grooved into the DNA memory processes of the brain.

By now the chase meant nothing to Hooker. In any case he should have been incapable of original thought.

They had come up along the galactic axis. Hooker, looking into the scope screen, saw the galaxy face-on. It was not bright, but it was wide. The galaxy showed like varicolored dyes poured into viscous ink, red dye and yellow and blue and green, but mostly red. Then the whole mass swirled around the center of the pot, so that the center glowed all colors—a continuous mass of stars packed so closely as to blot out the blackness behind, but it was not bright. There is dust even in intergalactic space. Nearly one hundred thousand light-years of dust shaded the galaxy from Hooker's view. The arms were almost black, the glowing areas spotted with black gaps and dust clouds. Everything was reddened and dimmed by Doppler shift.

He could not see Loeffler.

Habit used his fingers to magnify the view, slowly. The

galaxy, already wide enough to fill the scope screen, expanded. In the core, individual, red giant stars appeared, bigger than anything in the arms. A blue-white spot appeared, and grew.

It grew until it filled the screen. There was a black dot in the center. And that grew too.

Hooker had watched for nearly an hour before the thought stirred in his brain. That hadn't happened for a long time, but it did happen. Hooker's memory capacity was nearly full, but his brain was in good working order, and he was guaranteed sane.

I wonder how much damage I did.

The thought threatened to skip away, but he grabbed for it, sensing somehow that it might be important. *I held my com laser on him for hours. I may have damaged him. I've never seen him broadside; I'd have no way of knowing. But if his ship is badly hurt, I could finish the job with my laser. It never burned out. His did.*

He'd have to wait until Loeffler got closer. The thought slipped away . . . and returned two days later. *I wonder how much damage I did?*

How would I find out?

Every day he remembered the problem. A month and a half after he had first thought of it, he thought of the answer.

He could turn the ship sideways to fire the fusion drive laterally. Loeffler would imitate him to keep him from sneaking past and home. That would put Loeffler broadside to him.

He had done it once before, trying to make turnover for Wunderland. But Loeffler had been too far away for the scope to show details. If he did it now . . .

He did.

Then he focused one of the side scopes on Loeffler, enlarged the image as far as it would go, and waited.

The time came when he should have gone to the steam room. He was half out of his seat, but he couldn't leave. Loeffler hadn't turned yet. The ships were light-hours apart. Hooker forced himself to sit down and to stay down, gripping the arms of the control chair with both hands. His teeth began to chatter. He shivered. A deadening cold spread through him. He sneezed.

The shivering and the sneezing continued for a long time, then passed. Steam-room time was over.

Loeffler began to turn.

And Hooker knew why he had never turned for home.

There was no lifesystem at all. The lifesystem had always been the most fragile part of the ship. Aeons ago Hooker's laser had played over Loeffler's lifesystem and melted it to slag. Nothing was left but tattered shards, polished at the edges by gas molecules slipping through the ramscoop shield.

Loeffler hadn't died fast. He'd had time to program the autopilot to arrange a collision course with Hooker's ship.

Loeffler might have given up the chase long ago, but the autopilot never would, never could.

Hooker turned off his scope screen and went down to the steam room. His schedule was shot to hell. He was still trying to readjust when, years later, Loeffler's ramscoop field swept across his ship like an invisible wing.

Two empty ships drove furiously toward the edge of the universe, all alone.

THE HANDICAPPED

WE FLEW ON skycycles over a red desert, under the soft red sun of Down. I let Jilson stay ahead. He was my guide, and I hadn't been flying a skycycle long. I'm a flatlander. I had spent most of my life in the cities of Earth, where any flying vehicle is illegal unless fully automated.

I liked flying. I wasn't good at it yet, but there was plenty of room for mistakes with the desert so far below.

"There," said Jilson, pointing.

"Where?"

"Down there. Follow me." His skycycle swung easily to the left and began to slow and drop. I followed more clumsily, overcorrecting and dropping behind. Eventually I spotted something.

"That little cone?"

"That's it."

From up here the desert looked lifeless. It wasn't, any more than the deserts of most inhabited worlds are lifeless. Down there, invisible at this height, were spiky dry plants with water stored in their cores; flowers that bloomed after a rain and left their seeds to wait a year or ten years for the next rainfall; insect-things with four legs, unjointed; skinny warm-blooded quadrupeds from the size of a fox on down, who were always hungry.

There was a five-foot hairy cone with a bald, rounded top. Only its shadow made it visible as we dropped toward it. Its lank hair was the exact color of the reddish sand.

We landed next to it and got off.

I was beginning to think I'd been played for a fool. The thing didn't look like an animal. It looked like a big cactus. Sometimes a cactus had hair just like that.

"We're behind it," said Jilson. He was dark and massive

and taciturn. On Down there was no such animal as the professional guide. I'd talked Jilson into taking me out into the desert for a fair fee, but it hadn't bought his friendship. I think he was trying to make that clear. "Come around in front," he said.

We circled the hairy cone, and I started to laugh.

The Grog showed just five features.

Where it touched flat rock, the base of the cone was some four feet across. Long, straight hair brushed the rock like a floor-length skirt. A few inches up, two small, widely separated paws poked through the curtain of hair— the size and shape of a Great Dane's forepaws, but naked and pink. A yard higher two more paws poked through, but on these the toes were extended to curving, useless fingers. Finally, above the forepaws was a yard-long lipless gash of a mouth, half-hidden by hair, curved very slightly upward at the corners. No eyes. The cone looked like some Stone Age carved idol or like a cruel cartoon of a feudal monk.

Jilson waited patiently for me to stop laughing. "It's funny," he admitted with reluctance. "But it's intelligent. There's a brain under that bald top, bigger than yours and mine combined."

"It's never tried to communicate with you?"

"Not with me nor with anyone else."

"Does it make tools?"

"With what? Look at its hands!" He regarded me with amusement. "This is what you wanted to see, wasn't it?"

"Yes. I came a long way for nothing."

"Anyway, now you've seen it."

I laughed again. Eyeless, motionless, my potential customer sat like a fat lap dog in begging position. "Come on," I said, "let's go back."

A fool's errand. I'd spent two weeks in hyperspace to get here. The fare would come out of business expenses, but ultimately I'd pay it; I'd own the business one day.

Jilson took his check without comment, folded it twice and stuck it in his lighter pocket. He said, "Buy you a drink?"

"Sure."

We left our rented skycycles at the Downtown city limit and boarded a pedwalk. Jilson led the way from crossing to crossing until we were sliding past a great silver cube with a wriggling blue sign: CZILLER'S HOUSE OF IRISH COFFEE. Inside, the place was still a cube, a one-story building forty meters high. Padded horseshoe-shaped sofas covered the entire floor, so close you could hardly squeeze between them, each with its little disk of a table nestling in the center. From the floor a tinsel abstraction rose like a great tree, spreading its wide, glittering arms protectively over the customers, rising forty meters to touch the ceiling. The bartending machinery was halfway up the tree.

"Interesting place," said Jilson. "These booths were built to float." He waited for me to express surprise. When I didn't, he went on: "It didn't work out. Lovely idea though. The chairs would swoop through the air; and if the people at two tables wanted to meet, they'd slide their booths together and lock them magnetically."

"Sounds like fun."

"It was fun. The guy who thought it up must have forgot that people come to a bar to get drunk. They'd crash the booths together like bumper cars. They'd go as high as they could and then pour out their drinks. The people underneath didn't like that, and maybe there'd be a fight. I remember seeing a guy get thrown out of a booth. He'd have been dead if that tinsel centerpiece hadn't caught him. I hear another guy did die; he missed the branches."

"So they grounded the booths."

"No. First they tried to make the course automatic. But you could still pour drinks on the people below, and there was more skill in it. It got to be a game. Then one night some idiot figured out how to short the autopilot, but he forgot the manual controls had been disconnected. His booth landed on another and injured three important people. *Then* they grounded the booths."

A floating tray served us two chilled glasses and a bottle of Blue Fire 2728. The bar was two-thirds empty this early, and quiet. When the freeze-distilled wine was half gone, I explained why they call Blue Fire the "Crashlander's Peacemaker": the shape of the flexible plastic bottle, narrow-necked with a flaring mouth, plus the weight of the fluid inside make it a dandy bludgeon.

Jilson was turning almost garrulous now that I was no longer his employer. I was talking a lot too. Not that I felt like it; it was just—well, hell, here I was, light-years from Earth and business and the good people I knew, way out at the edge of human space. Down: a former Kzinti world, mostly empty, with a few scattered dots of civilization and a few great scars of old war, a world where the farmers had to use ultraviolet lamps to grow crops because of that red dwarf sun. Here I was. I was going to enjoy it if it killed me.

I *was* enjoying it. Jilson was good company, and the Blue Fire didn't hurt at all. We ordered another bottle. The noise level rose as cocktail hour drew near.

"Something I've been wondering," said Jilson. "Mind if we talk business?"

"No. Whose business?"

"Yours."

"Not at all. Why ask?"

"It's traditional, to us. Some people don't like giving away their tricks of the trade. Others like to forget work completely after hours."

"That makes sense. What's the question?"

"Why do you pronounce *Handicapp*ed as though it had a capital *H?*"

"Oh. Well, if I said it with a small *h,* you'd think I meant humans, wouldn't you? Potential paranoids, albino crashlanders, boosterspice allergics, people with missing limbs and resistance to transplants—handicapped like that."

"Yah."

"Whereas what I deal with are sentient beings who evolved with minds but with nothing that would serve as hands."

"O-oh. Like dolphins?"

"Right. Are there dolphins on Down?"

"Hell yes. Who else would run our fishing industry?"

"You know those things you pay them off in? They look

like a squirt-jet motorboat motor with two padded metal hands attached."

"The Dolphin's Hands. Sure. We sell 'em other stuff, tools and sonic things to move fish around, but the Dolphin's Hands are what they mainly need."

"I make them."

Jilson's eyes jerked up. Then ... I could feel him withdrawing, backing off as he realized that the man across from him could probably buy Down. Damn! But the best I could do now was ignore the fact.

"I should have said, My father's company makes them. One day I'll direct Garvey Limited, but my great grandfather will have to die first. I doubt he ever will."

Jilson smiled, with little strain. "I know people like that."

"Yah. Some people seem to dry out as they get older. They get dryer and tougher instead of getting fat, until you think they'll never change again; and they seem to get more and more energetic, like there's a thermonuclear source inside them. Gee-Squared is like that. A great old man. I don't see enough of him."

"You sound proud of him. Why does he have to die?"

"It's like a custom. Dad's running the company now. If he gets in trouble, he can go to *his* father, who ran the company before him. If Gee-Prime can't handle it, they both go to Gee-Squared."

"Funny names."

"Not to me. That's like a tradition too."

"Sorry. What are you doing on Down?"

"We don't deal only with dolphins." The Blue Fire made me want to lecture. "Look, Jilson. We know of three sentient beings without hands. Right?"

"More than that. Puppeteers use their mouths. Outsiders—"

"But they build their own tools, dammit. I'm talking about beasts who can't even crack themselves a fist-ax or hold a lighter: dolphins, bandersnatchi, and that thing we saw today."

"The Grog. Well?"

"Well, don't you see that there must be Handicapped

species all over the galaxy? Minds but no hands. I tell you, Jilson, it gives me the shivers. For as long as we expand to other stars, we're going to meet more and more handless, toolless, helpless civilizations. Sometimes we won't even recognize them. What are we going to do about them?"

"Build Dolphin's Hands for them."

"Well, yes, but we can't just *give* them away. Once one species starts depending on another, they become parasites."

"How about bandersnatchi? Do you build Hands for bandersnatchi?"

"Yes. Lots bigger, of course." A bandersnatch is twice the size of a brontosaur. Its skeleton is flexible but has no joints; the only breaks in its smooth white skin are the tufts of sensory bristles on either side of its tapering blank head. It moves on a rippling belly foot. Bandersnatchi live in the lowlands of Jinx, browsing off the gray yeast along the shorelines. You'd think they were the most helpless things in known space ... until you saw one bearing down on you like a charging mountain. Once I saw an ancient armored-car crushed flat across a lowlands rock, straddled by the broken bones of the beast that ran it down."

"Okay. How do they pay for their machines?"

"Hunting privileges."

Jilson looked horrified. "I don't believe you."

"I hardly believed it myself, but it's true." I hunched forward across the tiny table. "Here's how it works. The bandersnatchi have to control their population; there's only so much shoreline to feed on in the lowlands. They also have to control boredom. Can you imagine how bored they must have been before men came to Jinx? So what they've done is, they've made a treaty with the Jinx government. Now, say a man wants a bandersnatchi skeleton, he's going to build a trophy room under it. He goes to the Jinx government and gets a license. The license tells him what equipment he can take down to the lowlands, which is inhabited only by bandersnatchi because the atmospheric pressure is enough to crush a man's lungs and the temperature is enough to cook him. If he gets caught taking extra weapons, he goes to prison for a long time.

"Maybe he makes it back with a body; maybe he doesn't come back. His equipment gives him odds of about sixty-forty. But either way, the bandersnatchi get eighty percent of the license fee, which is a thousand stars flat. With that, they buy things."

"Like Hands."

"Right. Oh, one more thing. A dolphin can control his Hands with his tongue, but a bandersnatch can't. We have to build the control setup directly into the nerves, by surgery. It's not difficult."

Jilson shook his head and dialed for another bottle.

"They do other things," I said. "The Institute of Knowledge has instruments in the lowlands—laboratories and such. There are things the Institute wants to know about what happens under lowland pressures and temperatures. The bandersnatchi run all the expcriments, using the Hands."

"So you came here for a new market."

"I was told there was a new sentient life-form on Down, one that doesn't use tools."

"You've changed your mind?"

"Just about. Jilson, what makes you think they're sentient?"

"The brains. They're huge."

"Nothing else?"

"No."

"Their brains might not work like ours. The nerve cells might be different."

"Look, we're about to get technical. Let's drop it for tonight." And with that, Jilson pushed the bottles and glasses to one side and stood up on the table. He peered around Cziller's House of Irish Coffee, swinging his head in a slow arc. "Hah! Garvey, I've spotted a cousin and one of her friends. Let's join 'em. It's almost dinnertime."

I thought we'd be taking them to dinner. Not at all. Sharon and Lois built our dinner, handmade, starting with raw materials we picked up in a special store. Seeing raw food for the first time, practically in the state in which it had emerged from the ground or been cut from a dead beast, made me a little queasy. I hope I didn't show it. But dinner tasted fine.

After dinner and some polite drinking and talk, back to the hotel. I went to sleep planning to hop a ship the next morning.

I woke in total darkness around oh four hundred, staring at the invisible ceiling and seeing a round-topped cone with reddish lank hair and a faintly smiling mouth. Smiling at me in gentle derision. The cone had secrets. I'd come *that* close to guessing one this afternoon; I'd seen something without noticing it.

Don't ask me how I knew. With a crystalline certainty that I could not doubt, I *knew*.

But I couldn't remember what I'd seen.

I got up and dialed the kitchen for some hot chocolate and a tuna sandwich.

Why should they be intelligent? Why would sedentary cones evolve a brain?

I wondered how they reproduced. Not bisexually; they couldn't get to each other. Unless—but of course there must be a motile stage. Those leftover paws . . .

What would they eat? They couldn't find food; they'd have to wait for it to come to them, like any sessile animal: clams, sea anemones, or the Gummidgy "orchid" I keep in my living room so I can shock hell out of guests.

They *had* a brain. Why? What did they do with it, sit and think about all they were missing?

I needed data. Tomorrow I'd contact Jilson.

At eleven the next morning we were in the Downtown Zoo.

Behind a repulsor field something snapped and snarled at us: something like an idiot god's attempt to make a hairy bulldog. The animal had no nose, and its mouth was a flat, lipless slit hiding two serrated horseshoe-shaped cutting surfaces. Its long, coarse hair was the color of sand lit by red sunlight. The forepaws had four long, spreading toes, so that they looked like chicken feet.

"I recognize those feet."

"Yah," said Jilson. "It's a young Grog. In this stage they mate. Then the female finds a rock and settles down. When she's big enough, she starts having children. That's the theory, anyway. They won't do it in captivity."

"What about the males?"

"In the next cage."

The males, two of them, were the size of Chihuahuas, with about the same temperament. But they had the serrated horseshoe teeth and the coarse reddish hair.

"Jilson, if they're intelligent, why are they in cages?"

"If you think that's bad, wait'll you see the lab. Look, Garvey, what you've got to keep in mind is that nobody's proven they're intelligent. Until somebody does, they're experimental animals."

They had an odd, almost pleasant, odor, faint enough so that you stopped noticing it in two or three seconds. I peered in at the snapping motile-stage female. "What happens then? Does everyone suddenly get ashamed of himself?"

"I doubt it. Do you happen to know what humans did to dolphins while trying to prove they were intelligent?"

"Brain probes and imprisonment. But that was a long time ago."

"The scientists were trying to prove dolphins were intelligent, so they had to be treated like experimental animals. Why not? It makes sense. In the end they did the species a service. If their assumption had been wrong, they'd only have wasted time on animals. And it gave the dolphins a hell of an incentive to prove they *were* intelligent."

We reached the lab shortly after noon. It was the Laboratory for Xenobiological Research, a rectangular building beyond the outskirts of the city, surrounded by brown fields marked with rectangular arrays of ultraviolet lamps on tall poles. In the distance we could see the Ho River, with flocks of water skiers skimming across its muddy surface behind puller units.

A Dr. Fuller showed us through the lab. He was an obvious crashlander: a towering albino, seven feet tall, with a slender torso and tapering, almost skeletal, limbs. "You're interested in the Grogs? I don't blame you. They're very difficult to study, you know. Their behavior tells nothing. They sit. When something comes by, they eat it. And they bear young."

He had several presessile cones, the bulldog-sized quadrupeds, in cages. There was another cage containing two of the little males. They didn't bark at him, and he treated them with tenderness and something like love. It seemed to me that he was a happy man. I could sympathize with him. Down must look like paradise to an albino from We Made It. You can walk around outside all year, the soil grows things, and you don't need tannin pills under the red sun.

"They learn fast," he said earnestly, "that is, they do well in mazes. But they certainly aren't intelligent. About as intelligent as a dog. They grow fast, and they eat horrendously. Look at this one." He picked up a very fat, round-bottomed female. "In a few days she'll be looking for a place to anchor."

"What will you do then? Turn her loose?"

"We're going to raise her just outside the lab. We've picked her a good anchor rock and built a cage around it. She'll go into the cage until she changes form, and then we can remove the cage. We've tried this before," he added, "but it hasn't worked out. They die. They won't eat, even when we offer them live meat."

"What makes you think this one will live?"

"We have to keep trying. Perhaps we'll find out what we're doing wrong."

"Has a Grog ever attacked a human being?"

"To the best of my knowledge, never."

To me, that was as good an answer as No, because I was trying to find out if they were intelligent.

Consider the days when it was first suspected that the cetaceans were Earth's second sentient order of life. It was known, then, that dolphins had many times helped swimmers out of difficulty and that no dolphin had ever been known to attack a human being. Well, what difference did it make whether they had *not* attacked humans or whether they had done so only when there was no risk of being caught at it? Either statement was proof of intelligence.

"Of course, a man may simply be too big for a Grog to eat. Look at this," said Dr. Fuller, turning on a microscope screen. The screen showed a section of a nerve cell. "From a Grog's brain. We've done some work on the Grog's nervous system. The nerves transmit impulses more slowly than human nerves, but not much more. We've found that a strongly stimulated nerve can fire off the nerve next to it, just as in terrestrial chordates."

"Are the cones intelligent, in your opinion?"

Dr. Fuller didn't know. He took a long time saying it, but that's what it boiled down to. It distressed him; his ears turned red beneath the transparent skin. He wanted to know. Perhaps he felt he had a right to know.

"Then tell me this. Is there any evolutionary reason for them to have developed intelligence?"

"That's a much better question." But he hesitated over the answer. "I'll tell you this. There is a terrestrial marine animal which starts life as a free-swimming worm with a notochord. It later settles down as a sessile animal, and it gives up the notochord at the same time."

"Amazing! What's a notochord?"

He laughed. "Like your spinal cord. A notochord is a rope of nervous connection which branches into the trunk nerves of the body. More primitive forms have sensory connections, but arranged without order. More advanced forms wrap a spine around the notochord and become vertebrates."

"And this beast gives up its notochord?"

"Yes. It's retrograde development."

"But the Grogs are different."

"That's right. They don't develop their large brains until after they settle down. And, no, I can't imagine an evolutionary reason. They shouldn't need a brain. They shouldn't have a brain. All they do in life is sit and wait for morsels of food to hop by."

"You speak almost poetically when you turn your mind to it."

"Thank you—I think. Mr. Garvey, will you come this

way? You too, Jil. I want to show you a Grog central nervous system. Then you'll be as confused as I am."

The brain was big, as advertised, and globular, and a strange color: almost the gray of human gray matter but with a yellow tinge. It might have been the preservative. The hindbrain was almost unnoticeable, and the spinal cord was a limp white string, uselessly thin, tapering almost to a thread before it ended in a multiple branching. What could that monstrous brain control, with practically no spinal cord to carry its messages?

"I gather most of the nerves to the body don't go through the spinal cord."

"I believe you're wrong, Mr. Garvey. I've tried without success to find supplementary nerves." He was smiling slightly. Now I had a piece of the problem. We could *both* stay awake nights.

"Is the nervous material any different from the motile form's brain?"

"No. The motile form has a smaller brain and a thicker spinal cord. As I said, its intelligence is about that of a dog. Its brain is somewhat larger, which is to be expected when you consider the slower rate of propagation of the nerve impulse."

"Right. Does it help you to know that you've ruined my day?"

"It does, yes." He smiled down at me. We were friends. He was flattered to know that I understood what he was talking about. Otherwise I wouldn't have looked so puzzled.

The big soft sun was halfway down the sky when we got out. We stopped to look at the anchor pen Dr. Fuller had set up outside: one big flat rock with sand heaped around it, all enclosed in a wide fence with a gate. A smaller pen against the fence housed a colony of white rabbits.

"One last question, Doctor. How do they eat? They can't just sit and wait for food to pop into their mouths."

"No, they have a very long, slender tongue. I wish I

could see it in use sometime. They won't eat in captivity; they won't eat when a human being is anywhere near."

We said our good-byes and took our skycycles up.

"It's only fifteen ten," said Jilson. "Do you want another look at a wild Grog before you leave Down?"

"I think so, yes."

"We could get out into the desert and back before sunset."

And so we turned west. The Ho River slipped beneath us and then a long stretch of cultivated fields. Long pink clouds striped the sky.

They can't be intelligent, I was thinking. *They can't.*

"What?"

"Sorry, Jilson. Was I talking out loud?"

"Yah. You saw that brain, didn't you?"

"I did."

"Then how can you say they're not intelligent?"

"They've got no *use* for intelligence."

"Does a dolphin? Or a sperm whale, or a bandersnatch?"

"Yes, yes, no. Think it through. A dolphin has to hunt down its food. It has to outwit hungry killer-whales. A sperm whale also has the killer-whale problem, or used to. Then there were whaling ships. The smarter they were, the longer they could live.

"Remember, cetaceans are mammals. They developed some brains on land. When they went back to the sea, they grew, and their brains grew too. The better their brains were, the better they could control their muscles, and the more agile they were in water. They needed brains, and they had a head start."

"What about bandersnatchi?"

"You know perfectly well that evolution didn't produce the bandersnatch."

A moment of silence. Then, "What?"

"You really don't know?"

"I've never heard of a life form being produced without evolution. How did it happen?"

I told him.

Once upon a time, a billion and a half years ago, there

was an intelligent biped species. Intelligent—but not very. But they had a natural ability to control the minds of any sentient race they came across. Today we call them Slavers. At its peak the Slaver Empire included most of the galaxy.

One of their slave races had been the tnuctip, a highly advanced, highly intelligent species already practicing biological engineering when the Slavers found them. The Slavers gave them limited freedom, after they found the worth of those freethinking brains. In return the tnuctipun had built them biological tools. Air plants for their spacecraft, stage trees with shaped solid-fuel rocket cores, racing animals, bandersnatchi. The bandersnatch was a meat animal. It would eat anything, and everything but its skeleton was edible.

There had come a day, a billion and a half years ago, when the Slavers found that most of the tnuctip gifts were traps. The rebellion had been a long time building, and the Slavers had underestimated their slaves. To win that war they had been forced to use a weapon which exterminated not only the tnuctipun, but every other sentient species then in the galaxy. Then, without slaves, the Slavers too had died.

Scattered through known space, on odd worlds and between stars, were the relics of the Slaver Empire. Some were Slaver artifacts, protected against time by stasis fields. Others were more or less mutated tnuctip creations: sunflowers, stage trees, ships' air plants floating naked in space in cellophane bubbles; and bandersnatchi.

The bandersnatch had been a tnuctip trap. It had been built sentient so that it could be used as a spy. Somehow the tnuctipun had made it immune to the Slaver power. Thus it had lived through the revolution.

For what?

The Jinxian bandersnatchi spent their lives in a soupy, pressurized fog, browsing off the ancient food yeast that still covered the ocean a foot deep in cheesy gray scum. No data reached their senses but for the taste of yeast and the everlasting gray mist. They had brains to think with but nothing to think about ... until the coming of man.

"And it can't mutate," I concluded. "So you can forget the bandersnatch. He's the exception that proves the rule. All other known Handicapped needed brains before their brains developed."

"And they're all cetaceans from Earth's oceans."

"Well—"

Jilson made a razzing noise. Hell, he was right. They *were* all cetaceans.

We'd left the plowed lands far behind. Gradually the plains became a desert. I was beginning to feel more comfortable with the beast under me—this platform with a saddle, and an oversized lift-belt motor, an air pump, and a force-field generator to stop the wind. Feeling less likely to make a mistake, I could fly lower, with less room to correct before I hit sand. From this close the desert was alive. There, rolling before the wind, was a wild cousin to the tumbleweeds I'd seen in the Zoo of Earth. There, a straight stalk with orange leaves around the base, fleshy leaves with knife-sharp edges to discourage herbivores. There, another, and a fox-sized herbivore cleverly eating out the center of a leaf. It looked up, saw us, and disappeared into motion. There, a vivid flash of scarlet, some desert plant which had picked an odd time to bloom.

The soft red sun made everything look like the décor in a nightclub I know. It's decorated as Mars ought to be, as Mars was before space flight. A distance illusion: red sand; straight canals running with improbably clear, pure water; crystal towers reaching high, high, toward big fat crescent moons. Suddenly I wanted a drink.

I dug in my saddlebags, hoping to find a flask. It was there, and it was heavy with fluid. I pinched the top open, tilted it to my lips—and almost choked. Martini! A half-pint martini, a little too sweet, but far colder than ice cold. I sipped at it, twice, and put it away. "I like Downers," I said.

"Good. Why?"

"No flatlander would think to put a martini in a rental skycycle unless he was asked to."

"Harry's a nice guy. Woop, there's a cone."

I looked down and right, searching for sand-colored hair against sand. The cone was in its own shadow; it practically jumpèd at me. And equally suddenly, I knew what had awakened me in the dark morning.

"What's wrong?" asked Jilson. I realized that I'd gasped.

"Nothing. Jilson, I don't know all I should about Downer animals. Do they excrete solids?"

"Do they—? Hey, that was nicely put. Yes, they do." He tilted his vehicle down toward the cone.

It sat firmly on a tilted flat rock, which lifted one edge out of the sand. The rock was absolutely clean.

"Then Grogs do too."

"Right." Jilson landed.

I drifted in beside him, dropping the skycycle joltingly hard. The Grog sat facing us, faintly smiling.

"Well, where's the evidence? Who cleans up after this thing?"

Jilson scratched his head. He walked around the base of the Grog and came back, looking puzzled. "Funny, I never thought of that. Scavengers?"

"Maybe."

"Is it important?"

"Maybe. Most sessile animals live in water. The water carries everything away."

"There's a sessile thing from Gummidgy—"

"I've got one. But the orchid-thing lives in trees. It attaches itself to a nice thick horizontal tree-branch, with its tail hanging over the edge."

"Mmm." He seemed uninterested. No doubt he was right; some scavenger cleaned up after the Grog. But it didn't sound right. Why would the parasite animal do such a good job?

The Grog and I faced each other.

As a rule the Handicapped seem to suffer from sensory deprivation. Cetaceans live underwater; bandersnatchi live in heated, pressurized fog. Maybe it's too early to make such rules, but it's for sure that a Handicapped will have trouble experimenting with his environment. Experiments generally require tools.

But the Grog had real troubles. Blind, numb in all its extremities—due to the nearly useless spinal cord—unable even to move to a different location, what could be its picture of the universe?

Somehow I found myself staring at its hands.

Hands. Useless, of course, but still hands. Four fingers with tiny claws set around the tiny palm like the fingers of a mechanical grab.

"It didn't evolve at all. It devolved!"

Jilson looked up. He was using his skycycle as the only convenient thing to sit on for miles around. "What are you talking about?"

"The Grog. It's got vestigial hands. Once it must have been a higher form of life."

"Or a climbing animal, like a monkey."

"I don't think so. I think it had a brain and hands and mobility. Then something happened, and it lost its civilization. Now it's lost its mobility and its hands."

"Why would it stop moving?"

"Maybe there was a shortage of food. Not moving conserved energy." And because that was the sheerest guesswork, I added, "Or maybe it got in the habit of watching too much tridee. I know people who don't move for weeks."

"During the Interworld Playoffs my cousin Earnie— Hell with it! You think that's the answer, do you?"

"Yes. It's in a trap. No eyes, no sensory input, no way to do anything with what it does think about. It's like a blind, deaf, and dumb baby with glove anesthesia all over."

"It's still got the brain."

"Like our appendix. It'll lose that too."

"You're the one who was worried about the Handicapped. Can't you do anything for it?"

"Euthanasia, maybe. No, not even that. Let's go back to Downtown." I walked through sand toward my cycle, sick with discouragement. Bandersnatchi had needed men to tell them about the stars. But what could you tell a hairy cone?

No, it was back to Downtown for me, and then back to

Earth. There are people no doctor and no psychiatrist can help, and there are species equally beyond aid. With the Grogs there was no place to start.

A few feet from the cycle I sat down cross-legged in the sand. Jilson got down beside me. We faced the Grog, waiting.

By and by Jilson said, "What are we waiting for?"

I shrugged. I didn't know. But Jilson didn't move, and neither did I. I knew with a crystalline certainty that we were doing the right thing.

Simultaneously, we turned from the Grog to look into the desert.

Something the size of a rat came hopping toward us, kicking up dust. Behind it, another and another. They hopped laboriously across the sand, springing high, and stopped in an arc facing the Grog.

The Grog turned toward them—not the way you'd turn your neck, but turning all over. It looked sightlessly at the sand rats, and the sand rats perched on their hind legs and looked back.

The Grog's mouth opened. It was a cavern, and the tongue was coiled on its pink floor. The tongue moved like a lash, invisibly fast, flick, flick. Two of the rats were gone. The mouth (*not* too small for a man) dropped shut, smiling gently.

The third rat was there on its hind legs. None of them had tried to run. They might just as well have—

Again the Grog's mouth dropped open. The last sand rat took a running leap and landed on the coiled tongue. The mouth closed for the last time, and the cone turned back to face us.

I had the answers all at once, intuitively, with the same force of conviction that now had me sitting cross-legged on the sand.

The Grog was psychic or something similar. It could control minds, even minds as insignificant as a sand rat's.

That was the purpose of the Grog's large brain. Its intelligence was a side effect of its power. For aeons the Grogs had called their food to them. They did not hunt after childhood. Once the brain had developed, they never needed to move again.

They didn't need eyes; they had little need of other sensory perceptions. They used the senses of other animals.

They directed the scavengers who cleaned their rocks, and their pelts too, when necessary. Their mind control brought meat animals to their presessile female young, directed their breeding habits, and guided them to proper anchor rocks.

They were now feeding information directly into my brain.

I said, "But why me?"

I knew, with a crystalline certainty I was learning to recognize. The Grogs were aware of what they were missing. They had read the minds of passers-by: first Kzinti warriors, then human miners, explorers, sightseers. And my business was the Handicapped. They had learned of the Dolphin's Hands. They had primed Jilson and others to *know,* without evidence, that the Grogs were sentient, and to say so when the right person should appear.

Without evidence: that was important. They had to know what they were getting into before they committed themselves. Men like Dr. Fuller could investigate if they liked; it would look suspicious if they were prevented. But *something* kept them from noticing the handlike appearance of those tiny forepaws, the lack of biological wastes around a wild Grog.

Could I help them?

The question was suddenly an obsession. I shook my head to fight it off. "I don't know. Why did you wait so long to show yourselves?"

Fear.

"Why? Are we that terrifying?"

I waited for an answer. None came. There was no sudden, utterly convincing bit of information in my brain.

Then they feared even me. Me, helpless before a flicking tongue and an iron mind. Why?

I was sure that the Grogs had devolved from some

higher, bipedal form of life. The tiny hands, like mechanical grabs, were characteristic. As was that eerie mental control ...

I tried to stand up, to run. My legs wouldn't lift me. I tried to blank my thoughts, to hide what I'd guessed, but that was useless. They could read my mind. They knew.

"It's the Slaver power. Your ancestors were Slavers." And here I sat, with my mind wide open and helpless.

Soothingly, with characteristic crystal certainty, I realized:

That the Grogs knew nothing of Slavers. That as far as they knew, they had been there forever.

That the Grogs *couldn't* be idiot enough to try for a takeover bid. They were sessile. They couldn't move. Their leftover Slaver power could reach less than halfway around the world, with all the Grog individuals working together. How could they dream of attacking a species who controlled all space in a thirty-light-year-diameter sphere? Fear alone had kept them from letting mankind know what they were—fear of extermination.

"You could be lying about how far you can reach. I'd never know."

Nothing. Nothing touched my mind. I stood up. Jilson watched me, then got up and mechanically brushed himself off. He looked at the Grog, opened his mouth, closed it, gulped, and said, "Garvey! What did it do to us?"

"Didn't it tell you?" In the same moment I was certain it hadn't.

"It made me sit down; it put on a show with sand rats ... you saw it too, didn't you?"

"Yes."

"Then it left us sitting awhile. You talked to it. Then suddenly we could get up."

"That's right. But it talked to me, too."

"I *told* you it was intelligent!"

"Jilson, can you find your way back here in the morning?"

"Absolutely not. But I'll set your skycycle to record your course so you can get back. If you're sure you want to."

"I'm not. But I want the choice."

The sun was a smoky red glow in the west, fading over a blue-black horizon.

I'd laughed.

The hotel rooms didn't have sleeping plates. If you slept at all, you slept on a flat, cushiony surface, and liked it. I'd slept all right last night, until the Grog's call came to wake me in the small hours. But how could I sleep now?

Unbeknownst to yours truly, Sharon and Lois had been expecting us for dinner. Jilson had phoned them before we set out for the zoo. Tonight we'd eaten some kind of small bird, one each. Delicious. You didn't dare touch anything afterward, not until you'd wiped your hands on hot towels.

And we'd talked about the Grogs. The cone had left Jilson's mind practically untouched, so that he'd have something like an unbiased opinion. His unbiased opinion was that he wasn't going back there for anything, and I shouldn't either. The girls agreed.

I'd laughed at the Grog. Who wouldn't?

Dolphins, bandersnatchi, Grogs—you laugh at them, the Handicapped. You laugh *with* a dolphin, really; he's the greatest clown in known space. You laugh the first time you see a bandersnatch. He looks like something God forgot to finish; there's no detail, just that white shape. But you're laughing partly out of nervousness, because that moving white mound would no more notice you than a land tank would notice a snail under its treads. And you laugh at a Grog. No nervousness there. A Grog is a cartoon.

Like a doctor using a stomach pump in reverse, the Grog had shoved its information down my throat. I could feel the bits of cold certainty floating in my mind like icebergs in dark water.

I could doubt what I had been told. I could doubt, for instance, that all the Grogs on Down could not reach out to twist the minds of humans on, say, Jinx. I could doubt their terror, their utter helplessness, their need for my help. But I had to keep remembering to doubt. Otherwise the doubt would go, and the cold bits of certainty remained.

Not funny.

We ought to exterminate them. Now. Get all men off Down, then do something to the sun. Or bring in an old STL ramscoop-fusion ship and land it somewhere, leave the ramscoop running, twist every vertebrate on the planet inside out.

But: They had come to me. To me!

They were so secretive, so mortally afraid of being treated like savage, resurrected Slavers. Dr. Fuller could have been told half the truth, and he would have stopped his experimenting; or he could have been stopped in his tracks by the reaching Grog minds. But, no; they preferred to starve, to keep their secrets.

Yet they'd come to me at the first opportunity.

The Grogs were eager. Man, what a chance they'd taken! But they needed—something. Something only mankind could provide. I wasn't sure what, but of one thing I was sure: It was a seller's market. They wanted to do business. It was no guarantee of their good faith; but if I could think of such guarantees, I could force them through.

Then I felt those crystalline certainties again, floating in my mind. I didn't want any more of those.

I got up and ordered a peanut-butter, bacon, tomato, and lettuce sandwich. It arrived without mayonnaise. I tried to order mayonnaise, but the kitchen dispenser had never heard of it.

A good thing the Grogs hadn't revealed themselves to the Kzinti, back when they owned the planet. The Kzinti would have wiped them out or, worse, used them as allies against human space. Had the Kzinti used Grogs for food? If they had, then ... But no. The Grogs would make poor prey. They couldn't run.

My eyes were still seeing red light, so that the stars beyond the porch seemed blue and bright above a black plain. I thought of going down to the port and renting a room on some grounded ship, so that at least I could float between sleeping plates. Nuts.

I could not face a Grog. Not when it had to talk to me by—

That was at least part of the answer. I phoned the desk computer and told it what I wanted.

By and by other parts of the answer came. There was a mutated alfalfa grass which would grow under red sunlight; the seeds had been in the cargo hold of the ship that brought me. It was part of Down's agricultural program. Well . . .

I flew back to the desert the next morning, alone. The guy who owned the skycycles had set mine aside, with the course record intact so I could find my way back.

The Grog was there. Or I'd found another by accident. I couldn't tell, and it didn't matter. I grounded the skycycle and got off, tensing for the feel of little tendrils probing at my mind. There was nothing. I was sure it was reading my mind, but I couldn't feel it.

With crystalline certainty there came the knowledge that I was welcome. I said, "Get out of there. Get out and stay out."

The Grog did nothing. Like the knowledge I'd gained yesterday afternoon, the conviction stayed: I was welcome, welcome, *welcome*. Great.

I dug in my saddlebags and pulled out a heavy oblong. "I had a lot of trouble finding this," I told the Grog. "It's a museum piece. If Downers weren't so hell-bent on doing everything with their hands, I'd never have found one at all."

I opened it a few feet from the Grog's mouth, inserted a piece of paper in the rollers, and plugged the cord into a hand battery. "My mind will tell you how to work this. Let's see how good your tongue is." I looked for a good seat, finally settling my back against the Grog, under its mouth. I could read the print from there. There was no feeling of lese majesty. If the Grog wanted me, I was doomed—period.

The tongue lashed out, invisibly fast. PLEASE KEEP YOUR EYES ON THE TYPEWRITER, it printed. OTH-

ERWISE I CANNOT SEE IT. WOULD YOU MOVE THE MACHINE FARTHER AWAY.

I did. "How's that?"

GOOD ENOUGH. YOU ARE OVERCONCERNED WITH PRIVACY.

"Maybe. This seems to work. Now, before we begin, would you read my mind about ramscoop motors?"

I SEE. CONSIDER THE POINT MADE.

"Then I will. What can you offer us in trade?"

JUST WHAT YOU THINK. WE WILL HERD YOUR CATTLE. IN TIME THERE MAY BE OTHER THINGS WE CAN DO. WE COULD MONITOR THE HEALTH OF ZOO ANIMALS AND BE EXHIBITS AT THE SAME TIME. WE CAN DO POLICE WORK. WE WILL GUARD DOWN. AN ENEMY COULD DESTROY DOWN, BUT NO ENEMY COULD INVADE DOWN. Despite the speed of its flicking tongue, the Grog typed as slowly as a one-finger typer.

"Okay. You wouldn't object to our seeding your property with mutated grass?"

NO, NOR TO YOUR MOVING CATTLE INTO OUR TERRITORY. WE WILL NEED SOME OF THE CATTLE FOR FOOD, AND WE WOULD PREFER THAT THE PRESENT DESERT ANIMALS REMAIN. WE DO NOT WISH TO LOSE ANY OF OUR PRESENT TERRITORY.

"Will you need new land?"

NO. PLANNED PARENTHOOD IS EASY FOR US. WE NEED ONLY RESTRICT THE PRESESSILES.

"We don't trust you, you know. We'll be taking steps to see that you don't control human minds. I'm going to get myself checked over very carefully when I go home."

NATURALLY. YOU WILL BE HAPPY TO KNOW THAT WE CANNOT LEAVE THIS WORLD WITHOUT SPECIAL PROTECTION. ULTRAVIOLET WOULD KILL US. IF YOU WISH A GROG IN THE ZOO OF EARTH.

"We can take care of that. It's a good idea, too. Now,

what can we do for you? How about some modified Dolphin's Hands?"

NO, THANK YOU. A DESERT ANIMAL WITH SOMETHING LIKE HANDS WOULD BE BETTER. WHAT WE REQUIRE IS KNOWLEDGE. A TAPE ENCYCLOPEDIA, ACCESS TO HUMAN LIBRARIES. BETTER YET, HUMAN GUEST LECTURERS WHO DO NOT MIND HAVING THEIR MINDS READ.

"Guest lecturers. That'll be expensive."

HOW EXPENSIVE? HOW MUCH ARE OUR SERVICES WORTH AS HERDERS?

"Good point." I settled myself more comfortably against the Grog's hairy side. "Okay. Let's talk business."

It was a year before I touched Down again. By then, Garvey Limited was almost ready to show a profit.

I'd driven through the roughest deal I could think of. As far as the planet Down was concerned, Garvey Limited had a monopoly on Grogs. They couldn't have bought a pack of tabac sticks except through us. We paid fat taxes to the Downer human government, but that expense was almost minor.

We'd had major expenses.

The worst was publicity. I hadn't tried to keep the secret of the Grog power. That would have been futile. And that power was scary. Our only defense against a panic that could have covered human space like a blanket was the Grogs themselves.

Grogs were funny.

I'd kept pushing, pushing, pushing pictures: Grogs operating typewriters, Grogs guiding Down's expanding herds of cattle, Grogs in a spacecraft cabin, a Grog standing by during a tricky operation on a sick Kodiak bear. The Grog always looked just the same. To see one was to laugh, and never to fear ... unless there were unnatural crystalline certainties poking into the crevices of your brain.

The really important jobs for Grogs were just coming into existence. Already Wunderland had changed its laws to allow Grogs to testify in a courtroom, as expert lie-

detectors. A Grog would be present at the next summit
meeting between human and Kzinti space. Ships venturing
into unknown space would probably carry Grogs, in case
they met aliens and needed a translator.

Fuzzy Grog dolls were being sold in the toy stores. We
didn't make a dime on that.

I took a day to rest up after landing, to say Hi to Jilson
and Sharon and Lois. Next morning I flew out into the
desert. Now there was grass covering a lot of what had
been barren land. I found a circle of white far below, and
on a hunch, I dropped.

The white was a flock of sheep. In the center of the
circle nestled a Grog. She boomed up at me in an am-
plified voice: "Welcome, Garvey."

"Thanks," I said, not trying to shout. She would be
reading my mind, and answering through the nerve-
implanted vocal equipment we'd started manufacturing in
quantity two months ago. That had been another major
expense, and a necessary one.

"What's all this about dolls?"

"We can't make any money on that. It's not as if there
was a copyright on the Grog form." I circled the skycycle,
landed, and got off.

We talked of things other than business. She wanted a
Grog doll, for instance, and I promised her one. We went
through a list of "lecturers," arranging them in order of
priority. Getting them here would involve nothing more
than paying their way and paying them for their time.
None of them would have to make any kind of speech.

Neither one of us mentioned the ramscoop.

It was not on Down. Put a weapon on Down and the
Grogs could simply have made it their own; it would be
no defense. We'd put it in close orbit around the Downer
sun, closer than Mercury would have been. If the Grogs
ever became a threat, the electromagnetic ramscoop-field
would go on, and Down's sun would begin behaving very
strangely.

Neither of us mentioned it. What for? She knew my
reasons.

It was not that I feared the Grogs. I feared myself. The

ramscoop was there to prove that I had been allowed to act against the Grogs' best interests, that I was my own man.

And I *still* wasn't sure. Could the last man aboard have sabotaged the motor? Could the Grogs reach that far? There was no way to find out. If it was true, then anyone who boarded the old ship would report that it was A-okay, ready to fire, don't worry about it, Garvey. Forget it. Sleep easy.

Maybe I will. It's easy enough to believe that the Grogs are innocuous, helpful, desperate for friendship.

I wonder what we'll meet next.

GRENDEL

THERE WERE THE sounds of a passenger starship.

You learn those sounds and you don't forget, even after four years. They are never loud enough to distract, except during takeoff, and most are too low to hear anyway; but you don't forget, and you wake knowing where you are.

There were the sensations of being alone.

A sleeper field is not a straight no-gee field; there's an imbalance that keeps you more-or-less centered so you don't float out the edge and fall to the floor. When your field holds two, you set two imbalances for the distance you want, and somehow you feel that in your muscles. You touch from time to time, you and your love, twisting in sleep. There are rustlings and the sounds of breathing.

Nobody had touched me this night. Nothing breathed here but me. I was dead center in the sleeping field. I woke knowing I was alone, in a tiny sleeping cabin of the *Argos*, bound from Down to Gummidgy.

And where was Sharrol?

Sharrol was on Earth. She couldn't travel; some people can't take space. That was half our problem, but it did narrow it down; and if I wanted her, I need only go to Earth and hunt her up in a transfer-booth directory.

I didn't want to find her. Not now. Our bargain had been clear, and also inevitable; and there are advantages to sleeping alone. I'll think of them in a moment.

I found the field control-switch. The sleeper field collapsed, letting me down easy. I climbed into a navy-blue falling jumper, moving carefully in the narrow sleeping cabin, statted my hair and went out.

Margo hailed me in the hall, looking refreshingly trim and lovely in a clinging pilot's uniform. Her long, dark hair streamed behind her, rippling, as if underwater or in free fall. "You're just in time. I was about to wake everyone up."

"It's only nine-thirty. You want to get lynched?"

She laughed. "I'll tell them it was your idea. No, I'm serious, Bey. A month ago a starseed went through the Gummidgy system. I'm going to drop the ship out a light-month away and let everybody watch."

"Oh. That'll be nice," I said, trying for enthusiasm. "I've never seen a starseed set sail."

"I'll give you time to grab a good seat."

"Right. Thanks." I waved and went on, marveling at myself. Since when have I had to work up enthusiasm? For anything?

Margo was Captain M. Tellefsen, in charge of getting the *Argos* to Gummidgy sometime this evening. We'd spent many of her off-duty hours talking shop, since the *Argos* resembled the liners I used to fly seven years ago, before my boss, Nakamura Lines, collapsed. Margo was a bright girl, as good a spacer as I'd been once. Her salary must have been good too. That free-fall effect is the most difficult trick a hairdresser can attempt. No machine can imitate it.

Expensive tastes . . . I wondered why she'd left Earth. By flatlander standards she was lovely enough to make a fast fortune on tridee.

Maybe she just liked space. Many do. Their eyes hold a dreamy, distant look, a look I'd caught once in Margo's green eyes.

This early the lounge held only six passengers out of the twenty-eight. One was a big biped alien, a kdatlyno touch-sculptor named Lloobee. The chairs were too short for him. He sat on a table, with his great flat feet brushing the floor, his huge arms resting on horn-capped knees.

The other nonhumans aboard would have to stay in their rooms. Rooms 14-16-18 were joined and half full of water, occupied by a dolphin. His name was Pszzzz, or Bra-a-ack, or some such impolite sound. Human ears couldn't catch the ultrasonic overtones of that name, nor could a human throat pronounce it, so he answered to Moby Dick. He was on his way to Wunderland, the

Argos' next stop. Then there were two sessile grogs in 22, and a flock of jumpin' jeepers in 24, with the connecting door open so the Grogs could get at the jumpin' jeepers, which were their food supply. Lloobee, the kdatlyno touch-sculptor, had room twenty.

I found Emil at the bar. He raised a thumb in greeting, dialed me a Bloody Marriage, and waited in silence for my first sip. The drink tasted good, though I'd been thinking in terms of tuna and eggs.

The other four passengers, eating breakfast at a nearby table, all wore the false glow of health one carries out of an autodoc tank. Probably they'd been curing hangovers. But Emil always looked healthy, and he couldn't get drunk no matter how hard he tried. He was a Jinxian, short and wide and bull-strong: a topflight computer-programmer with an intuitive knack for asking the right questions when everyone else has been asking the wrong ones and blowing expensive circuits in their iron idiots.

"So," he said.

"So," I responded. "I'll do you a favor. Let's go sit by the window."

He looked puzzled, but went.

The *Argos* lounge had one picture window. It was turned off in hyperspace, so that it looked like part of the wall, but we found it from memory and sat down. Emil asked, "What's the favor?"

"This is it. Now we've got the best seats in the house. In a few minutes everyone will be fighting for a view because Margo's stopping the ship to show us a starseed setting sail."

"Oh? Okay, I owe you one."

"We're even. You bought me a drink."

Emil looked puzzled, and I realized I'd put an edge in my voice. As if I didn't want anyone owing me favors. Which I didn't. But it was no excuse for being a boor.

I dialed a breakfast to go with the drink: tuna fillet, eggs Florentine, and double-strength tea. The kitchen had finished delivering it when Margo spoke over the intercom, as follows: "Ladies and Gentlemen and other guests, we are dropping out some distance from CY Aquarii so that you may watch a starseed which set sail in the system of Gummidgy last month. I will raise the lounge screen in ten minutes." Click.

In moments we were surrounded. The kdatlyno sculptor squeezed in next to me, spiked knees hunched up against the lack of room, the silver tip of the horn on his elbow imperiling my eggs. Emil smiled with one side of his mouth, and I made a face. But it was justice. I'd chosen the seats myself.

The window went on. Silence fell.

Everyone who could move was crowded around the lounge window. The kdatlyno's horned elbow pinned a fold of my sleeve to the table. I let it lie. I wasn't planning to move, and kdatlyno are supposed to be touchy.

There were stars. Brighter than stars seen through atmosphere, but you get used to that. I looked for CY Aquarii and found a glaring white eye.

We watched it grow.

Margo was giving us a slow telescopic expansion. The bright dot grew to a disk bright enough to make your eyes water, and then no brighter. The eyes on a ship's hull won't transmit more than a certain amount of light. The disk swelled to fill the window, and now dark areas showed beneath the surface, splitting and disappearing and changing shape and size, growing darker and clearer as they rode the shock wave toward space. The core of CY Aquarii exploded every eighty-nine minutes. Each time the star grew whiter and brighter, while shock waves rode the explosion to the surface. Men and instruments watched to learn about stars.

The view swung. A curved edge of space showed, with curling hydrogen flames tracing arcs bigger than some suns. The star slid out of sight, and a dully glowing dot came into view. Still the view expanded, until we saw an egg-shaped object in dead center of the window.

"The starseed," said Margo via intercom. There was cool authority in her public-speaking voice. "This one appears to be returning to the galactic core, having presumably left its fertilized egg near the tip of this galactic arm. When the egg hatches, the infant starseed will make its own way home across fifty thousand light-years of space. . . ."

The starseed was moving fast, straight at the sensing eye, with an immediacy that jarred strangely against Margo's dry lecture-voice. Suddenly I knew what she'd done. She'd placed us directly in the path of the starseed. If this one was typical of its brethren, it would be moving at about point eight lights. The starseed's light-image was moving only one-fifth faster than the starseed itself, and both were coming toward us. Margo had set it up so that we watched it five times as fast as it actually happened.

Quite a showman, Margo.

". . . believe that at least some eggs are launched straight outward, toward the Clouds of Magellan or toward the globular clusters or toward Andromeda. Thus the starseeds could colonize other galaxies, and could also prevent a population explosion in this galaxy." There were pinpoints of blue light around the starseed now: newsmen from Down, come to Gummidgy to cover the event, darting about in fusion ships. "This specimen is over a mile in thickness, and about a mile and a half in length. . . ."

Suddenly it hit me.

Whatinhell was the kdatlyno watching? With nothing resembling eyes, with only his radar sense to give form to his surroundings, he was seeing nothing but a blank wall!

I turned. Lloobee was watching me.

Naturally. Lloobee was an artist, subsidized by his own world government, selling his touch-sculptures to humans and Kzinti so that his species would acquire interstellar money. Finagle knew they didn't have much else to sell—yet. They'd been propertyless slaves before we took their world from the Kzinti, but now they were building industries.

He didn't look like an artist. He looked like a monster. That brown dragon skin would have stopped a knife. Curved silver-tipped horns marked his knees and elbows, and his huge hands, human in design, nonetheless showed eight retractile claws at the knuckles. No silver there. They were filed sharp and then buffed to a polished glow. The hands were strangler's hands, not sculptor's hands.

His arms were huge even in proportion to his ten-foot height. They brushed his knees when he stood up.

But his face gave the true nightmare touch. Eyeless, noseless, marked only by a gash of a mouth and by a goggle-shaped region above it, where the skin was stretched drumhead taut. That tympanum was turned toward me. Lloobee was memorizing my face.

I turned back as the starseed began to unfold.

It seemed to take forever. The big egg fluttered; its surface grew dull and crinkly and began to expand. It was rounding the sun now, lighted on one side, black on the other. It grew still bigger, became lopsided ... and slowly, slowly the sail came free. It streamed away like a comet's tail, and then it filled, a silver parachute with four thread-like shrouds pointing at the sun. Where the shrouds met was a tiny knob.

This is how they travel. A starseed spends most of its time folded into a compact egg shape, falling through the galaxy on its own momentum. But inevitably there come times when it must change course. Then the sail unfolds: a silver mirror thinner than the paint on a cheap car, but thousands of miles across. A cross-shaped thickening in the material of the sail is the living body of the starseed itself. In the knob that hangs from the shrouds is more living matter. There are the muscles to control the shrouds and set the attitude of the sail; and there is the egg, fertilized at the Core, launched near the galactic rim.

The sail came free, and nobody breathed. The sail expanded, and filled the screen, and swung toward us. A blue-white point crossed in front of it, a newsman's ship, a candle so tiny as to be barely visible. Now the sail was fully inflated by the light from behind, belling outward, crimped along one side for attitude control.

The intercom said, "And that's it, Ladies and Gentlemen and other guests. We will make one short hyperspace hop into the system of Gummidgy and will proceed from there in normal space. We will be landing in sixteen hours."

There was a collective sigh. The kdatlyno sculptor took his horn out of my sleeve and stood up, improbably erect.

And what would his next work be like? I thought of human faces set in expressions of sheer wonder and grinning incredulity, muscles bunched and backs arched forward for a better view of a flat wall. Had Lloobee known of the starseed in advance? I thought he had.

Most of the spectators were drifting away, though the starseed still showed. My tea was icy. We'd been watching for nearly an hour, though it felt like ten minutes.

Emil said, "How are you doing with Captain Tellefsen?"

I looked blank.

"You called her Margo a while back."

"Oh, that. I'm not really trying, Emil. What would she see in a crashlander?"

"That girl must have hurt you pretty bad."

"What girl?"

"It shows through your skull, Bey. None of my business, though." He looked me up and down, and I had the uncomfortable feeling that my skull really was transparent. "What would she see? She'd see a crashlander, yes. Height seven feet, weight one sixty pounds—close enough? White hair, eyes blood-red. Skin darkened with tannin pills, just like the rest of us. But you must take more tannin pills than anybody."

"I do. Not, as you said, that it's any of your business."

"Was it a secret?"

I had to grin at that. How do you hide the fact that you're an albino? "No, but it's half my problem. Do you know that the Fertility Board of Earth won't accept albinos as potential fathers?"

"Earth is hardly the place to raise children, anyway. Once a flatlander, always a flatlander."

"I fell in love with a flatlander."

"Sorry."

"She loved me, too. Still does, I hope. But she couldn't leave Earth."

"A lot of flatlanders can't stand space. Some of them never know it. Did you want children?"

"Yah."

In silent sympathy, Emil dialed two Bloody Marriages. In silent thanks I raised the bulb in toast, and drank.

It was as neat a cleft stick as had ever caught man and woman. Sharrol couldn't leave Earth. On Earth she was born, on Earth she would die, and on Earth she would have her children.

But Earth wouldn't let me have children. No matter that forty percent of We Made It is albino. No matter that albinism can be cured by a simple supply of tannin pills, which anyone but a full-blooded Maori has to take anyway if he's visiting a world with a brighter-than-average star. Earth has to restrict its population, to keep it down to a comfortable eighteen billion. To a flatlander, that's comfortable. So ... prevent the useless ones from having children—the liabilities, such as paranoia-prones, mental deficients, criminals, uglies, and Beowulf Shaeffer.

Emil said, "Shouldn't we be in hyperspace by now?"

"Up to the captain," I told him.

Most of the passengers who had watched the starseed were now at tables. Sleeping cubicles induce claustrophobia. Bridge games were forming, reading screens were being folded out of the walls, drinks were being served. I reached for my Bloody Marriage and found, to my amazement, that it was too heavy to pick up.

Then I fainted.

I woke up thinking, *It wasn't that strong!*

And everyone else was waking too.

Something had knocked us all out at once. Which might mean the ship had an unconscious captain! I left the lounge at full speed, which was a wobbly walk.

The control-room door was open, which is bad practice. I reached to close it and changed my mind because the lock and doorknob were gone, replaced by a smooth hole nine inches across.

Margo drooped in her chair. I patted her cheeks until she stirred.

"What happened?" she wanted to know.

"We all went to sleep together. My guess is gas. Stun guns don't work across a vacuum."

"Oh!" It was a gasp of outrage. She'd spotted the gaping hole in her control board, as smooth and rounded as the hole in the door. The gap where the hyperwave radio ought to be.

"Right," I said. "We've been boarded, and we can't tell anyone about it. Now what?"

"That hole . . ." She touched the rounded metal with her fingertips.

"Slaver disintegrator, I think. A digging tool. It projects a beam that suppresses the charge on the electron, so that matter tears itself apart. If that's what it was, we'll find the dust in the air filters."

"There was a ship," said Margo. "A big one. I noticed it just after I ended the show. By then it was inside the mass limit. I couldn't go into hyperspace until it left."

"I wonder how they found us." I thought of some other good questions, but let them pass. One I let out. "What's missing? We'd better check."

"*That's* what I don't understand. We aren't carrying anything salable! Valuable, yes. Instruments for the base. But hardly black-market stuff." She stood up. "I'll have to go through the cargo hold."

"Waste of time. Where's the cargo mass-meter on this hulk?"

"Oh, of course." She found it somewhere among the dials. "No change. Nothing missing there, unless they replaced whatever they took with equivalent masses."

"Why, so we wouldn't know they were here? Nuts."

"Then they didn't take anything."

"Or they took personal luggage. The lifesystem mass-meter won't tell us. Passengers move around so. You'd think they'd have the courtesy to stay put, just in case some pirates should—ung."

"What?"

I tasted the idea and found it reasonable. More. "Ten to one Lloobee's missing."

"Who?"

"Our famous, valuable kdatlyno sculptor. The third kdatlyno in history to leave his home planet."

"One of the ET passengers?"

Oh, brother. I left, running.

Because Lloobee was the perfect theft. As a well-known alien artist who had been under the protection of Earth, the ransom he could command was huge. As a hostage his value would be equal. No special equipment would be needed; Lloobee could breathe Earth-normal air. His body could even use certain human-food proteins and certain gaseous human anesthetics.

Lloobee wasn't in the lounge. And his cabin was empty.

With Lloobee missing, and with the hyperwave smashed, the *Argos* proceeded to Gummidgy at normal speed. Normal speed was top speed; there are few good reasons to dawdle in space. It took us six hours in hyperdrive to reach the edge of CY Aquarii's gravity well. From there we had to proceed on reaction drive and gravity drag.

Margo called Gummidgy with a com laser as soon as we were out of hyperspace. By the time we landed, the news would be ten hours old. We would land at three in the morning, ship's time, and at roughly noon Gummidgy time.

Most of us, including me, went to our cabins to get some sleep. An hour before planetfall I was back in the lounge, watching us come in.

Emil didn't want to watch. He wanted to talk.

"Have you heard? The kidnapers called the base a couple of hours ago."

"What'd they have to say?"

"They want ten million stars and a contract before they turn the kdatlyno loose. They also"—Emil was outraged at their effrontery—"reminded the base that kdatlyno don't eat what humans eat. And they don't have any Kdat foodstuffs!"

"They must be crazy. Where would the base get ten million stars in time?"

"Oh, that's not the problem. If the base doesn't have funds, they can borrow money from the hunting parties, I'm sure. There's a group down there with their own private yacht. It's the contract that bothers me."

Gummidgy was blue-on-blue under a broken layer of white, with a diminutive moon showing behind an arc of horizon. Very Earth-like, but with none of the signs that mark Earth: no yellow glow of sprawling cities on the dark side, no tracery of broken freeways across the day. A nice-looking world, from up here. Unspoiled. No transfer booths, no good nightclubs, no tridee except old tapes and those only on one channel. Unspoiled.

With only half my mind working on conversation, I said, "Be glad we've got contracts. Otherwise we might get him back dead."

"Obviously you don't know much about kdatlyno."

"Obviously." I was nettled.

"They'll do it, you know. They'll pay the kidnapers ten million stars to give Lloobee back, and they'll tape an immunity contract too. Total immunity for the kidnapers. No reprisals, no publicity. Do you know what the kdatlyno will think about that?"

"They'll be glad to have their second-best sculptor back."

"Best."

"Hrodenu is the best."

"It doesn't matter. What they'll think is, they'll wonder why we haven't taken revenge for the insult to Lloobee. They'll wonder what we're doing about getting revenge. And when they finally realize we aren't doing anything at all . . ."

"Go on."

"They'll blame the whole human race. You know what the Kzinti will think?"

"Who cares what the Kzinti think?"

He snorted. Great. Now he had me pegged as a chauvinist.

"Why don't you drop it?" I suggested. "We can't do anything about it. It's up to the base MPs."

"It's up to nobody. The base MPs don't have ships."

Right about then I should have accidentally bitten my tongue off. I didn't have that much sense. I never do. Instead I said, "They don't need ships. Whoever took Lloobee has to land somewhere."

"The message came in on hyperwave. Whoever sent it is circling outside the system's gravity well."

"Whoever sent it may well be." I was showing off. "But whoever took Lloobee landed. A kdatlyno needs lots of room, room he can feel. He sends out a supersonic whistle—one tone—all his life, and when the echoes hit the tympanum above his mouth, he knows what's around him. On a liner he can feel corridors leading all around the ship. He can sense the access tubes behind walls, and the rooms and closets behind doors. Nothing smaller than a liner is big enough for him. You don't seriously suggest that the kidnapers borrowed a liner for the job, do you?"

"I apologize. You do seem to know something about kdatlyno."

"I accept your apology. Now, the kidnapers have definitely landed. Where?"

"Have to be some rock. Gummidgy's the only planet-sized body in the system. Look down there."

I looked out the window. One of Gummidgy's oceans was passing beneath us. The biggest ocean Gummidgy had, it covered a third of the planet.

"Circle Sea. Round as a ten-star piece. A whale of a big asteroid must have hit there when Gummidgy was passing through the system. Stopped it cold, or almost. All the other rocks in the system are close enough to the star to be half molten."

"Okay. Could they have built their own space station? Or borrowed one? Doubtful. So they must have landed on Gummidgy," I concluded happily, and waited for the applause.

Emil was slowly nodding his head, up, down, up, down. Suddenly he stood up. "Let's ask Captain Tellefsen."

"Hold it! Ask her what?"

"Ask her how big the ship was. She saw it, didn't she? She'll know whether it was a liner."

"Sit down. Let's wait till we're aground, then tell the MPs. Let them ask Margo."

"What for?"

Belatedly, I was getting cautious. "Just take my word for it, will you? Assume I'm a genius."

He gave me a peculiar look, but he did sit down.

Later, after we landed, we favored the police with our suggestions. They'd already asked Margo about the ship. It was a hell of a lot smaller than the *Argos* ... about the size of a big yacht.

"They aren't trying," Emil said as we emerged from City Hall.

"You can't blame them," I told him. "Suppose we knew exactly where Lloobee was. Suppose that. Then what? Should we charge in with lasers blazing and risk Lloobee catching a stray beam?"

"Yes, we should. That's the way kdatlyno think."

"I know, but it's not the way I think."

I couldn't see Emil's face, which was bent in thought two feet below eye level. But his words came slowly, as if he picked them with care. "We could find the ship that brought him down. You can't hide a spaceship landing. The gravity drag makes waves on a spaceport indicator."

"Granted."

"He could be right here in the base. So many ships go in and out."

"Most of the base ships don't have hyperdrive."

"Good. Then we can find them, wherever they landed." He looked up. "What are we waiting for? Let's go look at the spaceport records!"

It was a waste of time, but there was no talking him out of it. I tagged along.

The timing was a problem.

From where the kidnaping took place, any ship in known space would take six hours to reach the breakout point. If it tried to go farther in hyperspace, CY Aquarii's gee well would drop it permanently into the Blind Spot.

From breakout it had taken us ten hours to reach Gummidgy. That was at five-gee acceleration, fusion drive and gravity drag, with four gees compensated by the internal gee-field. CY Aquarii was a hot star, and if Gummidgy hadn't been near the edge of the system, it would have been boiling rock. Now, the fastest ship I'd ever heard of could make twenty gees . . .

"Which would take it here in five hours," said Emil. "Total of eleven. A one-gee ship would—"

"Would take too long. Lloobee would go crazy. They must know *something* about kdatlyno. In fact, I'll bet they're lying about not having kdatlyno food."

"Maybe. Okay, assume they're at least as fast as the *Argos.* That gives us five hours to play in. Hmmm . . . ?"

"Nineteen ships." On the timetable they were listed according to class. I crossed out fifteen that didn't have hyperdrive, crossed out the *Argos* itself to leave three. Crossed out the *Pregnant Banana* because it was a cargo job, flown by computer, ten gee with no internal compensating fields. Crossed out the *Golden Voyage,* a passenger ship smaller than the *Argos,* with a one-gee drive.

"That's nice," said Emil. "*Drunkard's Walk.* Say! Remember the hunting party I told you about, with their own yacht?"

"Yah. I know that name."

"Well, that's the yacht. *Drunkard's Walk. What* did you say?"

"The owner of the yacht. Larchmont Bellamy. I met him once, at Elephant's house."

"Go on."

By then it was too late to bite my tongue, though I didn't know it yet. "Not much to tell. Elephant's a friend of mine, a flatlander. He's got friends all over known space. I walked in at lush-hour one afternoon, and Bellamy was there, with a woman named . . . here she is, Tanya Wilson. She's in the same hunting party. She's Bellamy's age."

"What's Bellamy like?"

"He's three hundred years old, no kidding. He was wearing a checkerboard skin-dye job and a shocking-pink Belter crest. He talked well. Old jokes, but he told them well, and he had some new ones too."

"Would he kidnap a kdatlyno?"

I had to think about that. "He might. He's no xenophobe; aliens don't make him nervous, but he doesn't like them. I remember him telling us that we ought to wipe out the Kzinti for good and all. He doesn't need money, though."

"Would he do it for kicks?"

Bellamy. Pink bushy eyebrows over deep eyes. A mimic's voice, a deadpan way of telling a story, deadpan delivery of a punch line. I'd wondered at the time if that was a put-on. In three hundred years you hear the same joke so many times, tell the same story so many ways, change your politics again and again to match a changing universe ... Was he deadpan because he didn't care anymore? How much boredom can you meet in three hundred years?

How many times can you change your morals without losing them all? Bellamy was born before a certain Jinxian biological laboratory produced boosterspice. He reached maturity when the organ banks were the only key to long life, when a criminal's life wasn't worth a paper star. He was at draft age when the Kzinti were the only known extrasolar civilization, and a fearful alien threat. Now civilization included humans and nine known alien lifeforms, and criminal rehabilitation accounted for half of all published work in biochemistry and psychotherapy.

What *would* Bellamy's morals say about Lloobee? If he wouldn't kidnap a kdatlyno, would he "steal" one?

"You make your own guess there. I don't know Bellamy that well."

"Well, it's worth checking." Jilson bent over the timetables. "Mist Demons, he landed a third of the way around the planet! Oh, well. Let's go rent a car."

"Hah?"

"We'll need a car." He saw he'd left me behind. "To get to their camp. To find out if they rescued Lloobee. You know, the kdatlyno touch-sculptor who—"

"I get the picture. Good-bye and good luck. If they ask who sent you, for Finagle's sake don't mention me."

"That won't work," Emil said firmly. "Bellamy won't talk to me. He doesn't know me."

"Apparently I didn't make it clear. I'll try again. If we

knew who the kidnapers were, *which we don't,* we still couldn't charge in with lasers blazing—"

But he was shaking his head, left, right, left, right. "It's different now. These men have reputations to protect, don't they? What would happen to those reputations if all human space knew they'd kidnaped a kdatlyno?"

"You're not thinking. Even if everyone on Gummidgy knew the truth, the pirates would simply change the contract. A secrecy clause, enforced by monetary penalty."

Emil slapped the table, and the walls echoed. "Are we just going to sit here while they rob us? You're a hell of a man to wear a hero's name!"

"Look, you're taking this too personally—huh?"

"A hero's name! Beowulf! He must be turning over in his barrow about now."

"Who's Beowulf?"

Emil stood up, putting us eye to eye, so that I could see his utter disgust. "Beowulf was the first epic hero in English literature. He killed monsters barehanded, and he did it to help people who didn't even belong to his own country. And you—" He turned away. "I'm going after Bellamy."

I sat there for what seemed a long time. Any time seems long when you need to make a decision but can't. It probably wasn't more than a minute.

But Emil wasn't in sight when I ran outside.

I shouted at the man who'd loaned us the timetables. "Hey! Where do you go to rent a car?"

"Public rentals. Dial fourteen in the transfer booth, then walk a block east."

So the base did have transfer booths. I found one, paid my coin, and dialed.

Getting to Public Rentals gave me my first chance to look at the base. There wasn't much to see. Buildings, half of them semipermanent; the base was only four years old. Apartment buildings, laboratories, a nursery school. Overhead, the actinic pinpoint of CY Aquarii hit the weather dome and was diffused into a wide, soft white glow. There were few people about, and all of them were tanned the same shade of black for protection against the savage, invisible ultraviolet outside. Most of them had goggles hung around their necks.

That much I saw while running a block at top speed.

He was getting into a car when I came panting up. He said, "Change your mind?"

"No, but ... hoo! ... you're going to change yours. Whew! The mood you're in, you'll fly straight into ... Bellamy's camp and . . . tell him he's a lousy pirate. Hyooph! Then if you're wrong, he'll ... punch you in the nose ... and if you're right, he'll either ... laugh at you or have you ... killed."

Emil climbed into the car. "If you're going to argue, get in and argue there."

I got in. I had some of my breath back. "Will you get it through your thick head? You've got your life to lose and nothing to gain. I told you why."

"I've got to try, don't I? Fasten your crash web."

I fastened my crash web. Its strands were thin as coarse thread, and not much stronger, but they had saved lives. Any sharp pull on the crash web would activate the crash field, which would enfold the pilot and protect him from impact.

"If you've still got to look for the kidnapers," I said, "why not do it here? There's a good chance Lloobee's somewhere on the base."

"Nuts," said Emil. He turned on the lift units and we took off. "Bellamy's yacht is the only ship that fits."

"There's another ship that fits. The *Argos.*"

"Put your goggles on. We're about to go through the weather dome. What about the *Argos?*"

"Think it through. There had to be someone aboard in the first place to plant the gas bomb that knocked us out. Why shouldn't that same person have hidden Lloobee somewhere, gagged or unconscious, until the *Argos* could land?"

"Finagle's gonads! He could still be on the *Argos!* No he couldn't; they searched the *Argos.*" Emil glared at nothing. At that moment we went through the weather dome. CY Aquarii, which had been a soft white patch, became for an instant a tiny bright point of agony. Then a spot on each lens of my goggles turned black and covered the sun.

"We'll have to check it out later," said Emil. "But we can call City Hall now and tell them one of the kidnapers was on the *Argos*."

But we couldn't. Where the car radio should have been was a square hole.

Emil smote his forehead. With his Jinxian strength it's a wonder he survived. "I forgot. Car radios won't work on Gummidgy. You have to use a ship's com laser and bounce the beam off one of the orbital stations."

"Do we have a com laser?"

"Do you see one? Maybe in ten years someone'll think of putting com lasers in cars. Well, we'll have to do it later."

"That's silly. Let's do it now."

"First we check on Bellamy."

"I'm not going."

Emil just grinned.

He was right. It had been a futile comment. I had three choices:

Fighting a Jinxian.

Getting out and walking home. But we must have been a mile up already, and the base was far behind.

Visiting Bellamy, who was an old friend, and looking around unobtrusively while we were there. Actually, it would have been rude not to go. Actually, it would have been silly not to at least drop by and say hello while we were on the same planet.

Actually, I rationalize a lot.

"Do one thing for me," I said. "Let me do all the talking. You can be the strong, silent type who smiles a lot."

"Okay. What are you going to tell him?"

"The truth. Not the whole truth, but some of it."

The four-hour trip passed quickly. We found cards and a score pad in a glove compartment. The car blasted quietly and smoothly through a Mach four wall of air, rising once to clear a magnificent range of young mountains.

"Can you fly a car?"

I looked up from my cards. "Of course." Most people can. Every world has its wilderness areas, and it's not worthwhile to spread transfer booths all through a forest, especially one that doesn't see twenty tourists in a year. When you're tired of civilization, the only way to travel is to transfer to the edge of a planetary park and then rent a car.

"That's good," said Emil, "in case I get put out of action."

"Now it's your turn to cheer me up."

Emil cocked his head at me. "If it's any help, I think I know how Bellamy's group found the *Argos*."

"Go on."

"It was the starseed. A lot of people must have known about it, including Margo. Maybe she told someone that she was stopping the ship so the passengers could get a look."

"Not much help. She had a lot of space to stop in."

"Did she? Think about it. First, Bellamy'd have no trouble at all figuring when she'd reach the Gummidgy system."

"Right." There's only one speed in hyperdrive.

"That means Margo would have to stop on a certain spherical surface to catch the light-image of the starseed setting sail. Furthermore, in order to watch it happen in an hour, she had to be right in front of the starseed. That pinpoints her exactly."

"There'd be a margin of error."

Emil shrugged. "Half a light-hour on a side. All Bellamy had to do was wait in the right place. He had an hour to maneuver."

"Bravo," I said. There were things I didn't want him to know yet. "He could have done it that way, all right. I'd like to mention just one thing."

"Go ahead."

"You keep saying 'Bellamy did this' and 'Bellamy did that.' We don't know he's guilty yet, and I'll thank you to

remember it. Remember that he's a friend of a friend, and
don't start treating him like a criminal until you know he
is one."

"All right," Emil said, but he didn't like it. *He* knew
Bellamy was a kidnaper. He was going to get us both
killed if he didn't watch his mouth.

At the last minute I got a break. It was only a bit of
misinterpretation on Emil's part, but one does not refuse a
gift from the gods.

We'd crossed six or seven hundred kilometers of veldt:
blue-green grass with herds grazing at wide intervals. The
herds left a clear path, for the grass (or whatever, we
hadn't seen it close up) changed color when cropped.
Now we were coming up on a forest, but not the gloomy-
green type of forest native to human space. It was a riot
of color: patches of scarlet, green, magenta, yellow. The
yellow patches were polka-dotted with deep purple.

Just this side of the forest was the hunting camp. Like a
nudist at a tailors' convention, it leapt to the eye, flagrant-
ly alien against the blue-green veldt. A bulbous plastic
camp-tent the size of a mansion dominated the scene,
creases marring its translucent surface to show where it
was partitioned into rooms. A diminutive figure sat outside
the door, its head turning to follow our sonic boom. The
yacht was some distance away.

The yacht was a gaily decorated playboy's space boat,
with a brilliant orange paint job and garish markings in
colors that clashed. Some of the markings seemed to mean
something. Bellamy, one year ago, hadn't struck me as the
type to own such a boat. Yet there it stood, on three wide
landing legs with paddle-shaped feet, its sharp nose pointed up at us.

It looked ridiculous. The hull was too thick and the legs
were too wide, so that the big businesslike attitude jets in
the nose became a comedian's nostrils. On a slender needle with razor-sharp swept-back airfoils that paint job
might have passed. But it made the compact, finless
Drunkard's Walk look like a clown.

The camp swept under us while we were still moving at

Mach two. Emil tilted the car into a wide curve, slowing and dropping. As we turned toward the camp for the second time, he said, "Bellamy's taking precious little pains to hide himself. Oh, oh."

"What?"

"The yacht. It's not big enough. The ship Captain Tellefsen described was twice that size."

A gift from the gods. "I hadn't noticed," I said. "You're right. Well, that lets Bellamy out."

"Go ahead. Tell me I'm an idiot."

"No need. Why should I gloat over one stupid mistake? I'd have had to make the trip anyway, sometime."

Emil sighed. "I suppose that means you'll have to see Bellamy before we go back."

"Finagle's sake, Emil! We're here, aren't we? Oh, one thing. Let's not tell Bellamy why we came. He might be offended."

"And he might decide I'm a dolt. Correctly. Don't worry, I won't tell him."

The "grass" covering the veldt turned out to be knee-high ferns, dry and brittle enough to crackle under our socks. Dark blue-green near the tips of the plants gave way to lighter coloring on the stalks. Small wonder the herbivores had left a trail. Small wonder if we'd seen carnivores treading that easy path.

The goggled figure in front of the camp-tent was cleaning a mercy-rifle. By the time we were out of the car, he had closed it up and loaded it with inch-long slivers of anesthetic chemical. I'd seen such guns before. The slivers could be fired individually or in one-second bursts of twenty, and they dissolved instantly in anything that resembled blood. One type of sliver would usually fit all the lifeforms on a given world.

The man didn't bother to get up as we approached. Nor did he put down the gun. "Hi," he said cheerfully. "What can I do for you?"

"We'd like—"

"Beowulf Shaeffer?"

"Yah. Larch Bellamy?"

Now he got up. "Can't recognize anybody on this crazy

world. Goggles covering half your face, everybody the same color—you have to go stark naked to be recognized, and then only the women know you. Whatinhell are you doing on Gummidgy, Bey?"

"I'll tell you later. Larch, this is Emil Horne. Emil, meet Larchmont Bellamy."

"Pleasure," said Bellamy, grinning as if indeed it was. Then his grin tried to break into laughter, and he smothered it. "Let's go inside and swallow something wet."

"What was funny?"

"Don't be offended, Mr. Horne. You and Bey do make an odd pair. I was thinking that the two of you are like a medium-sized beach ball standing next to a baseball bat. How did you meet?"

"On the ship," said Emil.

The camp-tent had a collapsible revolving-door to hold the pressure. Inside, the tent was almost luxurious, though it was all foldaway stuff. Chairs and sofas were soft, cushiony fabric surfaces, holding their shape through insulated static-charges. Tables were memory plastic. Probably they compressed into small cubes for storage aboard ship. Light came from glow strips in the fabric of the pressurized tent. The bar was a floating portable. It came to meet us at the door, took our orders, and passed out drinks.

"All right," Bellamy said, sprawling in an armchair. When he relaxed, he relaxed totally—like a cat. Or a tiger. "Bey, how did you come to Gummidgy? And where's Sharrol?"

"She can't travel in space."

"Oh? I didn't know. That can happen to anyone." But his eyes questioned.

"She wanted children. Did you know that? She's always wanted children."

He took in my red eyes and white hair. "I ... see. So you broke up."

"For the time being."

His eyes questioned.

That's not emphatic enough. There was something about Bellamy ... He had a lean body and a lean face, with a straight, sharp-edged nose and prominent cheekbones, all setting off the dark eyes in their deep pits beneath black shaggy brows.

But there was more to it than eyes. You can't tell a man's age by looking at his photo, not if he takes booster-spice. But you can tell, to some extent, by watching him in motion. Older men know where they're going before they start to move. They don't dither, they don't waste energy, they don't trip over their feet, and they don't bump into things.

Bellamy was old. There was a power in him, and his eyes *questioned*.

I shrugged. "We used the best answer we had, Larch. He was a friend of ours, and his name was Carlos Wu. You've heard of him?"

"Mathematician, isn't he?"

"Yah. Also playwright and composer. The Fertility Board gave him an unlimited breeding-license when he was eighteen."

"*That* young?"

"He's a genius. As I say, he was a good friend of ours. Liked to talk about space; he had the flatland phobia, like Sharrol. Well, Sharrol and I made our decision, and then we went to him for help. He agreed.

"So Sharrol's married him on a two-year contract. In two years I'll go back and marry her, and we'll raise our family."

"I'll be damned."

I'd been angry about it for too long, with nobody to be angry at. I flared up. "Well, what would *you* have done?"

"Found another woman. But I'm a dirty old man, and you're young and naïve. Suppose Wu tried to keep her?"

"He won't. He's a friend, I told you. Besides, he's got more women than ten of him could handle, with that license of his."

"So you left."

"I had to. I couldn't stand it."

He was looking at me with something like awe. "I can't remember ever being in love that hard. Bey, you're overdue for a drunk, and you're surrounded by friends. Shall we switch to something stronger than beer?"

"It's a good offer, but no, thanks. I didn't mean to cry on your shoulder. I've had my drunk. A week on Wunderland, drinking Vurguuz."

"Finagle's ears! Vurguuz?"

"I said to myself, why mess around with half measures? said I. So—"

"What does it taste like?"

"Like a hand grenade with a minted sugar casing. Like you better have a chaser ready."

Silence threatened to settle. No wonder, the way I'd killed the conversation by spilling my personal problems all over everything. I said, "So as long as I had to do some traveling, I thought I'd do some people some favors. That's why I'm here."

"What kind of favors?"

"Well, a friend of mine happens to be an ET taxidermist. It's a complicated profession. I told him I'd get him some information on Gummidgy animals and Gummidgy biochemistry. Now that the planet's open to hunters, sooner or later people like you are going to be carting in perforated alien bodies."

Bellamy frowned. "I wish I could help," he said, "but I don't kill the animals I hunt. I just shoot them full of anesthetic so they'll hold still while I photo them. The same goes for the rest of us."

"I see."

"Otherwise I'd offer to take you along one day."

"Yah. I'll do my own research, then. Thanks for the thought."

Then, being a good host, Bellamy proceeded to work Emil into the conversation. Emil was far from being the strong, silent type who smiles a lot; in fact, we were soon learning all about the latest advances in computer technology. But he kept his word and did not mention why we had come.

I was grateful.

The afternoon passed swiftly. Dinnertime arrived early. Most of the people on Gummidgy accommodate to the eighteen-hour day by having two meals: brunch and dinner. We accepted Bellamy's invitation.

With dinner arrived a dedicated hunter named Warren, who insisted on showing us photos of everything he'd caught since his arrival. That day he'd shot a graceful animal like a white greyhound, "but even faster," he said; a monkeylike being with a cupped hand for throwing rocks; and a flower.

"A flower?"

"See those tooth marks on my boot? I had to shoot it to get it to let go. No real sport in it, but as long as I'd already shot the damn thing . . ."

His only resemblance to Bellamy was this: He carried the same indefinable air of age. Now I was sure it had nothing to do with appearance. Perhaps it was a matter of individuality. Bellamy and Warren were individuals. They didn't push it; they didn't have to demonstrate it; but neither were they following anybody's lead.

Warren left after dinner. Going to see how the others were doing, he said; they must be hot on the trail of something, or they'd have been back to eat. Not wanting to wear out our welcome, we said our good-byes and left too. It was near sunset when we emerged from the camp-tent.

"Let me drive," I said.

Emil raised his brows at me, but moved around to the passenger seat.

He did more than raise his brows when he saw what I was doing.

I set the autopilot to take us back to the base, and let the car fly itself until we were below the horizon. We were a mile up by then, and a goodly distance away. Whereupon I canceled the course, dipped the car nearly to ground level, and swung back toward the forest. I flew almost at treetop level, staying well below the speed of sound.

"Tell me again," I said, "about Beowulf the hero."

"What kind of game are you playing now?"

"You thought the size of the *Drunkard's Walk* cleared Bellamy, didn't you?"

"It does. It's much too small to be Captain Tellefsen's pirate."

"So it is. But we already know there was a pirate on board the *Argos*."

"Right."

"Let's assume it's Margo."

"The *captain?*"

"Why not?"

I'll say this for him, he got it all in one gulp. Margo to release the gas. Margo to tell Bellamy where to meet the *Argos* and to hold the ship in one place long enough to be met. Margo to lie about the size of Bellamy's ship.

And me to keep Emil in the dark until now, so he wouldn't blow his lines when he met Bellamy.

He gulped, and then he said, "It fits. But I'd swear Bellamy's innocent."

"Except for one thing. He didn't invite me to go hunting with him."

A yellow patch of forest streamed away beneath us. The purple polka dots we'd seen from high up turned out to be huge blossoms several feet across, serviced by birds the size of storks. Then we were over scarlet puffballs that shook in the wind of our passage. I kept us low and slow. A car motor is silent, but a sonic boom would make us more than conspicuous.

"That's your evidence against him? He didn't want you hunting with him?"

"And he gave lousy reasons."

"You said he hated ETs. He's a flatlander. To some flatlanders, we'd both look like ETs."

"Maybe. But the *Drunkard's Walk* is still the only ship that could have landed Lloobee, and Margo's still our best bet as the kidnaper on the *Argos*. Maybe the pirates *could* have found the *Argos* by guess and hope, but they'd have a damn sight better chance with Margo working with them."

Emil glared out through the windshield. "Were you thinking this all the time we were in the camp?"

"Not until he turned down the chance to take me hunting. Then I was pretty sure."

"You make a first-class liar."

I didn't know how to deny it, so I said nothing. None-theless, Emil was wrong. If I'd spilled my personal prob-lems in Bellamy's lap, if I'd accepted his hospitality, pro-fessed friendship, drunk his liquor, laughed at his jokes and made him laugh at mine—it was not an act. Bellamy made you like him, and he made you want him to like you. And Emil would never understand that, in my eyes, Bellamy had done nothing seriously wrong.

Six years earlier I'd tried to steal a full-sized spacecraft, fitted more or less for war, from a group of Pierson's puppeteers. I'd been stopped before the plan got started, but so what? The puppeteers had been blackmailing me; but again, so what? Who says the aliens of known space have to think we're perfect? *We* know we're not. Ask us!

"I'm sorry," said Emil. "Excuse my mouth. I got you into this practically over your dead body, and now, when you do your best to help out, I jump on you. I'm an ungrateful ..." And what he said then about his anatomi-cal make-up probably wasn't true. He was married, after all. He concluded, "You're the boss. Now what?"

"Depends. We don't have any evidence yet."

"You really think Bellamy's the one?"

"I really do."

"He could be holding Lloobee anywhere. Hundreds of miles away."

"We'll never find him thinking that way. He wasn't in the camp-tent. Even Bellamy wouldn't have that much nerve. If he'd been in the ship, we'd have seen the airlock open—"

"Closed."

"Open. Lloobee couldn't sense anything through a ship's hull. In a closed ship that size he'd go nuts."

"Okay."

"We know one thing that might be helpful. Bellamy's got a disintegrator."

"He does?"

"The holes in the *Argos*. You didn't see them, did you?"

"No. You think he might have dug himself a hideout?"

"Yah. Bellamy isn't the type to let a tool like that go to waste. If he's got a Slaver disintegrator, he'll use it. It's a fine digging-tool. A big roomy cave would take you an hour, and even the dust would be blown hundreds of miles. Disintegrator dust is nearly monatomic."

"How are you planning to find this cave?"

"Let's see if the car has a deep-radar attachment."

It didn't. Rent-a-cars usually do, on worlds where there are swampy areas. So now we knew Gummidgy wasn't swampy. Everything on the dash had its uses, and not one of them was sonar.

"We'll have to make a sight search," said Emil. "How close are we to Bellamy's camp?"

"About thirty miles."

"Well, there's a chance they won't see us." Emil sat forward in his chair, hands gripping his knees. His smile was thin and tight. Obviously he had something. "Take us up to ten miles. Don't cross sonic speed until we've got lots of room."

"What can we see from ten miles up?"

"Assume I'm a genius."

That served me right. I took the car up without quibbling.

Ten miles down was the wandering line of the forest border, sharply demarcated from the veldt. At this height all the magnificent colors of Gummidgy vegetation blurred into a rich brown.

"Do you see it?"

"No."

"Look for two nearly parallel lines," said Emil. "A little lighter than the rest of the forest."

"I still don't see it."

"It shows on the veldt too."

"Nope. Hah! Got it." Crossing the rich brown of the forest was a strip of faintly lighter, faintly more-uniform brown. "Hard to see, though. What is it?"

"Dust. Blown for hundreds of miles, just like you said. Some of it settled on the tops of the trees."

So dim was the path that it kept flickering in and out of the visible. But it was straight, with edges that slowly converged. It crossed the veldt too, in a strip of faintly dimmed blue-green. Before its edges met, the path faded out; but one could extend those edges in the mind's eye.

I let the car fall.

Unless we were building dream-castles, Lloobee's cave must be at the intersection.

When we got too low, the dust path disappeared in the colors of forest and veldt. Bellamy's hypothetical cave was half a mile into the forest. I couldn't land there, for reasons involving too many big plants and too many pirates. I dropped the car in a curve of the forest.

Emil had been fumbling in the back. Now he pressed something into my hand and said, "Here, take this." To my amazement I found myself holding a sonic stunner.

"That's illegal!" I whispered furiously.

"Why are you whispering? Kidnaping kdatlyno is illegal too. We may be glad we've got these before we're finished."

"But where did you get police stunners?"

"Let's say some criminal slipped them into my luggage. And if you'll look at the butts, you'll see they aren't police stunners."

They'd started life as police stunners, but they weren't anymore. The butts were handcarved from big cultured emeralds. Expensive. Dueling pistols?

Sure, dueling pistols. Lose a duel with one of these, and you'd lose nothing but face. I hear most Jinxians would rather lose an arm, permanently. They were not illegal— on Jinx.

"Remember," said Emil, "they only knock a man out for ten minutes."

"I can run a long way in ten minutes."

Emil looked me over rather carefully. "You've changed. You could have driven me straight back to base, and I'd never have been the wiser."

"I never thought of that."

"Bah."

"Would you believe I've decided to be an epic hero? Whatever that is."

Emil shrugged and moved into the forest. I followed.

I wasn't about to explain my motives to Emil. He'd put me in an unpleasant situation, and if he wanted to worry about my backing out, let him worry.

Back out? I couldn't. It was too late.

There had been a time when I knew nothing about Lloobee's kidnapers. I might suspect Margo, but I had no evidence.

Later, I could suspect Bellamy. But I had no proof.

But Emil had pressured me into confronting Bellamy, and Bellamy had been pressured into putting on an act. If I quit now, Bellamy would continue to think I was a fool.

And when Bellamy confronted Margo, Margo would continue to think I was a fool. That would hurt. To have Margo and Bellamy both thinking that I had been twice an idiot ...

It wasn't Bellamy's fault, except that he had voluntarily kidnaped a valuable kdatlyno sculptor. It was partly my fault, and mostly Emil's. I might be able to leave Margo out of this. But Bellamy would have to pay for my mistakes.

And why shouldn't he? It was *his* antisocial act.

The vegetation was incredibly lush, infinitely varied. Its chemistry was not that of terrain life, but the chemical it used for photosynthesis was similar to chlorophyll. For billions of years the plants of Gummidgy had had oversupplies of ultraviolet light. The result was life in plenty, a profusion of fungi and animals and parasites. On every branch of the magenta trees was an orchid-thing, a sessile beast waiting for its dinner to fly by. The air was full of life: birdforms, insectforms, and a constant rain of dust and spores and feathery seeds and bits of leaf and bird dung. The soil was dry and spongy and rich, and the air was rich with oxygen and alien smells. Somewhere in the spectrum of odors were valuable undiscovered perfumes.

Once we saw a flower-thing like the one in Warren's photo. I found a dry branch and stuck it down the thing's blossom, and pulled back half a branch.

Again, four feet of snake flew by. Emil stunned it. It had two small fins near the head end, and its hind end was a huge, leathery delta wing. Its mouth was two-thirds back along the body.

With typical abruptness, the flowering magenta trees gave way to a field of scarlet tubing. No branches, no leaves; just interlocking cables, three feet thick, moving restlessly over each other like too many snakes in a pit. They were four or five deep. Maybe they were all one single plant or animal; we never did see a head or a tail. And we'd never have kept our footing if we'd tried to cross.

We circled the area, staying in the magenta trees because we were getting too close to where the hypothetical cave ought to be. That brought us to a small round hill surmounted by a tree that was mostly wandering roots. We started around the hill, and Emil gripped my arm.

I saw it. A cave mouth, small and round, in the base of the hill. And leaning against the dirt slope of the hill, a woman with a mercy-gun.

"All *right!*" I whispered. "Come on, let's get out of here!" I pulled at Emil's arm and turned toward freedom.

It was like trying to stop a warship from taking off. Emil was gone, running silently toward the cave with his gun held ready, leaving me with numb fingers and a deep appreciation of Finagle's First Law. I swallowed a groan and started after him.

On flat ground I can beat any Jinxian who ever ran the short sprint. My legs were twice the length of Emil's. But Emil moved like a wraith through the alien vegetation, while I kept getting tangled up. My long legs and arms stuck out too much, and I couldn't catch him.

It was such a crying pity. Because we had it! We had it all, or all we were going to get. The guarded cave was our proof. Bellamy and his hunter friends were the kidnapers. That knowledge would be a powerful bargaining point in our negotiations for the return of Lloobee, despite what I'd told Emil. All we had to do now was get back to base and tell somebody.

But I couldn't catch Emil!

I couldn't even keep up with him.

A bare area fronted the cave, a triangular patch of

ground bounded by two thick, sprawling roots belonging
to the treelike thing on the hill. I'd lost sight of Emil;
when I saw him again, he was running for the cave at full
speed, and the woman with the gun was face up in the
dirt. Emil reached the darkness at the mouth of the cave
and disappeared within.

And as he vanished into the dark, he was unmistakably
falling.

Well, now they had Emil. With blazing lasers ... !
Proof wasn't enough. He'd decided to bring back Lloobee
himself. Now we'd have to negotiate for the two of them.

Would we? Bellamy was back at the hunting camp.
When he found out his men had Emil, he'd know I was
somewhere around. But whoever was in the cave might
think Emil was alone. In which case they might kill him,
right now.

I settled my back against the tree. As a kind of afterthought I focused the dueling pistol on the woman and
fired. I'd have to do that every ten minutes to keep her
quiet.

Eventually someone would be coming out to see why
she hadn't stopped Emil.

I didn't dare try to enter the cave. Be it man or booby
trap, whatever had stopped Emil would stop me.

Too bad the dueling pistols didn't have more power.
The craftsmen who had carved their emerald butts had
scaled them down; because, after all, they would be used
only to prove a point. It would take a shopful of tools to
readjust them, because readjusting them to their former
power would violate Jinxian law. Real police stunners will
knock a man out for twelve hours or more.

I was sitting there waiting for someone to come out
when I felt the prickly numbness of a stunner.

The sensations came separately. First, a pull in my
ankles. Then, in the calves of my legs. Then, something
rough and crumbly sliding under me. Separate sensations,
just above the threshold of consciousness, penetrating the
numbness. A sliding Bump! Bump! against the back of my

head. Gritty sensation in the backs of my hands, arms trailing above and behind my head.

Conclusion, arrived at after long thought: I was being dragged.

I was limp as a noodle and nearly as numb. It was all over. Nobody had walked innocently out of the cave. Instead, the man in there with Lloobee had looked out with a heat sensor, then used his sonic on anything that might possibly be the temperature of a man.

Things turned dark. I thought I was unconscious, but no, I'd been dragged into the cave.

"That's a relief," said Bellamy. Unmistakably, Bellamy.

"Bastard," said a woman's voice. It seemed familiar: rich and fruity, with a flatlander accent that was not quite true. Misplaced in time, probably. A dialect doesn't stay the same forever.

My eyes fell open.

Bellamy stood over me, looking down with no expression. Tanya Wilson sat some distance away, looking sullenly in my direction. The man named Warren, standing behind her, carefully did something to her scalp, and she winced.

"There," said Warren, "you go back to the camp. If anyone asks——"

"I was scratched by a flower-bird," said Tanya. "The rest of you are out hunting. Will you please assume I've got a mind?"

"Don't be so damn touchy. Larch, you'd better tie them up, hadn't you?"

"You do it if you like. It's not necessary. They'll be out for hours."

Oh, really?

Tanya Wilson got up and went to the cave mouth. Before leaving, she pulled a cord hanging at the side. Warren, who had followed her, pulled it again after she was gone.

The cord was attached to what looked like a police stunner, the same model as Emil's guns. The stunner was mounted on a board, and the board was fixed in place over the mouth of the cave, aimed downward. A booby trap. So easy.

The numbness was gone. My problem was the opposite: It was all I could do to keep from moving. I was stretched full-length on a rocky floor, with my heels a foot higher than my nose and my arms straight above my head. If I so much as clenched a fist . . .

"I wonder," Bellamy said, "what made him turn against me."

"Who? Shaeffer?"

I could see four in the cave. Bellamy was standing over me; Warren was nearer the cave mouth. The two others were near the back, near a line of plastic crates. One was a man I'd never seen. The other—huge and frightening in the semidark, a monster from Man's dimmest past, when demons and supernatural beings walked the home world— was Lloobee. They sat silently facing each other, as if each were waiting for something.

"Yes," said Bellamy. "Beowulf Shaeffer. He seemed such a nice guy. Why would he go to so much effort to get me in trouble?"

"You forget, Larch." Warren spoke with patient understanding. "They are the good guys; we are the bad guys. A simple sense of law and order—"

"Too much law and order around, Warren. There are no more frontiers. We sit in our one small area of the universe called known space, sixty light-years across, and we rot. Too much security. Everyone wants security."

"That's Shaeffer's motive. He was backing up law and order."

"I don't think so. Bey's not the type."

"What type is he?"

"Lazy. A survival type, but lazy. He doesn't start to use his brain until he's in obvious, overt trouble. But he's got pride."

"Could the other one have talked him into it?"

"I suppose so."

There was an uncomfortable silence.

"Well," said Warren, "it's too bad. What'll we do with them?"

Bellamy looked unhappily down at me. He couldn't see my eyes behind the goggles, not in the dim cave light. "They could be found half-eaten. By one of those big hopping things, say. The ones that prey on the gray plains herbivores."

"The carnivore that did it would be poisoned. It would have to be found nearby."

"Right." Bellamy pondered. "It's vital that there be no evidence against us. If we tried to square a murder rap in the contract, they'd chivvy our price down to nothing. You were bright to use the sonic. A mercy-needle would have left chemicals."

A small, sharp rock was pressing against the side of my neck. It itched. If I was planning to leap to my feet from this ridiculous position, I couldn't delay too long. Sooner or later I'd reach to scratch. Sooner or later Bellamy or Warren would notice the butts of Emil's altered police stunners and know them for what they were.

"First we need a plains carnivore," said Warren. "Do you think we can starve it into—"

Lloobee leapt.

He was five yards from the man who was guarding him at the back of the cave. The man fired instantly, and then he screamed and tried to dodge. The kdatlyno slammed into him and knocked him sliding across the floor.

I didn't see any more. I was running. I heard panicky shouting, and then Bellamy's roar: "Relax, you idiot. He was unconscious before he left the ground." And Warren's, "Relax, hell! Where's Shaeffer?"

I barely remembered to pull the trigger cord on Bellamy's booby trap. The cave entrance was long and low, sloping upward. I took it at a crouching run. Behind me was more confusion. Could the first man through have pulled the trigger cord *again?* That would give me time I needed.

Outside the cave I turned sharp right. The winding, half-exposed roof was almost Emil's height. I went over it like a spider monkey, and then under it, hiding under its protective bulk.

CY Aquarii was directly behind me, minutes from sunset. Its white light threw a sharp black shadow along the side of the root.

I started crawling uphill, staying in the shadow. Two sets of pelting footsteps followed me from the other side of the root.

Voices came from below, barely audible. They didn't sound like a search in progress. Why not? I looked back and saw no pursuit. Halfway up the hill I slid out of my blue falling jumper, tucked it as far under the root as it would go, and went on, thinking kindly thoughts about tannin pills. Now I'd be all but invisible if I stayed in the shadows. All but my white hair.

Why had Lloobee made that grandstand play? It was as if he'd read my mind. He must have known there was no chance of escape for him. But I'd have had no chance without his diversion. Had he known I was conscious?

Could kdatlyno read minds?

At the top of the hill I stopped in a cleft between two huge roots. The magenta tree seemed much too small to need all that root area; but the sunlight was rich, and maybe the soil was poor. And the roots would hide me.

But where were my pursuers?

I knew they needed me. They couldn't dispose of Emil until they had me. Granted that they could find me as soon as it got dark; I'd stand out like a beacon on a heat sensor. But suppose I reached the car first?

The car!

Sure, that was it. While I was crouching somewhere or taking a tangled trail that would keep me hidden at all times, Bellamy or one of his men was taking the shortest, straightest route to my car. To move it before I could reach it.

I pounded my head to get it working. No use. I was stymied. The cave? I'd find guns in there, hunting guns. The anesthetic slivers probably wouldn't work on human beings, but they might be poisonous—and they would certainly hurt. But no, I couldn't attack the cave. There'd be no way around the booby trap.

But there'd be someone in there to turn the booby trap

on and off and to guard Lloobee. Another on the way to the car; that made two.

The third would have found some high point, chosen days previously for its view of the surroundings. He'd be waiting now for a glimpse of my snow-white hair. I couldn't break and run for the car.

Maybe.

And maybe the third man had been the first to come charging after me. And maybe he'd snatched at the trigger cord as he passed, to turn off a police stunner that was already off. And maybe he'd run through the beam.

Maybe.

But if anyone reached the car, I was cooked.

I spun it over and over, while handfuls of needed seconds passed me by. There was no other way to figure it. Tanya was back at camp. A second man was in the cave; a third was on the way to the car. The fourth was either waiting for me to show myself or he wasn't. I had to risk it.

I came out from under the roots, running.

I'm good at sprinting, not so good at a long-distance run. The edge of the forest was half a mile away. I was walking when I got there, and blowing like a city-sized air pump. There was no sign of anyone, and no sign of the car. I stood just within the forest, sucking wind, nerving myself to run out into the fern grass.

Then Bellamy emerged to my left. He dogtrotted fearlessly out onto the veldt, into the fern grass, and stood looking around. One of Emil's sonics dangled from one hand. He must have known by then that it was only a dueling pistol, but it was the only sonic he had.

He saw something to his right, something hidden from me by a curve of forest. He turned and trotted toward it.

I followed as best I could. Multicolored things kept tripping me, and I didn't dare step out into the fern grass. Bellamy was going to get there first ...

He was examining the car when I found him. The car was right out in the open, tens of yards from any cover. Any second now he'd get in and take off.

What was he waiting for? Me?

I knelt behind a magenta bush, dithering. Bellamy was peering into the back seat. He wanted to know just what we'd planned before he made his move. Every two seconds his head would pop up for a long, slow look around.

A black dot in the distance caught my eye. It took me a moment to realize that it was in the plastic goggles, blotting out the dot of actinic sunlight. The sun was right on the horizon.

Bellamy was opening the trunk.

. . . The sun.

I started circling. The magenta bushes offered some cover, and I used it all. Bellamy's eyes maintained their steady sweep, but they hadn't found me yet.

Abruptly he slammed the trunk, circled the car to get in.

I was where I wanted to be. My long shadow pointed straight at the car. I charged.

He looked up as I started. He looked straight at me, and then his eyes swept the curve of forest, taking their time. He bent to get into the car, and then he saw me. But his gun hand was in the car, and I was close enough. The dots on his goggles had covered more than CY Aquarii. They'd covered my approach.

My shoulder knocked him spinning away from the car, and I heard a metal *tick*. He got up fast, empty-handed. No gun. He'd dropped it. I turned to look in the car, fully expecting to find it on the floor or on the seat. It was nowhere to be seen. I looked back in time to duck, and his other hand caught me and knocked me away. I rolled with it and came to my feet.

He was standing in a relaxed boxer stance between me and the car.

"I'm going to break you, Bey."

"So you can't find the gun either."

"I don't need it. Any normal ten-year-old could break you in two."

"Then come on." I dropped into boxer stance, thanking Finagle that he didn't know karate or ju-whatsis or any of the other illegal killing methods. Hundreds of years had passed since the usual laws against carrying a concealed weapon were extended to cover special fighting methods, but Bellamy had had hundreds of years to learn. I'd come up lucky.

He came toward me, moving lightly and confidently, a flatlander in prime condition. He must have felt perfectly safe. What could he have to fear from an attenuated weakling, a man born and raised in We Made It's point six gee? He grinned when he was almost in range, and I hit him in the mouth.

My range was longer than his.

He danced back, and I danced forward and hit him in the nose before he got his guard up. He'd have to get used to the extra reach of my arms. But his guard was up now, and I saw no point in punching his forearms.

"You're a praying mantis," he said. "An insect. Over-specialized." And he moved in.

I moved back, punching lightly, staying out of his reach. He'd have to get used to that too. His legs were too short. If he tried to move forward as fast as I could backpedal, he wouldn't be able to keep his guard up.

He tried anyway. I caught him one below the ribs, and his head jerked up in surprise. I wasn't hurting him much ... but he'd been expecting love pats. Four years in Earth's one point oh gee had put muscle on me, muscle that didn't show along my long bones. He tried crowding me, and I caught him twice in the right eye. He tried keeping his guard intact, and that was suicide because he couldn't reach me at all.

I caught that eye a third time. He bellowed, lowered his head, and charged.

I ran like a thief.

I'd led him in a half circle. He never had a chance to catch me. He reached the car just as I slammed the door in his face and locked it.

By the time he reached the left-hand door, I had that locked too, and all the windows up. He was banging a rock on a window when I turned on the lift units and departed the field of battle.

He'd have to get used to my methods of fighting, too.

As I took the car up, I saw him running back toward the hunting camp.

No radio. No com laser. The base was a third of the way around the planet, and I'd have to go myself.

I set the autopilot to take me a thousand miles north of the base, flying low. Bellamy was bound to come after me with a car, and I didn't want to be found.

Come to that, did he have a car? I hadn't seen one.

Maybe he'd use— But that didn't bear thinking about, so I didn't.

A glove compartment held a small bar. Emil and I hadn't depleted it much on the way out. I ordered something simple and sat sipping it.

The forest disappeared behind me. I watched the endless plain of fern grass whipping underneath. Mach four is drifting with the breeze if you're a spaceman; but try it in a car, with the altitude set for fifty yards. It wasn't frightening; it was hypnotic.

The sun had been setting. Now it stayed just where it was, on the horizon, a little to my left. The ground was a blur, the sky was a frozen sphere. It was as if time had stopped.

I thought of Margo.

What an actress she would have made! The confusion she'd shown after the kidnaping. She hadn't remembered the cargo mass-meter; oh, no! She hadn't even known Lloobee was one of her passengers! Sure she hadn't.

She'd taken me for a fool.

I had no wish to harm her. When I told the MPs about Bellamy, she would not be mentioned. But she'd know that I knew.

I wondered what had brought her into this.

Come to that, what had brought Bellamy? He couldn't need the money that badly. Simple kicks? Had he wanted to strike at human-alien relationships? The races of known space are vastly richer for the interstellar trade. But Bellamy had lived through at least three human-Kzinti wars; he'd read of things that looked like Lloobee in his children's books.

He was a man displaced in time. I remembered the way he'd said *stark naked*. I'd used a nudist's license myself on Earth, not because I believed the incredible claims for nudism's health-giving properties, but because I was with friends who did. Come to that, I was nude now. (Would I have to buy a license when I reached the base?) But Bellamy had laughed when he'd said it. Nudism was funny.

I remembered the archaisms in his speech.

Bellamy. He'd done nothing seriously wrong, not until he decided to kill Emil and me. We could have been friends. Now it was too late. I finished my drink and crumpled the cup; it evaporated.

A black streak on my goggles, at the edge of my right eye.

... Much too late. The black blotch of Bellamy's fusion flame was far to the north, passing me. He'd done it. He'd brought the *Drunkard's Walk*.

Had he seen me?

The ship curved around toward the sun, slowed and stopped in my path. It came down my throat. I swerved; Bellamy swerved to meet me.

He flashed by overhead, and my car, moving at Mach four, bucked under the lash of the sonic boom. The crash field gripped me for an instant, then went off.

He turned and came from behind.

SLAM! And he was disappearing into the blue-and-green-and-orange sunset. What was he playing at? He must know that one touch of fusion flame would finish me.

He could end me any time he pleased. The *Drunkard's Walk* was moving at twice my speed, and Bellamy moved it about like an extension of his fingers. He was playing with me.

Again he turned, and again the hypersonic boom slapped me down. The blur of veldt came up at me, then receded. Another such might slap me into the fern grass at Mach four.

He wasn't playing. He was trying to force me to land. My corpse was to carry no evidence of murder.

SLAM! And again the black blotch shrank against the sunset.

It was no playboy's yacht he was flying. Such an expensive toy would have been long and slender, with a superfluous needle nose and low maneuverability due to its heavy angular movement. The *Drunkard's Walk* was short, with big attitude jets showing like nostrils in the stubby nose. I should have known when I saw the landing legs. Big and wide and heavy, folded now into the hull; but when they were down, they were comically splayfooted, with a wide reach to hold the ship on almost any terrain.

The playboy's flashy paint job was indirection only. The ship . . .

The ship made a wide loop ahead of me and came slashing back.

I pulled back hard on the wheel.

The blood left my head, and then the crash field took hold. I was in a cushioned shell, and the crash field held my shape like an exoskeleton. As I curved up to meet him, Bellamy came down my throat.

Give him a taste of his own medicine!

If I hadn't been half loaded, I'd never have done it.

A crash now was the last thing Bellamy wanted. It would leave evidence, not only on the car, but on the *Drunkard's Walk*. But space pilots crack up more cars. They can't get used to the idea that in the atmosphere of a planet, Mach four is *fast*. He must have been doing Mach eight himself.

He pulled up too late.

I smashed into the ship's flank at a low angle. Without the crash field I'd have been hamburger. As it was, I blacked out instantly.

I woke in the midst of a flaming maelstrom, gripped in a vise that wouldn't let me breathe, with agony tearing at my hands. The car was diving out of the sky at four times sonic speed, with its aerodynamic stability smashed to hell. I could feel the terrific deceleration in my inner ear.

I tried to use the controls. Not that they would have worked; the ship was obviously stone dead. But I tried it anyway, and then the pain came. My hands had been outside the crash field, naturally; how else could I control the car? Half the joints had been dislocated in the crash.

The ground came up, rotating. I tried to pull my hands back, but deceleration pulled me hard against the crash web, and the crash field held. I was embedded in glass.

I hit.

The car was on its nose in high fern grass. All the plastic windows had become flying shards, including the windshield; they littered the car. The windshield frame was crushed and bent. I hung from the crash web, unable to unfasten it with my crippled hands, unable to move even if I were free.

And I watched the *Drunkard's Walk*, its fusion drive off, floating down ahead of me on its gravity drag.

I didn't notice the anomaly then. I was dazed, and I saw what I expected to see: a spaceship landing. Bellamy? He didn't see it either, but he would have if he'd looked to the side when he came down the landing ladder.

He came down the ladder with his eyes fixed on mine and Emil's sonic in his hand. He stepped out into the fern grass, walked over to the car, and peered in through the bent windshield frame.

"Come on out."

"I can't use my hands."

"So much the better." Bellamy rested the sonic on the rim of the frame, and pointed it at my face. With his other hand he reached in to unfasten the crash web and pull me out by the arm. "Walk," he said. "Or be dragged."

I could walk, barely. I could keep walking because he kept prodding the small of my back with the gun.

"You've helped me, you know. You had a car crash," he said. "You and Jilson. Then some predators found you."

It sounded reasonable. I kept walking.

We were halfway to the ship when I saw it. The anomaly. I said, "Bellamy, what's holding your ship up?"

He prodded me. "Walk."

"Your gyros. That's what's holding the ship up."

He prodded me without answering. I walked. Any moment now, he'd see ...

"What the—" He'd seen it. He stared in pure amazement, and then he ran. I stuck out a foot to trip him, lost my balance, and fell on my face. Bellamy passed me without a glance.

One of the landing legs wasn't down. I'd smashed it into the hull. He hadn't seen it on the indicators, so I must have smashed the sensors too. The odd thing was that we'd both missed it, though it was the leg facing us.

The *Drunkard's Walk* stood on two legs, wildly unbalanced, like a ballet dancer halfway through a leap. Only her gyros held her monstrous mass against gravity. Somewhere in her belly they must be spinning faster and faster . . . I could hear the whine now, high-pitched, rising . . .

Bellamy reached the ladder and started up. He'd have to use the steering jets now, and quickly. With steering jets that size, the gyros—which served more or less the same purpose—must be small, little more than an afterthought.

Now was my chance!

I struggled to my feet and staggered a few steps. Bellamy looked down, then ignored me. He'd take care of me when he had time. Where could I go? Where could I hide on this flat plain?

Some chance. I stopped walking.

Bellamy had almost reached the airlock when the ship screamed like a wounded god.

The gyros had taken too much punishment. That metal scream must have been the death-agony of the mountings. Bellamy stopped. He looked down, and the ground was too far. He looked up, and there was no time. Then he turned and looked at me.

I read his mind then, though I'm no telepath.

Bey! What'll I DO?

I had no answer for him. The ship screamed, and I hit the dirt. Well, I didn't hit it; I allowed myself to collapse. I was on the way down when Bellamy looked at me; and in the next instant the *Drunkard's Walk* spun end-for-end, shrieking.

The nose gouged a narrow furrow in the soil; but the landing legs came down hard, dug deep, and held. Bellamy sailed high over my head, and I lost him in the sky. The ship poised, braced against her landing legs, taking spin from her dying flywheels. Then she jumped.

The landing legs acted like springs, hurling her somersaulting into the air. She landed, and jumped again, screaming, tumbling, like a wounded jackrabbit trying to flee the hunter. I wanted to cry. I'd done it; I was guilty; no ship should be killed like this.

Somewhere in her belly the gyroscope flywheels were coming to rest in a tangle of torn metal.

The ship landed and rolled. Bouncing. Rolling. I watched as she receded, and finally the *Drunkard's Walk* came to rest, dead, far across the blue-green veldt.

I stood up and started walking.

I passed Bellamy on the way. If you'd like to imagine what he looked like, go right ahead.

It was nearly dark when I reached the ship.

What I saw was a ship on its side, with one landing leg up. It's hard to damage hullmetal, especially at the low subsonic speeds the *Drunkard's Walk* was making when she did all that jumping. I found the airlock and climbed in.

The lifesystem was a scrambled mess. Parts of it, the most rugged parts, were almost intact; but thin partitions between sections showed ragged, gaping holes. The flywheel must have passed here.

The autodoc was near the back. It looked intact, and I needed it badly to take the pain from my hands and put them back together. I'd as soon have stepped into a bandersnatch's mouth. You can get the willies thinking about all the things that can go wrong with a 'doc.

The bouncing flywheel hadn't reached the control cone.

Things lighted up when I turned on the communications board. I had to manipulate switches with the heel of my hand. I turned on everything that looked like it had something to do with communications; rolled all the volume knobs to maximum between my palms; and let it go at that, making no attempt to aim a com laser, talk into anything, or tap out code. If anything was working on that board—and something was delivering power, even if the machinery to use it was damaged—then the base would get just the impression I wanted them to have. Someone was trying to communicate with broken equipment.

So I settled myself in the control cone and smoked. Using my toes was less painful than trying to hold a cigarette in my fingers. I remembered how shocked Sharrol had been the first time she saw me with a cigarette between my toes. Flatlanders are less than limber.

Eventually someone came.

I picked up the open bulb of glass that Margo had called a snifter and held it before me, watching the play of light in the red-brown fluid. It was a pleasure to use my hands. Twelve hours ago they had been useless, swollen, and blackening—like things long dead.

"To the hero's return," said Margo. Her green eyes sparkled. She raised the snifter in toast and drank.

"I've been in a 'doc the past twelve hours," I said. "Fill me in. Are we going to get Lloobee back?"

"Lloobee and your friend too." Satisfaction was rich in her voice; she was almost purring. "The kidnapers settled for a contract of amnesty and antipublicity, with a penalty of ten thousand stars to the man who causes their names to be published anywhere in known space. Penalty to apply to every man, woman, and child on Gummidgy— you and me included. They insisted we list the names. Did you know there are half a million people on Gummidgy?"

"That's a big contract."

"But they never made a tenth-star. They were lucky to get what they did. With their ship wrecked, they're trapped here. Lloobee and your friend should be arriving any minute."

"And Bellamy's death should satisfy kdatlyno honor."

"Mm hm." She nodded, happy, relaxed. What an actress she could have been! How nice it would have been to play along . . .

"I didn't kill him deliberately," I said.

"You told me."

"That leaves us only one loose end."

She looked up over the snifter. "What's that?"

"Persuading Emil to leave you out of it."

She dropped the snifter. It hit the indoor grass rug and rolled under the coffee table, while Margo stared at me as at a stranger. Finally she said, "You're hard to read. How long have you known?"

"Practically since your friends took Lloobee. But we weren't sure until we knew Bellamy really had him. You'd lied about his ship."

"I see." Her voice was flat, and the sparkle in her eyes was a long-forgotten thing. "Emil Horne knows. Who else?"

"Just me. And Emil owes me one. Two, really."

"Well," she said. "Well." And she went to pick up the snifter. Right then, the rest of it fell into place.

"You're old."

"You're hard to fool, Bey."

"I've never seen you move like that before. It's funny; I can tell a man's age within a few decades, but I can't tell a woman's. Why don't you move like that all the time?"

She laughed. "And have everyone know I'm a crone? Not likely. So I hesitate when I move, and I knock against things occasionally, and catch my heel on rugs ... Every woman learns to do that, usually long after she's learned not to. Too much poise is a giveaway." She stood with her feet apart, hands on her hips, challenging. Now her poise was tremendous, a shocking, glowing dignity. Perhaps she had been an actress, so long ago that her most-devoted admirers had died or forgotten her. "So I'm old. Well?"

"Well, now I know why you joined the kidnapers. You and Bellamy and the rest; you all think alike. No persuasion needed."

She shook her head in mock sadness. "How you simplify. Do you really think that everyone over two hundred and fifty is identical under the skull?

"Piet Lindstrom disliked the idea from the beginning, but he needed the money. He's been off boosterspice for years. Warren's loved hunting all his life. He hadn't hunted a civilized animal since the Kzinti wars. Tanya was in love with Larch. She'll probably try to kill you."

"And you?"

"Larch would have gone ahead without me. Anything could have happened. So I saw to it that I was flying Lloobee's ship, and I declared myself in."

She was so damn vivid. I'd thought she was beautiful before, but now, with the little-girl mannerisms gone, she *glowed.*

I thought of the brandy.

"You loved him too," I said.

"I'm his mother."

That jolted me to my toes. "The brandy," I said. "What was in the brandy?"

"Something I developed long ago. Hormones, hypnotics ... a love potion. You're going to love me. Two years from now I'll abandon you like an empty beer-bulb. You won't be able to live without me." Her smile was cruel and cold. "A fitting revenge."

"Finagle help me!" I hadn't drunk the brandy, of course, but what the hell ... Then it penetrated. *Two years.* "You know about Sharrol?"

"Yes."

"I didn't drink the brandy."

"There's nothing in it but alcohol."

We grinned at each other across the length of the couch. Then the ghost was between us, and I said, "What about Bellamy?"

"Larch took his chances. He knew what he was doing."

"I can't understand that." I couldn't understand why she didn't hate me. Worse, all my questions were sure to be the wrong ones. I picked one that might be right, and asked, "What *was* he doing?"

"Dying. He'd run out of things to do. He'd have taken greater and greater chances until one of them killed him. One day I'll reach the same point. Maybe I'll know it in time."

"What will you do then?"

"Don't ask me," she said with finality. I never did again.

"And what will you do now?"

"I have an idea," she said carefully, watching me. "Sharrol Janss is bearing children on Earth, for you to raise. I can't have children myself. My ovaries have long since run out of ova. But is there any reason why we shouldn't spend two years together?"

"I can't think of any. But what would you get out of it?"

"I've never known a crashlander."

"And you're curious."

"Yes. Don't be offended."

"I'm not. Your flattery has turned my head." After all, there were two years to fill, and Margo was lovely.

I was alone on Jinx, two years later, waiting for the next ship to Earth. As it turned out, Lloobee's latest works were there too, on loan to the Institute of Knowledge. To the Institute I went, to see what my protégé had produced.

Seeing them was a shock.

That was the first shock: that they should make sense when seen. Touch-sculpture is to be felt: it has no meaning otherwise. But these were busts and statuettes. Someone had even advised Lloobee on color.

I looked closer.

First: a group of human statuettes, some seated, some standing, all staring with great intensity at a flat pane of clear glass.

Second: a pair of heads. Human, humane, handsome, noble as all hell, but child's play to recognize nonetheless. I touched them and they felt like warm human faces. My face and Emil's.

Third and last: a group of four, a woman and three men. They showed a definite kinship with the ape and a second admixture of what must have been demon blood. Yet they were quite recognizable. Three felt like human faces, though somehow ... repellent. But the fourth felt horribly dead.

The kidnapers had neglected to include Lloobee in their contract. And Lloobee has been talking to newsmen, telling them all about how his latest works came to be.

LARRY NIVEN

*"A shining example of what can be
done by the technologically
oriented writer of science fiction."*
—Algis Budrys

WORLD OF PTAVVS
> In which a telepathic alien almost takes over
> the planet.

A GIFT FROM EARTH
> Which saves the inhabitants of Mount Look-
> itThat from the organbanks (human organs,
> that is).

NEUTRON STAR
> A superb collection which includes the Neb-
> ula Award winning title story.

ALL THE MYRIAD WAYS
> In which a topflight writer can seduce his
> readers into believing the incredible—in-
> cluding teleportation . . .

RINGWORLD
> Winner of the Nebula Award for the best
> science fiction novel of 1970.

> "An excellent . . . s.f. story. Contains one
> genuinely mind-boggling concept—a ring-
> shaped artificial world, large enough to circle
> its sun . . ."—*A.J.*

NOTABLE SELECTIONS
FROM THE PUBLISHER OF
THE BEST SCIENCE FICTION
IN THE WORLD

THE WORLD'S BEST ADULT FANTASY
BALLANTINE BOOKS

THE KING OF ELFLAND'S DAUGHTER
        Lord Dunsany   95¢

THE WELL AT THE WORLD'S END VOL. I
        William Morris   95¢

THE WELL AT THE WORLD'S END VOL. II
        William Morris   95¢

THE WOOD BEYOND THE WORLD
        William Morris   95¢

THE SILVER STALLION   James Branch Cabell   95¢

THE HIGH PLACE   James Branch Cabell   95¢

SOMETHING ABOUT EVE   James Branch Cabell   95¢

TITUS GROAN   Mervyn Peake   95¢

GORMENGHAST   Mervyn Peake   95¢

DON RODRIGUIZ:
  The Chronicles of Shadow Valley   Lord Dunsany   95¢

VATHEK   William Beckford   95¢

THE ISLAND OF THE MIGHTY
        Evangeline Walton   95¢

LUD-IN-THE-MIST   Hope Mirrlees   95¢

PHANTASTES   George MacDonald   95¢

LILITH   George MacDonald   95¢

AND MORE!

To order by mail, send $1.00 for each book to Dept. CS, Ballantine Books, 36 West 20th Street, New York, N.Y. 10003.